INNOCENT AS SIN

The Innocents Mystery Series: Book Two

C.A. Asbrey

Innocent as Sin
Copyright© 2018 C.A. Asbrey
Cover Design C.A. Asbrey & Livia Reasoner
Prairie Rose Publications
www.prairierosepublications.com

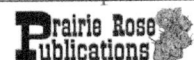

All rights reserved.
ISBN-13: 978-1721187959
ISBN-10: 1721187952

This is a work of fiction. The characters, incidents, and dialogues are products of the author's imagination and are not to be construed as real.

No part of this book may be used or reproduced in any manner whatsoever without written permission of the publisher, except in the case of brief quotations embodied in critical articles and reviews.

Chapter One

Wyoming, 1869

"Hands up!" barked Jake Conroy as his sapphire eyes scanned the room for risks and pitfalls.

"We're The Innocents. Everyone do as you're told and we'll be out of here before you know it, folks. We never hurt bystanders. We just want the money." The second man, wearing a black hat spoke with authority, and his adamantine eyes spoke of a man who would brook no opposition, not that anyone considered mounting any. Nat Quinn was backed up by some formidable fire power.

One of the outlaws chewed tobacco, moving his mask to spit on the floor. He closed the last of the blinds to obstruct the scene from casual passersby while the bank staff were corralled into a corner and patted down for concealed weapons.

Jake noted the heightened nerves of the manager whose color rose as he glanced toward the office with anxious eyes. The gunman didn't like nervous people. They tended to make rash decisions in the heat of the moment, and usually ended up doing something stupid. Despite the manager's best efforts to look elsewhere, his gray eyes continued to dart toward the closed door.

Jake Conroy strode over to the office door as he raised his gun and aimed it at the manager. "Is there somethin' I should know?" Jake's steel-edged voice made the manager tremble even more. "Who's in the office?"

"Please. No. My fiancée is in there. Don't hurt her. I'm begging you."

"A woman? Of course we ain't gonna hurt her." Nat's glower

underscored his indignation. "What kind of men do you think we are?"

"You're criminals." A voice wavered from somewhere at the back of the room.

"We're The Innocents," Nat said. "We're thieves, not savages; she'll be just fine."

"Ma'am?" Jake Conroy knocked at the door. "Come out with your hands up. This is a hold up. Ain't no one gonna hurt you. We're gonna take the money and leave."

They all stood listening to the sound of silence.

"Ma'am." Jake's voice underscored his determination, "either you come out, or we come in and get you. Move. Now!"

They heard a scuffling movement on the floorboards before the doorknob turned and the door opened by inches.

Nat and Jake stared at the petite, dark, curly-haired figure who emerged from the office.

"Well." Jake sucked in a breath as Nat strode forward, trying to head off any gasps of recognition he might make.

"Ma'am? What's your name?" Nat's eyes narrowed as he examined her, drinking in the wide eyes and enticing generous mouth he knew so well. What name would she give today?

"Abigail." She sounded uncertain as she spoke with a clear American accent. Did the gang make her nervous, or did her uncertainty stem from the possibility of being exposed as a liar?

He nodded, a sardonic smile lifting the corners of his eyes. "Well, Abigail. Why don't you go over there and join your *fiancée* and keep your hands where we can see them?"

She raised her hands under direction of his guiding gun barrel and walked over to join the bank staff forming a tight knot in the corner. Nat fixed on the extravagant diamond cluster on the third finger of her left hand. That ring was real; too real and too big to be part of a cover story.

His certainty the bank manager had no idea of his fiancée's real identity firmed in Nat's mind as he watched the manager fret over her welfare at the hands of the outlaws. If he had known more about Abigail MacKay he'd know The Innocents had more to worry about from her than the other way around. Why would she lead an honest man on like that? Did she care for him? Had she been drawn in while working undercover? He felt a stab of—what? Jealousy? Regret? Irritation? He wasn't sure. Nat arched a brow. "Quite a ring you got there, ma'am."

Abigail glowered at him as real anger flared. "Don't touch it. I'll hunt you down myself if you dare to even try. It was Robert's grandmother's. It's special."

Laughter rippled through the robbers before one of them cackled at the manager. "That's a wildcat you got there, mister. She looks like butter wouldn't melt, but—" Chuck dissolved in unsavory mirth.

"No. It would sizzle." Nat snorted. "Keep your ring, lady. It isn't what we came for."

The manager dropped his voice to a whisper. "Don't be scared, darling. Stand behind me. I'll look after you.".

"I think the lady'll be just fine, sir, as long as no one does anything stupid." Jake Conroy's flat monotone betrayed no emotion.

Nat glanced over to the safe at the back of the office before striding over behind the counter, each long step full of purpose, leaving his trusted lieutenant in charge.

Nat's dark eyes sparkled with humor, watching the manager's nerves jangle while the woman observed with a cool detachment. She was noting every detail of the robbery unfolding in front of her. No change there, then; Abigail MacKay was still a Pinkerton, and never off duty.

"Melvin, Chuck, take the men into the office and tie them up. Gag them tight." His blue eyes crinkled at the corners, his smile concealed by the mask. "Leave her here for now."

The manager blustered before Jake Conroy thrust his gun in his face. "Sir, your lady'll join you in there soon enough. Be a gent and save her from being tied up any longer than necessary."

"Go ahead, Robert. I'll be fine." Abigail tried to calm him, her voice smooth and proud. "The Innocents don't hurt people.

Just do as he says."

The man's doubtful eyes darted between Abigail and Jake Conroy, but he stood his ground. "I can't." He raised his chin in defiance and glared at Jake. "I'm staying with her."

Jake nodded. "I respect your courage, sir, but I gotta insist. We got work to do and we don't need you hangin' around."

"Then she comes with us."

The blue eyes hardened. "No, sir. She don't, and I'll remind you, you're in no position to give the orders."

"Robert, please. I'll be fine."

"What man would walk out of here and leave you with men like these?"

"The man who's smart enough to make sure you all walk out of here in one piece." Jake nodded to the outlaws standing behind the bank staff to step forward. "Now, you got a choice. You walk in that room, or two men drag you in there. Do you want to upset the lady, or do you want it all to be as civilized as possible?"

"Why? Why keep her here?"

Abigail closed her eyes and sighed before she spoke. "Because I think he recognizes me, Robert."

All eyes turned to the woman who stood in the corner with her hands still raised as someone let out an audible gasp.

"My guess is he's suspicious of a familiar face and needs to question me about it. Go, Robert. Once he realizes I'm a passenger from a train he once robbed, he'll move on. I can tell he's suspicious from the way he's been staring at me. I made a bit of a fuss about not wanting any criminals to touch me when they helped me from the train, but they were perfect gentlemen. I'm sure it'll be fine."

"You didn't tell me that," Robert said.

"No, Robert. I didn't. I don't like talking about it. I may have made a bit of a fool of myself. Please let him ask what he needs to so I can join you. Don't make this worse."

Jake darted her a look laden with meaning. Trust her to talk her way out of this. "She's a smart lady, sir." He glanced at

Abigail. "You guessed."

"I saw you looking at me. I knew you couldn't place me. Please, Robert, do as he says."

Robert glowered at Jake. "If you hurt her—I swear I'll find you and I'll kill you."

Jake Conroy nodded. "Sir, if I hurt her, I'll deserve it. I'd do the same to a man who hurt anyone of mine. Now, go with Chuck and Melvin. I won't ask again."

The outlaws watched as the staff marched through to the manager's office before the gunman strode over to Abigail and pulled down his mask to reveal the face she knew so well. Both Jake and Nat shared the same high cheekbones, but the uncle's jaw was heavier and offset by almost boyish dishwater-blond tousled hair, where his nephew Nat's hair tended to be straight brown with auburn highlights.

"So? What the hell are you doin' here, Miss Abigail MacKay?" Jake's hot breath burned into her cheek as he spoke, inches from her face now that they were alone. "Are you here for us? Who else is with you?"

Her facade dropped, along with her hands, and she reverted to her own Scottish brogue, the American accent now gone. "I'm on my own. How could I know you were coming here? I was visiting Robert."

A mirthless laugh slipped from his lips. "You got all kinds of ways of knowin' things. What are you doin' here?"

Her full mouth firmed into an obstinate line. "You can go to hell, Jake. You know I'll never tell you any details about any job I'm doing."

He tilted his tousled head as his eyes narrowed. "Abi, we need assurances. There's no truce, now. We ain't on the same side this time. Don't make this hard."

She threw him a wide grin and leaned forward, propping herself up on her toes before she dropped a light kiss on his cheek. "We both know you don't have it in you. Look, I'm not here for you. Take the money and then leave me in the office with the rest of them. Just let me get on with my job and I'll let you get on with yours. Then go. Leave here and don't come back. It's the best thing you can do."

He shook his head in bemusement. "You're a Pinkerton. I can't trust you. You're the law."

She flicked up an eyebrow. "That's rich. I was your prisoner for almost two weeks and I was left handcuffed to a door. I can't trust *you*. Anyway, what have I ever done to you?"

"As much as I'm prepared to allow, darlin'."

"I'm not after you." She shrugged. "You know me too well for me to try to bring you in. I'd be useless. I'm on another job."

"I ain't sure about this. I need to speak to Nat. We can't trust you, Abi. This could be a trap."

"I take it he's breaking into the safe." She shook her head in reproach. "You need to take me into the office. Right now. I don't need any awkward questions from Robert."

"Questions like what's your real name? Why are you pretendin' to be engaged?" Jake snickered. "Why have you got those handcuffs in your purse?" He threw her a wicked grin. "Or has he already enjoyed those?" He laughed as she colored from the neck up.

"I'm *not* that type of woman," she hissed.

"I know, more's the pity. You'd be no more than a sweet memory to Nat if you were. As it is, you're still a worry to me."

"Jake, please? This matters. They can't suspect."

"Then why didn't you disappear? There's a window. I've seen you. You can break into almost anywhere. Why not get out of here?"

"It's screwed shut and it has bars. It's a bank. I'm good with locks, but I can't shift screws with my bare fingers."

They turned as a now-unmasked Nat walked back into the room, beige sackcloth heavy with loot thrown over his shoulder. His brown eyes burned over his chiseled cheekbones and his mouth firmed into an uncompromising line. "What are you doing here, Abi?"

"Unfortunately, I'm not here to stop *your* thieving ways, Mr.

Quinn. I'm working, but I'm not interested in you. Not this time."

"Chuck and Melvin are tyin' up the men," Jake said. "I'm gettin' nowhere with her."

Nat nodded and indicated with his head toward the vault. "Abi, come with me. Now!"

Outrage spread over her face. "I will not. I won't be ordered around."

His eyes narrowed and he strode over and grasped her by the wrist. "I don't have time for this." He shouted through the door to the office as they passed. "Watch them. We'll be out of here in a minute."

Nat dragged her into a back room and thrust her against the wall, his intense eyes burning into hers. "Abi, give me one good reason why I shouldn't deal with you. Right now."

Indignation exploded over her expressive face. "You can't blame me because our paths cross in all innocence. You wouldn't look at me twice if you didn't know my real identity. Anyway, what do you mean 'deal with me'?"

"There ain't much *innocent* about you, lady."

"That's rich, coming from you. I don't have a reward on my head." Her brow creased in surprise at his genuine anger. "Mr. Quinn, you said it yourself. I'm useless around you, you know me too well. If this was a trap, wouldn't they get someone you can't identify to do whatever it is you suspect me of? I could have disguised myself."

He frowned. "You are damn good at that."

"You didn't answer me. What do you mean? Just how are you going to deal with me?"

Nat paused, ignoring her question. She was capable of avoiding being spotted with her skills. "What case are you working on?"

Determined anger flashed across her face. "You know I'll never tell you that. Just leave it. Now, back to that threat to deal with me. What do you mean? I demand an explanation."

His dark eyes drifted over her lavender silk dress with

lustrous pearls decorating her neck. "You look beautiful." Nat smiled, watching her involuntary response flicker and glow as her breathing changed and her pupils dilated. Part of him had almost forgotten the glorious fire in her spirit, in particular, the sparks which flashed up his own bursts of exhilaration. He sighed. "Being a banker's rich fiancée suits you better than a maid in a brothel. It's been a long time. What, six or seven months?"

"Seven. It was last November." She gulped down the knot of emotion filtering through her voice. "Please, take me into the office and leave me there with the men. I have important work to do here. You go your way and I'll go mine. People will be looking for you. Leave here and don't come back to this area."

"Work? How important?"

"Life or death. Please. I don't care about your arrest at the moment." Her dark eyes stared into his. "You know I care more about crimes against the person than crimes to property. I'll never ask you for another favor, but I need to stay here, and I need to be credible. Please. It matters."

He examined the woman he had seen in every mood, every shade of emotion from raging fever to masterful intellect. The concern looked real, but then, she was as good at acting as well as anyone gracing the stage. "Whose life or death?"

She paused, her eyes darkening. "I can't tell you that."

"Who got killed?"

"No one. Yet. I'm here to try to prevent it."

His eyes bored into her as his concern grew. Abigail took risks he would never countenance, despite being more like him than anyone he'd ever met. "How dangerous is it?"

"Less than a night with you." Her grin filled with a lightness he wasn't buying. "Shouldn't you be making a break for freedom by now? You've robbed the bank. Get out of here."

His eyes swirled with unreconciled concern and annoyance. She had stepped all over his carefully planned robbery. "I'll leave you for now, but we need to talk." He nodded toward the engagement ring. "About quite a few things. Where are you staying?"

"Mr. Quinn, I can't tell you that, either."

The right side of his mouth slid into an uneven smile. Her determination not to get too close to him meant she always called him Mr. Quinn, but it never ceased to amuse him how much warmth seemed to infuse such a formal address.

"Meet me, or I'll come back. You'll be easy to find now that you're engaged. You've got ties." His eyebrows rose over provocative brown eyes.

Her face flickered with—what? Excitement? Fear? Irritation? "I can't."

"I mean it, Abi."

"It's far too dangerous. People will be looking for you. Leave here and don't come back."

"I'll take my chances. But if you want to play it that way, maybe you should come with me instead?"

She dropped her head, knowing how determined he could be when he put his mind to it. "Fine. Just one meeting, then you leave me to get on with my job. Now, for heaven's sake take me to the office and tie me up."

His cheeks dimpled in feral delight. "If you insist, darlin'. If only I'd known you were intrigued by that. Think of the fun we might have had."

Her eyes narrowed. "You never give up, do you?"

His face dimpled. "I'll go through any door that's open, Abi. Nothing risqué, nothing gained."

"You're incorrigible. I'm in the Bentwood Inn on Oak Road. I'll be in the garden at nine o'clock on my own. There's a summerhouse." She walked over to the door. "I want a clean gag, and don't tie me too tight. I'll see you at about ten, after you've finished lurking about, checking to see if I'm really alone." Abigail paused. "And be prepared to explain that 'deal with you' comment. You don't get off so easy."

Chapter Two

The heady scent of jasmine drifted on the warm night air as Abigail sat in the summer house at the end of the garden. The quaint, thatched, wooden affair was perfectly in keeping with the twee boarding house. The clapboard and carved wooden fascias were picked out in beige and brown until it looked like a giant gingerbread house. Mrs. MacPhee had a whimsical sense of the quaint, and barely a surface or furniture leg remained unmolested by the frills, doilies, or embroidered leg curtains which she imagined inhabited the fine homes of the East.

It had been at least half-an-hour since Abigail thought she had heard the faint crack of a twig, but she continued to sit, waiting for her cautious tryst to be kept. A slight rustle off to her left indicated the visitor had arrived at last. "Good evening, Mr. Quinn. I take it you've ascertained I'm on my own at last."

A shadowy figure in the darkness drifted forward through the gloom until it became close enough to transform into a human shape. Nat stepped into the summer house and leaned forward to drop a light kiss on the top of her head before he sat beside her.

"Where's Jake?"

"He's around," he answered, the moonlight catching a flash of white as he grinned through the darkness. "So? How've you been?"

"I've been well, thanks. You?"

"Fine. How did you get on after our last meeting? What did Pinkerton say when you went back empty-handed?"

"I *didn't* go back empty-handed. I returned with two

murderers. It went well."

"But not with Quinn and Conroy. How did you explain that? What did you say to Pinkerton?"

"I told him the truth." Her soft laugh tinkled. "He's not the type of man you lie to."

Nat sucked in a breath. "The whole truth?"

She tilted her head in equivocation. "Most of it. You came out of it nobly enough, if that's what you're worried about." He chuckled as she continued. "I told him I had been injured by the Pattersons and you rescued me and nursed me through my fever."

"The truth, so far."

"Then I had to abandon the pursuit of Nat Quinn and Jake Conroy as you two knew what I looked like, so I pursued a different case, instead. That's also fundamentally true."

"True, but he didn't send you for anyone else."

"I had sent to Boston for information, so he already knew what I was doing. It's good publicity for the agency with the motto, '*We Never Sleep*'. When unable to deal with one case, I went on and caught two murderers and acted in the public interest. I'll have to explain the robbery today, though. He'll know you would have recognized me, even if you aren't supposed to have found out I'm a Pinkerton."

"What are you goin' to tell him?"

"Again, a version of the truth. You recognized me and I convinced you I had become engaged. The fact you kept me back to question me should corroborate it. You didn't have to know I'm using another name."

"Abigail Ansell."

"How did you know?"

His voice chimed with laughter. "You aren't the only one who can ask questions, Abi."

He knew of her engagement to the bank manager, so it took little skill to find out about what part she was playing this time. "Yes, servants are always ready to talk to a handsome stranger."

"Handsome?" He lit with delight. "I'm at your disposal

anytime, Abi. All you've got to do is ask real nice. Even a smile will do. I'm not fussy."

"How much do you know?"

"You're supposed to be the daughter of an Eastern gentleman. You came to research the dime novels you write. You've been here for four months and been engaged to Robert Metcalf for a month." He shook his head. "What are you playing at, Abi? That's plain cruel if you're playing a part. I hadn't marked you down as that sort of woman. You don't play those games."

She slammed him with angry eyes. "How I conduct myself is none of your business."

"He doesn't know, does he?" Her eyes glittered in the moonlight, her refusal to answer telling him everything he needed to know. "He cares for you. He was worried sick about you in that bank. I felt real bad for him, knowing you're in complete control."

"I know he does. He's sweet, and he cares for me." She dropped her head, her voice laden with guilt. "I hate it."

"Abi, you could have refused him, or put him off. You don't return those feelings." He paused. "Or do you?"

"He's kind, that's all. I couldn't put him off. I really couldn't. I had my reasons, but I wouldn't go as far as saying I was in complete control. Not with you two around. "

He sighed. "So? What now? You stick around and marry him?"

"Mr. Quinn, I can't see what difference it would make to you if I did."

"I'll take that as a no. At least you got the sense not to go that far." He sat back and stretched out his long legs. "He has no idea? Your kisses must be the most potent lies you tell."

"I don't usually reveal myself, and Mr. Metcalf doesn't have your powers of persuasion." She snorted, remembering that night at the cabin. "But then, not many men do."

"Mr. Metcalf. Is that what you call him?"

"I call him Robert. Why?"

He moved closer and slipped an arm through hers. "Good. I don't want you calling just anyone 'mister'. It's our thing."

"Why are you here, Mr. Quinn? This is none of your concern."

He turned his head and looked deep into her eyes. "I wanted to see you again. That's not a crime, is it?"

"It depends on what else you're doing while you're around."

She felt the rumble of his laughter against the arm he held. "I'm a bad man, Abi. Want to find out how bad? I wish I'd known back at the cabin how far you were prepared to go to get a job done. We'd have had a lot more fun."

"I do not lead men on for fun." She shrugged him off and stood. "Mr. Quinn, what do you want? I have a job to do."

"I'm joking, Abi. I guess that means I'm different, since you didn't play those games with me. You know I find you attractive." He sat back and folded his arms, his broad smile catching the moonlight. "I want to make sure you're safe. You tend to take risks I don't think are acceptable. I also just wanted to see you for old time's sake."

She closed her eyes as her stomach sank, guilt closing in. "I'm protecting someone's life. That's all you have to know. I have to stick around, no matter what, until I'm told otherwise. I'll do what it takes to get it done." She paused. "To a point. There are lines I never cross."

"A guard? You?"

She bristled at his disbelief. "Don't start. Just because I'm a woman."

"And what a woman." He leaned forward and fixed her with a determined stare. "Just how good are you with a gun?"

"That's none of your business, Mr. Quinn. In any case, I'm not *that* sort of bodyguard."

He shook his head and stood too. "Madness. I don't know what the world's coming to. I need to go, but can I see you again? Dinner, perhaps?"

"I can't. I agreed to meet you once. That's it."

"No, it's not." He walked over and stroked her cheek as his

intense eyes burned into her. "I'll be in touch."

Her eyes fixed on him, genuine desperation floating in the depths of the blackness. "Please. Don't. I really mean this. You have to keep away. Stay as far away as possible. Go anywhere else but here, and lie low for at least three months." He grinned at her, but she grabbed onto his arm, her fingers digging into his flesh. "Promise me. You must keep away! I've never been more serious in my life. If you ever believed in me at all, listen to this warning and leave here. Now!"

He gathered her face in both hands dropped a kiss on her lips. "Goodnight, Abi." Nat stared into her eyes before he sighed and stepped back. In less than a few seconds, he disappeared into the enveloping darkness.

Abigail walked back into the house with a knot of angst forming in her stomach. She had sworn to do her job to the best of her ability, but she hated duplicity and double dealing.

"How did it go?"

She looked at the tall blond man who stood in the kitchen, his strange, pale blue eyes appraising her. She nodded at Frank McCully, holding the thick-necked man's cold gaze. "Just as expected, Frank. He wants to see me again."

He nodded and smiled. "Good. I guess Jake was around, too, for protection, but after a few dates, neither of them will suspect what they're walking into. With men like Conroy, it's always better to catch them unawares. The longer Quinn and Conroy think you're emotionally involved, the more they'll be lulled into a false sense of security. This makes the whole thing even smoother. Meet Quinn a few more times and let Conroy drop his guard. Then, we'll strike."

She dropped her head. "I hate this. They saved my life, you know."

The bounty hunter stepped forward and put a reassuring hand on her shoulder.

"I know. You got a rotten job, here. You have to string the

bank manager and Quinn along at the same time, but if anyone can do it, you can. I trust you."

"I'll do my job, don't worry about that," she answered. "I know they're criminals."

"I know you will. Are you sure they don't suspect?"

"Would you? All I've done is try to avoid them and put them off because I know they can't resist a challenge. There's no way they suspect this whole thing's a set up. After all, put a successful bank with a large payroll coming in this close to The Innocents main area of operation, it's only a matter of time before Quinn and Conroy walk into this trap."

Frank McCully drained the last of his coffee and put his cup on the table with a clatter characteristic of his overall roughness.

"A good night's work. Not long now. I'm turning in. It's not going to be long before we snare two of the most wanted men in the country."

Abigail smiled at him before her face dropped into a blank expressionless mask, her eyes almost black in the lamp light. "Yes. Not long now," she murmured.

"What's so fascinatin' about those bank books, Nat? You've been examinin' them for almost a week."

Nat sighed and shut the ledger with a snap. "They don't add up, Jake. They look real good, but they aren't right. Not against the amount of cash we took from the vault. The bank's holdings are almost double those declared in the books. In any case, I always get suspicious when there's another set of books. I took these from the vault after I saw a full set in Metcalf's office. I think we got to the money before he did. "

Jake grinned. "He's a thief? As bad as us?"

"Looks like it."

"I guess that's what she's doin' there."

Nat shook his head. "She says she's guarding someone."

Jake Conroy snorted with laughter. "And you believed her? Does she look like a bodyguard to you?"

Nat sat back, his eyes glittering with amusement. "Nope, but she never struck me as looking like a sixty-year-old woman, either."

Jake flicked up a questioning eyebrow. "Do you think she can shoot?"

"I've no idea but I don't think we can dismiss it."

"I don't want you seein' her again, Nat. It's too risky. I like her, but I don't trust her an inch."

Nat smiled. "I'm with you there, partner, but have you ever been fascinated by somebody who isn't good for you?"

Jake's eyes reflected the pensive memories of his lost love. "Yeah, the girl from St. Louis with hair like gold, eyes like diamonds, and a heart of solid ice. I guess you warned me. I didn't want to hear it. I was too wrapped up in what she had to offer. I just don't want you makin' the same mistakes as me."

Nat eyes danced with mischief. "I'm gonna take her these books, Jake. Are you coming?"

"Why can't you just leave it?" Jake groaned.

"I didn't think I'd ever see her again." Nat collected his hat. "I guess this is my last chance before she moves to another job."

"It's gotta be on my terms. I don't trust her. I want to know more about what she's doin' here."

Nat sighed. "Sure, Jake. There's no point in arguing with you when you're like this. You check what you've gotta check. Your caution is what keeps us alive."

Jake Conroy watched Mrs. MacPhee's boarding house from the shrubbery for four hours noting everyone who came and went. He'd been a cautious man at the best of times, but when his nephew took stupid risks like this, he went the extra mile. He was able to place the people coming and going against the names he had extracted from the maid—a young girl who'd been happy to talk to the tall, handsome stranger who had carried her basket back from the store.

He found her an irritating, shallow girl with a habit of giggling at nothing in particular, but he personified charm itself, and by the time he handed over the basket of provisions at the back gate, he knew the names of everyone in the boarding house along with a their descriptions and a rough idea of where their rooms were.

He had seen everyone except for the female Pinkerton, who occupied a room in the upper floor, and the someone named 'Frankie' who stayed in the right-hand back bedroom—and who had business with Abigail. His vigil paid off at last when a six-foot tall man with cropped, white-blond hair stopped at the gate. He tipped his hat to a woman passing in the street, pushing her child in the perambulator for the world to see.

Jake's breath stilled in horror. He knew that man; Frank McCully was the bounty hunter who never brought anyone in alive. *Carcasses are the only ones that can be transported without escape attempts* was his motto. He only went after those wanted dead or alive. One shot through the head, and it was money in the bank until the next job.

Wanted men's wives and children had been found killed by a single shot to their heads after bodies were turned in because it was easier for the ruthless bounty hunter to transport cadavers than prisoners, and witnesses got in the way. All the while, random people in towns, farms, and homesteads were found murdered in the same arbitrary fashion wherever McCully made arrests. Inconvenient people got slaughtered wherever McCully worked. Never had a more selfish, venal, and ruthless man worked in what passed for law enforcement, and if Abigail had gotten involved with him, she had serious questions to answer.

Jake Conroy's determination to get those answers hardened. His breathing quickened, and a familiar tingling feeling crept from his numb fingers until it branched through his arms and into his chest. Cold sweat pricked at his skin as a familiar ball of leaden nausea firmed in his belly.

Nat always called it his red mist, but Jake's vision remained unaffected. Instead, it impacted his ability to reason and process. Past and present blurred as his mind filled with the sights and sounds of long-ago horrors, forcing him to re-live the worst moments of his life. He usually kept them at bay by being the best with a gun. It made him feel more confident about keeping loved ones safe, but the prospect of another loss could cause the attacks to surge to the forefront and play a frantic loop in his brain. These horrors went with him everywhere, rising unbidden at times of trouble. That poisoned prism now distorted the way he saw Abigail.

Chapter Three

It took another half-hour before Jake saw her neat, feminine figure approaching, her light blue dress standing out against the sun-parched dust of the streets. By this time, his breath came in rapid, shallow pants until his fingers prickled and his head spun. The everyday sounds of the town swamped his senses until they crashed around his skull in an echoing cacophony. Her voice reverberated, unusually strident and harsh, echoing between the screaming and shouting from years ago in his head.

"Jake?" Abigail's eyes darted around drinking in the surroundings, looking for danger. Why greet her openly in the street, near her gate? His glazed eyes sparkled and the pupils looked enormous, but he didn't seem drunk.

"Abi, come with me. It's urgent."

Her dark eyes were pools of worry as she gazed into his, unaware of the danger lurking in their depths. "Why? What's happened?"

"It's Nat. He needs you."

Jake Conroy watched her blanch as a delicate hand reached out to him."Oh, my goodness! What happened? Is he hurt?"

He steered her toward the tethering post where he had left his mount, trying not to sneer at her concern as they walked. "We need to ride two-up. Time's short."

Abigail's hung back, obviously not trusting Jake's words. "Do we need a doctor? Or a lawyer, maybe?"

"We ain't got time. We need to go." He checked the girth strap on his saddle and led the animal out.

"What do you mean we haven't got time? What's wrong?"

He saw the determination in her face and snapped at her. "Are you comin' or not?"

He threw his long leg over his mount and stretched out an arm to draw her up behind him.

Abigail paused. "If Nat's hurt, or in jail, he needs professional help more than a visit from me." She tensed. "If it's gun power, why choose a woman with a Derringer? What's wrong, Jake? Where is he?" She stepped back and she refused to take his hand, her breathing quickening.

"A cabin near here."

"Why me? Why would you bring me? Why not a doctor or a lawyer? You need real help."

Jake Conroy let out a snort of impatience and leaned over, wrapping a long arm around her waist. He lifted her, dropping her in front of him on the saddle as though she weighed next to nothing.

She bucked in his arms. "What are you doing?"

Abigail felt the hard, unmistakable butt of a gun barrel in her ribs as his rasping voice whispered in her ear. "Lady, I ain't got the patience for this. If you want to do it the hard way, it'll be real hard. I'd keep my voice down if I were you unless want innocent bystanders involved in this."

She sat stung into silence as she sensed the menace in his words, her breath coming in rapid, shallow gasps. "You wouldn't, Jake. It's me. Tell me what's wrong. I can help."

"You?" he snarled. "What if I tell you who I saw at your boardin' house? I know the murderin' scum you brought lookin' for us? Explain why I shouldn't play by the same rules."

He felt her take a sharp intake of breath as his words landed. She knew. The certainty hardened his resolved. "Looks like you're mixin' with folks who don't care much for our welfare, so I guess it works both ways."

"Jake—"

"Save it. I don't want to hear it. It'll all be lies and manipulation." He kicked his horse into action. "You got time to think of somethin' good before we get where we're goin'. It's a shame for you I'm in no mood for listenin'."

♦◊♦

The maid stopped halfway down the path, disappointed to see the attentive, handsome, blond man walk off with Miss Ansell. She thought he'd come to see her when she'd seem him loitering around the gate, but she was nothing if not fickle, and was mollified to see a stunning man with auburn highlights in his brown hair walking straight toward her.

"Is Miss Ansell at home, miss?"

"No. She went that way. With the blond man. A Mr. Black."

Nat smiled, recognizing the alias Jake Conroy sometimes used. "I know him. Are you sure?"

"Oh, yes. We spoke earlier, and he helped me with the shopping. I thought he was calling for me, but it seems everyone loves Miss Ansell." She tossed a pale brown curl over her shoulder, miffed at being overlooked.

"Everyone?"

"Oh, yes! Even Frankie—" She blushed at her indiscreet slip, hinting at a more intimate relationship. "Mr. McCully. He sent me out to see where she had gone."

Nat's blood ran cold. "Mr. McCully. Not Frank McCully?"

"Yes. Do you know him? Blond, and as handsome as they come, but then everyone seems so good-looking today."

The maid bit back her words as old Clayton, the town drunk, doffed his battered hat to her as he passed by. He gurned a toothless grin through his gray stubble as he wove his way along the street like a mule performing dressage.

"And is Mr. McCully at home? Has he spoken to anyone?"

"Oh, yes. Arrived home about half-an-hour before Miss Ansell." Her face fell. "Then she left with Mr. Black."

Nat's heart turned to lead as he understood the leap Jake Conroy had made. If he had seen Frank McCully with Abi then only one thing could have happened, especially if he had also spoken to this woman.

"Does Miss Ansell know Mr. McCully?"

"Oh, yes. I believe they're good friends. If she's not spending time with her fiancé, she's spending it with Mr. McCully. It doesn't seem quite right, but rich folks seem to have different rules."

He stared off along the street. "What way did they go?"

"I saw her go off with him on his horse." She pointed out of town as Nat's stomach sank. "That way. All I can say is, I wouldn't stay engaged for long if I went off with as many men as she does."

♦◊♦

The horse battered out of town for about two miles, Jake's arm like an iron band around her waist while the thumping echoed in her tight chest. Abigail fought to remain controlled and calm, but she knew betrayal was now driving the enraged man. She felt his hot breath pant in angry snorts against her neck as the countryside flashed by as fast as the strategies that ran through her mind. She quickly dismissed them all. There was nowhere to run, and this man could draw and fire before she even reached her ankle holster. The musky scent of horse drifted up as they pounded across the hard ground, mingling with the metallic taste of fear creeping from the hard lump of emotion forming in her gullet.

Jake's raw protectiveness toward his nephew gave him his sole reason for living. The certainty that she had betrayed them to a bullet in the head, courtesy of Frank McCully, was surely spinning around his addled mind. The gunman's fury didn't come as the explosive, hot, venting variety. It crept in as the cold, calculating, and circumspect type; as piercing as a stiletto. He didn't explode; he'd begun to implode—and wasn't listening. The trust he'd given so grudgingly had begun to unravel until he was entangled in a web of rage. What would he do?

He drew his sweating horse to a walk and started toward a copse of trees. Her heart thumped and her breath came in ragged gasps of panic. She was in trouble, and she knew it. She steeled herself to control her breathing, to breathe deep and slowly, because hysteria would only make the matter worse. Everyone in their world knew what McCully did, and anyone who would be prepared to hand them over to a man like him deserved no mercy. She knew that.

Her mind debated the best course of action, wondering if she should try to talk to him…or give in and beg. He'd never been a cruel man. Maybe begging was a good idea?

He stopped the horse and dismounted before tethering it to a tree and glaring at her with chilling blue eyes. "Get down."

His hard hands still held the reins and the pommel of the saddle, in complete control of the mount.

"Jake—"

"Get down, or I'll drag you off that damned animal."

Her stomach lurched as she looked into the eyes swirling with hate and decided she should remain quiet. Pride was all she had left, and she refused to plead just for the sake of it. She slipped a leg over the horse and slid to the ground, holding eye contact with him all the while, resigned to whatever fate awaited her. A spark of surprise burned in the back of her mind that a man she considered a friend would deliver the final blow.

"So, what have you got to say?"

She shook her head. "You've already said you're not going to listen. Just do what you're going to do and get it over with." Her voice broke with emotion. "You're wrong, but you've decided. You'll kill a friend, Jake."

His hands formed into fists, the knuckles showing hard and pale through the taught skin. "No defense? You were going to hand us over to Frank McCully. The man's a murdering animal."

Her eyes fixed on his, declaiming her denial. "I wouldn't. Not ever. Don't you know me well enough by now?"

He leaned over and yelled right in her face. "I saw him!"

"Yes, but it's not what you think—"

"I suppose I ain't bright enough to work it out? Maybe I ain't as dim as you think?"

She backed off as he advanced on her, shaking her head

from side to side. "I don't think you're dim, Jake. Far from it."

"He's a cold-blooded killer and you were goin' to hand us over to him."

"No." She stepped back once more as he advanced on her. "I'd never do that."

"Enough!" He grasped her by the arm and dragged her into the clearing before swinging her into the center of the copse. "You know what he does. Why else would you be so scared? Why wouldn't you have warned Nat that McCully is here?"

"Because I wanted him to leave, and he'd have stayed for my sake." Abigail closed her eyes. "I'd never hand anyone over to him. I was—"

He reached out and dragged the bonnet from her head, catching her hair, making shards of pain lance across her scalp.

"I can see you better now." He prowled around her, looking at her from head to toe as her stomach churned in trepidation. Jake Conroy would fight like a lion when his kin were threatened, and life didn't get any more dangerous for a wanted outlaw than Frank McCully. "Just what am I supposed to do with you now?" he growled.

A worm of hope ate through her cold fear at his words. She'd expected a quick death as his temper took over, but he was more controlled and considered than she expected. But was that a good thing or a bad thing?

"It's really not what you think, Jake."

"You expect me to believe that? That's the best you can come up with?"

She dropped her head in resigned hopelessness. "Because it's the truth. Please, take some time to think about this. I didn't even want to meet Nat, and I did my best to send him away. It's all a coincidence. I'm working on something here, and you turn up to rob the bank. That's not my fault."

"I don't believe in coincidences," he snarled, a spot of hot spittle hitting her face. His following whisper was more intimidating than his snarl. "You know McCully. You know what he does. Give me one good reason why I shouldn't do the same to you."

She raised her head and looked straight into his eyes. "Because I'm doing everything in my power to stop that happening to you or anyone else."

"You expect me to believe you?" he bellowed.

"Yes. It's the truth, and deep down you know it. I've been here for months, and I had nothing to do with you turning up. You know how you chose which bank to rob and I had no influence on your choice."

He gazed into her rich, cinnamon eyes, so full of earnest determination. He trembled as his emotions engulfed him. Confusion mixed with his fury, his mind unable to define which path he should take. His face drained of color before he snarled his reply. "I don't know anythin' about you anymore."

He stepped forward and grasped her dress at the throat with one strong hand, visions of Nat's crumpled body floating around his head, mingling with memories of his sister's blood filling the troughs and cracks between the cobblestones flooding back from his childhood. Never again, not if he could help it, but a germ of uncertainty wormed into his mind that prevented him from making the ultimate move. "Tell me why you're with McCully."

She hesitated, struggling to speak against the tightening fabric of her dress crushing her windpipe, her nails dragging at Jake's tight wrist as she stared into his cold, blank eyes. His pupils narrowed as his mind gave in to the haunting horrors of the past. His mind shut down, playing only the fears, and blocking out the here and now until he was lost to reality and to the harsh effect of his throttling grasp as his hand twisted the cloth even tighter.

"Jake!"

They both turned at the sound of beating hooves as Nat galloped into the clearing on a sweating horse. He took in the scene and dropped from his horse before he walked over to them, maintaining eye contact with Jake all the way. "Jake, I know about McCully. Let her go." Nat's voice remained steady and composed as though he was calming a skittish horse.

Jake ignored him, lost in the nightmare of his youth.

Nat frowned and took in the furious man before him. He had seen Jake like this before, during the war, when they had come across the remains of a family decimated by a marauding party.

One straggler had still been there, taking his time with an unconscious thirteen-year-old girl. Jake Conroy had descended into a spiral of ferocity. There was little point in trying to reason with him when he was like this. He was running purely on emotions and nightmarish traumas from his childhood, so Nat had to depend on the decent essence at the man's core. He knew Abi was struggling for air, but he also knew she'd be dead by now if Jake Conroy really meant to kill her.

His best tactic was to distract Jake and bring him back to reality, leading him away from his fractured past and toward the man he had become. Experience had taught Nat that telling Jake what to do would enrage him more. Jake wasn't reasoning. He was emoting.

Nat's gaze turned to Abigail's before he returned to Jake. He raised his eyebrows in query. "Did she tell you she was handing us over to McCully?"

"She didn't have to!"

Abigail's face was turning puce but Nat was in no hurry. "What did she say?"

"She lied. What do you expect?"

Nat put his weight on one leg as he hooked his thumbs in his belt and continued. "So? How you gonna kill her then?"

Abigail punched at Jake's arm in desperation as she dropped to her knees, able to suck no more than a tiny amount of air. "You gonna strangle her with your bare hands? Not sophisticated, but it'll get the job done I suppose."

Jake turned his chilling gaze back to the woman writhing at the end of his arm before Nat drew his attention back to him again. "A shot to the head would be quicker. Want me to do it?"

Abigail's eyes watered as she choked and struggled against

Jake's grip, while Nat's brown eyes drifted over to her, drawn by her fight for life. "There's a river over there. How about drowning? Drowning'd work."

Nat pondered and seemed to think the better of it. "No, you're right. Too wet. Or hanging maybe? What about hanging? One thing's for sure. I wouldn't do it that way."

Jake snorted in frustration.

"We both got knives. No, I guess you've thought it through. Far too messy."

Nat examined Jake's grip before looking straight into his face. "Maybe both hands and put them right around her throat? That fabric's starting to tear." He toyed with the grass with the toes of his boots for a few seconds before he spoke again. "Or a rope? You want me to get you a rope?"

Jake Conroy exploded at his annoying partner. "Oh, for cryin' out loud! You know how to do everythin' better, don't ya?"

Jake threw Abigail aside and strode over to Nat, facing him down, irritated beyond belief at his constant criticism, while Abigail lay on her side gasping for air and ineffectually trying to crawl away.

Nat gave Jake a satisfied nod and shook his head with a smile of relief. He grabbed his uncle by both arms and smiled a life-affirming grin. "No. Now that you ask. I don't want either of us to do it. It took you a while, but we got there in the end." Nat led Jake over to a tree and pushed him to a seated position. "Take a minute. I'll see to her. It's all fine, Jake. We're all safe. Relax. Breathe, and sit still. You were strangling her." Nat watched Jake's empty eyes fill with both humanity and confusion.

"I never! I just grabbed her."

"You were twisting the collar of her dress, Jake. It got so tight she was going bright red and dropped to her knees."

Jake paused, his missing memories confounding him. "No. I just grabbed her. I wanted answers. I would never—"

Nat patted his arm. "You got her real winded. What you saw

wasn't what you were doing. It was like Kansas again. You haven't been like this for years. I know what came over you. I found out about McCully." He glanced over at Abi pushing herself to a sitting position. "She's fine. Sort yourself out while I get to the bottom of this."

Nat walked over to Abigail and crouched, gathering her in his arms and examining her before giving her a smile. When he was satisfied her injuries were only superficial, he supported her to the side of the clearing before propping her against the same tree as Jake.

"Stay there." His eyes transmitted an unnecessary warning. She was too winded to go anywhere.

He smiled at Jake. "I knew you didn't have it in you. Not even for a woman who was going to hand us over to McCully. You ain't that man."

"I wasn't—" Abigail's voice croaked.

"We'll deal with you in a minute," answered Nat.

Jake closed his eyes and dropped his head. "McCully? Gettin' us arrested is one thing, but McCully? I can't believe she would do that to us."

Nat gave him a wry smile. "So, what did she say about it?"

"She denies it, but she would, wouldn't she?"

"Well. Let's see, shall we?"

He towered over her, his dark eyes penetrating her soul. "Well?"

She stared back at him, her chest rising and falling in fear and exertion.

"Nothin' to say? Not much of a defense..." His dropping of his 'g's told her Nat's anger robbed his accent of its polish.

"I can't tell you anything. I really can't. But I'm not prepared to see you hurt."

Nat crouched, leaning on his knees, reading her every move. "Abi, listen carefully. I need you to tell me what's going on, otherwise things could get unpleasant for you. I'm sorry about that, sorrier than you'll ever know, but if you don't tell me you'll leave me no alternative."

"No alternative to what?" Abigail's eyes turned to his, full of resignation and fear. "You'll have to do what you need to. I can't tell you anything. Lives depend on it."

"Whose life?"

"Many lives over time but—" She stopped, biting back her words. She'd already said too much.

He watched her mute stare, wondering why she didn't dare speak. Why was she refusing to defend herself? He knew her well enough to know she was articulate enough to try to bluff her way out of this. The stakes had to be high.

"Is someone going to die soon?"

Her eyes opened, almost pleading. "No one will die if you let me go back. Nobody. Just leave here as soon as you can."

He scrutinized her. She looked like she was telling the truth; in fact, she appeared to be placing her own safety behind her current assignment in the habit he found infuriating. She obviously had no idea what he might have planned for her. Nor could she be sure whether or not Nat would really do something to her if his life was at stake—yet she stuck to that damned secrecy which drove him insane.

He scratched his cheek and thought back to what she had told him. It was a matter of life or death. She was guarding someone. She didn't need gun skills. Frank McCully was in the equation. Who could she be protecting? His agile mind ran through the fragments, doing his best to piece them together into a viable theory. It hit him like a kick from a horse, right between the eyes.

He sucked in a breath and stared at her. "Abi? It's us. You're here to protect us."

Her eyes widened and filled with tears and confusion. "How? How did you know?"

"Who else needs protecting when McCully's around? It's got to be criminals—and who else is around Everlasting with a price in their heads? This is our territory."

"You sure about this, Nat?" Jake's jaw dropped open. "She could be tryin' to draw us out for him."

He shook his head. "Nope. She's done everything she can to stop me from seeing her. She almost begged in the summerhouse. She's drawing out McCully."

"Why? Why would the law care about that? He kills criminals."

"Yes, he does, but he also makes criminals fight to the death when we try to bring them in." Abigail spoke at last, knowing the game was lost. "They kill the law because they think we're all as bad as he is. In the last year, three Pinkerton agents have been killed because the outlaws think they'll be shot anyway. We have to stop McCully and let them know we consider murder to be murder. They need to know the law is fair and applied equally. They can do their time and then live as free men. We can't live by the gun like this."

"Why us?"

"Mostly your reward money." Unblinking eyes looked straight into his. "Intelligence told us he was after you. We leaked it to him you had nursed me when I was shot by the Pattersons and then let me go after a few emotional entanglements. He has no idea I'm a Pinkerton. In fact, he doesn't even know there *are* female Pinkertons. He's paying me to stay in Everlasting and pose as Abigail Ansell, even going so far as making eyes at the bank manager to make sure I could be around when *you* robbed the bank. I got engaged on his orders. He thinks he's running the show and it was only a matter of time before you robbed a bank in this area."

"And to make arrangements to see us?"

She shook her head. "He knows you're too sophisticated than to fall for that. He thinks I'm setting you a challenge, knowing you can't resist one."

Nat arched a dark eyebrow as his eyes bored into her. "It could be argued you did exactly that."

"No. You were never supposed to be there, and I tried my best to keep you away when you arrived. We have agents planted to rob the place, but if they had done it too quickly, it would have looked suspicious. The agents can pass for you both to someone who's never seen you and was going on your descriptions alone. I'm supposed to plan assignation and McCully's gun will have been tampered with so we can catch him in the act of killing without provocation. The tampering is my job. The only problem is you two turned up and almost ruined the whole plan."

"How do you know he's never seen us?"

"He told me so."

Nat narrowed his eyes and stood, letting out a long slow breath. It figured because they never mixed with criminals unless they were working and the gang was tested and loyal. So, McCully had never seen Quinn and Conroy, but they had made sure they had seen him. Their lives depended on it.

"Why didn't you tell me this before now, Abi?" asked Nat.

"I couldn't. I wasn't allowed to, and it couldn't get out, but you guessed. Even if this didn't work out we had to find a way of winning him over so he'd use me again if he went after someone else. He's a mass murderer, and he'll continue to kill unarmed people. If he's not stopped, he'll undermine the rule of law and endanger more of my colleagues as criminals treat all arrests like life or death. And he's not just killing criminals; he's also killing men, women, and children who don't stand a chance. They're defenseless. For that reason alone, I have to do this. He's a cold-blooded murderer." She dropped her head. "Besides, if I had told you there would be no way you'd keep out of this. You're too damned bloody-minded for your own good."

"You're no better. What if he found out about you?"

She looked him straight in the eye. "We all know what he'd do. He shoots unarmed men in the head while their hands are handcuffed behind their backs, so a woman who double crosses him wouldn't be a problem, but there would be someone else to take my place."

Nat shook his head as he bit his lip. "I can't let you risk your life for mine, Abi. Does he know your real name?"

"Yes. Why not? If any one of The Innocents had talked, I

could have been exposed. You might have told them my real name. It wasn't worth the risk to lie."

"The Innocents don't talk, Abi. I make sure of that. I also don't tell the gang about people like you. You need to protect yourself more." He rubbed his face and turned toward Jake who was staring at them, transfixed with horror at how he had treated her.

"This could be a lie," he muttered. "She could have been settin' us up to hand us over."

"Except for one thing, Jake." Nat shook his head. "She pushed and pushed for me to keep away."

"Double bluff? She's a real good liar."

"She's not bad, but she ain't a poker player. In fact, she's real easy to read for anyone skilled at it. Right from the first day in the cabin, remember?"

"You sure?"

"It's a gamble, but I'll stake my life on it."

Jake mused on everything he'd heard before he spoke again. "It sounds like you have, Nat."

Jake turned to her, struck by Nat's certainty. He leaned over and stretched out a hand toward her bruised neck. Shame kicked him in the guts as she flinched at the approaching hand, and he stopped short.

He was suddenly caught in a vortex of abhorrence, seeing himself through her eyes as his stomach turned over. Adrenaline still filled his system from his episode of anxiety, and it charged every emotion with a special power. The bile rose in his gullet, fired by his anxious episode, until he clutched a hand to his mouth and ran behind a tree, revolted at what he might have done. He had turned into one of the men he hated. He was as bad as one of the gang who had cheered as Mary's body had smashed onto the street to escape the fire back in Philadelphia.

Abigail glanced at Nat in surprise as the loud retching and heaving drifted over to them. He smiled tenderly and gave her a reassuring pat on the back of her hand. "I guess Jake believes you, too. It's his way of saying sorry."

He straightened and looked into the trees, following Jake's movement. His pensive eyes dropped to Abigail and drank in the woman whose confusion melded with her clear irritation at the men who were treading all over her carefully-planned operation. "Catch your breath. I need to speak to Jake so we can decide what we're going to do with you."

Fire flashed in her eyes. "You're going to let me get on with my job. Too much time has gone into this and it could cost dozens of lives if we have to start again. I simply won't tolerate interference. Not this time. Am I clear?"

He turned and fixed her with a cold grin as he removed the Derringer from her ankle holster. "I hear you, but you're unarmed in the woods with two criminals, and are in no position to give orders. Am *I* clear?" His eyes softened but the set of his jaw told her he meant business. "Rest a while. We'll talk, but I'm in no mood for ultimatums, Abi."

He pinned her with a hard glare and allowed his warning to sink in. "I need to speak to Jake. Stay there. Listen to a warning for once in your damned life."

The outlaw leader was still shaking his head in frustration as he strolled back to his uncle. Jake was pacing the copse as though he was trying to shake off the malignant spirits dogging his every step.

"You all right?"

Jake turned bleary, red-rimmed eyes on his nephew. "You believe her, don't you?"

Nat's eyes glittered with sympathy. "Yup. She's not the sort to allow anyone to be slaughtered, it goes against her values. I got to know her mind when I questioned her in the cabin. I explored her and tested her. I even know her breaking point. It wasn't pretty." He turned and sat on a fallen tree, lost amongst the troubling memories which came flooding back to him from that night. "You didn't see that side of her until now. You didn't have the chance to know her that deeply. Don't beat yourself up over it."

"Just how hard were you on her?" Jake asked, his face drawn and weary.

"Real hard." Nat flickered a reassuring smile. "Harder than you were. I broke her, remember? I took her right to her worst fears. I had to. She was too strong to fall for anything less." He dropped his head. "I felt like a shit, too, and I wondered what I'd turned into. Why was I even considering treating a woman like that? But I had to find out the truth to save our lives." Nat placed a hand on his uncle's shoulder. "We've turned the wrong corner when we're hurting innocent people to save our skins. It's time we reconsidered a lot of stuff, huh? We fell into this life. I guess we've fallen too far."

Jake sucked in a breath. "The thought of what I might have done is killin' me. I didn't even realize. I lost my mind, Nat. What's wrong with me?"

"Nothing. Not one thing. You're human enough to be scarred by all the hurt you've seen. Being human is nothing to apologize for," said Nat with a shake of his head. "It's not in you to hurt her. If you really wanted to kill her, she'd have been dead before I got here. Your instincts took over, but the real you won."

"Fine, so I ain't the brains of the outfit."

"I wouldn't say that. You see things I miss all the time. It's clever, just a different type."

"Huh? Instincts so good I half-strangle an innocent woman?"

Nat laughed softly. "Oh, Jake. You can say a lot of things about Abigail MacKay, but innocent isn't one of them. She'd turn us in, but she wouldn't let anyone kill us. That's about as far as I'll go. Besides, you've got a medical reason for what happened. She hasn't. She's with McCully, and she has some explaining to do. Why don't they just arrest the bastard?"

Jake dropped down onto a log and supported his pale face in his hands. "I was hit by what I nearly did; I was like the men who hit our place in Philly when we were kids. My stomach turned over at the thought of it. My sister's body layin' there at that angle. No human body could make that shape without being broken. She jumped to escape the fire they set. How could grown men cheer the death of a girl just because she was Irish?"

"Yeah. The Know Nothings? Evil bastards. They claimed to hate Catholics, but the way they hungered for violence, I think they hated everyone and anything." Nat gripped Jake's forearm reassuringly, knowing the visions which filled his mind with nightmares. "You ain't that man. You're better than that, or I wouldn't be sitting here with you, family or not."

He laid an arm on Jake's shoulder. "Well, partner. The question is where do we go from here? Do we high tail it outta here and let McCully target someone else, or do we get involved and help her?"

"She don't want our help. She's got agents ready to take our place."

"They ain't got the vested interest we got."

"True." Jake sighed.

Nat paused. "We got two big advantages, though."

"What?"

"We know what he looks like, but he doesn't know what we look like."

"And the other?"

His grinned widened. "We got you. You lied about us being brothers to keep us together in the orphanage when our folks were killed. You're the man who feigned a bad chest to stop from getting adopted, and taught me to do the same. The same man who took me from the orphan train going across country trying to sell us off as cheap labor to farmers, and found us a good home with Pearl. If you could do all that when you were a little kid, what can you do now? There's grown men who can't keep a family together. You're remarkable. You're way better'n McCully at every single thing you do. Especially with a gun."

Jake raised his deep blue eyes to his nephew. "I could've killed her, Nat."

"But you didn't. You chose not to because you're better than that, even in the middle of an attack. I know you get the horrors from what you saw that day and I know what brings them on. I guess I was too young, and you protected me from it. You get dreams as well as waking flashes and tremors. Your mind went to the wrong place, but you still couldn't follow through. She'll understand. I guess we've got to tell her more about our past so she understands...everything."

"What am I gonna say to her?"

The sound of hooves clattered in the background and both men turned. Nat groaned. "How about, *why are you stealing Nat's horse, Abi?*" He leaped to his feet. "Stay here, I'll get her. That damned woman is impossible."

Chapter Four

She was lighter on Nat's mount, but Nat was a superior horseman on a larger animal, and it didn't take long before she heard the percussive pounding of the horse battering across the dry road toward her. Abigail turned. She could see Nat high in the saddle with a forward seat, urging his mount on faster and faster toward her. She gritted her teeth and pressed in with her heels, but the pulsating thumps behind her were getting inexorably closer. The adrenaline flooded her system and her heart beat like a drum which filled her ears, but somehow, the horse refused to go any faster. The mare's ears flicked back listening to the pursuit, but the thump of the hooves got louder, which told her Nat was gaining on her. Her dress fluttered in the wind as she rose in the saddle, the petticoats annoying her as they flapped around, robbing her of everything but comic value.

Her peripheral vision caught the shadow of the chasing man closing in, an arm outstretched. A hard hand grasped at the reins, tightening them and pulling the beast to a halt.

"Whoa, there, Gypsy. Good girl." Nat glared at her. "That was aimed at the horse. Not you. What the hell are you playin' at, Abi?"

"If he didn't want me taking his horse, he shouldn't have brought me out here."

"That's *my* damned horse. This isn't over. You can't go running off."

She raised her chin. "Oh, it's well and truly over. You need to put as many miles between yourself and Everlasting as possible so I can get on with my job."

Nat gathered the tethers in his hands, his jaw firming. "No, it isn't. For a start, you need to understand what happened back there...and why."

She tilted back her head, eyes flashing. "Your uncle nearly strangled me while you discussed more convenient ways to kill me. What else is there to discuss?"

"There's why." He paused, his voice softening. "He was diagnosed by a doctor in the orphanage as having irritable heart. That's what you saw today."

Her brows gathered. "Irritable heart? He has a bad heart?"

He shook his head. "He's as strong as an ox. It's more a melancholia which comes with attacks of panic or the horrors. It's his reacting to a terrible event from his past that never leaves him. It shifts his reality back to when the damage was done; when he was first traumatized. He doesn't get it often now. It can come when he's asleep as bad dreams." He paused and gazed at her pointedly. "Or when he's forced to face the things which it caused it in the first place, like the loss of a loved one. They diagnosed a lot of soldiers with irritable heart after the war, but some children saw enough to have it, too."

"Children?" Her brow creased. "He wasn't a child during the war. He'd have been, what? Maybe twenty-three or twenty-four when it started."

Nat's horse shifted under him. "The damage was done by then. Have you ever heard of the Know Nothings?"

She shook her head. "Who? No."

"We came here from Ireland in the eighteen forties. The potato famine caused a lot of us to emigrate. There was a big influx of German Catholics, too, and the change worried a lot of Protestants. They felt outnumbered and threatened. They formed a political movement called the Native Party, but everyone called them the Know Nothings because they'd commit violent crimes in public, and everyone in the community would *know nothing* when the authorities tried to do anything about it. They weren't interested in what Catholic witnesses had to say. We didn't count." His face hardened. "They did terrible things, and our folks got caught up in it." He paused and dropped his head. "Nobody cared. Nobody helped Jake. He saw it all, and it damaged him."

Her jaw dropped open. "Where was this? What happened?"

"Philadelphia. Our folks lived in a rundown house. Three families in one place, and we had the room right at the top. The men were back from work for the day, and everyone was in there. Jake was twelve, and had been sent to deliver work the women had done at home. Piece-work, decorations for hats, that sort of thing. I went with him, to get me out from under their feet. I was only about four, and worshipped my uncle Jake. When we got back, the place was alight and surrounded by a baying mob that'd blocked the doors back and front. Mary, one of Jake's sisters, climbed out of the attic window and tried to escape across the roof. She fell." He swallowed hard and dropped his head. "She was my aunt. They say her head split right open, but I don't remember it. Jake made sure I didn't see, I think—I'm not sure. He watched everything…and was never the same again. It's how we were orphaned. They all died, and he heard them scream as they burned to death."

"Oh, Nat!" She reached out and grasped his arm.

"He did everything he could to keep us together by lying to the authorities and saying we were brothers. We pretended to be too sick to get adopted as cheap labor. Then, we ran away and he looked after me all by himself." His shrug was weak. "He doesn't have these episodes often, but it's not the real him. It's what happened to him. It's like an old wound or a scar that plays up. He starts breathing too fast, he gets tingling, and his head buzzes. He can't think straight. It takes something to set him off, and the thought of McCully putting a bullet in our heads was enough. I'm sorry you experienced that. Yelling at him or fighting him wouldn't have helped. That's why I talked to him the way I did when he had you by the throat. He needed to be diverted, not confronted. That would have made him worse."

Her mind ran through everything she knew about the gunman, picking out his squeamishness around violence connected to women, and remembering the man who had fixated on the little girl they'd seen when they had broken into the undertaker's office in Bannen. His breathing had changed and his body stiffened; she'd had to nudge him out of his trance. Words from her training came back to her. The woman who had trained her talked of the mental state of traumatized warriors and how dangerous they could be when they snapped. Her blood ran cold at the rider to the lesson ringing in her ears, *"They often take their own lives. Their greatest danger is to themselves, but they can occasionally run with a folly which puts them right back in that moment and they don't see what is really going on around them. Be aware."*

Her brow creased. "Poor Jake. Can't anyone help?"

He shook his head. "Nope. I've tried to read about it, but there isn't much out there."

Soft brown eyes fixed on him. "I'm sorry, Mr. Quinn."

His cheek pitted with a joyless dimple. "Back to Mr. Quinn again? I was *Nat* a few seconds ago."

She dropped her head. "A few seconds ago, you were four years old and watching your family die horribly. I'm so sorry. I really am."

He urged his mount into action, ponying her mare along with him. "Good, because that's why you and him need to clear the air, for both your sakes."

Her brows curved in surprise. "Why for *my* sake?"

"Because I'm not finished with you yet, Abigail MacKay. Not by a long shot, and if you're going to be around, you need to understand a few things about us."

She opened her mouth, but he kicked the pace to a canter and left her reply hanging in the air.

Chapter Five

Jake Conroy walked back into the clearing and fixed Abigail with eyes full of contrition and shame. "I'm sorry Abi. Real sorry."

Soft eyes drifted over to him, her physical vulnerability hitting him like a blow to the stomach as Nat lifted her from the horse. Her tiny waist was only about the size of his thigh, and her soft, white hands with their long, delicate, fingers plucked at her skirts where she subconsciously worked at the fabric. How could he have even have thought about grasping her around the throat?

Her weak smile warmed her face as she walked over to him. "I'm sorry, Jake." She embraced him before she pulled back and examined him. "I'm fine. Honestly. Come and sit. Talk to me." She wandered over to a tree and settled down, patting the ground next to her.

He crouched beside her and looked at her throat, the burning redness and congestion already promising intense bruising, especially where now-torn fabric had dug in to her pale flesh. His stomach rolled with self-reproach. She was no more than five-foot-four and built like a sparrow. What chance did she stand in a physical confrontation with a man who had at more than seventy pounds on her?

"I thought you were going to get us killed. I was wrong."

She nodded. "I know what you thought. Come. Sit with me."

She drew her knees up and wrapped her arms around them in a gesture he read as self-protection as he closed his eyes and slid his back down the tree trunk until he dropped on the ground beside her.

"Look, I think we got off on the wrong foot somewhere. You thought I would shoot a boy, and we sorted that out. I thought you'd hand us over to a man like McCully. I hope you'll forgive me."

"I do forgive you. You run on your instincts and act too fast sometimes." She shrugged. "A wise man once told me we all do that, at times. It's fine. I understand."

He looked at her, her eyes downcast, still staring off at her feet through her long, black lashes. "It would help if you could bear to look at me."

She gave him a sideways look, her rueful smile lit with regret. "We're really not that different, you know. It's the past. It marked us. If things hadn't turned out like they did, I'd have been married and running a home. I'd be a different person. So would you. I can't blame you for that. I understand it."

His voice dripped with sorrow. "And kids. Maybe even kids."

She turned her head to look at him properly, picking up on the tone and sensing he was no longer talking about her. "Yes. Definitely children."

"And a home. Just stay in one place and make friends. Build a future." He stopped himself, realizing he was getting caught in his feelings again, and met her gaze.

She smiled at him. "Go on."

He shook his head and narrowed his eyes with a blue twinkle, realizing she was drawing him out. "You had no time for a man in your life? You've got no need to run."

"No need? I have every need; it's just not the same reason as you." She shrugged. "I'm too much like hard work for most men. I won't do as I'm told, as you've probably noticed. There's no place for women like me in this world. I don't fit in." She reached out and took his hand. "That's hard, but I've carved out an area to make the next best thing."

He caught the angst in her voice, knowing better than anyone how it felt to be misunderstood. "Abi, can you forgive me? I promise I'll never do anythin' like that again."

"There's nothing to forgive." She gave huge sigh before she stood and shook the grass from her skirts. "It's a dangerous life. I have to expect a few bruises."

"Not from me, you don't."

"I know, Jake. Don't overthink this. It's another lesson, huh? We know one another better, now." She walked off toward the river, but he stood and followed her, standing right in front of her with a nervous smile. "Remember you did this in Bannen to make me talk?"

She stopped and regarded him with gentle eyes before her face broke into a smile. "Yes, Jake, if you want my forgiveness then you have it, freely and from my heart. It's fine. It's forgotten. But will you leave this place? Take your nephew and go. Go as far away from here as you can, and don't come back. It is dangerous for you here, but not because of me." She took his hand and drew it to her lips, kissing the knuckles with velvet lips. "We're even. No bad feelings, huh? I need to go and think about how I'm going to explain all this to McCully. Someone will have seen us, and he'll know. Just give me time before we go back, please."

He watched her back recede as she walked away to bathe her wounds in the river as he felt Nat's hand in the center of his back.

"Just let her be, Jake. She's right. Someone'll have told McCully."

"What did you tell her, Nat?" He gulped down a knot of angst before Nat spoke again.

"The truth." Nat folded his arms and shifted his weight onto one leg. "Just be glad she's not angry at you. She has a Scottish temper; remember what she did in the cabin? She smashed me on the head with a jug."

"I'd be happier if she smashed me with somethin'. I deserve it." He mulled over her words, suddenly coming to a decision as he fixed Nat with a determined gaze. "You wanted to know if we should leave or get involved. We stay. We get involved."

"Are you serious?"

"Ain't never been more serious in my life. McCully doesn't know what we look like, and if anythin' goes wrong, she'll get a bullet in her brain. I ain't gonna let that happen. I owe her. Then, we're even."

Nat threw his uncle a huge grin. "We'd need to be real careful. The men from the bank could recognize our voices."

"So we don't go to the bank. There must be a way to trap McCully?"

Nat's eyes sparkled as only his could. "There's a way to trap anyone, Jake. I bet nobody ever tried to pull a flim flam on McCully before. In fact, I don't think he'd be expectin' it at all."

◆◊◆

Abigail returned from the river, dabbing at her neck with a damp handkerchief trimmed with delicate lace.

"I want to know why you don't just arrest McCully?" asked Nat.

"Being a bounty hunter isn't illegal. We need to prove he's killing people." Abigail's chin set with determination. "I work on getting a conviction in court, Mr. Quinn. I don't go around exacting revenge."

Nat folded his arms. "Are you alone in that boarding house? Surely, they wouldn't put a woman in there with McCully without backup?"

"Of course I'm alone. It would be too easy to spot backup."

"Unbelievable," muttered Jake. "It's like puttin' a kitten in a box with a rattlesnake."

"Hardly." Abigail scowled. "This is what I *do*. I'm aware of the danger."

Jake shook his head in exasperation. "Bein' aware doesn't stop a bullet to the head. That's how he kills witnesses. That's how he'll kill you."

A range of emotions flickered over Abigail's face. "Well? What have you decided?"

Nat's cheek dimpled. "We're goin' to take you back. You're

right. It would cost lives to start again and I couldn't have that on my conscience. But we stick around to make sure you're safe."

"You can't!"

"I can, and I will, Abi." Nat examined her neck. "We need an explanation for that." He leaned over and released the clasp on her string of pearls before dropping them into his jacket pocket as she cried out in indignation.

"Those are from the agency. Mr. Pinkerton will want them back."

Nat's lingering look dripped with thinly-veiled exasperation. "Lady, he needs to thank his lucky stars he gets *you* back. You got robbed, they stole your necklace. That's how your neck got bruised. You went to the first man you found for help and he rode you around to look for them. That man was Jake." His eyes glittered at her to quieten the objection on her lips. "The maid saw you with him. You need a story to go back with. Don't crowd me, lady, or I might change my mind completely."

♦◊♦

"All my male boarders sleep on the ground floor, dear. Only the ladies are allowed upstairs. No men. This is a respectable place."

Mrs. MacPhee peered through her round spectacles as Jake Conroy saw himself reflected in the twinkling crescents of the thick lenses. She drank in the man in the crisp suit and starched collar before her. He looked decent enough, but there was a rawness about him which worried her enough to find out more.

"Respectable? Of course. That's why I chose it, ma'am."

He threw her his most charming smile as he put down his hat and tried the wrought iron bed. The springs squeaked as he bounced, his arms akimbo like a child. "Comfy, ma'am. Real comfy."

"What business did you say you were in, Mr. Black?"

"I didn't, ma'am."

"Oooh?" she vocalized a range of notes querulously. "I do

like to know who's in my home. It's only right."

"Sure it is. If you were my mother I'd be makin' sure myself. You got any family, Mrs. MacPhee?"

"No, Mr. Black. Mr. MacPhee died years ago, and we were never blessed."

"How sad. Mrs. Black and I have a boy and a girl. I couldn't imagine life without them. Especially my baby girl." He tilted his head and observed her. "I bet you'd have been a wonderful mother. You have such kind eyes. Very beautiful."

"Oh, you flirt!"A hand leapt to her chest as the landlady's train of thought slammed to a halt. Jake stepped into the void.

"I'll take it. It's got a real family feel to it. Who wants a room near a saloon bar? A man'll never get any sleep." His eyes swept across the frilly curtains, the doilies, and the Broderie Anglaise trimmed pillows, yet he managed to speak without a trace of irony. "It's just what I'm lookin' for."

◆◇◆

"This is my new boarder. Mr. Black."

All the faces lining the long dining table turned to face the newcomer as Abigail choked on her glass of water as she took in Jake Conroy's sapphire eyes and tousled hair.

Mrs. MacPhee bustled over to an empty place and pulled out a chair. "This is your place, Mr. Black. I like to try to maintain boy, girl, boy, girl, like they do at fine dinner parties."

"Fine dinin' is fine, ma'am." Jake grinned.

"This is Miss Ansell, and Miss Pickering." She indicated the man opposite. "This is Mr. McCully, and at the end there, we have Mr. Stanton. He travels in ladies' underwear."

A man as plump as a bear preparing for hibernation smiled in welcome at the newcomer.

"Ya, do?" Jake smirked at the salesman and took his seat between Abigail and a pretty, young blonde with large, clear, blue eyes set in a porcelain face. He smiled a greeting to Abigail. "Miss Mansell." He deliberately mispronounced her name as he nodded to her, before turning to the other woman to begin a powerful charm offensive. "Miss Pickering, it's a great pleasure."

"Mr. Black." Abigail tapped his shoulder, knowing the maid had seen them together. "We've met before, haven't we?"

He feigned irritation at being interrupted in his pursuit of the blonde by his side. "We have? At church maybe?"

"You helped me look for the robber. I'm much recovered, thank you. They never caught the man you helped me look for." Her fingers leapt to her bruised neck, hoping he would pick up on her cover story.

"I'm sorry to hear that, ma'am. Real sorry." His brow creased with concern and he hoped he was displaying the right level of indifference before suddenly remembering her. "Oh, yes. How are you? I rode you around to see if you could see him."

"Yes, I'm fine. Thank you."

"Did the sheriff find the men responsible?"

"I just told you that they didn't." Her dark eyes glittered at him, pushing her next point with great meaning. "I'm sure arrests are imminent," she purred. "Very soon."

Jake Conroy nodded. "I hope so, ma'am. It's an awful business when a woman can't walk the streets in safety. Someone said you'd been in a bank robbery too? The Innocents, no less. You appear to be a magnet for troublemakers. I'll have to avoid you."

"I've been unfortunate," she answered. "I do seem to be making a habit of being in the wrong place at the wrong time."

"That's quite a run of bad luck. I'd stay indoors if I were you. They say these things always come in threes."

She fixed him with her dark eyes. "Oh, no, Mr. Black. My problems definitely come in twos." He ignored the obvious jibe and grinned at her as she spoke again.

"Are you staying long?"

"I'm not sure. That depends on my work." He smiled, and turned his back to Abigail again, shutting off her line of questioning.

"What line of business did you say you were in?"

The question came from Frank McCully who observed him

coolly from across the table.

"I didn't, Mr.—"

"McCully. Frank McCully."

Jake turned and faced him. "I'm a security consultant, Mr. McCully. And you?"

"Me? I'm in Asset Recovery."

"What does that involve?" Jake's stomach tightened, knowing what he recovered and how.

"Oh, it's not too far from your line. When something valuable goes missing, I try to recover it...or, at least, a proportion of the value."

"Interestin'. We must have a long talk."

"And what are you here for?" asked McCully. "The bank was robbed recently. Are you here about that?"

Jake shook his head, refusing to disclose a thing. "Nope."

"Here for long?" asked McCully.

"It depends."

"On what?"

"On many things." Jake Conroy's grin widened, refusing to disclose more as Frank McCully sat back and narrowed his strange, pale eyes. The outlaw turned back to the young blonde beside him. To the casual observer, Jake was consumed by her explanations on how she taught school to all ages, ignoring the dark-haired woman beside him.

"Mr. Black?" The brown-haired maid he had flirted with recognized him as soon she entered the dining room.

"Meg? I was hoping to see you." His eyes flicked back to Mrs. MacPhee who sat scowling at the head of the table. "It was due to her I chose this place. She spoke so highly of it."

"I hope so. I don't hold with anyone carrying on with the help."

"No, ma'am. I helped a pretty girl with her heavy shoppin'. My Ma raised me to be a gentleman. Ain't seen her before or since. Ain't that right, Meg? Besides, I'm a married man."

"Yeah. I saw you go off with Miss Ansell, though. Do you know her?" demanded a wounded Meg.

"Who?"

"Miss Ansell. She went off with you on your horse."

All eyes darted between them.

"Ah, yes. The panicked young lady who had her necklace stolen." He said as she turned back to Abigail. "It's all go around here, ain't it?"

"It was a traumatic day." Her hand darted to her bruised throat.

"Pleased to be of assistance, ma'am."

The downward intonation in his sentence made it clear he was dismissing her to resume his quest for the blonde on his left hand side. Abigail had clearly underestimated his ability to think on his feet. She pushed back the half-empty soup bowl in front of her and resolved to get him on his own. What exactly was Jake Conroy up to?

Chapter Six

Nat pushed himself to a sitting position on his bedroll as the faint sound of a metallic tinkling drifted over from the door. Jake had already sprung up, his gun drawn, before Nat issued a subduing hand signal.

He took his place behind the door as it slowly opened and a shadowy figure crept in, clicking the door closed as Jake struck a match and filled the room with an expanding bubble of golden light from the oil lamp.

"Good evening, Abi. We've been expecting you."

She whirled round to the voice behind her and saw Nat holding a gun on her while a grinning Jake sat in the bed.

"Put the gun away," she hissed, before she turned her back on a bare-chested Jake. "And are you going to put some clothes on? I need to talk to you."

"Why? If you break into a man's room, you've gotta expect things like this," he answered with a broad smile. "You never got dressed for near enough two weeks at the cabin."

Her face flushed. "And whose fault was that?" She turned back to Nat. "Are you going to put that gun away?"

"Nope, if you come sneaking into our room, you take what's coming. What do you want?"

She glowered at him before crossing over to the bed and sitting on the end. Jake grinned at her, his well-muscled torso glinting in the lamplight as she hoped he only sat naked from the waist up. Maybe breaking into their room hadn't been such a good idea after all?

"What are you two doing here?" she demanded, looking

away from Jake's distractingly tight body.

"We paid for a room." Jake answered. "There was no need for Nat to sleep outside when we've got this. Not when it's on the ground floor and he can get in through the window."

"It's my turn for the bed tomorrow, Jake," said Nat.

"Put your gun down, Mr. Quinn. It's not a toy."

Nat strode over to her, his pistol still drawn, but pointing at the floor. "I can't trust you, Abi. There may be back-up coming. You're here on a Pinkerton operation, after all."

"Och, for heaven's sake. Do you think I'd have turned up here if I had a gang with me? McCully would have noticed them right away. Who do you think it is? Meg? Stanton, with his ladies' underwear?"

"If you have, we've got a hostage." Nat eyes twinkled at her.

"Behave yourself, Mr. Quinn." She shook her head, her long curls tumbling around her waist. "I've come here to find out what you're playing at. Are you mad? He's *Frank McCully*. You're playing with fire."

Jake crossed his muscular arms and smiled at her. "We've come to help you. He's *dangerous*."

"I don't need any help. Especially not from you. You might as well wear a target." She arched a brow. "But wearing anything would be pretty good right now."

"Pinkerton shouldn't be puttin' you in places like this on your own," Jake answered with determination. "We ain't askin', Abi. There ain't anythin' you can do about it."

"No?" Her determined eyebrows rose.

His eyes glinted like flint in the lamplight. "Then maybe Nat should take you out of here and leave this to me? It's the only way I can make sure you're safe."

"Leave this to *you*? Are you talking about killing him?" She gasped in horror. "You wouldn't dare."

"Abi, Jake is quite determined to make sure you're safe after yesterday. He feels he owes you, and wants to deal with this for you." Nat gave her a mischievous flash of his eyebrows. "I'll look after you. I can be real entertaining when I put my mind to it."

"I've already seen most of your repertoire, Mr. Quinn." Abigail rolled her eyes. "I have a job to do, and you two are going to mess this up. What if someone recognizes you? Just what are you doing? I can't sit back and let you kill McCully anymore than I would let him kill you."

Jake looked wounded. "We ain't gonna kill him. We ain't killers, Abi. We're way more sophisticated than that."

"What, then? Why are you here?"

"I'm here to make sure you're safe. I hurt you, so I owe you. I need to make up for it."

Her face softened at his earnest tone. "You don't owe me anything, Jake. Get out of here. Please. You're the ones who are in danger."

"Nope. I scared you real bad, and your neck's still bruised. I hurt you like I never hurt a woman in my life. Either you come with us, or I stay here. It's a straight choice, but one way or another, I'll make sure you're safe. I owe you, and you need back-up around McCully."

"Jake, this is too dangerous. I can't let you do this. You've held up the bank in this town. This is just plain crazy. This job is no worse than anything else I've done over the years. If you really want to help, then don't give me anything else to worry about."

"You aren't going to change his mind, Abi. Not when he's in this mood." Nat put his gun away and walked over to stand in front of her. "He feels he owes you, and you may not think this is any different, but it is. Frank McCully is treacherous. As dangerous as they come. I wouldn't be surprised if he was already planning on putting a bullet in your brain if he thinks it'll save him from paying you once you've outlived your usefulness."

"Don't you think I've thought of that?"

Jake shook his head and muttered in exasperation. "Your ma must lie awake every night."

Abigail glared at him, refusing to speak as a grin of

realization spread over Nat's face. "She doesn't know, does she?"

Her porcelain brow wrinkled as she tilted her head provocatively. Nat chuckled, darting a look at Jake. "What does she think you do?"

"None of your business."

"I bet she'd have a conniption fit if she knew you were in a bedroom in your dressing gown with two outlaws at two in the morning."

"And one of us as naked as the day he was born." Jake chuckled.

She stood and pushed her way past Nat, heading for the door. "If you don't get out of here, I'll have to let Allan Pinkerton know. He may send someone out for you himself. Don't say I didn't warn you."

Nat shot out a hand and caught her arm. "You aren't gonna do that, Abi. Otherwise, you would have already told him."

She glared at his hand as his face dimpled in a smile.

"No?" she muttered in challenge as she met his eyes.

"Nope." He shook his head slowly. "You're gonna let Jake look out for you. You do your job. He'll do what he has to in the background, and no one's upset. More importantly, no one's hurt. Look on the bright side. We won't have time to rob anything when we're looking out for you."

She glanced over at Jake, still trying not to look at his rippling torso. "You don't have to do this."

"I do, Abi. I sickened myself in those woods, so God only knows what you must have thought." He beamed a determined smile at her. "I'm gonna make sure you're safe, one way or another. At least, this way, I'm just a businessman in the background."

Her chocolate eyes glittered in poor light. "You make sure you *stay* in the background!" She whirled away and stood with her back to him, sure of his nakedness, as he tugged back the sheets to stand. "And more importantly, right now, you stay in bed."

♦◊♦

"What do you want?" Abigail groaned as she stared into Nat's laughing eyes.

He watched the maid's departing back and took a seat in the ornate parlor beside the huge fronds of the potted palm which filled the corner of the room with lush vegetation. He made sure he spoke loud enough to be heard by her. "You've missed your publishing deadline. I called to see you yesterday, but you were out."

"Deadline?"

He dropped his voice to a whisper. "Yes. Your cover for McCully. You publish dime novels, remember? I'm your publisher."

She sat simmering at him as his face displayed his unconstrained amusement at her obvious annoyance. "This isn't a game."

"Get McCully in here. On some pretext or other."

"Why? I thought you weren't here for him?"

"*Jake* isn't. *I* never said anything of the sort."

Abigail glared at him. "Get out of here, right now."

"Nope. I need to speak to him. If he thinks a publisher's around, he might be less likely to get trigger-happy. He may think he's being watched and written about."

"I'm warning you."

"Leave it, Abi. What's the harm in a little subterfuge?"

"When you're involved, the potential harm is unquantifiable."

Nat chuckled as she stood and stormed toward the door. Abigail turned the handle and pulled it open. "I think you'd better leave."

"Who should?" A male voice demanded from the hallway. Abigail's stomach sank as she saw the unmistakable cropped, blond hair of Frank McCully enter the parlor, his broad shoulders betraying his bullish body language.

"Meg said you had a visitor. I thought I'd come and see who

was calling, this far from your home town."

He pushed the door fully open and looked around the room as Nat stood and proffered a hand in greeting.

"Walter Perceval. Miss Ansell promised me a draft of her story about her time with Quinn and Conroy. It's late."

Frank McCully's eyes darted over to Abigail as he closed the door behind him and leaned on it, blocking the exit from the room. His chilling blue eyes transmitted an earnest warning. "My name's Frank McCully, and she's workin' for me. It ain't her real name, mister. Suppose you tell me the truth?"

The smile dropped from Nat's eyes, but the grin remained as thought set in ice. "I know that. I wasn't aware anyone else did. Suppose you explain how *you* know it?"

"I'm payin' her."

Nat nodded and sat again, but Abigail noticed he concealed a Derringer in his right hand, crossing his legs casually before he glared at Abigail.

"What are you playing at, lady? You promised *me* the story; exclusive! Now, I find you've been dealing with—" He threw out a hand toward McCully. "—Mr. McThing here."

"McCully. Frank McCully. And I ain't a publisher."

"No?" Nat enquired, innocence oozing from every pore. "What are you and what business do you have with this woman? I have a contract, and she has a legal obligation to fulfill it."

"That ain't none of your business." McCully's eyes narrowed. "What's her real name? If you know her, you know it."

Nat looked Abigail full in the face before he turned to McCully. "Her name's MacKay, and she's the only woman ever to be held by Nat Quinn and Jake Conroy. I want that story, mister, and I'm prepared to fight dirty to get it. I have a female readership that'll pay dearly for it."

"How'd you find her?" McCully demanded.

"Her mother. She writes to her. Now, suppose you answer my questions. Who are you, and what do you want with her? If you think, for one second, I'm about to lose out another prize to Street and Smith, you got another thing coming."

McCully paused, sensing the anger simmering beneath the surface of a man so single-minded in pursuing the prize.

"I told you. I'm Frank McCully!"

Nat snorted dismissively. "You keep saying that as though it's supposed to mean something. Am I supposed to know who you are?" He tensed. "You work for the New York Daily Tribune, maybe? The name's vaguely familiar. I promise you, if you're planning on running a series, I'll tie you up in court for years."

"I'm McCully. You must have heard of me." The man turned puce, his starched collar looking tight and uncomfortable around his thick neck. "You publish books about men who're either fantasists or liars. Do you really think all those tales are true?" He thrust a thumb toward his chest. "There are true heroes out there who face down the worst criminals in the West, and you're not interested? Men like me!"

Nat shook his head and affected a slightly mystified air. "Nope. I can't place you. Are you a friend of her mother's? She mentioned a florist called Mac—something. Or, her hairdresser, maybe?"

McCully glanced at Abigail, his annoyance growing. "I did more'n a woman keeping company with a couple of outlaws. I'm a bounty hunter. *The* bounty hunter."

"Bounty hunter?" Nat shook his head in confusion. "Nope. Never heard of you. Who are you after, around here?"

McCully paced across the room and glared at the smiling man who refused to be intimidated by his bellicose demeanor.

"Surely if you were that good I'd have heard of you? Who've you brought in?" Nat pressed, seemingly oblivious to McCully's mounting ire.

McCully's hands formed into fists, but Nat was comfortable enough to push him.

"Some of the most dangerous men in the country."

"Yeah?" He looked vaguely interested. "Like who?"

McCully opened his mouth to respond as Nat's head turned

to face the opening parlor door. Jake Conroy strolled casually into the room, a newspaper thrust under his arm. His blue eyes glittered around the room before he spoke. "I hope I ain't interruptin' anythin'?"

"Nope. Just ready to leave Mr.—" Nat stood and smiled at Jake.

Jake Conroy thrust out a hand. "Black. Jonathan Black."

Nat's eyes lit like a Christmas tree in recognition of the name. "Not *the* Jonathan Black?"

Jake adopted a coy look and dropped his head. "Yes. Have we met?"

"No. But I'd like to have the honor." Nat eyes sparkled as he strode ever to meet him. "*The* Jonathan Black. You are exactly the type of man I want to speak to. Walter Perceval. Knight Perceval Press. We're always interested in speaking to men like you. I'd like to publish your story."

"I've never heard of Jonathan Black. What's he done that's so all fired important?" McCully interjected.

Nat's eyes glittered in McCully's direction. "Sir, if you knew anything about the West, you'd know who he is."

Nat stood and put an arm around Jake's shoulders as they wandered out to the hall, leaving Abigail with a seething McCully. Nat's voice drifted behind them as they walked away. "You have so many tales and I'd like to talk to you about a publishing deal. I can arrange a ghost writer—" He turned at the doorway and looked straight at Abigail. "Miss MacKay, we have a contract. I need the first draft by Tuesday, and no excuses."

◆◇◆

Meg snapped open the leather valise, her eyes darting around as she realized she had made more noise than she had intended. She paused, sure her rasping breath could be heard even in the hallway. She was not an experienced malefactor but she was the most obvious choice of accomplice to search Jonathan Black's bags as a maid had a ready excuse for being in anyone's room.

Frank McCully had worked his magic on the gullible girl until he had persuaded her she was the most bewitching creature he had ever laid eyes on, and their fortunes would be inextricably linked from this point on. She had to find out about the mysterious stranger attracting the publicity and money that should be going to her Frank so he could afford to marry her.

Her trembling hands raked through the clothing and paused on the battered notebook. She opened it, and out dropped two folded documents. Wanted posters. There was nothing out of the ordinary about them as few bore more than a rudimentary description, as the cost of reproducing photographs was prohibitive. Nat Quinn and Jake Conroy were wanted dead or alive—everyone had heard of them, but why would he be carrying these around with him?

The notebook contained cryptic notes; lists of banks with an amount of money beside each one, trains and stagecoaches also had a price beside each one along with a place name. As she flicked through the pages she could see a few rudimentary maps one of which was labeled 'G.C.'. The rest of the scribbling meant nothing to her, so she tucked it back under the blue shirt and picked up the bank book.

She gasped as she saw the quantity of money in Mr. Black's account, every penny of it paid in sums of thousands of dollars. The most Meg had ever seen in one pile had been one hundred and seventy-two dollars, so a total of over sixty thousand dollars was unimaginable to her. Jonathan Black was a rich man. Probably the richest man she had ever met.

"Lookin' for somethin'?" Jake Conroy stood in the doorway staring at her with a furious glower.

Meg dropped his bank book and twirled round to face him, her heart thumping against the panic rising in her breast. "I'm sorry. I—I was just—"

He strode over to her and snapped the bag shut, towering over her as he stood inches from her face. "Give me one good reason why I shouldn't get you sacked? Right now."

She shook her head furiously, her light-brown ringlets

dancing against her shoulders as her blue eyes widened in entreaty. "Please, I need this job. I've never done anything like this before. I was—" Her voice drifted off to a choked grizzle, unable to finish the sentence against the scrutiny of his chilling gaze.

He opened the bag and rifled through the contents before he closed it again, satisfied everything was still inside. He arched a threatening eyebrow.

"It looks like everythin's there, but you never know. Maybe I should search you?"

She gasped and backed off. "I never. I never stole anythin' in my life, mister."

"No? Then you'd best tell me why you were in my bag. What were you lookin' for?"

His hot breath burned into her face as she stammered her reply. "I was curious. Search the bag. Nothin's missin'. Honest."

His eyes narrowed as he stared into her eyes, appraising her before dismissing her with a curt twitch of his head. "Go. Get out of here, before I change my mind, but if I find anythin's missin' later, I'll skin your hide."

"There's nothin'…honest," she stammered as she bolted for the door. "Please don't tell Mrs. MacPhee."

Jake Conroy watched the maid's retreating back, his grim face brightening with a wry smile after the door was closed behind her. So, the first bite of the bait had been taken. She had seen the fake bankbook. It would soon be time to play in earnest.

♦◊♦

"I don't understand. What was in the notebook?"

"Directions to a place called G.C., and lists—lots of lists of banks, railways, and coaches with prices beside them—huge prices."

"Prices or amounts? Amounts stolen, perhaps?"

"I don't know." Tears welled in her eyes as she felt browbeaten and put upon. "He caught me. He's really scary when he's angry. I was lucky to get out of there alive."

"Why? What did he do? What did he say?"

She shook her head. "It wasn't *what* he said, it was *how* he said it."

Frank McCully sneered, disingenuous about how frightening the man he knew as Mr. Black could be when he put his mind to it. Hardened criminals took pause at one glance, so it didn't take much to scare a simple farm girl.

"You stupid—" He bit back his words, aware he might still need to use her. He strode over to the window and gazed out at the back garden, trying to ignore Mrs. MacPhee's substantial bloomers fluttering on the line and using the moment to swallow his irritation at the girl. "I'm sorry. You ain't used to this life." He turned and smiled at her. "Only two wanted posters? Quinn and Conroy, lists of what could be holdups, and a map to various places, one called G.C.? You don't remember details?"

"No. Why should I?"

"Hmmmm. He's got a real interest in Quinn or Conroy. He was probably listing all their jobs. G.C.? Ghost Canyon, maybe? They're rumored to lie low there, sometimes." He turned to face her again. "Did you see any other names?"

"No."

He paused, ruminating on her potential usefulness before he spoke again. "Can you bring me the book?"

"No! He's dangerous. I'm not going near him. If you want that book, do it yourself."

He glowered at her through narrowed eyes, realizing he had to string along an annoying, dim-witted woman even though she had outgrown her usefulness. It would be easy enough to avoid her though, as Mrs. MacPhee was determined to keep rigid social boundaries in place. He smiled. "I don't want to place you in any danger, Meg. Leave this to me."

◆◇◆

"Mr. Black?" Jake Conroy looked up from his newspaper, into the crystal blue eyes of Frank McCully. "Do you have a moment?"

Jake dropped his paper, leaving it open at the page he had been reading. The newspaper was local, and over a week out of date. McCully pretended not to notice as his eyes flicked back up to meet Jake's.

"I can spare you five minutes. Is it to do with a commission, perhaps?"

McCully sat in the opposite chair. "I couldn't even discuss anythin' like that until I got a better idea about what it is you do, exactly."

"What, then?"

"That publisher fella knew you real well. I can't say I've heard of you, but he knew you."

Jake gave him a wry smile.

"I guess that works both ways, mister. I ain't never heard of you, neither."

McCully tugged at his collar, clearly irritated. "I've worked as a bounty hunter for the last eight years. There ain't nobody who can compare with my record."

"If you say so, sir."

McCully's color rose. "So? What exactly do you do? What's he know you for?"

Jake Conroy delivered his best enigmatic smile. "You'd best ask him that, but I'd say it was discretion and success. I don't aim for fame. I get on with my work. The quieter the better in my mind. I'm not interested in his publishing deal."

McCully's gaze dropped to the newspaper. "That's an old copy. It's out of date."

"I know. I always like to get up-to-date in a new town."

"You're readin' about the robbery. The Innocents. Do they interest you?"

Jake folded the newspaper and tilted his head at McCully. "Robberies always interest me. They probably interest you, too."

"Sure do. But why that one in particular?"

"I never said it was that one in particular. If you'd arrived five minutes ago, you'd have seen me read about the town drunk doin' ten days for startin' a fight with a horse. You think I'd have a specific interest in that?"

"I think you're interested in Quinn and Conroy."

"You're welcome to your opinion, sir, as long as you know that's all it is."

McCully leaned forward and fixed Jake with determined eyes. "Look, if you're after them, we could be conflictin' with one another. I'm out for them, too, and we could get in each other's way."

Jake's brow creased. "Why are you tellin' me this? Surely, if we're competin' with each other, it makes more sense for you to keep me in the dark?"

"Who else could you be here for? There ain't anyone else for miles around who's got a bigger bounty on their head, and you turn up right after the robbery."

Jake sat back and began to tap the arm of the plump chair with his long fingers. "Are you suggestin' a partnership?"

"Could be. If you're interested?"

Jake nodded and leaned forward. "Or, are you tryin' to find out what I'm doin' and what I know?"

"No. There ain't no point in competin', standin' on each other's toes while we both miss out. It makes sense to pool our resources and get at least half each."

He sat back again and faced McCully with a grin. "Did you send the maid into my room?"

"No—"

Jake chuckled. "Yeah, right. If that's the standard of your work, I don't want nothin' to do with you."

"I didn't."

"She don't look like she'd be too hard to break. Do you want to reconsider your answer?"

McCully paused, assessing the hard eyes and understanding for the first time why Meg had been so afraid of him. "I wanted to know what you were doin' here."

Jake's mirthless laugh rang through the room. He stood, folding his newspaper and jamming it under his arm. "I guess that's the difference between a professional and a keen amateur. You ain't heard about me because I keep my head down and can blend in when I have to. Law enforcement and those in the know have heard all they need to about me. I don't care about anyone else, and I'm not interested in bein' famous. Is that clear?"

"Maybe you'll reconsider when you've had time to think. It's bad enough tryin' to bring in Quinn and Conroy without trying to duck each other, as well."

He turned as he reached the door. "You don't have to worry about tryin' to duck me. I ain't interested in Quinn and Conroy; leastways, not at the moment. They're all yours. I got bigger fish to fry."

"Bigger?"

"Too big for you, sonny. All you need to worry about is keepin' on the right side of the law so I ain't involved in lookin' for you, too."

McCully's jaw firmed. "Some people might say that sounded like a threat."

Jake Conroy opened the door, the ghost of a smile playing around his lips. "Really? I must have said it wrong. I didn't want to leave you in any doubt."

♦◊♦

Nat's suppressed laughter gurgled against his closed lips, trying not to alert anyone to the presence of another occupant in the room. "You think he bought it?"

Jake shrugged. "Dunno. Maybe? One thing's for sure. He's got no idea who either of us really are."

"Stage two?"

"Stage two. Shame. I've enjoyed sleepin' in a real bed."

"True, but it's my turn for the bed tonight, Jake."

"Yeah. I ain't happy leavin' Abi, though. I don't think she's got any idea how dangerous he is. We all know McCully killed

Seth Matthew's wife and kids, all the family killed the same way. A bullet to the brain before Seth's body was turned in a week later."

Nat nodded, his face serious. "We can't control what she does, Jake, but at least we can distract him."

"I don't think that's enough." Jake's eyes glittered like diamonds through the half-light of the room. "Seth was tryin' to go straight. He hadn't done a thing since he married Elizabeth." His mouth formed into a hard line "McCully's the most dangerous man either of us has ever faced, and I don't think she has the any idea what he's capable of."

Nat sighed and sat back against the metal bedstead. "That's her choice, Jake. All we can do is make her aware of everything we know about him so she can make an informed decision."

"We can't let a woman walk into that kind of danger, Nat. It ain't right."

"What do you suggest? We can't force her to do things our way. She won't have it. Besides, she's not your usual woman."

"Nope, but I wouldn't let any law man walk into it either."

"She won't be there. Everything's leading him away from here—away from her."

"Only if it all goes right, Nat."

"When have I ever let you down?"

Jake leaned forward to glare at his partner. "Don't get me started. What about that time you promised me, *promised* mind you, that we'd walk straight into the bank and there'd be a full safe sittin' in there. Easy as pie, you said. Who did we find there instead?"

♦◊♦

Jake swallowed the last of his coffee before he stood, dropping his snowy napkin on the table. He paused to glare at a cringing Meg before stepping over to Mrs. MacPhee and handing her a wedge of notes.

"I'd like to pay for the next two weeks, if I may. I have business in the area, which means I will probably have to stay away, but things are—well, they're a bit up in the air. I could be back at any time, and I would like to reserve the room, if that's all right?"

Mrs. MacPhee's eyebrows rose in surprise. She had never been asked this before, and she wasn't sure if she wanted to continue to do business with such an irregular guest. The size of the sum he offered, however, was not to be scoffed at, so she swallowed her reservations and accepted the money.

"Will you need the room after that?"

"I doubt it, Mrs. MacPhee. I expect to finish my business here soon, maybe even tomorrow. I may need to finish paperwork and things in the area though, so I'd like to keep the room. I will recommend your accommodation to the Governor himself. He likes his men to stay in good, wholesome accommodation."

"The Governor? Of the state? *This* state?"

Jake winked. "The very same. The name *Mrs. MacPhee* will be on his lips before too long."

Her large cornflower blue eyes sparkled at him as she clasped her hands in delight. "Oooh, Mr. Black. Can you imagine him staying here?"

"I'll be recommendin' it in person soon enough. Until then, it might be best to keep quiet about my work here."

He tapped the side of his nose, indicating he required her discretion, knowing all the while a snowball had more chance of surviving in the depths of hell than a delighted, posturing matron in a small town staying silent about an elevated social position for her business.

But then, he needed her to talk about his departure, his connections, and the importance of his business. He could rely on her to boost his status and reputation despite her complete ignorance of him and his vocation. The more McCully heard people talking about his competitor's impending success and reputation, the more pressure he'd put on himself through injured vanity. She had to remind everyone he could be back at any time with his job concluded. The pressure was starting to show in McCully's tense posture and pacing back and forth in the hallway.

"Will you be gone for long, Mr. Black?"

Jake turned at the sound of Violet Pickering's voice. She was still as attractive as the first evening he had arrived with bright, glossy blonde hair and clear china blue eyes set in a heart-shaped face.

He turned on his most magnetic smile. "That depends, Miss Pickering."

"Oh? I was hoping you'd be back by the weekend." She blushed and fluttered coy lashes at him. "There's a dance."

Jake grinned. "I'd like that, ma'am. I'll see what I can do."

She flushed prettily, embarrassed by her obvious approach. "I don't make a habit of asking men to dances, you know. I'm sorry if I've been a bit distant, but you've grown on me. I thought we'd have more time together, so I could be more…subtle. It seems I was wrong."

He admired her porcelain skin and the pert, turned-up nose. "You don't look like a lady who needs to do the askin'. If I don't make it back, I'm sure there'll be plenty standin' in line to take my place."

She turned her face to his, full of longing. "What does it matter if I don't want them?"

Jake Conroy smiled. "I'll do my best Miss Pickering."

"You promise?"

"I do. I promise to try. I can't promise when I'll be back. That ain't in my control."

"As long as you do your best, Mr. Black, That's all I ask. If you're not here, I won't go to the dance. It won't be worth it without you."

"I can promise that, Miss Pickering. I will do my best."

"Violet," she whispered as she stared intently into his eyes. "Call me Violet."

He nodded. "I'll do my best, Violet."

Chapter Seven

Jake lay back and placed his hat over his face and crossed his arms behind his head with a gaping yawn. "Remind me again why we have to sit on this hill, Nat? I ain't complainin', but now the sun's goin' down it's gettin' kinda borin', especially when there's a hot blonde and a cool drink down there."

Nat lowered his brass telescope and raised his eyebrows.

"You know why. Abi won't speak to me. It's the only way I can find out when she's meeting the Pinkertons who are pretending to be us. We've got to see who McCully's following."

"So you stay here. What does it matter if Abi's not speakin' to you? Violet's speakin' to me, and sayin' real nice things, too."

Nat glowered at Jake's satisfied smirk. "Did the maid tell her you were rich?"

Jake lifted the brim and cast a cynical gaze in his direction. "That ain't gonna work, Nat. She was sweet before anyone found the fake bank book, she's just warmed more. Quite a bit, in fact. I think it was me goin' away that did it. She started to miss me before I even went."

"It'll soon be time to move nearer to watch the place. We can't watch it from here in the dark."

"What makes you think it'll be so soon?"

"'Cause you got McCully worried, Jake. He's going to rush this, so he'll make mistakes. We need to be ready for him. The minute you're out of there, he'll make a move to make sure he's clean away before you get back. He'll want to get Quinn and Conroy before you do."

Jake pushed himself upright, leaving his hat on the grass.

"How come it's always Quinn and Conroy? Why ain't it ever Conroy and Quinn?"

Nat shrugged. "I dunno. It's how folks always say it. It's easier to say, I guess."

"I mean, it ain't like it's alphabetical," said Jake. "It ain't even as though you were famous first. I was runnin' a gang long before you came along with all your safe crackin' and schemes."

"It flows better, like bread and butter; salt and pepper; smoke and mirrors; fire and brimstone; milk and honey."

"More like ladies and gentlemen or Cain and Abel," Jake answered.

"Pearls before swine?"

"A fool and his money?" Jake replied. He paused. "How'd you think we'd have done if we'd never been told McCully was after us?"

Nat shrugged. "Who knows? I don't want to find out, either. We know what he looks like, though, so it'd be hard to surprise us. Especially you."

They sat quietly on the hill until Nat spoke again. "Do you think I'm getting too involved?"

Jake threw a cheeky grin at his nephew. "Don't even try to tell me you treat Abi the same as a man. When did you last meet a hairy-assed sheriff in a summerhouse? This one's down to me, though. I insisted on stickin' around."

Nat chuckled as he turned twinkling dark eyes toward his partner. "She isn't even the same type of law man as a sheriff, but no. I wouldn't let a sheriff deal with McCully on his own, either. He's a murderer. I think most men'd take the help, though. She's stubborn."

"Too stubborn, Nat." Jake shot a warning glance at his nephew. "We gotta get outta here as soon as we can."

His nephew nodded and threw a smile back. "As soon as we can, we head back to Ghost Canyon. Who'd have thought we'd feel safer on the run than in a boarding house with pretty women?"

"We took a real wrong turn somewhere, Nat."

"I guess we did." Nat stood and threw the contents of the coffee pot over the smoldering flames of their fire, shaking off the pensive turn the conversation had taken.

"Well, I suppose that's a good start."

"What?"

The older man's lips twitched into a grin. "Destroy the evidence of your last serious crime."

Jake Conroy ducked away with a laugh as Nat launched the pot at his head. "I swear, if you ever have a go at my coffee again—"

"I won't. Sometimes poison's as good a weapon as a gun."

♦◊♦

Quinn and Conroy lurked in the background and made sure they could see both front and rear access to the boarding house. It was their third night's vigil, sure any visitation would take place before the wee hours, as it was dressed up as an assignation with the fake outlaw.

They watched two mounted men leave from the rear of the building, followed within minutes by a lone horseman. Nat was about to emerge from his concealment when the rattle of a bridle made him dive for cover again, just making it before another mounted figure, smaller than the last, slipped by into the night.

Jake moved forward and hissed at the shadowy figure skulking against the shrubbery.

"Nat. We gotta move fast. Looks like there's more than one of them."

"Damn it! I thought this might happen. I think that was Abi. It looked like a woman." He strode into the center of the road and crouched, waiting for the wispy cloud to sail away from the silver face of the frail moon which hung in the sky above them. "I thought so," he murmured as his fingers trailed over the surface of the hoof print. "She hasn't got the sense she was born with."

"What?"

Nat's eyes glinted from under the brim of his hat as he tilted his head up to his uncle. "It's Abi's horse. I made sure I marked the hooves so I'd know by the tracks if she went out."

Jake snorted. "That woman don't know what's good for her."

"Bear her in mind if the shootin' starts, Jake."

His face was obscured by darkness but Nat could hear the scorn in Jake's voice as he barked his retort. "I came here to make sure she was safe because I owe her. Do you really think I'm gonna blow her head off?"

♦◊♦

They trailed the little party for about three miles, in a furtive game of tag, following their quarry, who was following McCully, who, in turn, was following the Pinkerton agents. The hooves and tack were wrapped to muffle against unnecessary noise as they used all the lessons they had learned over the years of felony to conceal their approach.

They knew it was unlikely McCully would try to corner the men on the road. He thought he was facing Quinn and Conroy, so only a fool would try to draw on them in an open road. He would follow them to ground and try to split them up and pick them off one at a time. That gave them the luxury of time, especially if McCully didn't know he was being trailed.

After some time, they saw the warm glow of a light from a small cabin nestling amongst the trees. The smoke from the chimney billowed into the still night air like a malignant mushroom, telling them that the occupants had arrived home and had settled for the evening.

The light from the uncovered window also told them anyone inside could be easily targeted by a marksman hidden outside in the darkness. It was a fatal mistake, but it was also where McCully would be most likely to take position to pick off his victims.

But the real Quinn and Conroy would be waiting for him.

♦◊♦

It took hours before they saw a shadowy figure creep over by inches to the window shining out into the darkness.

They had pre-arranged their tactics. Nat was to take McCully, while Jake took care of the bigger picture, so they adopted the roles which were so well-arranged they were almost instinctive.

McCully crept from his crouching position and peered into the cabin through the corner of the window. He removed his gun from the holster and slowly raised his hand to the level of the window sill.

He matched the pistol's sight to the back of the figure seated in front of the range. The man's hat was pushed to the back of his head as he sat reading the newspaper spread out in front of him.

McCully's pale blue eyes narrowed as he pulled the trigger, ready to blast the back of the man's head clean away. The long finger curled around the trigger, retracting it as he squeezed, driving the metal back against the metal housing.

He bit his lip in frustration, nothing happened. Not even a click. What the hell was wrong with his gun? He was about to turn it up to examine it in the light from the window when a voice hissed in his ear.

"Drop that. Right now."

McCully's heart thumped as he complied with Nat's demand, the weapon clattering on the gritty ground.

"Stand up. And keep your hands where I can see them."

The man stood, his hands raised. He was about two inches taller than Nat, and the light from the full moon lit the scene, cut with slashes of shadows from the surrounding trees.

"I guess your usual method of execution ain't gonna work this time, McCully. Now walk over to the well."

"Don't I even get to see who you are?"

"Why?" sneered Nat. "Elizabeth Matthews and her kids never got to see *you* coming, did they?"

The man stiffened before he replied. "You a friend of the family, then?"

Nat felt his distaste for the man slither down his spine as he narrowed his eyes. "You don't even try to deny it, do you?"

"What's the point? You'd never believe it wasn't me, would you?"

Disbelief dripped from every syllable as Nat spoke again. "You gonna tell me you're innocent? That you never killed anyone?"

McCully's harsh snort of laughter cut through the night air. "Of course I killed! I ain't never killed a woman or a child, though. I ain't got the stomach for it."

"Now, why would you expect me to swallow that?"

Nat's heart froze as he felt cold gunmetal against the back of his ear as a female voice caught him by surprise by her proximity. "Because *I* did it. Now drop that gun right now, or you'll get the same treatment."

Jake Conroy's voice cut across the woman's as he stepped forward, his arm raised, aiming his weapon straight at her head. His anger at himself for allowing this situation to develop spilled over into his taught, harsh voice. When he had seen the figure lurking in the shadows he had assumed it was Abigail, not Violet Pickering, who now stood with her gun pointed straight at his nephew's brain.

"No. *You* drop it, and do it fast. I ain't too particular to shoot a woman in the head if the situation demands it. Do as you're told. *Now!*"

Violet stood, coldly appraising the situation, not even reacting to Jake's yell before she dropped her arm with a snort as Nat whirled round to look into the face of the woman who was obviously McCully's partner in crime.

"It's Violet. Violet Pickering," yelled Jake.

"You're with McCully?" demanded Nat. He reached out and snatched the gun from her hand.

She glared at him, refusing to answer as the door to the cabin opened and two men, one blond, one dark, piled out of the door with their weapons in their hands. They took in the group outside as they raised their guns, the dark man pointing at

Nat, the blond one covering Jake.

"Drop those guns." The dark man examined Nat. "Who the hell are you people?"

The blond man abruptly stopped as his eyes came to rest on the unmistakable face and cropped blond hair of Frank McCully.

"We're friends," Nat stepped forward with his hands raised. "Keep McCully and the woman covered. They're the problem. He was about to shoot one of you through the window, but Abi obviously got to his gun, thank God."

"Abi? You know Abi?" The blond man threw his partner a significant look.

"Who the hell are you two? Who do you work for?" demanded the dark Pinkerton.

"We work for ourselves, but we know you're Pinkertons and our paths have crossed with Abi before. We've been watching McCully too." Nat hoped he was giving enough detail to be believable while still remaining vague as to his true identity.

"We thought he was going to kill someone tonight so we followed him out here." He darted a look at Violet Pickering. "We didn't reckon on *her*, though."

"What're your names?"

"Jonathan Black, and he's Walter Perceval," answered Jake. "I'm a bounty hunter, but McCully's bad for business."

The two men nodded. "Where is Abi?" asked the dark one.

"I dunno," Nat answered. "She wouldn't talk because I thought her job was too dangerous for a woman. You know what she's like when she decides to keep a secret. I've been operating on guesswork, but seeing her around McCully could mean only one thing. I marked the hooves of her horse and followed her here, but I ain't seen her."

"You idiot!" McCully snapped at the woman, "Couldn't you have stolen someone else's horse? You led them straight to us."

"Abi's not here?" Jake queried.

"Not without a horse, she ain't," said Nat, his parochial speech a clue to his heightened emotions. "I guess she's still back at the boarding house."

"Either of you two got cuffs on you?" asked the blond man.

"Nope." Nat's airy tone signaled apparent unconcern at meeting Pinkerton agents. "We saw McCully riding out followed by what we thought was Abi. We followed them on impulse. You?"

The dark man nodded. "In the cabin, you two." He gestured with his gun to McCully and Violet. "Move, now!"

Chapter Eight

Nat sat on his horse in Everlasting and watched the Pinkertons head over to the sheriff's office with their prisoners. "Well, I guess there's no reason why we can't spend a night at the boarding house. The Pinkertons think we're bounty hunters, we've paid for a room, and McCully's in jail. We can head off in the morning—" his cheeks dimpled with satisfaction, "—after a spot of gloating to Abi." He chuckled, nudging his mount toward the stables. "I'm looking forward to that bit."

Jake nodded, his voice pensive. "Who'd have thought McCully would have a sister who looked like that?" He turned to his partner. "I'm real sorry, Nat. I saw her in the shadows, but I thought she was Abi, so I didn't do anythin'. She could've killed you."

Nat shrugged and smiled at him, understanding why he wouldn't shoot. "Well, it was a successful night, and you paid your debt, Jake."

Jake nodded. "Thank God that woman stole her horse and kept her in Everlastin'."

"Yup, sure did." Nat grinned. "She's gonna be mad we were involved with her colleagues when she was kept right out of it."

"Not completely. She got to his gun and disabled it. She also fooled him into goin' through with it."

The smile dropped from Nat's chastened face. "I know. We helped, that's all. Though God only knows what mess she'll be involved in next." He turned to Jake. "She worries me, you know. It's like she doesn't care about her own life."

Jake tugged at his reins to guide his mount. "I know what

you mean. There's a darkness deep in her. Someone who carries the same blackness can spot it easy. She needs real light cast on that shadow before she'll live a proper life again."

Nat glanced over at his uncle. He frequently condemned himself for his lack of intelligence beside Nat's quicksilver mind, but he was far from stupid. Jake just lacked a brain which could process vast quantities of data at the same speed as he could process the tiny cues in body language which told him when he needed to draw his gun.

"Let's hope it happens soon, eh?"

Jake glanced at him. "It can't be you, Nat. We both know that."

Nat frowned. "I don't know what you mean. I'm not in the market for anything serious."

"Nobody is until it hits them." Jake chuckled. "She's special. I can tell, and she'd be interested if you weren't a criminal. Thank God she's smart enough to make sure she keeps well away from you."

"She's attractive. That's all. I ain't dead. I'm not looking for anything serious."

"She stunnin' and she's got a mind that can tie yours in knots. That puts her in a different league from the farm girls and teachers you're used to sparkin'. We leave first thing in the mornin', Nat. No excuses."

◆◇◆

The stable doors creaked open and they led their animals in, ready to bed them down for the night. Nat strode over to the oil lamp hanging on the hook and lit it. A warm, cozy glow filled the stables, lighting the way for Jake as he led them forward toward the stalls.

He stopped dead in his tracks as the horses shied and whinnied in distress at the sight in front of them, yanking at his arm as they bucked and pulled back.

"Nat!"

Abigail's body lay in a pool of blood which trailed and

collected from a wound on the side of her head as her life source ebbed from her body. The congealing puddle ran off into the discolored hay of the stall. Her head was turned to the side, and the blood found numerous routes across her face, turning into gruesome streams which formed a ghastly mask over her pale, lifeless face.

Nat ran over, gasping in horror at the sight before him. "Abi?"

He dropped to his knees and gathered her body in his arms as burning tears hit the back of his throat. She hung, limp in his arms like a broken doll as he hugged her to him. "No—"

He stared at her as visions of her face floated around his mind, laughing, living and challenging the world to take her on.

A tangible pain ached at his core as his heart cracked at the thought of what he had lost before he'd had the chance to even realize what he'd found. It was a soreness which began as a knot before it spread across his chest and stomach until every nerve in his body jangled. It was one he had felt before—too often. He hugged her to him, sucking in her scent as he stared in disbelief.

"We need to get help, Nat."

"She's not breathing, Jake. She's dead." He darted hopeless brown eyes to Jake, blinking back tears as his anger surged to the fore. "Her horse! Violet killed her when she stole her horse. I'll kill her, that evil bitch—"

"She's in jail, and she ain't worth hangin' for. We'll be there when they do. We'll watch the law hang her, thanks to the work Abi already did. It ain't worth you goin' down for murder, too. She wouldn't want that."

He realized Jake was right as he swallowed his helplessness. A part of his future had died with her. She was like him in a way; the good side of him, the positive, worthy, valuable member of society he could have become if things had turned out differently, or he had made better choices. It was too late now. Too late for almost everything.

Nat dropped his head and nuzzled into her, his face red with her blood as his tears pooled before they tumbled down his cheeks, squeezed out by his futile attempts to blink them away.

Jake stepped forward and laid a gentle hand on his shoulder. "Stay with her, Nat. I'll go. I'll get someone."

♦◊♦

The dark Pinkerton strode forward as his colleague delicately helped Jake extricate Abigail's body from Nat's arms, his face and clothes stained with her blood. The man's dark eyes looked into Nat's as he softly spoke with professional kindness, crouching to touch his arm. "My name's Tom. Tom Bartlett. I used to be an army surgeon. I'm a doctor now. Let me look after her. I'll take real good care. She's a good friend of mine, too."

Nat's glittering eyes turned to the man, nodding mutely at him. Emotion swirled in the chocolate depths before he swallowed his caustic angst and handed her body over.

"Were they close?" The blond man whispered to Jake as he looked at the darkness engulfing the man before him.

"Not really. It's kinda complicated. Maybe? If she had lived? They kinda thought the same way. They were fond of each other. Real good friends."

The two men nodded in mutual understanding as Dr. Bartlett laid her on the straw and started to make the preliminary examinations to pronounce life formally extinct. He felt for a pulse, he pulled up her eyelids and looked into her dull, sightless eyes before he brought out a small mirror and held it under her nose.

He held it there for a while before his back stiffened and he examined it.

"Bring that lamp over here!"
"Sure."

He held the mirror to Abigail again before examining the surface in better light.

"She's still alive."
"What?"

"The mirror! The mirror misted over, faintly. It was so faint I wasn't even sure the first time. But I checked. She's still breathing—just."

The whole atmosphere suddenly changed in an instant as the stables exploded into activity as Abigail was gathered into the doctor's arms and carried over to the local doctor's office.

They ran in a huddle. The doctor's office was only a few doors away, and Jake reached it first, battering at the door with his fist.

"Can you save her?" Nat asked, desperation coming through in his voice as he questioned the doctor.

"She's lost a lot of blood. Maybe too much." Bartlett paused, his irritated foot thumping at the surgery door as he was getting no response from inside. "Oh, for God's sake, man. Open this door!"

"Allow me?" Jake Conroy took out his gun and shot the lock off, meeting the doctor's surprised eyes with raised eyebrows.

They stormed in, the shot finally gaining the attention of the local doctor who appeared in a ratty dressing gown, reeking of whiskey. The man held a guttering candle which cast a flickering light etching shadows into every wrinkle and crease on his face.

"What the hell?"

The men were in no mood to pander to him. "She's had a shot to the head."

He blustered, but the men were in no mood to pander to him.

"It's a glancing wound, but she's been lying over there in the stables bleeding for a long time. She needs a transfusion. Why didn't you answer the door, man?"

The doctor gazed at Dr. Bartlett with eyes swirling with confusion, his mad, frizzy gray hair surrounding his bald pate. "I was asleep. Transfusion? I've never done a transfusion."

Tom Bartlett looked at the man through narrowing eyes before glancing around at the equipment in the office in disdain. "Where'd you qualify?"

"I—Philadelphia."

Tom's eyes narrowed. "What university? Which doctor did you study under? How many years did you study?"

Without waiting for an answer Dr. Bartlett barked out an order, betraying his army roots. "Mike, get him the hell outta here. He ain't qualified. He's a quack." He laid Abigail out on the couch and rolled up his sleeves.

Bartlett was an adherent of Joseph Lister's new work in the prevention of infections, and kept everything clean and as sterile as possible. "I need water, boiled hard; to a rolling boil. And carbolic. Knock every door until you find it. There's a pharmacist down the street, try there." He turned and yelled at Nat. "Find bandages. Make them into a wad and put pressure on that wound."

"Carbolic? I'll go get it!" yelled Jake, running into the darkness as Mike heaved huge stockpots out from a kitchen cupboard and put all the water he could find on to boil.

Dr. Bartlett fixed Nat with determined eyes. "She needs blood. It's not always successful, but it's all we got. I can give a pint. Can you?"

Nat looked at her broken body on the table as he let out the breath he hadn't realized he had been holding. "Blood?" This concept was new to him, and the doubt flickered over his face.

"Yes. She's lost a lot." Bartlett wrapped rubber tubing around his own upper arm, pumping his fist until the veins stood out. "We use our blood to replace hers. It's our only hope. She's nearly gone."

Nat didn't hesitate for a second. "I'll give you as much as you need, Doc. Anything. Do me first."

♦◊♦

Tom Bartlett walked into the kitchen and poured himself a cup of coffee, his face tired and drawn as he turned to the men sitting around the kitchen table. Nat still looked gray and harrowed, but had washed Abigail's blood from his face at Jake's urging.

"She's better. Her breathing is stronger and her pulse is

regular. She has a long way to go yet, and she ain't out of the woods, but she has a chance. A small one, but it's still a chance. The bullet didn't penetrate her skull, it hit the superficial temporal vein. She was knocked out and left to bleed to death in the stable. God willing, she'll pull through. She had defensive injuries on her hands and arms. I'm guessing she caught Violet sneaking off and they had a fight."

He turned and leaned wearily against the range. "She's reacting well to the blood transfusion so far. It's a desperate act, and it's usually the last resort because most people die from them. We don't even know why." He sighed heavily. "But we might get lucky. A couple of soldiers had their lives saved that way in the war, but most died. I'll have to keep an eye on her to see if it took. If she turns yellow and gets a fever, there'll be no hope. It's given her the strength to have some fight so far, though."

"Thank you, Doctor."

"You're welcome, Mr. Quinn."

Jake's hand darted to his gun as the blond man smiled, and he sat back and folded his arms.

"We ain't idiots, Mr. Conroy, and Abigail told us everything." His eyes drifted to Jake's gun. "Leave that. We're all here for the same reason; to stop McCully…and now, to save Abi. Relax. We ain't interested in you two." He sat back and smiled at both of them. "Tom would be dead now if it wasn't for you. He was sitting right in front of that window. Sure, McCully's gun had been tampered with by Abi, but he would have gotten his sister's and used it. None of us knew about her. Dear God, we'd never have left Abi alone with her if we had. She's a treacherous witch. Who knows how many innocent people she's killed in cold blood to help her brother make a dirty living?"

The dark-haired doctor continued. "I saw something in you, right from the start. Real humanity, at the cabin and again at the stables with Abi. You saved my life, so you get a chance. All anyone needs to know is bounty hunters who knew Abi stepped in to help, then disappeared. Go. You gave her the best chance of life anyone could."

Jake scowled. "You mean that?"

"I sure do. I'm not even sure we'd have checked the stables at all. If she wasn't found until morning, she would definitely have died. You didn't do this to stop McCully catching you. You cared about the lives he took. I can see that."

Nat darted an anxious glance at the dark man who looked similar to him in coloring, but had a Roman nose as opposed to Nat's smaller, straight one. "Doctor Bartlett, how will she be? If she lives? It's a head injury. Will she be normal?" His eyes glittered with intensity, but the question was asked through a haze of distress.

"The bullet only grazed her. I think she fought and that stopped it being fatal. It hit a major blood vessel near her temple, that's why she lost so much blood. She'll have one hell of a headache, but I doubt there'll be brain damage. It didn't penetrate the skull." He smiled. "There's nothing to be gained by you staying here. Her biggest danger now is infection, and a reaction to the transfusion. That's my job. Get yourselves to safety. More agents will be arriving tomorrow and they may not be as philosophical as us."

The blond Pinkerton smiled at them. "She was always impressed by you two. Now we know why. The best advice I can give you is to get out of here while the getting's good."

The doctor's eyes met Nat's from across the room. "She's got a discerning eye, Mr. Quinn, and I have to say I share your excellent taste in women. Go—before we change our minds."

"Wait." Mike smiled at Jake before he turned to the doctor. "I can't see why they couldn't leave after a night's rest. Can you, Tom?"

Tom Bartlett's trained eyes glittered across at them, noting the men slipping into fatigue before he nodded. "I think it's a good idea."

"No, I think we should leave." Jake Conroy's voice was underscored with determination.

"Listen," Tom said. "You saved my life. The least I can do is let you have a night's sleep. Go. Rest, and you can look in on her in the morning before you go. I'm a fair man. Besides, it's what she'd want."

♦◊♦

Nat stared aimlessly ahead as they rode out into the bright expanse of the verdant valley. Mountains provided the rocky walls around the rich meadow, topped by a vault of jewel-blue sky. A spine of dotted clouds swept off into the far distance. It was a beautiful, bright clear day with a mellow touch of autumnal loam in the air and a gentle breeze kissing the skin with an ethereal balmy breath. The temperature was perfect; warm without any of the oppressive burning heat of recent days. Birds chattered and sang their little hearts out as they darted about catching insects and selecting only the juiciest berries and plumpest seeds before winter's icy grasp shriveled and wizened nature's bounty.

It was easy to be alive on a day like this—at least, it was for most people. Not for Nat Quinn.

Jake Conroy darted an anxious glance at his nephew. He'd barely said a word in the last twelve hours. Jake wanted to help, but he had his own problems. He had sworn to protect Abigail and he had stayed with the man he had thought was dangerous instead of guarding the victim. It was a stupid mistake, and one he would regret to his dying day if she didn't pull through.

Guilt sat in his belly like a ball of lead, but he tried to present as positive a front as he could to encourage the man who had been plunged into more emotional involvement than either of them had realized. It had snuck up on him, ambushing him totally and completely. One thing was sure, there was no denying the depth of his feelings for the woman he had left behind in Everlasting.

"How you doin', Nat?"

His answer was an indifferent shrug accompanied by an incomprehensible grunt.

"Look, she'll be fine. She was even stronger this mornin'.

The doc said so."

Nat groaned and shook his head. "It's too early to tell. He was being kind. That blood could still turn bad on her."

A flicker of a smile flickered over Jake's stony face satisfied Nat had broken the silence at last. "It's Abi, Nat. She's a fighter. If anyone can get through this, it's her."

"Yeah? And how will we know? Can we contact her family or her friends? How about we wait for someone to write to us?"

Jake paused, knowing he was right. The possibility of never knowing whether she was alive or dead weighed heavily on Nat's mind.

"She'll let us know. She'll find a way."

"So if we don't hear? Is she dead, or she can't find us? How would we know?"

They continued in silence as he tried to find a way to put a positive spin on the situation. "If we don't hear, it'll be because she'll have seen sense and gone home to her mother's. She'll surely quit this world after this. God knows I feel like walkin' away and livin' like a normal person. I'm sick to my stomach with this life. I wish I had a proper home to go to."

"Maybe she will, but maybe she won't. She might never be the same again if she lives. She might be fit and happy. We'll probably never know."

"She won't do that, Nat. She'll find a way."

He shook his head. "How? We found her by accident this time. Either way, it's over. It's all behind us. Part of her will always be dead because I'll never see her again, no matter what."

"I know." Jake sighed. "I'm just tryin' to help you. There's hope, though, and we need to credit her with the fight to see it through. Then, you get on with your life, because either way it'll carry on for you."

Nat nodded. "I'm sorry. I'll shake this off. It was the shock; thinking she was so safe at the boarding house. Everything she's done and it happens that way, just for a horse. There was no other reason. Violet didn't know why she was really a Pinkerton. Abigail was working for her brother and became an inconvenience when Violet tried to steal her horse. Abi was shot by someone stealing a horse. It's so pointless. You never know the minute."

"Nope, you don't. But she'd want you to live life to the fullest until it does."

"I guess." He paused. "I feel so responsible. She was there to stop McCully killin' us."

Jake bit back the thoughts swirling around his mind. He wanted to talk more about how Nat really felt and what had really happened between him and the woman he had known for such a short period of time; but he couldn't find the words. Part of him knew the answers, and most of him didn't want to face the possibility that Abigail provided a window on the world Nat could have had if he had done a better job of raising him. She rejected Nat because he was a criminal, and Jake felt responsible for Nat's dishonest career.

He had seen Nat that morning, sitting on the bed staring at her blood on the shirt he had worn the night before. His eyes had been as black as midnight, as though recalling the nightmare could somehow change things. He had hurriedly put the garment away when he realized Jake was awake.

It hadn't hit him in the same way as Nat. It wasn't even close. Had anything more happened between them or had it only been a meeting of two mercurial and cunning minds? Jake desperately wanted to break the silence to find out more. But he didn't. It didn't feel right to intrude there. It felt too intimate.

He stared off into the distance, feeling impotent and powerless, little realizing his solid, ever reassuring presence was exactly what Nat needed right now. The fog of bereavement was as debilitating for those trying to offer support as it was for the person in the eye of the storm.

Nat kicked his heels into his horse and cantered off before Jake urged his own horse forward to join him. They rode into one more day of many under acres of sky, and into one more day of wondering why they always chased the wrong prize.

Chapter Nine

The snow floated down in huge, feathery flakes which settled and nestled on the already frozen timber frame buildings of Pettigo. It silently covered the houses, sidewalks, and streets with a fresh covering of freezing fleece until the scene was blanched to fading shades of grays and white in the arctic landscape. January had been a particularly cold month, and the bad weather had trapped Quinn and Conroy in town until they had begun to worry about their lack of ready cash.

Robbery was not an option to increase their funds. There was no easy way to escape, and in any case, tracks clearly stood out in the new snow for any following posse. That was especially true in a town which had decided to supplement its winter income by holding a January poker festival. Law enforcement here was good. It had to be, given the sums involved on the tables, but they never mixed with criminals in their downtime. That was how you got caught. They arrived in Pettigo as innocent, law-abiding gamblers, but had been driven into taking casual labor by their dwindling nest egg.

An avalanche had swept down the mountainside, blocking the railway tracks under tons of snow, ice, and rocks. Blasting it was out of the question. The noise could trigger even more landslides. They had to rely on manual digging and a thaw for the town to get moving again. To make matters worse, a train had been caught in it. It had missed the worst of it and remained on the tracks, but it was still trapped by snow and rocks with people still stuck inside. Nat, Jake, and every other gambler trapped in Pettigo by the poker tournament had supplemented their income by helping to dig their way through the avalanche to clear the way.

News had come through that the train had finally arrived in town after being snowed in on the tracks for two days. Celebration was in the air as tired travelers made it through to warmth and safety. Down-on-their-luck gamblers were paid to help out, so Nat and Jake were among those who swarmed forward to help passengers from the freezing train to guide them to a meal and hospitality. Those without somewhere to stay were found spartan, but suitable, accommodation. The men had been instructed to leave the hotel to stay in the church to make room for women and children, while the school had been allocated to younger, single women. A uniting stoicism had brought people together, sharing food, keeping people from sleeping rough, and helping those too old or infirm to cope with the conditions. Nat and Jake were right in among them, doing their best to fit in and look like normal low-paid drifters.

"Down you come little man." Jake Conroy lifted a tiny boy from the train before reaching to help his older sister. "Stand over there, inside in the warm. There are ladies in the station who'll look after you." Jake threw a cheeky wink to the thirteen-year old girl who looked into his startling blue eyes with awkward shyness before he wrapped his long fingers around her waist and settled her beside her brother. He looked back up at their mother. "Ma'am?"

"Thank heavens, we're here at last." She held out her hand to Jake. "Thank you. Have you any idea what it's like to be stuck in the freezing cold for two days with eighteen bored children?"

Jake laughed and shook his head, the frigid temperature seizing his exhaled breath leaving it hanging in the air like a frigid ghost. "Pure torture I'd imagine, no matter the temperature. I'll bet you need adult company. The ladies are in the station to help, ma'am."

He glanced over at Nat before whispering in his ear. "Tempted to sneak into the baggage car and crack the safe?"

Nat chuckled and nodded. "It doesn't feel right just helping folks off, that's for sure."

He put out a hand to help a youth who shook his head, refusing help as he bundled his jackets around him against the freezing air.

"No. I can do it myself." His voice had the amusing high-low of a boy whose voice was starting to break. "I can jump. Help the women."

Nat smiled at him, recognizing the bravado and posturing of youth. "Sure, son. Go on."

The boy leaped, slipping slightly before recovering his balance and composure as the next passenger appeared at the door. The boy walked off toward the railway buildings and glanced back at Quinn and Conroy.

"The station house, boy." Jake pointed at the building. "There's soup and hot drinks. They'll find you and your folks a bed for the night, too. The women have everything organized."

◆◊◆

Later that night, Quinn and Conroy walked back from the bar making their way to the church and their palliasses, knowing the straw-filled mattresses would keep them warm, as they crunched though the fresh, crisp snow

"Darn it. That drafty church will be borin'," Jake said.

Nat shrugged. "We haven't got much choice. We need to save what little money we have. We've no idea how much longer we'll be stuck here."

"We'd have a chance of winnin' some cash back if all the big games stopped all the gamblin'. I can see the sheriff's point, though. It could lead to trouble in a cut-off town."

"Yeah, and we're not sitting in on an illegal game. Getting arrested for something that stupid is how folks like us get locked up."

Jake chuckled. "There are folks like us? I thought we were originals."

"We might have stood a chance of earning decent money, but all the big games were closed by the time we got here," Nat said. "Stake money doesn't last long when all you do is spend it."

"It's been a disaster from start to finish. Right from the first day, when our train was held up," Jake answered. "I hate public transport. Why didn't we ride here?"

"Because it's too far and too cold. It'd have taken twice as long." Nat stepped over a patch of ice. "I really thought you were gonna draw on that fella when the train was held up."

"He wasn't gonna get my gun or my money. It's lucky for him he changed his mind."

"Lucky for all of us, but I thought the coach ride was worse."

"I sure ain't getting in another coach with a pregnant woman, that's for sure." Jake frowned. "I'll never look at them the same way again. Whose idea was it to come out here, anyway?"

"You said I needed a break. It was far enough away that no one would recognize us, and the poker would put my mind on something else."

"You *asked* to come." Jake scowled. "You said it was the biggest tournament in months you were actually free for. You were desperate. You shoveled on loads of guilt about how much you needed a break and the distraction."

Nat grinned at the memory of the naked manipulation he had used, but he wasn't about to admit this to Jake and be held responsible for the catalogue of errors which had dogged them since they had left Ghost Canyon for the winter.

Jake whispered urgently to his nephew, still walking on. "Don't react. We're bein' followed. I'm sure of it."

Nat darted a concerned glance at him. "You want to hang back, or me?"

"You do it. I'll double back and cover you."

They strolled on together until they turned a bend and Nat dove behind a bush as Jake strolled ahead. A small, dark figure approached tentatively, looking at the footprints in the snow before staring at the divergence, noting one set suddenly disappearing.

Nat leaped out, snatching the lad, taking him by surprise, and knocking him onto his back. He held him down with his weight as he clasped a hand over his mouth. In a harsh voice, he whispered in the lad's ear as he pressed a cold blade against his throat. "Looking for something?"

Nat felt the boy relax. Bemused by the strange reaction, he barked a warning. "I'm gonna take my hand away. Don't try anything stupid."

He felt the small figure exhale before he removed his grip. It took a few seconds before he heard a quiet voice whisper close to his ear.

"Since you ask, Mr. Quinn. I'm looking for you."

His heart froze, unsure if he had heard what he thought he had. His dark eyes glittered through the darkness a few inches from hers.

"Abi?" he queried, the uncertainty coming over in his voice at the sound of her rich, warm voice and the rounded Celtic tones of her Scottish accent coming from a pubescent boy.

He felt a gentle rumble of laughter vibrate against his chest before she spoke again, slightly louder this time. "The very same."

"Abi!" He sat upright and looked at the "boy" as well as he could in the poor light, still sitting astride her as he replaced his knife in the sheath. Incredulity swirled around in his head before it finally hit him he wasn't imagining things. She was really here, despite the finality of her appearance in Everlasting. "Abi? My God. I've been so worried."

"I heard. I had to come and thank you for your care, for your blood. Without it, I would have—well. You know." Her whisper trailed off.

"Abi." His voice dropped to a purr as he lowered himself to her lips. He felt her hands start to press against his chest as she pushed him away, but he enveloped them in his own and pushed them over her head and he held them fast against the ground. "Not this time, Abi. Not this time."

He captured her mouth in a hungry kiss, pushing into her with eager fierceness before he pulled back and smiled. The light danced in his eyes again for the first time in months. "Do you know how worried I was? How devastated, when I thought— How are you? How did you find us?"

"Which question do you want me to answer first?" She gave him a weak smile. "They told me how you reacted. I was shocked."

"Not as shocked as me."

He felt her tug her arms against his hold and he released her before pulling her up and lifting her from the snow. He embraced her, trying to forget the last time he had nuzzled into her neck as he sucked in her scent. He filled his lungs with her essence, only to be reminded once again of that terrible night in the stables.

He shook his head, scattering his nightmare at the sight of her here in his arms, before running his lips softly against her generous lips, dropping butterfly kisses at each corner before working his way back to taste her again in a probing kiss. His heart missed a beat as he felt her return it, clinging to him with genuine affection.

"Abi?"

They turned at the sound of Jake's voice behind them. "How did you know it was her?" demanded Nat.

Jake shifted his weight to his right leg as he fixed Nat and the *boy* with a grin which caught in the moonlight. He snickered. "Judging by what I've just seen, it had better be."

Chapter Ten

They sat in the saloon, the "boy" clutching a glass of bourbon watered down with lemonade. Nobody turned a hair, as this was often the way youths were introduced to alcohol in an area where the only legislation was shaped firmly around being able to judge if the dead man had drawn first.

Nat stared at her, barely able to take his eyes off her. "I can't believe you're here, Abi. How did you find us?"

"An instinct." She shrugged. "You use a lot of poker terms. You talk about people using tells, bluffing, and the like. I know you don't mix with criminals in your recreation time, or we'd have more information on you. You don't tend to work in the winter, and that's obviously because it's too easy to track you through the snow." She eyed them, one to the other. "Put all that together, and a massive poker tournament reachable from your area was obvious winter entertainment. It was worth a try."

"Smart deductions, Abi." Nat sat back, his eyes glittering with caution.

"Too smart. We've gotta be more careful. And the disguise?" asked Jake.

"Boys can go unnoticed up and down alleys and the like. Women can't." she smiled. "It was also a lot more freeing to travelling in."

A saloon girl drifted by, eyeing the adolescent hopefully. Introducing young virgins to fleshly pleasures could be as lucrative as it was fast and undemanding. "Hi, there, handsome. You looking for any education tonight?"

Jake snorted into his glass while Nat marveled at the prosthetics and make up which gave the impression of fledgling stubble and a wispy moustache. Abigail looked into the girl's eyes after glancing at the men.

Jake flicked a censorious look at her, deciding to play her at her own game after her antics in the restaurant in Bannen on their first meeting. Abigail had embarrassed him in front of an attractive waitress. He faced the saloon girl. "Yeah, sure. How much, honey?"

Abigail stared at him in horror. "I don't think I can afford it."

Jake Conroy's huge grin said it all. "Don't worry about that, Albert. We'll pay."

The girl eyed Abigail expectantly as the men smirked, realizing that she had no way of knowing they were on their uppers.

"Well? I ain't got all night, sonny. Come on."

Abigail glowered at them as her shoulders sagged, admitting defeat. There was no graceful way out of this. "No, thanks, ma'am."

"Aaaah, go on, Albert." Jake laughed as he gave her a gentle punch to the shoulder. "Make a man of you. A real man."

She glared at him. "No. Really."

The men dissolved into laughter as the girl turned away with an annoyed harrumph and an indignant look spreading over her face. "I can't abide time-wasters, sonny. You'd best learn not to mess with the help if you intend to start comin' in places like this."

"Oh, Abi. You know there ain't any other woman we could joke with like this. Not ever." Jake laughed as she glared at them.

"Well." She folded her arms. "Things are getting back to normal. Real fast."

"There ain't anyone else who would show up the way you do." Nat snorted as he threw her a huge smile. It fell from his face as he turned serious again. "I was so shocked. So was Jake.

It made me realize we know nothing about you. You know us. You know almost everything, but we wouldn't even have known if you were dead."

She sighed. "I'm so sorry I put you in that position. It was never meant to be like this. It's all so complicated."

"What happened that night Abi?" Nat asked.

"I don't know. I really don't. Either I was unconscious or my mind has blocked it out. I remember nothing, not even going to the stables."

"The doc said you fought," said Jake.

"Maybe." She shrugged. "It sounds like me, anyway. I really don't remember. Maybe that's for the best, or I might wake up with the horrors." She glanced at Jake, especially at the muscle flinching in his jaw. She smiled and brought her hand to her temple. "Nature can be kind at times. I never even dream of it. The bullet left me with a physical scar, but not a mental one. You can't really see it unless you look hard. Most of it is covered by my hair. There's a little mark here." Her delicate fingers rested on a scar just under her wig; angry and red in the cold weather. "Tom assures me it'll fade completely soon; maybe even within a year if I use wool wax."

Nat instinctively put out a hand but stopped short, aware he couldn't grasp a boy's hand in the bar. "So? What now?" He was reluctant to ask, but needed to know the answer. "Are you working?"

"No. I came to let you know how I was."

His smile warmed with relief. "Jake said you would do that. I didn't dare hope."

Her dark eyes turned to Jake's under the brim of her hat, still resolutely feminine and undisguisable with their long, thick lashes.

"So, where've you been?" asked Nat.

"I went home to New York and spent time with my mother. She was told it was a robbery."

Nat sipped his drink. "And that poor bank manager? The one you were engaged too?"

"He was told I died." Abigail sighed. "It's very sad, but it does free him up to love again."

"Good. I hope you stay at your ma's, too." Jake's brows met in a frown.

"Where are you staying here?" asked Nat.

Her lips formed into a moue. "In the church with the rest of the men. I have to stay as a boy now, because they'll know no more strangers could have got into town, and they registered who came off the train."

"We're there, too. Well, you can stick around with us. We'll look after you." Jake Conroy's smile warmed as he fixed her with an intense gaze. "I guess I still owe you. If I'd stuck with you, you'd never have been shot. I'm sorry, Abi. I really am."

She dropped her gaze. "That's not fair to you." Her earnest brown eyes met his gaze. "And it's not that simple. I could have stayed in the boarding house. You did your best. Really. Let it go. You can't control the world. You'll go mad if you try. Trust me. I know."

Jake nodded. "Well, it's over now, and you ain't stupid enough to get sucked back in."

She shook her head. "Nope. I'm starting again. Really soon. I thought you should know I'm fine."

"Abi, no!"

"Yes, Jake. I really have to. People like Violet McCully would still be killing if I hadn't been a Pinkerton. There are more out there. McCully killed for money, but she seemed to relish the power. I think she enjoyed it, but together, they were even worse than they were apart. People didn't have to die at all for the arrests to be made. It gave her a thrill, I swear it did. McCully's sister was angry when I confronted her in her cell, but it wasn't because she was accused. I swear it was because I had lived to thwart her. She seems to think she has the power of life or death over anyone who gets in her way, even a little. Without women in the law, she'd have gotten away with it. She'd pose around as a helpless victim with a pretty face. Other women never fall for that nonsense. My evidence will make a difference."

The men shared a look of concern as she continued, remembering the cold, controlled reaction of the woman before she dropped her gun. Violet had been weighing her options trying to decide if Jake really meant to shoot her. Jake also couldn't help reflecting on how quickly the ice maiden had melted when all other methods of finding out what he was doing had failed. What else had she planned if Violet had gotten Jake alone?

"I looked in her eyes and I saw real evil," Abigail said. "She was the brains behind her brother's technique to bring in the criminals, and she cut right through anyone who got in her way, always taking them by surprise. She kills the way most people swat a fly. She seems to have no empathy or humanity, and was furious to have been caught. If Jake hadn't been there she would had killed you the minute you dropped your gun, Mr. Quinn. That's how they worked. On their own, they may never have killed anyone, but when they combined together, they made a hellish duo. We'll probably never know how many they killed. They chimed off one another, escalating the hunger to kill. They killed because it was the easiest way to make money. They also killed anyone who saw them or got in their way."

"Will they hang?" asked Jake.

"She will. Her brother's turned state's evidence against her and is singing like a bird. Add my evidence, and she's doomed," answered Abigail.

Nat's eyes glittered from a grim face. "So? You're going back. I don't suppose there's anything we can say to dissuade you?"

"What do you think?" She gave Nat an intense stare as she hooked him with a lopsided smile. "We all know how the court system fails to convict women or young people if a lawyer paints them in a sympathetic light or they have respectable connections. They get away with murder all the time. Newspapers have written exposés on the phenomenon for years. The juries are made up of men, and they simply can't see that a respectable-looking young woman is capable of killing, or any kind of wrongdoing. Sometimes they need another woman to state the obvious. My evidence doesn't get around the problem we have of juries being made up of men looking after their own social group when they appear in court, but I can try to get through to them how evil Violet Pickering is. She has some kind of sickness. She will kill again if they let her out. She's dangerous, especially as she's so unexpected." She sipped her drink and looked at each man in turn. "There's one more thing. Smitty commissioned McCully to bring you in."

"Smitty?" Jake exclaimed. "That rich sonofa—" He paused, dropping his voice to a hoarse whisper. "The son of the railway owner who thought we were stealin' his inheritance? The bastard who tried to set us up for murder?"

"Yes." She looked from one to the other. "Cornelius Schmitts Dewees. He absconded from his trial and is on the run. His family is obviously covering for him. More than that, he's clearly still after you. I came here to warn you two. He has it in for you for some reason. Are you sure you've never met him?"

"Nope." Nat shook his head. "Not that I know of, but until I get a look at him, I can't be sure."

♦◊♦

Abigail shifted on the straw-filled mattress in the church hall, Nat lying on her right, and Jake to her left. The place was clouded in the thick, sickly scent of gamey men who had decided it had been far too cold to bathe. As if that wasn't bad enough, it melded with the smell of cheap booze and tobacco. There was a point where the nose was overloaded and stopped detecting the obnoxious odors, but hers hadn't reached that point yet. The cloud of body odor mixed in with a hall full of men passing wind who had consumed soups and stews just that evening, bulked up with beans to stretch supplies. The stench was overbearing, and at times, nose-wrinkling. For the first time in weeks, she decided travelling as a woman may have been better. She rolled onto her side and glanced at Nat. Even in the darkness she could see his brown eyes glittering through the shadows at her.

A rustle of rough blankets could be heard as he stretched out an arm and felt the warmth of his fingers curl around hers. She tightened her grasp, rubbing his knuckles with her thumb. Somehow, her near-death experience had been freeing, making her seize the tender moment with an almost reckless abandon. It wouldn't last, but she also knew she wouldn't see him again. Her new posting was in a different state and further east. So right now, she was living for the moment and enjoying the simple touch of skin on skin in a life as frigid as the weather outside.

A scuffling sound near the door made them withdraw quickly, pulling their hands back under their own covers while the heavy breathing and panting behind Nat grew louder. She could make out the silhouettes of three figures in the darkness of the room. An unsteady man looked like he was being supported on both sides and the reek of cheap bourbon surrounded all three of them. The man was hefted onto the vacant mattress beside Nat, the exertion telling in the grunts of the men assisting him. They finally covered the man in blankets and padded back to the door. The man's drinking companions clearly weren't staying here. Who could blame them?

Nat leaned over and whispered through the darkness. "Let's hope he doesn't snore, huh?"

"Sssssh!" hissed someone nearby.

Abigail smiled silently into her blankets and turned over. Before too long, she was fast asleep.

♦◊♦

They waited until fairly late before guarding the latrines and wash rooms for Abigail to complete her ablutions in private. The hall was almost empty by the time she joined them, her disguise makeup fully re-applied, and hungry for the breakfast being served over at the saloon. She paused at her bed to fold her blankets and watched as the man in charge of the hall prodded and shouted at the drunk who'd been carried in during the night.

"Time to get up. C'mon. This ain't a flop house. We expect folks to get up at a reasonable hour around here."

Jake frowned, pausing to stare at the immobile figure lying on his back and kicked the man's foot. "Hey, pal. Time to get up."

Nat and Abigail exchanged a glance.

The man reached out and prodded at the sleeping figure on the shoulder with his broom. "Come on. I ain't got all day, even if you do." He dragged the blanket away and stepped back in shock at the deathly-gray face, a vivid burgundy stain contaminating one side. "Whoa. That ain't right."

"No, it's not." Abigail stepped forward, frowning heavily. She touched his skin. "So cold. This man's dead, and has been for a while."

"Died in his sleep, I guess." The man muttered with eyes wide as saucers. "I'll go get the doc."

"And the sheriff." She pulled back the covers all the way and started to unbutton the man's shirt. "He's been dead a long time, and has been moved after death."

"How do you know that, boy?" the man demanded.

"That mark there, all down the side of his face." She pointed to the burgundy mark staining his cheek. "That's called livor mortis, and it's caused by the blood settling on the lowest parts of the body after the heart stops pumping. It coagulates and gathers at the bottom with gravity. He was left on his side after death, and the blood pooled on that side." She pressed on the mark with a finger. "Nope, it's not changing color. That means the blood is already congealed and he's been dead for more than twelve hours. Someone brought him in here a good while after he died."

The caretaker propped his hands on his hips. "How the hell would a stripplin' like you know that?"

"I—" Abigail floundered.

"He's a medical student." Nat cut in. "He's my nephew, and quite the prodigy. We're all real proud of him."

"Huh? A porridgy?"

Jake shook his head. "It means he's smart. If he says he's been dead for a long time, he's probably right. Go fetch the doc and the sheriff. We'll keep an eye on things here."

◆◊◆

"I take it this is him?" The doctor frowned at the sight of a boy undressing an obvious corpse. "Is this the medical student? He's far too young to be a medical student. Stop that immediately."

Abigail stood, bowing her head to hide her face beneath the brim of her hat. "Sorry. I was trying to help."

The doctor was a handsome young man in his thirties, with wavy brown hair and expressive gray eyes. "So? What have we here? Yes, livor mortis does definitely indicate the body has been moved." He applied pressure to the dark red area in the same way as Abigail had. "He's been dead for over twelve hours." He tested the arm and fingers for mobility. "Probably nearer to forty-eight. Rigor has worn off. He's stone cold. Really cold."

"He's been stabbed, doctor. Once in the heart. It looks like a long, thin weapon like a stiletto. There's no blood on the clothes, and little on the body."

"You shouldn't have been meddling with evidence, young man." The doctor's voice dropped to a growl. "I admire keenness, but this is too much."

"I'm sorry, but I've made other observations, if you're interested?"

"Where's the sheriff, Sam?" The doctor barked at the caretaker. "Get this boy outta here before he does any more damage."

"I haven't damaged anyth—ow!" Abigail squirmed as Sam grabbed her ear. "Let me go."

"Hey!" Nat pushed the man's shoulder. "Get your hands off

him."

The caretaker kicked out at Nat.

"Don't push me." Sam grabbed Abigail by the arm and dragged her out of the hall. "You'd better git, boy, or we won't let ya sleep here tonight. It's too cold to be out on the street."

Jake seized her other arm and pulled her back. "We'll go, but there's no need to get rough with him. He was only tryin' to help."

"Ow! Will you all let me go?" Abigail bellowed, tugged between the pair.

"What's goin' on in here?" A burly man with extravagant gray muttonchops and a silver star on his jacket filled the door.

The doctor paused in his examination. "Sam's getting rid of the boy, Ben. He fancies himself as a bit of medical genius and was meddling with the evidence."

The lawman raised a thick brow. "You want to end up in my cells, boy?"

"No, sir." Abigail dropped her head and pouted in an adolescent manner as everyone released her. "I'm sorry."

"So you should be." He gestured with his head. "Now, git."

She stepped away from the caretaker and walked over to the door, followed by Nat and Jake. The men shared a glance; they could see she was ready to burst the way her shoulders heaved and tightened. She reached the door and swirled around, yelling at the top of her voice.

"There's something else. He's been redressed after his death and they're not his clothes. They're trying to hide his real identity by leaving him here looking like a tramp."

She jumped aside to escape Sam's booted kick before Jake stepped in front of the caretaker, staring him down with an arctic glower.

"Wait." The doctor frowned. "Why do you say that, boy?"

"A few things. There's no puncture wound in any of those clothes, or blood. He was dressed after he stopped bleeding. The clothes almost fit him, but not quite. That's not so surprising in a tramp as they often wear second-hand, but those clothes are covered in brick dust. He has soft hands, and neatly-cut nails. He's never done manual work in his life. His callous on the left hand shows he writes a lot and he's left-handed. The wear on those clothes shows a right-handed pattern of use in the cuffs, and on the fabric, in general." She paused, glancing nervously at the doctor and the sheriff. "And the trousers are far too short, but the ends are worn. How can you wear out the fabric if it's flapping around your ankles and not rubbing on anything?"

The doctor stared at the slip of a boy in disbelief. "What age are you boy?"

"Fifteen," Abigail said, inserting a voice-breaking trill.

"He told the caretaker the body had been dead for over twelve hours and had been moved before he told him to get you and the sheriff," Nat said. "He's a real smart kid. He knew about that red mark. He doesn't deserve to be pushed about for trying to help."

"You look younger than fifteen." The doctor frowned. "What's your name?"

"Albert," Abigail said, staring at her booted feet. "I've never been big for my age."

"Yeah," the sheriff said. "Real girly, but It's a man's brain you got there."

"Are you apprenticed to anyone?" asked the doctor.

"I've studied under Doctor MacIvor in Chicago. He qualified as a physician in Edinburgh, and wants me to go to university to study." She thought on her feet to explain her presence here. "My uncles are helping me to find work to raise the money."

"Edinburgh, huh?" The young doctor scratched his cheek. "One of the best in the world. Impressive. Sam, let him in. He might be some use, after all. My name is Doctor Fox. Where can I contact this Doctor MacIvor?"

Abigail walked tentatively forward. "He has a practice in Hyde Park, Chicago, and does work for the Pinkertons, too." She paused. "But the telegraph wires were brought down by the snow. You can't contact him, can you?"

"He don't miss a trick, this one, does he?" chortled the sheriff.

"No, he doesn't," the doctor answered. "Have you ever helped with an autopsy, Albert?"

She shook her head. "I've seen a few. I've never helped." She bit into her lip. "And Doctor MacIvor always calls them post-mortem examinations. He says autopsy comes from 'auto' in Greek and means 'self'. You can't examine yourself after you're dead, can you?"

A smile twitched at the doctor's lips. "Yeah, I can see Doc MacIvor's real particular. What university does he want you to go to?"

"Lind University in Chicago."

Dr. Fox turned to the sheriff. "He checks out. If you're all right with it, I'll use him as an assistant. He's been trained to notice things I haven't."

"He's fifteen." The sheriff's gaze hardened in protest.

"That's the age apprenticeships start for doctors." Dr. Fox shrugged. "They start doing menial work, but Albert's obviously bright. I can use him."

"He's supposed to be working with us," Nat said.

"I'll pay, so it'll go toward his university fund. How about a dollar a day?" He raised a hand to shut out the protest spilling from Nat's opening mouth. "It's more than boys usually earn. It's a good offer."

"It won't take long, Uncle Nat. It'll be a day. Two, at most," Abigail answered.

"Fine." He nodded. "Just for a day or so. I was looking forward to spending time with you."

Her eyes lit with warmth. "I know. It's why I came, but it won't take long."

"Good." The sheriff rubbed his hands. "Did anyone see the body being brought in?"

Chapter Eleven

The skin was folded back over the corpse's face and the domed top of the skull sat on the tray beside the body. The brain slipped out into Dr. Fox's hands, more firm and gelatinous than Abigail expected. She watched, fascinated at the events unfolding before her, the pull of new knowledge overwhelming any revulsion she felt.

He frowned. "This is partially frozen. How cold is that church hall?"

"It's freezing, but I wouldn't have thought it was *that* cold. We slept there."

"Can you hand me that scalpel, Albert?" He took the implement. "Now, what do we cut to remove this?"

"The optic nerves and the spinal column?" she asked.

"That's right. We also cut the carotid arteries and the pituitary stalk." He sliced as he spoke. "The temporal lobes are lifted, and the tentorium is cut with either scissors or a scalpel. The cervical spine is then cut as far down as possible. The pituitary is removed by fracturing the sella turcica." He turned the organ in his hands. "It looks healthy, but that's to be expected in an obvious stabbing." He deposited the brain on the tray and turned back to the body which lay open and on display; a large 'y' cut displayed the organs, the pinnacles of the 'y' starting just below each shoulder.

"It all looks fairly normal to the naked eye except for the wound to the heart. I'll examine it more closely when we remove it. Let's start with the liver." He plunged his hands into the abdomen his arched brows registering bewilderment.

"What is it, Doctor?"

His brows met. "It's stiff." He felt around in the abdomen. "It's frozen solid beyond the surface."

"Frozen?" She peered into the cavity. "He must have been left outside."

Dr. Fox shook his head. "Nope. I'd expect to see bites and animal activity, especially at this time of year when there's been a hard winter and there's little food around. I'd also expect him to have frozen from the outside in. This is more like he was frozen solid and started to thaw from the outside overnight. His skin was normal." He wiped his bloody hands on his apron. "Let's have a look at the heart. Yup, that's frozen solid, too. He must have been a block of ice when he was dragged into the church hall. He's hardly thawed at all. I thought he didn't smell much when I opened him."

"So he's been stored somewhere cold? Somewhere animals can't get to?" Abigail stared down at the gaping chest. "Does that sound like anywhere you can think of?"

"It sounds like *everywhere* I can think of." The doctor wiped his hands on a cloth. "Just about every place in town has outbuildings and root cellars, and the place has been as cold as the crypt for weeks, now. We'll never narrow it down by looking for somewhere cold and private. Not in this weather."

"We can't do much until he's thawed, can we?"

"Not much without damaging the organs, no."

She paused. "Can you tell how long he's been frozen? How long has it been cold enough for that to happen here?"

Dr. Fox shook his head again. "Nope, I can't tell. I've read of frozen bodies being recovered from the bottom of lakes with hardly a mark on them after years. It takes nearly a week for them to thaw out. Mind you, once you thaw them out, the cells start to lose their integrity and the body deteriorates. I'm going to have to do some reading on this." He turned to 'Albert'. "It's a damned shame the telegram wires are down. I could do with advice on this from your Pinkerton friend."

"We still might be able to contact him." Abigail removed her apron. "But maybe it's not a complete waste. We can examine the clothes to see what size man they were made for and the trajectory of the wound. Do you have a tape measure? We can compare the suit measurements to the corpse. We can estimate height from leg length, can't we?"

"Yes, we can. Tibia, fibula, and height of foot. Also, arm span. We'd have to estimate hand and finger length."

"We'll have to estimate foot height, but the trousers dragging on the ground should be a good indication." She stretched out the trousers. "I'd say the top of the thigh would be about here, wouldn't you?"

"Yes, but we can also check against the iliac height. I'm going to estimate it as being about here. Get a pencil and paper, Albert."

She grabbed a clipboard, taking notes.

"Subischial height—iliac height—get that jacket spread out. Let's get the arm span from that. We'll have to estimate the hands…we'll use an average of seven inches." He leaned over the bench, scribbling figures and working through equations, resting forehead on his left hand. He stood back his lips forming a line. "I'm estimating foot height and hand length. So I have to allow for error. By my reckoning, the man these clothes were made for was between five-foot-seven and five-foot-eight-and-a-quarter, allowing for any variations within the normal range."

Abigail noted the figure and compared it to the height of the corpse. "That's why the trousers were too short. He was five-foot-ten." She took the trousers, turning them inside out, and examined the stitches. "No label, it's probably too old for one." She peered at the seams. "The stitches are even. They look like they're done by machine." She held it out to compare to the work around the waist. "A watch pocket is hand-finished, and the stitches are different. I think it is machine-sewn and hand-finished. The legs are wide, indicating they were fashionable in the fifties. The legs tapered more in the sixties, and would be about the right timescale for them being relegated to work-wear by the late sixties, and largely at rags by 1869." She took a piece of paper and knocked the fabric until a red dust fell onto the sheet. She rubbed the grit between her fingers. "Brick dust...I thought so. Is there a brick factory around here? I've seen brick-fronted buildings."

"Yes, the brick factory is by the river on the road out of town."

"Maybe the body was stored there? Let's look at the pockets." She turned them out onto another piece of paper, bits of fluff, a white granular powder, and sawdust. Another piece of paper under the other pocket caught even more white powder. She raised questioning eyes to Dr. Fox. "What is it?"

He frowned. "Well, I can test it, but I need it to be pretty pure to get a good result. That means someone sitting and picking through all those grains to pull out anything which shouldn't be there. You start that, and I'll see if there's any more of it caught in his clothes."

She fixed him with dismayed eyes. "What? Sort through tiny grains to find stuff that's another tiny grain?"

"Yup." He strode over to a drawer and pulled out a pair of tweezers and a magnifying glass. He put them beside her with a clatter. "There you go, Albert. You might need these. That's why I'm paying you a whole dollar a day."

♦◊♦

Her shoulders ached and her eyes protested against the blurring of the magnifying glass, but the grains were beginning to look nicely organized on the sheet of paper. The sawdust was fairly easy to remove, but the tiny dark specks of the red brick dust were infuriatingly fiddly. In a few hours, she had made progress and a series of little piles sat in front of her. She pulled her arms out in a great stretching yawn and rolled her head around to release the tension in her neck.

"You've done really well." Dr. Fox smiled.

"It's tough work." She huffed. "Really fiddly."

"I'll bet." He poured another lot of the powder onto the

corner of her paper and grinned at her dismay. "I reckon there's about a quarter of an ounce in total. It was caught everywhere, in his shoes, the back of his neck, and so on. It must have been scattered everywhere where he was lying. We should have enough to test from all this, though."

"This'll take forever."

"I know." He pulled up a chair. "That's why I'm going to help. We've got to find something to do until he thaws out." He put on a pair of magnifying spectacles and started to work on sorting the grains.

"So, Albert." Dr. Fox paused before glancing over the lenses. "You know I'm a doctor. Anything you tell me will be in complete confidence."

She put down her tools and stared at him with a frown. "I know."

"So? Is there something you want to tell me, or do I ask the questions?"

She took a deep breath. "About what?"

He looked her full in the face. "I'm medically trained, but I could tell the difference between male and female since I was a kid. Sure, you can pass as a boy at a distance, or in passing, but not at close quarters or for long periods. Who are you, and why do you suddenly appear at the same time as a corpse?"

Her spreading smile surprised him as much as watching her rip off a fake pubescent moustache and pull off the shaggy wig. She switched back to her own Scottish accent. "My name is Abigail. Abigail MacKay. I work for Alan Pinkerton in the women's department. My being here has nothing to do with the body, which happened to be left on a mattress near us. I'm happy to help you with a murder, although I normally earn a lot more than a dollar a day." Her own hair was caught in a tight cap and clips in numerous pleats flat to her head. Long fingers worked at it until it hung in glossy dark curls to her thighs. She laced her fingers through her hair and rubbed furiously at her scalp. "Aah, that's better. All the tight hair starts to ache after a while when it's pulled up."

The doctor laid down his tweezers staring at her with amazement. "You expect the sheriff to believe this?"

"I have a chest in the left luggage office at the railway station. It contains equipment and disguises, not to mention identity papers."

He tilted his head. "A confidence trickster would have all of that, too."

"True, but would a confidence trickster have fought you all to make sure you didn't miss any evidence? She'd have kept her head down and walked away. I'm a trained detective, and I don't want whoever did this to get away with it."

He sat considering this information. "Those men. Your uncles—"

"Are of no concern to you, but they're not my uncles. I'm not related to them in any way." She smiled. "I know the telegraph wires are down, but provided they aren't broken farther along the line, I can show you how to tap into them and use them, anyway. The Pinkertons have been doing it since eighteen-fifty, and probably employ people who did it since the system was invented."

"What are you doing here in Pettigo?"

"At the moment, it feels like I'm counting angels on the head of a pin." She laughed. "I'm here on another matter. I'm not prepared to talk about that."

"And the doctor you said you'd trained under?"

"A colleague." She grinned. "He taught me a lot, but not how to become a doctor. He's an adherent of the scientific method of detection taking hold in Europe. You must meet him. He'd be impressed by your work and your eye for detail. I am."

"Just supposing I believe you." Dr. Fox sat back in his chair. "How do I know you have nothing to do with this murder?"

"Because if I had, you'd never have seen me at all. Do I strike you as an idiot?" She folded her arms. "Now, if you're looking for help I can try to use the telegraph wire to ask the agency about frozen bodies and to identify how long they've been dead. Somebody somewhere in the world must have done work on it, and they have experts who have nothing but time to look into it. It could help."

"You could be talking to anyone," the doctor answered.

"Bring the local telegrapher." She shrugged. "Let him send the message. I'll show him how to tap the wires, after that it's the same process he's used to. We have to tell them to reply at a certain time and date to make sure we'll be at the broken line to receive it."

"I have one more question, Abigail." His eyes glittered across the table at her. "How can I let you go back to a church hall full of men tonight? It's not right for a woman to sleep there."

"Trust me. With my *uncles* at either side of me, I've never been safer in my life. The smell is a whole other matter."

"Yeah, but I expect they're used to it if they work with you often enough." he chuckled at her eyes widening with indignation. "What? It's a pathology joke. If you've never heard jokes about the smell, you can't possibly be telling the truth."

"Very funny. Now, how about we try to work out the trajectory of the wound and the height of the person who made it?"

"Good idea. I suppose you know how to do that?"

"I do. I need a string and a tape measure." Her eyes narrowed. "You do, too, but you're quite right to check."

Chapter Twelve

"Abi?" Jake darted a discomfited glance at his 'nephew', dressed in boy's clothes but with her hair trailing to her knees as she and the doctor worked to match a stabbing movement with a straw protruding from the rib cage of a skeleton hanging from a frame. "He knows?"

"I do." Dr. Fox grinned at their concerned faces. "Come on in and join us. She's told me everything. She had to. It was obvious she was a female. I know you're Pinkertons. Why didn't you tell the sheriff?"

"We didn't want to tell anyone." Nat darted a hard look at Abigail. "We have another matter to deal with as soon as the town opens up, and we need to stay low. We didn't mean to stay here. We got stranded. Why've you got a bit of string tied to a skeleton?"

"We're trying to work out the height of the person who stabbed him from the position, and trajectory of the wound. We've set the skeleton to the victim's height and the straw shows the angle of entry." Abigail held the tape as Dr. Fox crouched and made a stabbing motion. "That looks about right. So an over-arm swing from someone smaller than him, say between five-foot-five and five-six. I'll take a note of that. Could it have been a taller person seated?"

"I'll look into that." Dr. Fox stood and faced the men. "If it's any help, I can offer you a bed here instead of the church hall."

Jake stared at the corpse covered by a sheet and the brain on tray on the workbench. "Here? No thanks."

The doctor's gray eyes followed Jake's gaze. "Not in here, in the house with me. I have one spare room, which will go to Miss MacKay, of course. You gentlemen are welcome to the parlor where we can put a couple of mattresses. Sleeping in front of the fire here's got to be better than the church."

"I'm sure Abi'll be happier in a bed than lying between us." Nat masked the regret in his eyes with a beaming smile. "That's real kind of you, Doctor. We'll be happy to accept."

"I'll have to tell the sheriff." Dr. Fox warned. "I'm not going to lie."

"That's fine, Doctor. I wouldn't expect anything less from you." Abigail pointed at the little piles of dust. "Maybe my colleagues could help separate the grains and I could try to intercept the telegraph wire to contact the agency about frozen bodies?"

"Frozen bodies?" asked Nat.

"Yes. We had to halt the examination. He's frozen solid inside, thawed on the surface. He'll take days to thaw out." Dr. Fox slid the brain into a jar and poured liquid over it. "He could have been frozen for weeks. I have no idea how long he's been dead. I also have no idea how to find that out without help."

"And these little piles of stuff?" Nat peered at Abigail's work.

"Traces found on the body. I need them separated out so I can test them," said the doctor.

"It's frustratingly tedious work. I thought you could maybe help out while I go out tomorrow? I need to tap into the telegraph lines to get a message to the agency. I need to ask them about frozen bodies," said Abigail.

"Tap into a telegraph system? I can do that in my sleep." grinned Nat. "You write out the message you want sent and I'll send it as a soon as we find a line."

Abigail's brows rose. "You can?"

"I guess this is one area where our skills overlap, Abi. There's no need for you to go tramping over miles of snow." His eyes gleamed, sensing she wanted a break from sorting piles of grains by passing the job onto him. "You can finish the easy work here in the doc's warm office."

Doctor Fox rubbed his hands together. "That's sorted then. I think we've done enough here for the day. How about some dinner while we get mattresses brought over? Mrs. Small won't have expected guests, so we'll have to eat out. I'll warn her breakfast will be for four, though. My name is Clarence, but everyone calls me Clancy." He turned back to Abigail. "So, do you stay as a boy or a woman?"

"A woman, I suppose. The genie is out of the bottle. If someone could get my chest from the station, I can change."

"Yeah, we'll do it," Jake answered. He proffered a hand. "Nat and Jake. Good to meet you, Clancy."

"No surnames?"

Jake's uncompromising blue eyes glittered at the doctor. "Nope. Just Nat and Jake is all you're gonna get."

♦◇♦

"Clarence?" The young woman, her nose pinched red by the cold, blinked around the table and paused to stare at Abigail. "I thought I saw you through the window of the restaurant."

"Constance." Clancy Fox dropped his napkin on the table and gallantly stood, along with Nat and Jake. "How lovely to see you here. What are you doing out in this cold weather?"

"I was coming back from the church with mother when she thought she saw you. You didn't tell me you were eating out."

Clancy smiled to the older woman wearing a black straw hat adorned with an extravagant hatpin standing by the door. "Mrs. Williams? Come over. Why are you standing there?"

"I don't want to interrupt your dinner." She sniffed, her blue eyes scanning the table. "You didn't say you had guests."

"Because I didn't, until now. Please, let me introduce you. This is Miss MacKay and her colleagues, Nat and Jake. This is my intended, Constance Williams, and her mother, Mrs. Williams."

"Colleagues? First names already. It all seems extremely

informal." The mother honed straight in on Abigail. "What kind of woman has *colleagues*?"

"A pleasure to meet you." Nat cut in at the sight of Abigail's eyes narrowing. "We're stuck here with all the snow and are helping the sheriff with the body discovered in the church hall. We have professional experience which may assist him."

The mother's lips sealed disapprovingly. "Really? A body?"

"Yes, really," Abigail said. "It's a pleasure to meet you both."

"Are you suspects?"

"No, Mrs. Williams. We're witnesses."

"I've been helping the women who are at the school house." Constance turned to Abigail, her cold eyes examining every thread, hair, and gesture. "I haven't seen you there. That's where the stranded women have been put up."

"You wouldn't have. I haven't been staying there." Abigail smiled sweetly. "I've been staying with friends."

"Oh? Who?" asked Mrs. Williams.

"Old friends. Have you and Dr. Fox been engaged long? You make a lovely couple. Quite the thing. You'll have beautiful children, I'm sure."

"Six months," Connie answered. "He didn't tell me about you."

"That's because he only met us this morning and we've been talking business. Miss MacKay is with us." Nat cast a look at a hungry Jake staring at his cooling steak. "I'm sure he'll tell you everything soon. We mustn't keep you. I'm sure you want your dinner, too."

"Good to meet you," Jake said.

The group silently smiled at the Williams women until Clancy dropped a gentle kiss on his fiancée's cheek.

She pursed her lips. "I'll drop in tomorrow morning. Don't work too hard." Constance turned back to Abi. "All those trapped people won't feed themselves. Maybe you'd like to help us? We need as many hands as we can get to chop all those vegetables."

Abigail's patience for her digging was running out. "I'd love to, but I'll be busy tomorrow chopping body parts with Dr. Fox. A corpse was found this morning, and I'm assisting him."

"Oh!" Constance paled. "You're a nurse?"

Abigail ignored the question. "It's been lovely meeting you, Miss Williams. I must insist we return to our meal, now. It's getting cold." She picked up her cutlery. "Have a lovely evening."

Constance nodded. "Of course. I'll see you tomorrow, Clarence." She glanced over her shoulder as she briefly hesitated at the door before it tinkled closed.

"I'm sorry about that." Abigail shrugged. "She doesn't like me much. I should dress as a boy and get back to the church again. I don't want to cause you any trouble in your private life. I'm less noticeable in disguise."

"I won't hear of it." Clarence resumed eating. "She'll have to learn to be less possessive. It's her mother. She's insecure. She questions every woman she sees me with. It gets wearing, if I'm being honest."

Nat and Jake exchanged a glance.

"I saw that." Clarence grinned. "I know what you're thinking."

"You do?" Nat cut into a lump of venison. "My sincere apologies. I've never been one for clingy women."

"I'm sorry, Doc. She's a lovely woman, and this pair need to shut the hell up." Jake cut in. "It ain't like you've had much choice in women, clingy or not, Nat."

"True." Nat tilted his head. "We never stay anywhere long enough."

"I mean it, Doctor," Abigail said. "This is why I dressed as a boy. It saves all these complications. People see a woman and immediately wonder which man to associate her with, whether as a brother, father or lover. I can get a hostile reaction from women who think I'm muscling in on their territory. I think Albert needs to make a return in the morning, especially as your housekeeper will be around."

"How will I explain that to Constance when she comes

around?"

"I'm staying with friends and you forget the name. Albert can be the little brother I left to do the donkey work."

Clarence frowned. "And what if she asks Albert?"

Her generous lips twitched into a lopsided smile. "Oh, Albert doesn't speak English. Let her ask whatever she wants."

◆◇◆

The chilled wind cut through the sinuses and bit at the skin of the four men riding their horses along the railway line. The whole scene faded to a monochrome tableau broken only by an occasional glimpse of steaming chestnut horseflesh or the ruddy nipped cheeks appearing over the scarves wrapped around their faces for protection. The bone-numbing rawness grew as they went farther and farther from town, but they made sure they kept a sharp eye out for animals. The wolves were getting closer to town, driven by sheer hunger to investigate any food source in the arctic landscape. They announced their presence every night in their plaintive moon song under frigid skies. The bridles jingled, the snow muffling the normal echoes of the hard landscape, creating a world which invaded every sense with nature's indifference to the frailty of flesh.

"What was it you said about not doin' that job in the Doc's office?" grumbled Jake.

"Yeah, like you'd have let Abi come out here without you," Nat said.

Sheriff Gibson turned to Nat. "Is that the way the wind blows with her? He's got a thing goin' on? I can't say I blame him now that I've seen her in women's clothes."

Nat avoided the man's eyes, looking straight ahead. "Nope. He's real protective of her. We both are. She's a fine woman. She ain't like that."

"Oh, well, I didn't mean nuthin' personal. I meant she's a looker when she ain't—" He cast a glance at the telegrapher who rode along behind and lowered his voice. "—got up like a boy."

"Yeah, she is."

"What're you two whispering about?" yelled the telegrapher. "I can't hear back here."

Sheriff Gibson turned and called behind him. "Nuthin', Jim. We were wonderin' when we'd find this broken wire."

"I dunno what I'm bein' dragged out here for." Jim's voice dripped with annoyance. "If'n he can tap into the wire, he knows enough to send the message."

"Yeah, but I've never met him before, Jim. I gotta make sure I'm really dealin' with the Pinkerton Agency. You're the only one who can tell me what's in the message and who it's bein' sent to."

"Sheesh, Ben. I ain't no lawman, but if'n I was tryin to dispose of a body I wouldn't put it on the mattress next to me and then wait around to talk to the law about how to find the killer. Of course he's a Pinkerton. Who else could he be?"

"I'm just checkin', Jim. I'm a cautious man. I won't need you when we come back for more messages when I've checked things out."

"Well, thank the good Lord for that. I'm freezing my dilberries off."

"We all are, Jim." Jake pointed to a post where a wire dangled impotently before it disappeared off under a covering of snow. "I think we might have found it."

"Yup, I think we have. It should be relatively easy to cobble up a temporary fix, too. Jim gave me a couple of climbing spikes and a belt from the office." Nat caught the trailing end in gloved hands and dragged it out of the snow; hand over hand, until he held the end in his fist.

He unwound the cable he had wrapped around his waist. Deft fingers knotted the ends together, ensuring the wires made contact. Another trailing piece was then wrapped around the joint before catching the joint in a huge bulldog clip.

He crunched through the snow, slipping and slithering on the siding before righting himself and reaching the pole. He tossed a thick leather belt around both the pole and himself before he attached the spikes to the sole of his boots and thrust them into the icy wood, foot over foot while leaning on the belt until he reached to top of the pole.

"Damn it." He fiddled with the screw on top of the ceramic junction box. "This is frozen solid."

He removed his glove, cursing as it fluttered to the ground like a dead bird. He blew on his fingers and worked at the screw until he could eventually remove the cover. From there it was an easy matter to slip a rubber pad out from his breast pocket to drag the cable and connect it. He quickly replaced the cover and slithered down the pole, blowing at his freezing hand to warm it. "Where'd my glove land?"

"It's fixed?" asked the sheriff.

"It's only temporary, but it should hold up until you can get an engineer out." Nat slipped on the glove handed to him by his uncle. He walked over to the wire still connected by the bulldog clip which dangled to the ground. "It's all yours, Jim. Get that telegraph key connected and send the message. Use this rubber pad to hold it. There can be up to a hundred and sixty volts running through the wire now that the circuit's restored."

Jim stared at the wire dangling from the bulldog clip. "That's it? You connect the machine? It kinda makes you wonder why anyone pays."

"Yup." Nat tried not to look at his uncle's amused face. "I guess you've got to know Morse code, too, though."

"Best not tell old Ma Gibbons about this. She's so tight she'd be shimmyin' up the pole four times a day." The lawman laughed.

"All connected." Jim looked at the sheriff. "Ya got that letter you want sendin' to the Pinkertons, Ben?"

They all watched the man's nimble fingers dance up and down on the key. He paused. "Frozen body?" asked the telegrapher.

"Don't ask," the lawman muttered.

"As long as we get back before we end up being frozen, too," Jim replied. The fingers clattered on for a few more minutes until he stood and disconnected the telegraph key. "So, what now? Do we pull this loose wire free?"

"Best not to." Nat grabbed it in the rubber mat. "It might break the connection. Jake, can you find me a stone or something heavy?"

"Will this do?" Jake shook the snow from a stick.

"Perfect." Nat tied it to the loose wire before pitching it high into the air until the cable settled into a huge loop high over the pole in the air. "We couldn't leave it dangling, either. It's too high to do any damage, now. Let's get back. There's a hot bath with my name on it."

◆◊◆

Constance Williams strolled into the doctor's consulting room, her knock no more than cursory as she opened the door as she walked straight in. "Clarence? Mrs. France told me you had no more patients." She glanced around the room, her brown eyes settling on the 'boy' sitting at the table doing something with a magnifying glass. "Miss MacKay isn't here?"

"No, she left earlier. She's gone back to her friends." The doctor walked over and dropped a kiss on her cheek. "How are you?"

"I'm well, thanks. Who's this?"

"That's Albert. Miss MacKay's brother. He's helping me with a *fiddly* job." He smiled.

She swept over and examined the little piles the 'boy' sorted through. "Hello, Albert."

Abigail glanced at her and smiled. "*Ciamar a tha sibh.*"

"Pardon?"

"Oh, I should have warned you, Constance. Albert doesn't speak English. His sister gave him his directions before she left."

Her brow creased. "His sister does. What language is that?"

Clancy glinted with amusement at Abigail. "Oh, a heathen Scottish tongue. Yes, his sister is well-educated. That's why she helped me out. Albert's learning English, now he's come to the

States."

"I see." She trailed her fingers lazily over the workbench. "How did you meet her?"

"Through the sheriff. Have you finished at the schoolhouse for the day?"

"Yes, mother's still there, though." She peered at Abigail while she carried on sorting grains. "He has long lashes for a boy. Much longer than his sister's."

"Really? I hadn't noticed."

"Yes, he's going to be rather good-looking when he grows up. He's like his sister, but those coarse features work better on a man."

"Did you want something?" asked a frowning Clancy.

"Just to ask you to dinner. Daddy says he hasn't seen you in ages."

"Sure, when?"

"How about tonight? We *do* own a hotel, so we can arrange a dinner at any time."

Clancy considered for a moment. "Yes. Why not? What time?"

"Eightish?" Constance lifted the cloth on a jar and shrieked. "Oh, Clancy. You should have warned me. That's horrible."

"It's a heart, Constance. You know what I do. If you don't like those things, don't go poking around in my surgery."

"It's disgusting."

"It's evidence. The man was stabbed through the heart. I have to examine it."

"He was stabbed. What's to know?"

"The type of weapon, the force required, the trajectory—"

"I don't see the point. He was stabbed. He's dead."

"There's more to it than that, Constance. We can tell all manner of things, like how long it took for him to die, and the type of weapon helps tell us what type of person killed him. This was a long, thin weapon, and unusual."

Constance's brows met. "Can't you take a mold to show what the weapon looks like? To make a model of it?"

"No, a wound in flesh never matches a weapon exactly. Flesh stretches, people move and struggle. The body is also full of cavities which would fill with whatever material you try to pour into the wound. It's only ever an estimation but we can be sure it was a thin implement, but we can't make a mold to create an image of it."

"It all sounds pointless." She stood on her toes and gave Clancy a peck on the cheek. "I'll see you later. 'Bye, Albert."

Abigail raised her head and nodded at her waving hand. Clancy turned back to her as the door closed behind his fiancée. "I'm sorry."

"For what?"

"Those cracks about your looks. They're totally unwarranted."

Her face broke into a smile. "It's fine. I'm used to hearing all sorts of comments when I'm in disguise. She's only doing it because she loves you."

"But still, it's impolite. I'll tell her I find it unattractive."

"That's brave. Don't do it on my account, though. I'm quite used to it. Her father owns the hotel?"

"Oh, yes. It's the biggest one in the county. They attract a lot of tourists in the summer to hunt and experience the West and the mountains. It's built next to the hot water mineral springs, so people come for their health, too. They have a fine chef, a string quartet, an ice house, and a rose walk. They hold a poker tournament in the winter to carry them over the down season. That's the main reason we have so many people stuck in town."

"It sounds wonderful. What a shame I never got to stay there. I suppose you have a built-in venue for your wedding celebrations."

"Definitely. Williams dotes on his daughter and would shoot me if I chose anywhere but the Regal Hotel for the wedding breakfast." He sat opposite and folded his arms. "Speaking of accommodations, I hope you all slept better than the church floor."

"Oh, much better, thank you. Shouldn't you tell the

housekeeper you won't be here for dinner?"

"Ah, yes. I should." He paused. "I've known Constance for three years now, and she can still surprise me. That question about the mold was really quite insightful, wasn't it?"

"For a squeamish person, it was surprising." She put down her magnifying glass and stretched. "I expect she came to make sure you and Miss MacKay weren't bonding over a cadaver."

"Probably. She hates it in here. She never comes in. The green eyed-monster huh?"

Abigail nodded. "Yes. It's best not to discuss anything else about the murder with anyone, though. You never know who she might talk to, and whether they might dispose of evidence because of it."

Clancy looked chastened. "I didn't think. I'm sorry."

"It's fine. You weren't to know. You're new to this." She stared at the little piles of granules. "I think I should be able to finish tomorrow. Is there enough to test? How do you know where to even start?"

"Well, we can take it as a given those are brick dust and wood shavings, but it's the granules I'm interested in. They look like an alkali metal nitrate. There's a flame test I can do to find which one. Different metals produce different colored flames."

"I'd like to see that." Abigail's eyes widened in interest.

"Then we'll do it together tomorrow. Finding out what those grains are could tell us where the body was lying."

Chapter Thirteen

"You look perished!"

The men's boots thumped against the door jamb as they shook off the snow. "If that means freezin', I sure am, Abi." Jake stumbled into the hallway and pulled off his coat. "Solid ice."

"How was your day?" asked Nat, wryly. "Warm and comfortable enough for you?"

"Beautiful, thank you. But don't try to make me feel guilty. I was perfectly prepared to go and deal with the telegraph. You insisted."

"Thank your lucky stars you didn't. We were nearly five miles out of town before we found the break. It's like the North Pole out there." Nat gratefully accepted the mug of coffee she held out. "It's sent, and a temporary fix has been rigged. The town should be able to communicate again."

"Great work. You can relax now. Clancy sent Mrs. France home. She's prepared dinner and it's keeping warm, so all you have to do now is let me know when you're ready. He's gone to the hotel. He's having dinner there with his fiancée."

Jake leaned back on the sofa, warming both hands on the cup. "I wondered why you were wanderin' around in a frock again."

"Do you need anything else?" She set the pot on the hearth.

"A hot bath wouldn't go wrong." Jake sighed.

"I'm way ahead of you. There's one in the kitchen."

Nat's eyes gleamed. "Don't toy with me, woman. I'd kill for a hot bath."

"I'm not. There are pans of water on the range to freshen it too. Who's going first?"

"Want to toss for it, Jake?"

The older man stood. "Nope, I know the tricks you play too well. I'm goin' first."

"How is that fair?" Nat protested.

"I've got a gun and you don't have to see me use it. That's as fair as you're gonna get. You went first last time." He stood. "Drink your coffee. I'll see you in a bit."

Nat turned back to Abigail. "The sheriff's signed us as deputies. Me with a star. Can you believe it?"

"I can, actually. You'd have been a good lawman."

His gaze dropped momentarily before the twinkle returned. "It's a good thing he did, really. We were getting really low on funds. We were honest about it, and he paid us a day's wage already."

Her brow creased. "Why didn't you tell me? I have money. I could have helped."

"I don't take money from women, Abi."

"Huh?" She snorted. "You'll take money from almost anyone. You're famous for it. They write dime novels about it."

He leaned forward. "No, I don't. I take from railways and banks; places with insurance, and I've got a good reason for doing it, too. I never take from ordinary people. Not ever."

"A good reason? I want to know more about that." Abigail frowned at his vociferous tone. "But, fine. I apologize. Still, I could have helped. It's not stealing if someone gives it to you."

"Nope." He shook his head, his tired face still ruggedly handsome after the exertions of the long day. "I don't take money from women."

"Not even a loan?"

"What part of my last sentence don't you understand?"

"I'm not just *any* woman." She stood and took the pot over to top off his coffee. "You'd take money from Jake."

He held out his cup. "He's my uncle. It's not the same."

"I'm your friend." She put the pot back down by the fire.

His mouth firmed into a line. "No, you're not. I'm not quite sure there's a word for what you are, but *friend* doesn't cover it. It's not enough. There's something about the idea that makes me feel hollow and lonesome. If the time or place was right, you'd be my whole world...but it ain't. There's a just a big, empty hole we pretend ain't there."

"Oh!" Her eyes rounded and she dropped into the nearest seat.

He drank deeply, staring at her over the rim of his cup. "You know that as a well as I do. It's why you're here. Now I'm left to wonder exactly why, because this damned case has gotten in the way. You had a long journey here from New York. You had weeks to decide what you wanted to say." He arched a brow. "We're alone now, so let's have it. Talk, Abi."

"I know. I—" She paused. "I wanted to come here and thank you for helping to save me yet again. I wanted to ask about the emotion they told me you showed. I wanted to say you matter. I wanted to tell you you're unique and special. It all sounds so weak and stupid now."

"Stupid? That doesn't sound stupid." His eyes danced with humor. "I *am* unique and special."

"Surviving that bullet changed me. It makes me feel like I have to grab life by the throat and snatch at everything which mattered. *You* matter—more than I was prepared to admit." She stood, wandering back and forth. "I wasn't anything but a human being right after that incident. I was living in the moment. I wasn't a Pinkerton, a daughter, or anything else. I was a woman who had nothing to do but follow my instincts. They brought me here. I didn't know what I was going to do once I got here. I thought those blanks would somehow fill themselves."

"So?" His brows met in a deep frown. "Why not be that woman?"

"It's difficult." Her shoulders sagged. "It's a leap into the dark."

"I'm here to catch you, darlin'. I'll make it a real soft place for you to land."

Her eyes closed slowly, before she gazed at the carpet. "It's a big step. It's throwing everything in my life away."

"Yes." His gaze gathered in intensity. "But you're not doing it alone."

"But where are we going? Where will we live? What will we do? I need answers. My past is full of death and emptiness, but I can't step into a void."

"Death?"

Abi gazed into the flames of the fire for a few seconds before she spoke. "My father was…was murdered. It's why I became a Pinkerton." She met his eyes once more. "I'm not like other women. I'm independent and what the Scots call *thrawn*. It means stubborn and intractable, with a touch of absolute conviction. Men generally aren't interested. I live in a world of isolation and disdain. I'm not looking for a man who can keep me or provide for me. I can do that for myself. I'm interested in a man who can meet me as a full partner and give me as much as I give him."

His dark eyes glittered with temptation as he stood to face her, the room filling with unspoken passions and want. "And you're here. Looking me in the eye. What do your instincts tell you now, Abi?"

"Yes, my instincts." She bit into her lip tentatively. "They tell me to ask you—"

The door opened. "Right, the bath's all yours. I put another pot on the stove for you so it's good and hot now." Jake strode into the room and tossed a towel at his nephew. At the pregnant silence, he looked around. "What? What's wrong?"

"Nothing." Nat sighed, the moment gone. "I'll go bathe."

♦◊♦

Jake stood at the door and buttoned his sheepskin coat. "I'll see you later."

"Where are you going?" asked Abigail.

He picked up his hat. "Out. The saloon."

"Without me?" asked Nat.

"Definitely without you. You two need to talk, and this is the first chance you've had to be alone since she arrived in Pettigo. We've had dinner and the doc ain't back. You carry on with whatever you were talkin' about before I barged in." He slipped his hat on and headed for the door. "I'll be back about ten."

She turned to Nat, who reclined on the sofa, one leg crossed at right angles over the other. "Did you tell him to do that?"

The lamplight made the auburn highlights in his brown hair glow brightly in a warm halo. "Nope. He knew. He's real smart, but you'd have to be dumb as a box of hair not to realize he'd walked in on something." He patted the cushion next to him. "Come. Sit. Talk to me."

He watched her carefully, examining her as she steeled herself for the coming conversation. "There's no need to be scared. You came here to do this, didn't you?"

"Yes, but it was all easier in my head."

Nat reached out a hand, his fingers curling around hers. "I knew something had hurt you, Abi. Hurt you so bad you didn't care about your own life. Jake and I both saw that in you, we talked about it. Were you close to your pa?"

"Very close. My mother always said I was like him in a frock. We thought the same way. I miss him." She nodded. "I suppose that's true, too. Work was a diversion. I thought I'd found something I could throw myself into." She turned to him. "Then you walked into that potato I was carrying in that railway station. What a way to meet."

His cheeks dimpled. "Yeah, you don't deny the moment we locked eyes now, huh?"

A smile twitched at her lips. "No. It was a kick from life, telling me to wake up and live."

He nodded. "I denied you mattered, but you sat at the back of my mind, constantly coming up to bother me. You were the one thing I tried to escape the most, but you were the place I kept heading back to."

"It was the same for me." Her grasp tightened around his

hand. "I put it aside, thinking it was only me who felt like that until Everlasting. Then…we couldn't deny it anymore." A tinkle of laughter escaped her lips. "Everlasting. What a name!"

"Yes," Nat answered. "Perfect for the place to realize you lost the rest of your life before you had the sense to grab it. I thought you were dead and everything slipped away from me. I never thought of the future until fate rubbed my nose in a life without you."

She sighed, turning to him. "Oh, Nat. What a mess. What can we do?"

"Do?" He leaned in inches from her face, his hot breath hitting her flesh. "We have another chance. We grab it with both hands."

"And do what?" Her eyes glittered with inquiring intensely. "I still won't be involved with a criminal. I won't live life on the run."

He reached out and stroked her cheek, his smile slipping so easily into the feral. "But you'd be so good at it."

"I'm not joking, Nat. We both know there's something deep here, but it's not a relationship until we move things on. Falling in love is a big enough gamble as it is without making things more dangerous."

He arched his brows, his face lighting. "Love? You love me?"

"One of us had to say it, and I'm no coward." She tilted her head proactively. "You have all the missing pieces of my soul. The question is, do I complete the puzzle and accept them?"

"Oh, neither of us have a choice in that. It's whether we learn to live with it or fight it." He rolled a hand into her hair, threading it between his fingers as he grasped the back of her head and pulled her to him. His kiss was fierce, flooding her senses and causing the world to fall away beneath her. He pulled back staring straight into her with an honesty more frightening than his lies. "Which is it?"

Her brows met in consternation. "I just told you I love you. Is that all you have to say?"

The lights in his eyes danced, the way only his devilment could. "Abi...of course I love you. Haven't I told you so in every breath since we met? Love isn't only a word. It's what we do." His fingers trailed lazily over her cheeks and down to her neck. He brushed her earlobe with velvet lips, moving to her neck. Her head rolled back and her lips parted involuntarily as he toyed with sweet spot on her neck. He was playing with her, making her wait for the crashing crescendo to flood her senses. His mellifluous baritone floated in her ear. "Come with me, Abi. Let me show you more."

His fingers interlaced with hers and he stood, pulling her to her feet, embracing her like a dancing partner. "Let me show how much I love you."

She reached out and drew him into a sensual kiss, running her hands through his thick hair. His hand dropped to her hip, moving her inexorably toward the door. It settled there and pulled her close to his hard chest. She groaned, anticipating his next move. She slipped one foot behind his and pushed hard.

Surprise crowded his face as he tumbled backward onto the floor. "What the hell—"

Her generous lips tugged into her lopsided smile. "You think I'm going to fall into your bed? Think again, Mr. Quinn. If you want to show me love, you can think of a way out of this mess first. Do something to show you deserve me."

He propped himself on his elbows, his brows gathering in a knot. The consternation was dispelled in an instant, quickly replaced by his trademark dimpled mischief. "You can't blame a man for trying, Abi." He clambered deftly to his feet, and arched an eyebrow. "I didn't lie to you. You might not like the truths I tell you, but I'll never lie."

She sighed heavily. "You'll excuse me if I reserve judgment on that? It's not unreasonable to expect you to prove yourself. Not under the circumstances."

They turned at the sound of the front door opening and someone walking along the hall. Clancy's smiling face appeared at the door. "Good evening. Was your meal good?"

Both of them quickly slipped into a front of normality as though they had years of practice. "Wonderful, thanks. We've done the dishes and cleaned the kitchen for Mrs. France," said Abigail.

"Jake's gone out to the saloon. He said he'll be back by ten," Nat answered.

"Left you to clean up, did he?" Clancy chortled. "Maybe I could tempt you to a nightcap? Brandy anyone?"

"A drink? That sounds great." Nat grinned.

"I could be tempted," Abigail answered.

Nat dropped his voice to a whisper as Clancy walked over to the sideboard and lifted a bottle. "I'm counting on that, Abi."

Chapter Fourteen

Clancy held the test tube which showed a clear, brown ring sitting in straw-colored liquid. "This shows it's a nitrate. Now, let's see what else is in there." He took a metal implement with a thin loop of wire at the end and dipped it into a jar marked 'Hydrochloric Acid' then pushed the loop into the flame of a Bunsen burner. "Now. Let's see what this does." He dipped the wire back in the acid before dipping it into the granular salts. He then held it into flame. It flickered and flared a bright lilac before dissipating back to a normal flame again.

"It changed color," said Nat.

"Yes. The color tells us which alkali metal is in here. This is potassium nitrate."

Abigail frowned. "So? Where would we have potassium nitrate scattered all over the place?"

"It's used in explosives and fertilizer. You can make it from clay, organic matter, or urine. It's found naturally in the south of the county, but not so much here." He scratched his head. "It's valuable stuff, it must have come from a burst bag of fertilizer or something."

"So a farm or a place where they make explosives?" Nat ventured. "Is there a place like that anywhere around here?"

"Explosives? No. Not anywhere I can think of." Clancy looked at them in turn. "There are literally hundreds of places that use fertilizer. I guess that's your job. I don't envy you."

"I guess it is," Jake said. "The sheriff should know about explosives, or at least, know who to ask."

"There's one more obvious thing to follow up, too," Abigail said. "His clothes were covered in brick dust and sawdust. There's a brick works in town. They use straw and sawdust as packing materials to protect the bricks in barrels so they can be rolled by one man. At least, that's what they do in Scotland. It's easier than getting a block and tackle to move them like they would have to with packing cases. I suspect it's the same here. That could account for two of the traces we found."

"You sure know a lot about bricks, Abi," said Jake with raised brows.

She shook her head. "The new buildings in Glasgow were being built when we moved there from the island. They were rebuilding the whole city. There were building sites everywhere. I watched them from our house when I was ill once. I used to be fascinated by the men rolling those huge barrels over ramps made of planks with almost no effort." She shrugged. "I'm nosey."

"No argument there." Jake laughed.

"So, what's the plan? You go and see the sheriff and I'll go to the brick works? Abi's supposed to be a boy, so she needs to go with one of us," Nat said.

"You take her," answered Jake. "She's got a good eye. She might notice somethin' there you wouldn't."

♦◊♦

The Cibecue Brick Works sat at the edge of town, near the spot where the river bent off into the trees. The edges of the confluence were set with gray boulders, softened occasionally by verdant fronds and the fizzing white lace of rushing water. The buildings were wooden, no more than sloping barns, with the enormous, conical brick chimney of the kiln thrusting at least sixty feet into the air. The yard outside had long, snow-covered mounds and looked like stock had been piled ready for dispatch. Nat wore his deputy's star, clearly visible, on the shearling coat which protected him from the biting cold, while

Abigail's disguise was bulked out by layers of jumpers and a borrowed blanket.

"Yeah? Can I help you?" The call came from a man in a bulky wool coat, with a scarf pulled over his hat and tied under his chin.

Nat raised his hand in a wave. "Hey, there. Who's in charge?"

The man crunched his way over the freshly frozen snow. "That's me, Oscar Janko. I'm the owner." He frowned at the star. "The law? I don't know you. How'd you get into town? We're cut off."

"Ben made me a deputy. I was got stuck here. He needed help when a body was found in the church hall, and I've been involved with the law before." Nat's creative instincts kicked in. "The name's Nat."

"So? What's a body got to do with me?"

"We had the body examined. The clothes on the body were covered in brick dust and sawdust. We're covering off the obvious. Nobody's accusing anyone of anything."

Janko's eyes widened. "You'd better come on in."

They followed him inside the nearest building buzzing with busy boys and men. At one end, boys slapped wet clay into wooden molds, and a little farther away, more adolescents turned them out when dried. Firing was an adult job, and the young men handed unfired bricks in a human chain to be stacked inside a huge brick structure with a domed roof, which culminated in the conical chimney they had seen from outside.

"Up here." Janko indicated rickety steps which led to an office on stilts where the entire works could be overlooked at a glance.

They followed him to a little square wooden office. Two walls were covered in notices, invoices, and missives too dirty to read, while the other two sides were windows which afforded a perfect view of the factory. He planted himself in a filthy leather seat and kicked out at a chair. "The boy can have the box over there." He frowned. "What's he doing here, anyway?"

"He's studying medicine. Clancy Fox thought he could learn something." Nat watched Abigail pull out a wooden crate and perch on it.

"Medicine, huh? What's he gonna cure here?" The man peered at the 'boy'. "He looks about twelve."

"Yeah, what can I tell you? I do as I'm told. He promised to be quiet. He's learning stuff."

"So, the body's connected to this place?" Janko asked.

"We don't know. It was covered in brick dust, and this is a brick yard. Have you lost anyone in the last few months?"

"Few months? The body was only found a few days ago."

Nat nodded. "Yes, but his clothes could have gathered that dust any time."

"I guess. We don't use itinerant workers much. They're all locals, and nobody's left since Carl retired and moved in with his daughter. That was October. He's alive and kicking. You can find him in the Jagged Tick Saloon every Friday. I guess your body didn't gather the dust here."

"So, you've nobody new? Nobody at all?" asked Nat.

"The last new boy was fourteen and he's related to my sister-in-law's cousin's father, on her half-brother's side. Ya gotta look after family. We tend to already know everyone we employ."

"I guess." Nat looked bemused. "Nobody left?"

"Nope. They stay. We're a good employer. We teach them a trade. Folks don't tend to leave."

Nat sighed, admitting defeat. He stood, extending his hand. "Thanks anyway. We had to check."

A shrill tooting sound cut through the factory, and Abigail scrutinized the rotund man striding across the floor blasting on a tin whistle as he strode across the building. "Lunchtime," said Janko. "You can ask any of the workers anything you want. It's on their time, but they'll tell you the same as I have. If your body has brick dust all over it, I'm guessing it ain't from here."

♦◊♦

Abigail stood silently at the bottom of the steps waiting for Nat. Janko followed closely and nodded farewell. "See ya. Ask what you want. I'm going home to eat."

Nat shook his head, looking around at the workers opening lunch pails and settling on piles of bricks to enjoy a break. "See anything?"

Abigail dropped her eyes. "Don't stare. Him over by the door putting on the coat. Notice anything?"

Nat shrugged. "It's huge on him. The fur collar and cuffs look pretty bad. Real mangy. It's horrible."

"Compare it to the rest of the coats here. That's expensive tweed, and not even close to being worn out. His work shirt and trousers are filthy and ragged."

"So? He's got an ugly new coat."

"Which is far too big for him. It's almost at his ankles. No, I want to know where he got his coat from and how long he's had it. It looks too new to be relegated to work wear in a brick yard."

"Fine, come on." They strode over, Nat smiling at the man. "Hi, I wonder if you can help me?"

The man's hazel eyes drifted to the star on Nat's chest. "Me? Why?"

"Where did you get the coat?"

The man puffed out his chest and swiveled proudly from the hip. "It's great isn't it. To think someone threw this away. It's a bit singed, but I think the fur covers it."

"Singed?" Nat frowned. "Who threw it away?"

"Dunno. I found it on Climax Hill. It was on a bonfire."

"When?" Abigail asked.

"About a month ago." he looked from one to the other. "What's the big deal? It's just a coat someone threw away."

Nat peered at the hem nearly touching his ankles. "What's your name?"

"Jethro Walters. Mr. Janko's known me all his life. I went to school with him. I do odd jobs and yard work for him, too."

"Mr. Walters, I need you to show me where this bonfire was." Nat gestured with his head. "Come with me."

"I'm workin' here." Jethro scowled in protest. "I can't leave."

"It's lunch break. The whistle blew. I've gotta insist you come with me and show me where you got your coat."

"We also need the date," said Abigail.

"Who is this pipsqueak? Are you babysittin' on the job?"

Nat rolled his eyes. "He's a medical student. Dr. Fox sent him."

"That?" Jethro snorted. "I wouldn't let him tend a cut finger. His balls ain't even dropped yet. What's a medical student interested in a coat for?"

"I'm not interested in the coat. I'm interested in the man who wore it before you. He may be a murder victim."

"Murder!" The man's voice echoed around the factory rafters. "I ain't killed nobody. Not never."

"What's the problem, Jethro? Are this pair accusin' you of murder?" A workmate headed a little knot of men who gathered behind him.

"Nope." Nat smiled with as much charm as he could muster. "A body was found, and we want Jethro to show us where he found his coat. It might be a clue. If it was one of your family lying in the undertaker's office, you'd want us to find out as much as we could, wouldn't you?"

"Well, yeah," muttered the lead-malcontent. "We ain't standin' by while Jethro's set up for it, though."

"Set up?" Nat's grin widened and gestured with a thumb toward Abigail. "How many lawmen bring an apprentice kid along when they're railroading someone?"

Abigail smiled winsomely under her fledgling moustache, trying to look as innocent as possible. "I'm not a kid," she squeaked, in character.

The crowd shuffled uneasily.

"I want him to show us where he found it and when. That's

all," said Nat. "Come on, Jethro. Mr. Janko said we can talk to anyone we want to. He's fine with it."

"I'm not under arrest?" Jethro demanded.

"The words never passed my lips," Nat answered. "I said I needed you to show me where you found the coat. I'm asking for help as a good citizen. What are we waiting for?"

"I 'spose. It was weeks ago, though. It'll be covered in ice and snow."

Chapter Fifteen

They stood on a natural terrace on Climax Hill, staring at a patch of snow. "That's it?"

"Yeah, that's it. I told you, it was weeks ago, and there's got to be at least three feet of snow on top of it."

"How can you be so sure this is the spot?" asked Abigail.

"'Cause this is where we all burn stuff. We've done it for years." Jethro pointed to the backs of the houses in front of him. "That one there is Mr. Janko's place, and I do the work for him. That's Mr. Morgan's place. He's the manager of the Golden West Trust Bank. Otto Schuster does his yard work, and up there's the Regal Hotel. Eugene MacGilfoyle and his son look after the grounds and do odd jobs there. This here is where we burn rubbish. It's flat, it's outta sight so it doesn't look messy, and the ground's stony, so it ain't gonna spread and set the whole place alight."

"This is waste ground?" Abigail asked.

"The hotel owns it but they never mind us usin' it 'cause it's kinda private and outta the way 'cause it's behind the outbuildings. Us men have been known to meet and chat at the end of a summer day around a fire here a few times to roast potatoes and put the world to rights. MacGilfoyle's a real smart man. A real philosopher." Jethro cast a hand out to the vista. "We sit on the boulders and we got a sunset, a view, a bottle of hooch, and good conversation. There are worse ways for a man to end a day of work."

Abigail scratched at the ground. "Think back. When did you find the coat? Why were you here? What exactly did you see?"

Jethro's brow crinkled. "He's keen, ain't he?"

A smile ghosted over Nat's lips. "Yeah, young 'uns, huh? So? Tell us."

The man looked to the left, staring at both the heavy sky and the memories in his head. "It must've been five or six weeks ago. No, I tell a lie. It was about two weeks before Christmas, so it was about five or six weeks. We had a little snow, but nothin' like this. Most of the snow came in January."

"Why were you here?" asked Nat. "Most of the outdoor work is finished by December."

"There was still prunin' and tidyin' to do. Mrs. Janko is real persnickety. She's from Denver, you know." Jethro added, as though her birthplace justified her peculiarities.

Abigail cut in. "So you tidied and came here with the rubbish? What time of day? Can you remember the date?"

"Dunno. Mrs. Janko will have it, though. There ain't much she don't keep notes on, and she'll note the money she paid me. As to the time, I reckon it was gettin' near four, because the light was startin' to go. There weren't nobody here, but a fire was already smoulderin'. This coat was on top, but I guess the fire hadn't hardly gotten to it yet 'cause when I pulled it away, it wasn't too bad. There were other clothes underneath, but they weren't worth savin'. The one on top barely got touched. The collar was worst, so I covered it with coney fur." He held out his arms. "Then I added the cuffs 'cause I had pelts left over after a big stew, and they match, and they were raggedy after I cut them down to size. Kinda swanky ain't it?"

"Lovely." Nat grinned. "The only problem is it might belong to a dead man."

"So? Half my clothes come from clearin' out after the dearly departed. That ain't no reason to let them go to waste."

"He means we need to examine it in case there's any evidence we can get from it," said Abigail.

"But I've been wearin' it for weeks. If there was anythin' in the pockets I'd have found it."

Abigail arched a brow. "We need that coat, Mr. Walters."

"But it's freezin'. I need a coat. I threw my other one away. It was a rag."

"We'll find you one. The church has loads of them, and if it's not the victim's, we'll give it right back." Abigai nodded.

Jethro's jaw dropped in dismay. "But it'll be a rag compared to mine. This is nearly new."

"I'm sorry," Abigail answered, glancing at Nat. "Maybe the deputy could take you by the church to take your pick of what's in the charity box there."

"The best'll be gone. The town's filled with moochers."

"I don't know what to tell you, my friend. We need that coat." Nat twinkled his most persuasive charm at the witness. "I'll get you the best one I can. I reckon your sacrifice deserves something in return. Let's go and see the parson. I'll make him feel guilty enough to get the best coat I can get from him, huh? Maybe a bit extra? A suit, maybe?"

Jethro relented at recognition of the game about to be played. "Sure. As long as it's warm enough. But I want somethin' stylish, too."

"I can't guarantee it'll have the style of your old one." Nat's dark eyes swept over the fur-trimmed ankle-length tweed. "That's one's special."

"You go. I'll see what I can find here. Are there any tools I can borrow nearby? A shovel?"

"Sure. Mrs. Janko will have some. I'll get it for you, but I dunno what you expect to find after all this time."

◆◇◆

The booted feet crunched over the ice and snow pausing next to the huge hole in the snow where a slight figure crouched over the exposed dark ground at the bottom. She turned, nodding a greeting to Jake, who folded his arms and grinned incredulously. "Was your pa a miner, Abi?"

She shook her head. "Nope. He owned a distillery. It's still the family business. That's how we knew Mr. Pinkerton. He was a cooper in Glasgow, and my father bought barrels from him."

"A distillery? Wait'll I tell Nat. That almost makes you the perfect woman. Now, if you could talk a lot less—"

"That's not going to happen." She threw him a smile. "*Almost* perfect, if you ignore my propensity for locking people up."

"It strikes me we've got pretty good at ignorin' it." He leaned forward. "Is that the ground? You've gotta be at least seven feet down."

"There's been a whole lot of snow. More than I thought. Thank goodness not many people have walked around here or it'd be packed too hard for me to dig through easily."

"Nat sent me to see you home. He's busy with a laborer who's performin' in the church hall with a box of coats."

She stopped digging and laughed out loud. "Are they still doing that? They left hours ago."

"Oh, yeah. Nat's fit to be tied. It's third time through. The pastor had to grab his own coat real fast, because it was in the rotation before he knew it."

"He was really fond of his fur-trimmed coat."

"Tell me about it. I think he's holdin' out for a new suit. He'd better shape up soon. Nat was losin' patience, and that's not somethin' anyone wants to see. Are you goin' to be much longer?" He glanced at the cerulean skies. "We're losin' the light."

"I'm almost done. I haven't found much other than old ashes. I've bagged them."

"Huh? You can analyze ashes to see what they were?"

"No, but there might be a rogue fibre in there. You never know."

"What can you tell from one fibre?" asked Jake.

"Who knows? It's worth seeing if a clever scientist can do something with it, though." She stood, stretching her aching back before she scrunched a paper bag thoroughly closed. She tossed it to Jake. "Here, catch."

He caught it deftly in a one-handed snatch. "Got it. Now you." He crouched and reached down. "Give me your hand.

Jees, Abi!" He hauled her from the hole as she dug her feet into the sides.

His brow developed into a scowl as he stared at her at the edge of the snow hole.

"I'm not that heavy," she said.

"You're blue around the lips." His brows met. "You ain't even got the sense to come in out of the cold, woman." He rubbed her arms vigorously. "I can't even hug you warm because you're got up as a boy and it ain't seemly." He slid a hand around her arm and dragged her along in his wake. "Come on. I want the doc to check you out. Nat'll kill me."

She trotted along in his wake. "Really? You're the famous gunman and you're worried about him?"

"He's family. Who else's opinion am I gonna worry about?"

♦◊♦

Clancy handed her a mug of hot milk with sugar. He stood back and smiled at the men who glowered at her before he walked back over to the sideboard. "She's fine. Just a bit cold. There's no need for you two to worry." He turned to Abigail. "How about a spot of whiskey in there? I have Scotch."

She grimaced. "Och, no. I hate the stuff."

"I thought your pa owned a distillery," said Jake.

She chuckled. "And my mother owned a wooden spoon she used to paddle us with. I wasn't fond of that, either. What's your point?"

"A distillery?" Nat grinned. "Really?"

"Yes, but I'm not keen on whiskey at all. You have brandy, though. I like brandy."

"Brandy? Sure, I'll put some in." Clancy turned back to the sideboard and grabbed a decanter. "Drink the warm milk and sit by the fire. You're looking better already."

"You have no idea what she's like, Doc." Jake cast a hand in her direction. "That woman has been close to death more times than I care to think about. See the mark on her head? It's a damned bullet wound. I despair around her, I really do. We ain't bein' unreasonable in bein' worried. She runs headlong into trouble."

Clancy stopped dead, apparently suddenly seeing Abigail through new eyes. "I did see it. I wondered."

"I only got a bit cold. There's no need to make a fuss."

"I agree. A fuss never got anyone anywhere," Clancy answered with a frown. "Let's leave her to get warm. We can all chat later." He bent at the waist and examined her carefully again. "She's doing fine."

"Did you get the coat?" She asked.

Nat nodded. "Eventually. Jethro extracted two suits and a coat in exchange, though."

"Can I see it?"

"Sure." He wandered out into the hall and quickly returned carrying it. She stood, casting aside her blanket, and quickly spread the garment out over the table.

"Is that stain blood? There's not much." Nat peered at the material. "I'd have thought it'd be covered. No wonder he was more worried about the scorching."

"Most of the bleeding was internal." Clancy nodded. "There wouldn't have been much on the clothes."

"The label says it was made in San Francisco by Frederick Carne and Sons. It must be expensive to have a label. The House of Worth only started doing that in Paris in 1858. Only the best fashion houses do that." She paused over the stain on both sides of the lining. "Very dark brown and quite stiff. It's possible it's dried blood. I can soon find out."

Jake frowned. "Can you tell?"

"Yes. We can apply hydrogen peroxide and guaiac resin. The hydrogen peroxide foams and the guaiac turns blue."

"It does?" Clancy arched his brows. "Why didn't anyone ever teach me that?"

"They probably hadn't discovered it when you were studying," Abigail answered. "It was only discovered in sixty-two. I've got some in my trunk. I'll go get it. We need to measure everything, too."

She returned with a small leather case which she flipped open. She took out a small bottle of liquid and dripped a couple of drops on the stain. It fizzed and foamed into life before their eyes. "Well, we know it's a protein." She took blotting paper she soaked with distilled water and gently rubbed at the stain until a little came off on the paper. "This is a tincture containing guaic." Abigail added a spot of fluid and hydrogen peroxide to the paper and watched it gradually change to a dull blue.

"Well, it seems pretty conclusive." Clancy frowned. "Can you prove it's human and not animal blood?"

"Nope. We have no way of doing that. We can't even prove it's his. All we can say is this coat had a blood stain on it." She held both sides of the front and scrutinized them, "and it's consistent with a chest injury in the same position as the victim's, wouldn't you say, Clancy?"

He nodded. "Pretty much. There wouldn't have been much blood. Less than you'd expect. The right ventricle was punctured, which is thinner than the left. When the pericardium was punctured, the pressure wouldn't build. The blood was pumped into the thoracic cavity instead. That'll be why the coat was still wearable and not totally covered in blood. There are a few marks on it, and I'm guessing that's where the weapon was pulled out. If the coat was open, it may not have gotten much blood on it at all. Most of it would have been on the shirt and suit beneath."

"What height was he again?" asked Abigail, stretching out a tape measure.

"Five-ten-and-a-half," Clancy answered.

"So allow about nine inches for the head, probably around fifteen for the drop to the ground—" she stretched out the tape and measured the full length of the heavy greatcoat, "—forty-six inches."

"Just right for a man of five-ten-and-a-half." Nat propped his hands on his hips. "I'm six-one, and it's too short for me. I guess we found the victim's overcoat. Unless he travelled all the time, we have to assume he bought the coat where he lived."

"He didn't wear a wedding ring. There was no mark for one on his finger, either," said Abigail. "A married man would generally shop for clothes with his wife, so he would do it in his home town."

"That doesn't mean a thing," Jake said. "Hardly any men wear a ring."

"True." Abigail avoided a Nat's eyes. "And there's a difference between the old world and the new. In Germany and Britain, men wear their wedding ring on their pinky finger. In the United States of America, most men won't wear one at all, but many follow the Latin habit of the third finger, like the women. The victim had no marks for a ring being worn on either finger. I noted it."

"They do? Their little finger? I didn't know that," Jake answered. "Is that what the men in your family do?"

A shadow flitted over her eyes. "There are few men left in my family, and they come from all over. They do whatever they were raised with." She quickly brightened and changed the subject. "So, we need to ask the agency about portly men missing from the San Francisco area, with receding brown hair, brown eyes, five-foot-ten-and-a-half. It could be any time, but we might be looking at a window of about the middle of December onward."

"Progress." Clancy rubbed his hands together. "It's more than I'd hoped for."

"We'll see. They might come up with nothing at all." Abigail shrugged. "But if we can figure out who he is, we can possibly connect him to someone in town."

♦◊♦

"Will you want your husband to wear a wedding ring, Abi?" The innocence of the question drifted through the air, but the intensity in Nat's eyes robbed the words of their lightness.

She looked up from her papers. "Yes, on his pinky, like a good old-fashioned Scotsman. If I wear one, he's going to, too."

He leaned against the desk trying to look casual. "Has anyone been close enough for you to consider buying one?"

She turned her seat to face him. "Why all the questions?"

He shrugged. "I guess what I don't know about you bothers me."

Her eyes widened, brightening with a smile, "Oh, Nat. Don't be silly."

"I know it's dumb. It's not like you ask me about other women."

One dubious brow arched. "And I'm not likely to. I can guess."

Indignation crowded his face. "Hey, that's unfair. They weren't all prostitutes."

She sighed. "Just when I thought I was special, there you go giving me unrealistic expectations of the grandeur of your past conquests."

"It's just that I never thought of you being with another man until I saw you engaged to that poor bank manager."

"Thanks." She pouted. "Which do you see as the biggest deterrent? My looks, or my personality?"

"That's not what I mean and you know it. Why are you making this so hard, Abi?"

"Me? I can't be with a *criminal*, Mr. Quinn. Not only will it break my heart to see you carted off to jail, but it's pretty hard to maintain a relationship with a man doing fifteen years hard labor. I need a commitment unlike anything you'll ever be asked for. I'm interested in till death do us part; I want you to leave all this. You're remarkable enough to start again."

"So what do you want me to do? I'll always be wanted. There's no statute of limitations in Wyoming. You could be caught stealing apples as a kid there and still be wanted at eighty-five."

She laid down her pen. "You could go where they'd never ever think of looking for you. Give them enough time and they'll forget you even existed."

"Ya think? They write dime novels about us. We're famous.

It's not going away any time soon."

"You could leave the country? Canada?"

He shook his head. "Too close. I'd be recognized. It's too cold, too."

She cast a hand over to the window. "Too cold? You came to Pettigo of your own free will. There's got to be at least seven feet of snow out there. What about Mexico?"

"I don't speak the language, and it's too hot."

"Too hot, too cold; are you expecting three bears at your destination?" She frowned. "There's a whole world out there. There's Europe, Australia, the whole of the British Empire. You could hide and reinvent yourself. What's the real reason?"

He hesitated, guilt flickering over his face. "Jake."

"Jake? So bring him."

"No, he can't leave." He paused avoiding her eyes. "He has—commitments."

"Commitments?" She closed her ledger. "What type of commitments?"

He darted an uneasy glance at her. "He's got kids. He'll never leave them. He feels bad enough about only seeing them a couple of times a year as it is."

Her jaw dropped open. "Jake's married?"

"Nope."

"Oh, I see. Where?"

His dark eyes dripped with suspicion. "You don't think I'm going to tell you that, do you? Apart from the fact that we're just getting to know one another, it's not my secret to tell."

"Would she come away and bring the children with her?"

Nat mused on the question. "I reckon her husband might complain."

Abigail shook her head. "She's married. How does Jake know the children are his?"

"He was with her before she gave in and found someone else. Her husband thinks she was a widow and that their uncle visits sometimes."

"This is my problem with getting involved with a criminal,"

said Abigail. "I don't want that kind of life."

"Where did you have in mind?"

"I don't know. Canada, Australia? How about Scotland?"

He shook his head once more. "I've heard your language. There's no way I could learn it. I can't even make the sounds."

"Most of us speak English. You'd be fine." She stood and walked over to him. "Maybe you need to be a lot more open with me. Where do you go when you disappear?"

A mischievous glitter danced in his dark eyes, but he remained mute.

"Or, where do you come from? I know you said Philadelphia, but where did you go after that? There's no sign of you in any records I could find." She toyed with his shirt, a gentle finger sliding between the buttons on the Henley beneath, and playing over the smattering of hairs on his chest. "And what about when you and Jake split? What caused it, and why did you get back together? Was it due to his woman? Did she get in the way? There's so much I don't know."

Her fingers slid deeper, sliding around his nipple until it contracted and rose. He caught his breath and grasped her hand. "Abi? This isn't like you."

"So what? I'm tired of waiting. Why don't we grab life by the throat?" Her face turned to his as she pressed against his firm body. "Don't you see what we're wasting? How long will it be before it's too late?" She drew up his hand and kissed the knuckles. "Look at what we're throwing away."

His arms reached around and pulled her close kissing her deep and hard. Everything went quiet, but for the sound of his own heart beating the primal rhythm of being alone with a person who mattered. She kissed him back, gently at first, but then becoming more demanding. When she pulled back, her lips were full and rich, engorged with hunger. "Come here, Nat. Nobody's home. It's only us, and that's all we need."

They fell together on the huge sofa, using kisses to explore one another in a wild, sensory overload. She unbuttoned his shirt, trailing her velvet mouth over his neck and down to his chest, pausing to gaze at him once more. "We could move somewhere Jake could visit from. Where is she?"

His hand slid up her skirts, causing a deep groan of exhilaration to slip from somewhere deep in her throat as he found her sweet spot. "Who cares," he answered.

"What's her name?"

"Jess."

"Jess what?"

His lips pressed against hers, slow, soft, and sensual, his body melding to fit her soft, yielding curves until there was nothing between them but too much clothing.

She pulled back her head. "You were trying shut me up weren't you?"

"No." his lips drifted to her cheek to suck at her ear lobe before nuzzling into her neck. He continued to her blouse, unbuttoning it and nosing the fabric aside to admire the mounds of her cleavage.

"Is it true you sometimes stay at a place called Ghost Canyon?"

He stiffened, and not in a good way. "Are you trying to question me, Abi? What are you doing?" His stomach turned over at the realization he almost walked into a trap. "What am *I* doing? You're the law! You're here to seduce us into jail."

He felt himself go into freefall, into the empty blackness of fear and betrayal spinning around him along with the echoing sound of Abigail's laughter.

♦◊♦

"*Nat!*"

His eyes opened to the darkness of Clancy's living room and the outline of Jake's irritated face lit by the still glowing embers in the grate.

"Will you shut the hell up? Some of us are tryin' to sleep here. What're you dreamin' about?"

He shook himself back to consciousness. "It was a dream?"

"A damned noisy one, too." Jake's grin widened. "There was

so much groanin' I couldn't work out if it was good or bad."

He sat, gulping back the knot of stress rising in his chest. "A bit of both. It was Abi. What a nightmare."

A deep chuckle rolled through the darkness from his uncle's mattress. "Can I be there when you tell her? Put it exactly like that. It should be good."

"I dreamed she was here to cheat us into jail." Nat listened to the burning silence from Jake's side of the room. "Is that it? You don't have an opinion?"

"Sure, I do. I want to make it through the night, though."

Nat rubbed his face. "This isn't a joke."

"I know." The sound of rustling blankets told of Jake settling down again. "What do your instincts tell you?"

"Maybe it was my instincts telling me to sit up and take notice?"

"Could be, but does your gut agree? I've always found your gut never overthinks a problem."

He paused, holding his sleepy head in both hands. "I don't know. I want to say she's on the level, but it's a huge risk."

"She ain't told anyone here. She could've turned us in a hundred times."

"I guess." More silence. "She's not acting much like she did in the dream, either. Well, it started like her, then it took a turn—"

"A good turn, huh?"

"Great, until she questioned me on your kids and where we hide."

Jake's voice tightened. "Nat, you didn't tell her about—"

The younger man cut in. "Of course I didn't. She never asks anything like that. It was only a stupid dream."

Jake's audible sigh underscored the sound of him settling back on his straw-filled mattress. "Nat, if I thought she was here to dig into our pasts to turn us in there wouldn't be enough snow to keep me in this town, and I'd take you with me if I had to lay you out across a horse. She's been kinda broken, and not just by the bullet. I don't think she knows why she's here, herself. I'd stake my life on her not bein' here for you." His soft laugh was muffled by his blankets. "Well, not in that way, anyway. Go to sleep."

"You're right." Nat settled back. "I guess the fear at the back of my mind is she's stringing me along until we're in a trap."

"If that's what you think, we need to go, Nat, but I've gotta wonder why she's trying to get information to turn us in sometime in the future when she could do it here and now."

"No, it's not what I think. It's what I'm afraid of, and it's my problem. There's no sign she's doing that. Go back to sleep, Jake."

"Yeah." The older man turned on his side. "Let me know when you figure out what you're really scared of. We ain't covered the half of it yet. G'night, Nat."

◆◇◆

The breakfast table was quieter than usual. The clatter of crockery and the rasp of butter on hot toast cut through the thick silence hanging over the room as Clancy walked in, followed by Abi. Nat and Jake gallantly made to stand, but she ushered them back into their seats with a hand signal.

"I'm not supposed to be a woman, remember. Treat me like a boy. Mrs. France will see."

Abigail examined the dark circles under Nat's bleary eyes. "Are you all right?"

"Fine."

"He had a bad dream." Jake grinned.

"You did?" She pulled out a chair. "What about?"

Nat glowered at his uncle. "Just stuff. Nothing. You know what dreams are. I ended up falling, then Jake woke me."

"Oh, I hate those. I wonder what brought that on?"

"Yeah, me too." Jake twinkled at Clancy's amused glance. "Remember, it's not the fall that kills you. It's the sudden stop at the end."

"We never hit the bottom in those dreams, do we?"

"I dunno about that." Jake smirked. "Did you find the

bottom, Nat?"

Nat choked on his coffee and clattered the cup on the saucer. He glared at his uncle as he wiped his lips with his napkin. Jake was enjoying this far too much.

"Shut up." Nat changed the subject. "What's the plan for today? Question all the various handymen?"

"I guess." Jake sipped at his coffee. "How'd you want to do this? Split them between us?"

Mrs. France entered the room, her hair as gray as the ashes of a neglected fire but her eyes as bright as sparks. "A telegram arrived, Doctor Fox." She glanced at Abigail's plate. "You need more than toast, young man. You don't hardly eat enough to keep a bird alive. You do want to grow into a strapping man, don't you?" She ladled out scrambled eggs and dropped bacon on top. "Eat! You won't get muscles from a bit of bread. You get the bed because you've been ill, so do your bit and eat everything put in front of you."

Abigail watched the woman bustle from the room and sighed. "Anyone want some eggs?"

"I'll have them." Jake reached out for her plate and shoveled them onto his own. "She'll be offerin' to bathe you next."

"I'm surprised she hasn't. She's quite powerful with the mothering, isn't she?"

Clancy opened the envelope. "It's for you. They think they have a match for the body."

Nat took it and read aloud. "Lymen Cussen, aged fifty-three, married, lay preacher. Thirteen children. Attended Pettigo to audit the Golden West Trust Bank. Last heard from arriving in Pettigo December late on the seventeenth. Sent a telegram to confirm arrival at the next town on the nineteenth but never checked into the hotel or audited the next bank."

Abigail's eyes widened. "The auditor? Oh, now that could provide a strong motive."

"It looks like your genius for numbers is about to come in handy, Nat." Jake pushed back his plate.

"Genius for numbers?" asked Clancy.

"He can spot accountin' errors the way a cat can spot a mouse," Jake answered.

"And what's your place in this trio, Jake? It strikes me you all three have particular skills?"

"Jake's pretty observant himself, but his main function is logistics and security," Nat answered. "And annoying me if I ever wake him in the middle of the night."

"You've got it all covered." Clancy agreed. "I can see why they team you three together."

The table remained a silent spot of knowing smiles until Nat broke the silence. "I suppose we head to the bank first and take it from there, huh?"

Chapter Sixteen

Sheriff Gibson held back his heavy coat as he propped his hands on his hips. "I'm sorry about this, Gabe. We've gotta check the books. I'm sure you'll understand. Now we've identified the body, we need to look for a motive."

"I understand. I have nothing to hide. We passed the audit with flying colors." Gabriel Morgan nodded. "Poor man. He's been dead all this time and nobody knew. His family must have been frantic with worry." He glanced over at Nat who pored over the accounts, taking occasional notes. "Who is he anyway?"

"A Pinkerton who got stuck in town." Ben Gibson indicated Jake, who stood by Nat's side. "He and his partner are helping me out with this one. It's a good thing, too. I wouldn't have known where to start, and they got the man identified already."

"Cussen was a quiet man. Real religious and diligent," the bank manager said. "He'd been coming here for about five years. He stayed at the Regent Hotel when he was in town. He only left to dine or go to church. I can't imagine why anyone would want to kill him."

"Robbery, maybe?" asked Jake.

"Maybe." Morgan shrugged. "He lived quite frugally, though. He ate plain food, didn't drink, and went to bed early to read the Bible. Between you and me, I found him kinda boring. I'm surprised he had anyone listen to him for long enough to take against him."

"Yeah, it looks like he never left town, but someone travelled to Lattimer to send a telegram to make it look like he did." The lawman sighed. "When did you last see him?"

"When he left the bank. I checked my diary, and it was on the eighteenth of December. He'd finished and was leaving the next day."

"You didn't meet him after work for a drink or a meal?" asked Jake.

"Like I said, he didn't drink." Morgan shuffled, frowning in discomfort. "He was pretty dull company. No, I didn't meet him. I went home to my wife and had a good dinner. Ask her. We made popcorn garlands for the Christmas tree with the kids."

"So he must have died either late on the eighteenth or early on the nineteenth, because there's no evidence he made it to Lattimer and then came back. Anyone could have sent the telegram that was supposed to make it look like he left town." Gibson stuck out his arm to shake the bank manager's hand. "I'll leave my man here to go through the books. I can't even think of anything else to ask." He turned to Jake. "Can you?"

"How about, did you kill him, or do you have any idea who did?"

Morgan's eyes widened and his face broke into a grin. "I guess that's a fair question. No. He was dull and stuffy. I'm surprised anyone stayed awake in his company long enough to murder him."

"Well, I guess I'll head to the hotel and ask a few questions there." Jake gestured with his head to 'Albert' who lingered nearby, chatting to the mail boy and another youth. "Are you comin'? I'm going to check out where he stayed."

"Why's he got a kid with him?" asked Morgan.

"Don't ask." The sheriff glanced sideways and spoke in a low mutter. "They had no control over who they got stuck here with. Just humor them."

♦◊♦

They trudged through the packed snow, frozen hard and glistening after weeks of biting cold. The relentless wind cut through to the bone, meaning the streets were deserted by all but those who needed to be outside. The breeze nipped at their numb noses until they made a good match with their iced-cherry cheeks, and dulled their extremities. As they tramped up the arctic hill toward the hotel, Abigail turned to the gunman beside her. "That was young Tommy MacGilfoyle I was talking to in the bank. He's sixteen. He can't remember anything about Cussen. He says he and his father never went far beyond the reception desk unless something needed to be repaired. They work outside most of the time, and they have a little workshop on the grounds. The office junior said the victim wasn't popular. Not disliked, just irrelevant. He came, he audited, and he left. He was a remote man with an air of detachment and rather uncommunicative."

"He's sure got a way with words for an office boy."

"Well, yes. I paraphrased. He was as dull as dishwater. That's something I didn't reword."

"I've gotta wonder what a man like that could've done to upset anyone." Jake looked down at his foothold in the icy conditions. "He never said boo to a goose. If it ain't the audit, I've got no idea where this is gonna go. It doesn't sound like a jealous wife or a rival in love."

"No, he doesn't sound the type, but they always say the quiet ones are the worst."

"Yeah, maybe in offices or banks, but not so much in bar rooms full of drunks. The danger's usually the most obvious thing to watch out for."

He reached out to grab her as they both slithered and slid on the hard-packed ice, the pair of them hobbling to the ruts cut by carts and wagons. People had scattered ashes in the streets to provide grit and traction on the worst inclines and cambers, and Climax Hill had plenty of those. For the rest of the climb, they stuck to the gritted grooves and tracks.

The building was a confection of brick decorated with ornate carved wood and pillars. The flat-rolled tin roof was covered in a downy blanket of fleecy snow, softening the geometric façade with nature's crystalline coat of curves. Bright amber lights glowed from the windows, promising warmth, comfort, and even normal traction—everything the two figures struggling up the steep hill dreamed of as they struggled ever upward.

"If Constance Williams and her mother are doing this in skirts every day, I have a new respect for them," said Abigail as they approached the gates of the Regent Hotel. They trudged onto the porch and opened the door to a warm, palm-fronded world of velvet splendor. A crackling fire roared in the hearth of a drawing room to their left and leeched the chill from their frozen bones with the nourishing comfort of blessed heat. A beetle-shaped man with shiny oiled hair smiled from the front desk in curiosity.

"We have no rooms, I'm afraid. We're full. They might be able to accommodate you in the church hall."

Jake pulled off his gloves and unbuttoned his coat to reveal the star on the jacket beneath. "Is the owner around? I'd like to speak to him."

"Mr. Williams? Sure, he's in the private quarters out the back. I'll get him for you."

"On second thought, you might as well take me there. If I get the chance to talk to the family, it might save another visit."

"Follow me, sir."

The clerk made his way over to a door marked 'Private' in gilt lettering and knocked before opening it at the urging of a baritone male voice.

"Mr. Williams, sir? I have a man from the sheriff's office who says he'd like to speak to you and Mrs. Williams."

The door was pulled open by a square little man with bright blue eyes. His expanding waistline was covered by highwaisted trousers which sat around the nipple-line, making his short legs look even stubbier. "The law?" He opened the door and motioned for Jake to enter while Abigail trotted in behind.

"Mr. Williams?" Jake dragged off his hat at the sight of Mrs. Williams and Constance sitting in the room. "Ben Gibson employed me and my partner to help with the murder of the man dumped in the church hall. We've identified him and he stayed here more than once. We'd like to know what you remember about him, if anythin' at all."

"We?" Constance's brown eyes widened in question as they fell on Abigail. "Why have you brought the boy?"

"He's a medical student. Dr. Fox thought he might learn a few things."

"What can he learn? He doesn't speak any English." Constance frowned. "I've met him before."

Jake stared at the *boy* by his side and shrugged impotently while Abigail peered around the room with blank uncomprehending eyes, sticking with her role.

"I did what I was told and brought him," said Jake.

"That woman has been worming her brother into Clarence's world. It's too much, it really is. I'm sure she's doing it to keep in contact with him." She stalked over to the door and held it open, pointing at 'Albert' and then out to the reception once more. "You go! Leave, get out. Do you understand?"

Abigail decided he didn't and smiled an annoying smile.

"Oh, you stupid boy," she walked over and grabbed 'him' by the gloved hand, pulling him over to the door and pushing him out. "Go." Abigail blinked and remained mute, feigning surprise. "Go away, and take that witch of a sister with you."

The door slammed in her face. She couldn't help but break out into a grin as she glanced about. The beetle at reception was dealing with a resident, so she seized the moment and wandered off toward the kitchen.

Jake took the seat offered to him and smiled at the family. "The man's name was Lymen Cussen. He came here to audit the bank's books for at least the last five years and always stayed here. A quiet man in his fifties, five-foot-ten-and-a-half, balding, came from San Francisco? Ring any bells?"

"Not for me, but then I do office work and the books and the like, so I don't tend to meet the guests unless I'm standing in at the front desk. Kathleen will sometimes do front of house stuff in the restaurant. Handing out menus, seating people, that sort of thing." He turned to his wife. "Do you remember him, dear?"

Her brow furrowed. "A man who audited the bank does sound familiar, but I can't place him."

"And Miss Williams? Would she know him?"

Williams shook his head. "No, Constance doesn't work. I've made sure of that."

Jake paused. "To be honest, we're scratching around. He was a teetotal lay preacher who kept to himself. We can't imagine what he might have done to end up being stabbed to death. Would any of the staff know him?"

"Lay preacher? Now, it rings a bell," Williams paused and turned back to his wife. "Kathleen, you're active in the church. Wasn't there a guest who attended services and did a few sermons? Is he the man? You told me about one."

"It sounds like him," Jake answered. "Does it help you remember anything, Mrs. Williams?"

She pursed her lips and shook her head. "There are so many guests. Who can say?"

Constance peered at her mother. "Wasn't there the man who talked about Massachusetts, Mother?"

"Massachusetts?" asked Jake.

"The Catholic riots," Constance said. "They were animals by all accounts. Drunken louts who disrupted the peace. He told us all about it. I was there when he told the pastor about it after the sermon. You must have heard, Mother. You were pouring out drinks."

"No, I don't remember that at all, Constance. You were clearly part of a conversation I wasn't part of. Riots? We don't have riots in Pettigo. And if people should talk of such things again I want you to walk away immediately."

"No, Mother he was talking about—"

Mrs. Williams's brows met in consternation. "Constance, I don't know anything about politics and I would suggest it's unladylike to get too interested in such things. We are there to serve the Lord, not to inflame any of our passions. Have you ever heard me talk of such things?"

She dropped her head. "Sorry, Mother."

"That's quite all right, Constance. Women brains are smaller. We can't cope with such matters. I'm trying to protect you."

Jake cut in. "When did this happen, Miss Williams?"

"A few weeks before Christmas," Constance replied. "Why? Does it help?"

"Not really, but it does give me somewhere else to ask questions. We're lookin' around for a motive." He stood. "Is your man MacGilfoyle around? I'd like to ask him a few questions."

"Questions?" asked Mrs. Williams.

"Yeah, his bonfire was used to burn the clothes, but we recovered the coat." Jake turned toward the door. "Thanks for your help."

"You have recovered clothes?" Mrs. Williams's eyes bulged. "On our land?"

"Yup, so we've a few more questions to ask." Jake opened the door. "Thanks for all your help, folks."

◆◇◆

A buxom woman turned at the sound of Abigail opening the kitchen door, her salt-and-pepper hair caught back in a mop cap. "This is private."

"I know. Miss Constance sent me here. I came with the deputy who is asking questions about a guest. She says I'm not allowed to stay with the adults for the interview."

"She did? You'd better come in then. You look freezin'. Would you like some warm milk?"

"Oh, yes, please. My name's Albert, ma'am."

"Mrs. Chatsworth. I'm the cook. Do you want sugar and cinnamon in your milk?"

Abigail smiled. "Yes, please, ma'am. Thank you very much."

"What a nice polite boy. What is the deputy doing, dragging you all the way here in this weather?"

"Dr. Fox thought I could learn something. I'm a medical student."

"At your age? What are you, twelve, thirteen?"

"Fifteen, ma'am."

Mrs. Chatsworth shook her head. "You don't look near that. You're no more'n a little scrap of a thing."

"I've always been small for my age."

"Oh, for heaven's sakes!" A skinny girl stormed in the back door, slamming it behind her. She dropped a basket of logs on the floor and peeled off her coat and hat, hanging them on a peg at on the door. "Where's MacGilfoyle got to? He should be doing this work."

"Tommy? I saw him in town," Abigail said. "He was at the bank. I was speaking to him there."

She paused, indicating toward the *boy* with her head. "Who's this?"

"Albert. He's here with someone seeing the Williamses. I'm making him warm milk."

"With sugar." Abigail added, in character.

"Hi, Albert. I'm Sarah. No, I didn't mean Tommy, I meant Eugene, the father. He's always slopin' off somewhere or other. He's an expert at hidin' from work. I don't know why we keep him on."

"'Cause he's thick as thieves with the missus, that's why. He makes sure he keeps on her right side." The cook poured the milk into a mug and grated in the lump sugar. "She's mad on her roses and he keeps them lookin' beautiful. No wonder, with all the manure he talks. I don't know why she can't see through him. He's a boozer. She must know he has a still in the grounds."

Abigail looked at the mug in front of her, a smattering of aromatic nut-brown powder floating on the top. "Thank you, ma'am."

Mrs. Chatsworth beamed. "Isn't he a lovely boy?"

"More polite than Tommy, that's for sure." Sarah opened the range and tossed in logs before clapping her hands clean and rubbing them on her apron. "You know him?"

"Not really. I've only talked to him once."

"Stay away from him. He'll get you into trouble."

"He's dishonest?" Abigail asked.

"A scrapper. He's always gettin' into fights over one thing and another. He's bad news. I'm sure he'll be a drinker like his pa, but he's violent enough sober."

"Good to know." Abigail sipped her milk. "What do you do

here, Sarah?"

"Maid of all works. So basically, if it moves I feed it, and if it doesn't, I clean it."

"Hard work, huh?"

"It sure is. There are a few of us, but I've been here the longest, so I work directly for Mrs. Williams, mostly. I keep the family quarters looking clean and do the public rooms." Sarah smiled proudly. "They don't want just anyone being the face of the Regal Hotel."

"Quite an honor."

"Yes, I'm aiming to be in charge of housekeeping once Mrs. Williams decides she wants to take things easier. She trusts me."

"Not all the time." Mrs. Chatsworth snickered. "Remember the fuss Constance made about the missing shepherdess. She blamed you."

"Shepherdess?" asked Abigail.

"An ornament," Sarah said. "And only until Mrs. Williams explained she'd broken it and was scared to admit it to her daughter. I can understand why. Constance is the type to hold a grudge and she does take on so."

"Yeah, it took her long enough, though. Nearly a week. I thought it was going to ruin Christmas. Miss Constance bought it for her mother's birthday. Of course, the staff were the first suspects. Typical, huh?"

"Are they a good family to work for?"

"Lovely, well, apart from Miss Constance. She's a bit spoiled. Mrs. Williams dotes on her daughter. She's marrying the doctor in June, so she'll be gone soon."

"Yes, it was Miss Williams who sent me here." Abigail smiled at the cook. "I'm glad she did. I wouldn't have gotten the warm milk."

"So tell us, what's the deputy here for?" Mrs. Chatsworth settled in a chair across the table and smiled conspiratorially. "Is it that body they found?"

"Yes. They say he stayed here. Lymen Cussen? He was a lay preacher and audited the bank?"

Sarah nodded. "The bank auditor? I remember him. Really

boring. I'm sorry he's dead, though."

"Stabbed," Abigail said. "Who'd want to do that to a preacher?"

"I've met a few who've been askin' for it." Sarah chuckled. "All fire and brimstone in the pulpit, but more arms than an octopus when they get you alone in their room."

"Was Mr. Cussen like that?"

Sarah shook her head. "Nope. An aspidistra was more interestin'. It was like he was made of wood."

"Oh, hush. Don't speak ill of the dead." The cook scolded. "And that's no way to speak around Albert."

"I don't mind, Mrs. Chatsworth."

"I mind. Drink your milk."

Abigail did as she was bid before she attempted one more question. "Did Mrs. Williams know Eugene MacGilfoyle before he worked here?"

"He came here about ten years ago," Mrs. Chatsworth answered. "He was interviewed along with a few others. Apparently, he knew a lot about roses, and that was enough for Mrs. Williams."

"And *does* he know about roses?" asked Abigail.

"He worked on an estate in Ireland for Lady Something-or-Other, so I guess so. They sure look good. It's beautiful in the summer."

"I expect they need a lot of fertilizer?" Abigail ventured.

"Horse manure." Sarah asserted. "He collects it from the street, and gets the men to pee on the big pile. It's disgusting, but he says it's the best. I think his other selling point to the missus was the ice. It is great to have ice cream when it's real hot in the summer. He can make it even in *hot* weather. It makes the hotel a real special place."

"He can *make* ice?"

Mrs. Chatsworth stood and took the empty mug from Abigail. "Yeah, the rich folks in Europe have been makin' ice for hundreds of years. He knows how. He won't tell anyone else so they can't get rid of him. It takes him ages and he can only make a little at a time, but it's a real treat in the summer. We charge the earth for it, too."

"I can see why she likes him," Abigail said. "He knows stuff."

"Albert?" They turned to look at the tall blond man with piercing blue eyes at the door. Sarah's jaw dropped open at the sight of the handsome deputy. "I've been lookin' for you."

"Well, you found—" Abigail stood, her words were cut off by the sound of a gunshot ringing through the air.

Jake's hand dropped to his gun quicker than anyone could have thought possible, and followed the sound of the scream ripping through the building. Abigail sprinted after him.

The desk clerk stood riveted in a near-catatonic state of voice-robbing shock at the open door to the private quarters, holding back anxious guests and staff. Jake's keen blue eyes scanned the lobby for danger. "What happened?"

The desk clerk shook his head ineffectually but his open lips remained mute. The sound of woman screaming lacerated the background noise, gradually changing cadence as it dissolved into deep, heaving sobs against an echoing silence.

"Speak, man! Where did the shot come from?" Jake grunted dismissively at the man's inaction and pushed him aside. He walked into the family quarters, gun raised, followed by Abigail.

Constance had dissolved into hysterics and dropped to her knees in the center of the room. She wept into her hands as her father stood by the door off to the right, a gun hanging from his right hand.

Jake raised his weapon. "Drop the gun, Mr. Williams."

The man turned vacant, glittering eyes to the room, looking at everyone and no one. "I didn't do it. She went into the bedroom after you left and then we heard a gun go off. I've killed her."

"You've killed who?" Jake's brows met in consternation. "She? Mrs. Williams?" He approached cautiously and quietly, like a hunter stalking his prey. He eventually stood off to the side and reached out. "The gun, Mr. Williams. Give me the gun."

He clumsily dumped the gun in Jake's hand, his fingers still hooked around it. "She'd never kill herself. It's an accident." Williams glanced at the heap of humanity on the floor. "Oh, my love! This is my fault. You told me you hated the thing, but I refused to get rid of it."

Jake's hand curled around the weapon until he pulled it away from the rictus fingers. He glanced over the man's shoulder at the blood-splattered wall and the crumpled body lying on the floor of the bedroom. He turned his head away as his stomach rolled over, and gestured with his head. "Abi—"

She nodded. "Sure—"

She entered the room, gazing at the gouts of brain matter and spots of blood splattered from floor to ceiling. There was no urgency to rush to Mrs. Williams, it was clear the wound to her head wasn't survivable. One side blossomed in a grotesque set of gory, meaty, petals and the woman lay face down in a pool of dark red blood. She approached tentatively, crouching to peer at the entry wound. It was circled by dark spots of black powder, displaying a tattoo of evidence the barrel of the gun had been close to the head when discharged. The further away the weapon was, the more scattered the pattern. This was tight and dark, so it was either against her head, or extremely close. She narrowed her eyes, fighting the deep sense of regret engulfing her heart. She had seen so many fight for every scrap of life. It hurt like hell to see people throw it away.

The bloodstained arm stretched out beside the body, and footprints in the pooling blood showed someone had walked through it after the act, and then tracked imprints over to where Mr. Williams now stood. It fitted with a distressed husband hurrying over to grab the gun. Why? It was pointless, but instinct told people to grab a weapon from a loved one. She'd seen it too many times. Her eyes fell on a blood splattered note on the nightstand. She leaned over and picked it up, glancing at the words, *'I killed Lymen Cussen. I can't live with the guilt any longer. May God have mercy on my soul. K.W.'*

She frowned and placed it in the breast pocket of her jacket and turned to the distraught husband at the door. "What happened?"

"The deputy left and she came in here. I heard a shot and rushed in." Williams clutched his head in both hands. "I grabbed the gun. She always told me she hated me having one. I never thought she'd use it. I never thought she'd even touch it." The catch in his voice dragged at her heartstrings. "Why? Why would she do this?"

"We'll find out, Mr. Williams." She laid a comforting hand on his forearm. "You need to tell us what she said and how she's been acting." She turned back to Jake. "Can you send someone for the sheriff?"

He gestured toward the sobbing girl. "Sure, you need to deal with her."

Abigail approached her, laying a soft hand on her arm. "Miss Williams? My name is Abigail MacKay. I'm a Pinkerton detective. I'm not a boy." The young woman's glistening eyes turned to her in confusion. "I'm sorry about misleading you. We simply thought we'd save you from worrying about a woman working with Clancy. We've been helping the sheriff investigate the murder of the man found in the church hall."

"You?" Constance spluttered.

"I'm sorry. Now I need you to tell me what happened."

"Mother went into the bedroom. I never paid any attention. I was reading my book. She wasn't in there for long before we heard a shot. Father rushed over to the door and we found—" She dropped her head into her hands and sobbed once more, her shoulders heaving against the rasping breaths catching in her throat. "Is she—"

Abigail helped her to her feet and seated her on the sofa. "Yes, she's gone. I'm so sorry."

Constance wailed once more.

"Did she seem down about anything? Upset at all over the last few weeks?"

"No." Constance pulled a handkerchief from her sleeve and blasted her nose. "She's been fine. She'd never kill herself, not ever. It's all a horrible accident."

"How can you be so sure?"

"She's a devout Christian. It's a mortal sin." Constance

shook her head in bewilderment. "She could never be buried in consecrated ground. She couldn't go to heaven, so she would never commit suicide. Absolutely not."

Abigail nodded and glanced at Mrs. Chatsworth who wrung her apron in anxious hands. "She's in shock. So is Mr. Williams. Can you make them hot sweet tea? I'm sure Dr. Fox will come up with the sheriff."

◆◇◆

Sheriff Gibson turned the note in his thick fingers. "Never. She was protectin' someone. Kathleen Williams wouldn't hurt a fly."

"You think?" Abigail shrugged. "You knew her better than me. Who would that be? Her daughter or her husband? I can't think of anyone else."

"You can't suspect Constance." Clancy scowled. "She's harmless."

"Self-defense? Most women can do more damage than men think they can. Trust me. I found that out the hard way."

Clancy shook his head. "She'd have told me if anything happened to her. She's an open book. She's not good at hiding her emotions."

Abigail sat. "How well did you know your prospective mother-in-law, Clancy?"

He pondered, his pale face betraying his stress in the thin lips and stiff jaw. "Socially, but nothing too intimate."

"Have you seen any changes in her over the last six weeks or so?"

"She was always a bit frigid and formal at the best of times." Clancy shrugged. "I didn't notice anything."

"What about friends?" Jake leaned back on a chair, "or other relatives?"

"Nope. Percy Williams has a brother somewhere, but he's back east. They keep in touch by letter. He was going to come to the wedding, but I've never even met him. Kathleen's parents died decades ago. So did her only sister, many years ago. That always seemed to be a deep tragedy to Kathleen. I believe her sister had been ill for years. There's nobody I can think of."

Abigail sighed. "How are they doing, Clancy? Constance and her father? They both looked devastated."

"Yeah, they are. I gave them something to make them sleep. The Morgans are going to take them to their house to look after them until their quarters are cleaned up. You know, the bank manager and his wife." Clancy turned weary eyes on the group. "I expect you've seen all this before. It's another day in the office for you."

Her brows met in a frown. "Not exactly," she answered. "It's shocking for us, too. Very shocking."

Jake silently stared at her, noting the muscle flex in her neck and reading the tension in her shoulders. "We'll go easy on your fiancée's family, doc. We know this is painful for everyone, but I guess the case is solved if she admitted to it, and she's dead."

Clancy shook his head. "I'll never believe she killed anyone. There's more to this."

"I agree. A great deal more to it. She was a committed Christian, too. Suicide was a mortal sin to her." Abigail rubbed the weariness from her face with both hands. "I think it's best not to tell anyone about the note yet. Let them think it was a tragic accident for now. It's kindest, and if she did kill him, she must have had a good reason. I'm going to look into it, but in the meantime, I suggest we protect the family from as much pain as we can."

"Women stayin' at the school have offered to come and clean the room," Ben Gibson murmured. "I was thinkin' of askin the men to do some repaintin', too. That mess goes way deeper than soap and water. We can't leave it to the family."

"Good idea." Jake stood. "I guess we need to speak to MacGilfoyle next, but it can wait until tomorrow. It's been a long day, and I need a drink." He hooked Sheriff Gibson with a questioning glint. "Surely, Nat ain't still goin' over those bank books. The place'll be shut."

"He's kinda single-minded when he's got work to do." the sheriff replied. "He doesn't strike me as a man who bothers about closin' time."

"Single-minded?" Jake's drained face lit with a wry smile. "Ben, you don't know the half of it."

♦◊♦

A shadowy figure ghosted into the shadows at the rear of the Morgan house, stealthily and silently checking each of the windows. The wraith paused where the edges of the drapes fluttered in the bone-chilling wind and quickly drew back, seeking the cover of the shrubbery. This had to be the place. It was too cold to leave windows open intentionally. It was time to wait and watch in the glittering white wasteland lit only by the silvery shafts of watery moonlight. That window was surely going to be the exit. The argent light from the clouded moon glistened on the pitted footprints testifying to this being a nefarious entry point for the underhanded. The burglar was bound to come out the way he went in.

The creeping cold stultified the bones until it reached right into the knees, but it was time to stay quiet and still. Immobility in the darkness was the best way to trick the eye into blending the outline with the surroundings, and this quarry was tricky.

It was the longest time before a gloved hand grasped the window sill. It was followed by a long leg which emerged from the house by inches. The silhouette slid out like a cat, the booted foot landing on the soft snow with an almost imperceptible crunch. Another followed, and within seconds, the interloper stood outside and slid the sash window closed, his cloud of breath hanging in the air in tiny condensing crystals.

The head turned from side to side, checking out potential dangers and pitfalls before stepping away from the house and making for the alley at the side.

"Drop the bag, Mr. Quinn." She emerged from the gloom. "Put your hands up."

He stopped dead, doing as he bid, before turning and fixing her with a beaming smile. "Abi? Why didn't you come in and join me like last time? You must be freezing out here."

"What's in the bag?"

"Come and see." The smile broadened. "Search me. I dare you."

"I knew it. This is what you did last time, when you stole those jewels in Paris. When you didn't come back after closing time at the bank I knew you were up to no good. That's the bank manager's house, and he's up at the hotel helping the Williamses."

"Put the gun away. You might hurt someone, and I'm not stealing anything. I'm investigating. I'm helping you."

Her eyes narrowed. "I heard all those excuses before. You almost made off with a bag of jewels from Paris. You've been checking to see if the bank manager had duplicate books at home. Haven't you?"

"That's what I've been doing, but they haven't. I've searched the bank and his safe. I went right through his study, too. It seems Gabe Morgan is that mythical creature we've all heard about but never met; an honest man. The books are straight. Cussen wasn't killed to cover any embezzlement." He snorted and dropped his arms, stooping to snatch the bag and toss it at her. "Enough of this. It's too cold. Catch."

It hit her with weighty thump, making her step back with the momentum and drop her arm. "You did that deliberately."

"That's pretty rich coming from a woman who held a gun on me." He strode forward and picked up the bag. He stood, his hot breath hitting her in the face. "If you want to treat me like a criminal, I'll behave like one." He leaned in and prized the Derringer from her gloved fingers. "Are you trying to provoke me, Abi?"

She turned and faced him. "I'm trying to stop you from stealing. Why didn't you tell me you were going to do this?"

"You want to know why I broke in?"

"Money?" she snorted.

"I didn't tell you because I was breaking and entering." He stared at her, his willful presence maintaining an intimidating closeness. "I was protecting you from the news. Now, if you're going to force me to choose between looking after you or myself, you might want to reconsider." He stepped closer.

"Want to test me?"

She held his gaze. "What's in the bag? It didn't feel like books."

"Fertilizer from their barn. I thought we could compare the samples."

Her brow creased. "Oh, that's a good idea."

His dark eyes twinkled through the shadows. "Careful, now. That was almost a compliment."

"What do you expect when you can't be trusted to be left alone?"

His voice danced with mischief. "I'm fine when I'm on my own, it's when I'm around you I need to be watched. There's something enticing in a woman who stares life in the eye and dares it to give her more. I'll give you as much as you want, honey."

"I thought you were using Mrs. Williams's suicide as cover to get up to no good."

He stopped dead, his jaw dropping. "She killed herself? I had no idea."

"Yes, shot herself in the head. She left a note confessing to Cussen's murder, too."

A frown flickered across his brow. "Did she say why?"

Abigail shook her head. "No. We're keeping it from the family and letting them think it was an accident while we dig deeper. The commonest theory is she was protecting someone."

"The daughter?"

"That's my favorite right now, but we'll see where the evidence goes." They walked a little more. "Mr. Quinn, it seems I owe you an apology."

"Oh, you owe me more than that, Abi. You pulled a gun on me. I know that peashooter you carry could hardly mark warm butter from that distance, but there's a principle at stake." He hooked an arm through hers and led her into the alley leading to the main street. "I have a reputation to maintain."

"I'm well aware of your reputation. That's why I was there waiting for you."

"I'm not talking about that one. I'm talking about my

credibility as a criminal. A leader of men." He walked her out into the main street where lights from the windows illuminated the scene. "It's a ruthless world, and they'll eat me alive if I let you off scot-free with something like that."

She pulled away, striding ahead through the fresh snow with a laugh. "As if you'll tell them. Do your worst."

"You mean that?" he chuckled.

Abigail turned, walking backward as she taunted him, the moonlight catching her beaming smile. "Oh, yes!"

"You asked for it." He stooped and scooped a handful of snow, pounding it into a ball.

"A snowball?" she laughed. "That's all you've got?"

"Throw one back, if you can reach me."

She bent and armed herself with a tight icy ball. Nat raised his arm, pulling it back and tossed high into the air. It spun off into the darkness, disappearing above the illumination at street level. She pulled her head back until she heard it land on the sloped stable roof above her with a muffled 'thunk'.

"Is that it? You couldn't hit a barn door." She chortled. "Quite literally. I'm right in front of one."

She pulled back her own arm and threw as hard as she could. The missile whipped through the air and caught Nat square on the chest. "Got you!"

She paused, turning her head to the sound grumbling above her. Flakes of snow of dropped on her face, causing her to blink in confusion. It grew in intensity until it developed to a rush as an avalanche of snow cascaded from the pitched roof above her. She dropped to her knees as it enveloped her in a swirling maelstrom of crashing ice and snow. It resounded in her ears, blinding her under a freezing, damp heap. She lay there catching her breath, shaking her head free of the blinding chill as Nat's booted feet crunched in the snow beside her.

"Do your worst, you said." He held out a hand to help her. "I wasn't going to do that, but you deserved more than a snowball."

She grimaced at the irritating grin dimpling over his face. "*Bod ceann!*"

"There you go with the Scottish stuff again. It doesn't intimidate me. I'm Irish. The women there are so scary the weak men got in a boat and went somewhere else. We call that place Scotland."

She struggled out of the snow pile, shaking off the flakes. "*Mhac na galla*. How did you do that?"

"I noticed how the snow was sliding off the roof when I passed earlier and thought it wouldn't take much to bring it down. It's called strategy. You note what's around you and remember it. You never know when you might need an advantage." His irritating grin got wider. "You should try it."

She kicked out and swung her legs around, kicking his feet out from under him. He tumbled to the ground with a thump. "Like that?"

"Ow!" He flopped flat on his back. "You little—"

She pushed herself to a sitting position, brushing off the snow. "I'm a quick study." She whacked a handful of snow in his face.

He lunged at her pushing her back into the snow. "You never know when to stop. Do you, Abi?"

"Like you're any better?" She threw another handful of snow. "You think you're getting away with pulling down a roof full of snow on top of me?"

He fell on her, pinning her to the ground and silencing her in a crushing kiss. His insistent lips increased their intensity, until every nerve was alight with craving. She drew up her hands and wrapped them in his hair, kissing him back with the same ferocity. The world went silent, like the gap between claps of thunder, crowded out by sensual want as they gave and took in equal measure.

A sharp voice cut through their passion, squelching the flames as surely as a wet mudslide.

"When you two are finished, there's stuff to be done. A woman just died, remember?" They turned in unison, fixing on an irritated Jake who glowered over folded arms. "I'm ashamed of you."

Abigail shook Nat off and sat bolt upright. "It's not what

you think," she stammered.

"It's *exactly* what I think," he growled. "You're ruttin' like animals in the street. I'm no prude, but I expected better of you, Abi. You're actin' like a cheap whore. What would Clancy or the sheriff think if they saw this? Clancy's mother-in-law is lyin' in the undertaker's with half her head missin' and you're cavortin' in the snow."

Her face froze in anger, the wound slicing deep into her fragile dignity. She climbed to her feet and dusted herself off, frozen flakes of ice falling from her clothes. Her words were conciliatory, but the delivery was clipped and as sharp as the gleam from her dark eyes. "You're right. It won't happen again. Not ever."

She stalked off, Nat jumping to his feet and running after her. She whirled around, her fists clenched in tight knots of anger. "Leave me alone! He's right. This is insanity. I'd never behave that way in any other sphere of my life. This is completely inappropriate. He woke me up to the craziness I almost embraced. I'm done here. The minute the railway is open I'm leaving."

"But, Abi—"

"I told you to leave me alone. I'm going back to Clancy's. From here on in, I'll dress and behave like a lady." Her eyes glittered with anger as she glanced from one to the other. "You two can do what you want. I'm done here."

She turned on her heel and disappeared off into the murky darkness.

Nat strode over to Jake. "Who the hell made you head of morals around here? Do you know how long it's taken me to get her to thaw enough to be, well, just damned normal? It's the first time she relaxed and got playful, and you march in here and stomp all over it. Why?"

The blue eyes narrowed. "A woman died. I was there. It was terrible."

"So? Is the whole world supposed to stop because a woman killed herself? You've seen dead people before, Jake."

A spot of angry spittle landed on Nat's face as Jake yelled

back. "It eats me up inside when it's a woman. They don't go fightin'. They don't deserve to die that way."

"Did I say she did?" Nat bellowed. "Is that any reason to speak to Abi like that? You've undone everything I built up with her just because you feel squeamish about a woman you didn't know."

"She was a mother. Her brains were splattered all over the wall. It was like Mary, all over again."

"Yeah, well when you go and see your kids, remember you stomped all over my chance to have the same with the woman I love." Nat's sharp finger jabbed at his uncle's chest. "You crushed every ounce of faith and affection she had in me."

"She's dallyin' with you. It's never gonna happen."

"Not *now* it ain't." Nat's jaw clenched, his anger ripping the veneer of education from his accent. "You ain't the only one who carries damage with them. She does too, and she was startin' to come out of her shell. She talked about us goin' off somewhere to live a quiet life and have a fresh start. I had a chance and you ripped it to pieces and threw it in my face!"

Jake paused. "She did?"

"Yeah, she did." Nat turned, yelling over his shoulder as he went. "When she leaves here, I might just go with her and damn you to hell."

Jake caught up and grabbed him by the shoulder. "Wait, you never told me—"

"Do I have to tell you every detail to get you to act like a human being?" Nat's dark eyes glared at the gloved hand. "Move that, or I won't be responsible for my actions. I've never felt more like beatin' the hell out of you than I do right now. If you've ruined this, I'll never forgive you." A pointed finger punctuated his fury. *"Not ever."*

Jake watched his nephew's stiff back as he stalked off along the main street, his loosening gut a swirling maelstrom of regret, anger, and trepidation. He knew he'd been too sharp, and Nat would forgive him once the Irish in him calmed. Abi was a whole other matter. Nat was right about his outburst crushing the delicate shoots of faith and confidence. If Jake had driven a wedge between them, it could be the end of the only family he was still close to.

He thrust his hands into his pockets and glanced along the street toward the glowing lights of the saloon. There was no point in trying to speak to Nat until he calmed down. He shuffled an undecided toe in the snow, deciding to go for a drink. With any luck, Nat would be asleep by the time he got back. He could work on this tomorrow. Maybe the bottom of a glass could provide a few answers on how to win over the woman he'd just slammed unfairly. If not, it might dull the pain.

A woman's character meant everything in this society; it was all men really afforded them, and he'd just stripped her of it as she made a tentative venture into their realm. No proud woman would walk into a world where people treated her so badly. Especially not a woman like Abigail MacKay.

Chapter Seventeen

"Good mornin'." Jake walked into the dining room and nodded to Clancy. He nodded to Nat whose dark eyes were as bitter as burnt coffee as he refused to respond. Jake's belly tightened as he braced himself to appear as normal as possible for Clancy's sake. "How's everyone?"

"Still a bit shocked," said Jake.

Clancy poured Jake a cup of coffee. "But I guess we get on with things as best we can, huh?"

"Yeah." Jake nodded, glancing at his nephew. "It always gets me when it's women and children."

"Me, too." Clancy nodded. "What have you got planned for today?"

"Dunno, what do you say, Nat? We go and question the handymen?"

Nat shrugged and chewed at a crust.

"What's Abi doin'?"

"She was about early. Before me," said Clancy. "She looked like she had something specific in mind." A door closed with a bang which resonated throughout the house. "That'll be her going out."

Nat stood, dropping his napkin on the table. "I'll go and see. Have a good day, Doc."

He strode from the room, leaving Jake and Clancy sitting in a thick silence filled only by the crackling fire and ticking of the mantle clock.

Clancy turned his perceptive gaze on his companion. "Is something wrong? You all seem a bit strange this morning."

Jake's face fell. "Yeah, I upset Abi real bad by lettin' my mouth run on. Nat, too. I was dumb."

Clancy nodded. "I thought there was an atmosphere. You all work in close quarters. Little things can seem magnified. It's a tempest in a teapot. I'm sure of it."

"Yeah." Jake didn't believe the platitude for a second. "I'm sorry. You have enough to deal with without worryin' about us. It'll be fine. It's only a stupid thing. I'll make it right."

"What did you say?"

Jake hesitated. "I told them off for laughing. We'd dealt with Mrs. Williams. That kinda thing bothers me, especially when it's a woman. I guess they handle it better'n I do."

"Is that all?" A smile cut through Clancy's grim countenance, brightening it for the first time that morning. "Listen, everyone deals with shock in their own way. Doctors and undertakers are the worst for dark humor. It's another way of coping. From what I've seen, neither of them are hard people. You must have come across it before now."

"I have, but I've never handled it well when it's women or kids."

"There's no right or wrong way. You process it any way you need to. It's really not worth losing friends over. Talk to them."

"It ain't that simple."

Clancy's brow creased. "Why?"

The gunman dropped his head along with his guard. "Where's the harm in tellin' you? You're a doctor. I saw my sister's head smashed open after a bad fall when I was a little 'un. I took it real bad, and the sight of that woman yesterday brought it back." His chest heaved. "I was real rough on them for livin' and laughin' when folks have lost loved ones. I let rip at Nat and Abi. The minute the words were out my mouth, I knew I was wrong. I cut Abi deep just for bein' alive. What's the point of life if you don't live it? I've done some dumb things in my life, but my head was so far up my own ass I could see breakfast."

"Go and find them. Tell them what you told me. Well,

maybe miss out the bit about breakfast when speaking to a lady."

Jake nodded, knowing getting them to listen would be the hardest part. "Yup, I guess I'd better finish the eggs and move on to a big dose of crow. Served cold. Real cold."

♦◊♦

He saw her ahead, her dark skirts standing out against the frosty, achromatic whiteness of the landscape. She slithered at the corner and disappeared off to the right before regaining her footing and appearing once more. She was headed for Climax Hill, so Nat increased his pace to catch her. He cursed under his breath as feet slipped on the icy ruts of the main street, finding it better to wade through fresh snowfall than skid and slip over the hard, compacted ice.

His legs were longer than hers, so he gained on her until he was close enough for her to turn at the sound of the approaching scrunch of his boots through the snow. Her face was pale and pinched, the only color coming from the cold nipping at her nose and brightening her generous lips.

"Go away."

"Abi, wait."

"There's nothing to say. I'm a whore. I now know where I stand."

She skidded and grabbed at a hitching post, and scrabbled to find her footing. Nat kept to the virgin snow at the edges and quickly gained on her. "Damn it, Abi. The last thing you are is a whore. If you were, this whole thing would be a lot easier. Where are you going?"

She scowled. "I'm maintaining this charade, so you needn't worry. I'm also going to get to the bottom of this, so I'm heading back to the hotel as myself to speak to the staff and the family. You can do whatever you want. Go to the saloon."

"I want to help."

"Then find a way out of town." She struggled over to the gritted part of the street and started climbing the steep incline.

"Will you stand still for a minute, woman?" Nat lumbered across the ice toward her. "I've told Jake I'll leave with you. I won't tolerate any man treating you like that. If he hadn't been my uncle, I'd have smashed him in the face."

"How lovely. That's just the world I want to be more immersed in." Her stiff, upright posture was even more dismissive than her words. "It's too late, Mr. Quinn. His words cut right to the bone. You bring things out in me nobody else does; stupid, dangerous, foolish things. I came here to find out what life would be like with you and I found out how the world would see me in one short sentence. Jake uttered it last night. I understand the world judging me harshly, but when your own family calls me a whore, I'm done. I won't be treated like that."

"And you never will be," said Nat. "Never again."

She turned to face him. "You're in no position to make any such promise, but I can decide to remove myself from your world. It's over." She pointed up the hill. "I am going to the hotel. Do not follow me. I mean it. Our cooperation has ended. I'm done. Don't push me. That would be the stupidest thing you ever do. Do you understand me?"

His eyes stung. "Abi, I love you."

"Too late. You should have answered me immediately when I said it to you." She blinked and dropped her head before staring him straight in the face. "You don't love me. Not enough. You love the idea of me, the thrill of a challenge, but you didn't want to do anything to achieve it. I asked you to come away with me, and you evaded it. I only matter when it's convenient. I've got it. I'm a whore when I show affection in public. I guarantee, it'll never be a problem again." She stomped on, whirling around at the sound of his pursuit and barked at him. "Go! How can I make this any clearer? It's ruined. It's done. It's over." Her voice rasped with emotion. "I don't want to see you again. I'm as done as I'll ever be." She tramped on up the hill, her voice carrying back to him as he stood stock still in the middle of the street. "And take your uncle with you."

He watched her receding back struggle through the arctic

landscape, continuing to climb the steep hill. A ball of lead sat in his gullet, but his resolve already ate into it. This wasn't over. Not by a long shot.

◆◇◆

"Abigail MacKay. I'm a Pinkerton." She nodded over to the Sheriff Gibson as she faced the staff at the Regent Hotel. "He's checked my credentials. I'm looking into the death of a man who was a guest here. Lymen Cussen? I need to speak to anyone who had contact with him, from the waiting staff to the chamber maids."

The desk clerk shook his head. "It's not a good time, ma'am. We had an accident here yesterday. We lost the owner's wife in a terrible accident."

"I'm aware of that. I was here yesterday. It was terrible, indeed." Her eyes widened at the sight of an army of aproned women carry mops and buckets walking into the family quarters. "Already? They can't clean yet."

"Why not? The folks need to get their home back to normal," Gibson answered.

"I haven't given it a full examination yet."

The lawman frowned. "What's to know?"

"A great deal. Follow me." She strode into the private rooms and yelled at the top of her voice, clapping her hands together to get their attention. "Ladies! Please stop for a moment." She glared at the matron who continued to scrub. "You there, in the blue. That includes you. Stop right now, or I'll have to get the law to do it."

The woman in the blue floral frock, stood upright, the African Violets on her hat trembling with indignation as Abigail continued.

"I'm grateful for your help in this matter. We need a few hours to go over the room to make sure there's nothing we missed. I'm sure the hotel staff will get you tea and coffee while you relax by a warm fire."

The lawman's mouth dropped open. "A couple of hours?"

"I'm afraid so. Details are vital."

"But it was an accident," said the desk clerk.

"The Pinkertons engage in the scientific method. It's better to ensure you've covered everything, rather than miss the chance entirely."

Gibson shrugged, noting the determined glint in her eye. "Jees, I guess we'd better do as she says, Dick." The rueful desk clerk nodded in agreement. "Can you arrange refreshments? We'll be as quick as we can."

♦◊♦

"You see those splatters." Abigail pointed at the bloodstained wall. "See the little tails on the spots. They indicate a direction of travel. In a gunshot wound, they splatter forward in a fine mist with a back spatter which has much larger drops. A Dr. Swinburne has been doing some work on that, as well as Dr. Bell." She indicated the bullet hole. "We know what happened here. There's no room for doubt. The point of impact is consistent with the victim sitting on the side of the bed and pulling the trigger. The powder burns show the barrel was right against her temple. Her skull fractured, and brain matter was driven against the wall, too. Her body found any outlet it could for the blood to be released, so it poured from her nose and ears. The eyes were forced forward by the power and protruded. She fell forward onto this rug, these footprints are also consistent with her husband rushing in and taking the weapon away from her. That's common. It's instinct."

"So?" Gibson demanded. "We knew all of that. Why did we need to search?"

"I have to submit a report to show I looked at all the details." Her dark eyes glittered at him. "But I need to search the rooms to see if I can find anything connecting Mrs. Williams or anyone in her family to Lymen Cussen. I can't do that with the place full of women, and the family will want to move back as soon as it's clean. Will you help?"

"Search? Sure. What are we looking for?"

"Anything. Letters, inscriptions on jewelry, writing on the endpapers of books showing they were an award or a gift from him or anyone from San Francisco."

"Books?" The sheriff's baneful eyes scanned the groaning bookcases. "All of 'em?"

"All of them. Now where do you want to start? How about Constance's room."

"Nuh-uh." The sheriff waved the idea away. "I ain't goin' through a young woman's unmentionables. It ain't decent."

"Fine." Abigail cleared the lamp from the nightstand so she could move it away from the pool of blood for examination. "I'll start here, then do Constance's room. You do the big bookcase in the living room, then the desk. Let me know if you find anything."

♦◊♦

She'd been through everything in the bedroom and found nothing of note. Mrs. Williams was no hoarder, but her lack of sentimentality was starting to worm into Abigail's brain. She kept little from her own past; sure, there was everything from her marriage, her daughter, and from building up the hotel. But nothing from her parents, her childhood, or her early life.

That wasn't too unusual, but it did provoke curiosity. Many poor people had nothing of value to hold onto and couldn't afford to get photographs done on a routine basis. It was something reserved for major occasions like weddings, or even a momento mori of a loved one before they were buried. Sometimes a picture after death was the only picture of a child at all.

Without other information it was fair to assume Kathleen Williams may have been poor. None of her jewelry was hallmarked which indicated it was probably from the United States. Europeans had hallmarked theirs for a long time, some countries for hundreds of years, but it meant she couldn't get a date of manufacture. So, the next thing to establish was whether the assumption of poverty was correct, and if so, where was she from? Could she have encountered Cussen before?

She paused on the way to Constance's room and glanced at the sad scene of Mrs. Williams's hat on the stand, still complete with the extravagant hatpin Abigail had admired at their first meeting. It was rather beautiful, but it looked like no more than colored glass and base metal formed into a ball. No hallmarks there, either.

Constance's room yielded little. There were a few *billets-doux* between her and various local admirers, including Clancy. She had jewelry and one wedding ring with a London hallmark from 1820. As one of the initials was A.W., it seemed this came from her father's side of the family as her name was Williams. A grandmother perhaps, or an aunt? It all added to Abigail's list of questions.

She walked back into the lounge, where the sheriff had started on Mr. Williams's desk. "Find anything?"

"There were a few books with notes. I left those out for you."

"Where did Mrs. Williams come from before they came here?"

"Back East somewhere." Gibson rifled through a stack of bills. "Near Boston, I think."

"Thanks." She walked over to the stack of books and flicked them open, looking at the inscriptions on the endpapers. There were dedications from each member of the family as a gift for Christmas or birthdays, but one small, black Bible was far more interesting. It was dog-eared and well-used, and the gilded lettering had almost worn off. Abigail opened it and read the now faded copperplate writing, '*To Kathleen Anne Powell on the occasion of her First Communion, July 1824.*' A scrawled signature sat underneath, but it was indecipherable.

Abigail raised her head. "Was her maiden name Powell?"

"I dunno. I reckon her family will be able to say."

She snapped the Bible closed and tapped on the spine, deep in thought. "What did you say the gardener's name was again? Eugene MacGilfoyle?"

"Yeah. That's him."

"I think I'll go speak to him next." She paused, scrutinizing at the rug. "Has someone moved the furniture in here?"

"I never moved anything."

"Are you sure?" She tilted her head looking at dents in the carpet. "Have you been in here before? Is the furniture always arranged like this?"

Gibson turned. "A couple of times." He scanned the room. "Yeah, it looks pretty much like it always does."

Her brows met. "There are dents on the carpet where there's no furniture on it." She cleared the chairs and side tables. "So if the furniture hasn't been moved, it means the rug has been turned. Those marks match the sofa legs, but they're on the opposite side of the room. Help me with this settee, please?"

They heaved the heavy couch aside and Abigail's eyes scrutinized the floor, scanning the patterned rug. She gasped and fell to her knees. "Look!" Her fingers traced out dark brown stains on the heavy Persian pattern. She pulled it up to look at the backing, where the stain was more visible. "I think this might be blood."

"How can you tell?" Gibson asked.

"I have chemicals in my kit which react to blood. We need to get this rug to Clancy's so I can test it."

"What do we tell the family?"

Abigail shrugged. "Evidence? Specialist cleaning? You tell me, but I need this carpet." She stood, inverting the mat in her mind. "So, if this was the other way around, the stain would be near the door to the private quarters. She knelt once more, crawling along the floor, peering at the wooden floorboards. She squinted in the gaps between the planks. "Is there a magnifying glass on the desk? May I borrow it?"

Gibson handed the brass instrument over and she peered at the floor, one eye appearing giant and distorted by the refraction of the lens. She reached into her hair and pulled out the lock pick she always carried there. She carefully inserted it, picking at a mark, until a flake came loose. "May I have a piece of paper?"

It was handed to her, and she dropped the flake on the page, poking at it and trying to smear it over the surface. Serious brown eyes turned to the lawman. "I think this is dried blood. They've tried to clean it, but it's still there between the floorboards." She scrambled to her feet. "You need to send those women home for today. I'm going to get my kit to test and determine what it is and what the distribution pattern is. Something happened here."

◆◇◆

Nat turned and walked wearily back to Clancy's house, his heart beating like the gavel of an angry judge. Somehow, the wind bit right through his clothing and the way was more treacherous than on the outbound journey. That had been alight with hope, even if it was fragile. He was walking back to nothing, and to make things worse, it was starting to snow again.

Huge feathery flakes drifted from a sky so pregnant with fractals the gray clouds were tinged with a hint of purple. They hung low over the town like a purple-tinged pall. His eyes narrowed at the sight of the approaching figure in a sheepskin coat, masked in swirling snow as a blizzard set in. Nat's shoulders stiffened and he continued to walk, weaving a wide berth around the approaching man.

"Nat."

He continued to walk.

"Nat!"

He had now overtaken Jake and was striding ahead.

"Ignatius Ebenezer Dunraven Quinn! You stop and get your ungrateful ass right back here." Nat stopped dead at his rarely-heard full name. It was a name he had always hated, one which caused ridicule at school, but it still held power. It was the name bellowed in full by his Irish mother in the throes of maternal exasperation, and a name he had disguised since he was four-years old. A heavy hand landed on his shoulder. "We need to talk."

"Go to hell, Jake. And stop using my real name. Do you want to put me in jail?"

Determined blue eyes confronted Nat. "I needed to get your attention. I know you hate it. You go around bein' 'Nat', but not many know it's short for Ignatius. They think it's Nathan or Nathaniel. Does Abi know you got an old man name?"

Nat pulled away. "Does it matter? She'll never talk to me again."

Jake's eyes glittered with contrition. "Nat, I'm sorry. I was every kinda wrong. I'm gonna do whatever I can to put it right." Nat scowled and made to walk away, but Jake continued, desperation lacing his voice. "Her head was split open. My mind went—well, if it went black, it'd be great, but it was more like fireworks goin' off. The pictures kept appearin' over and over like flashes, and they got mixed up with the sight of Mary lying in the street with her brains fallin' out. I walked about in the snow tryin' to clear my mind. When I came across you two in the street, I was right back there; in Philly, with a sister lyin' dead and a family burnin' to death before my eyes—while you were laughin'. I cracked. I'm sorry, Nat."

Nat glowered at his uncle under beetled brows. "That's not an excuse, Jake. This doesn't only concern me."

"No. It's not an excuse. It's a reason; not a good one, but a reason. It's still wrong. I'll do whatever I can to put it right. Just name it."

"It's too late." Nat shrugged off the hand reaching out to him. "She's finished. It doesn't matter how sorry you are. She's not prepared to listen to it. You've ruined my life with your tantrum."

"Nat, I'll get her to listen—"

"Wild horses complete with a marching band couldn't get that woman to listen to you. She ain't usual. You can hurt anythin' but her pride, and you pushed her too far." He turned, walking along the wide main street. "You called her a whore. Her? It's ridiculous. I've never worked so hard for a woman in my life."

Jake cursed under his breath and stomped after his nephew. He grabbed at his left arm, backing off when Nat whirled around with a raised fist.

Jake raised appeasing hands. "What'll it take? Name it. Will you forgive me if I can get her to see sense?" Jake stared into the uncompromising dark eyes. "Would it help to punch me in the mouth?"

"It'd help *me*," Nat growled, "but it'd confirm to Abi we're the animals she thinks we are."

"Then what? What can I do?"

A muscle flickered in Nat's jaw. "There's only one thing. Make her understand. If you don't, I'm gone."

Jake nodded, his pensive eyes searching for forgiveness. "I'll do it. I'll make her understand. Jees, if she forgave me for half-stranglin' her, she'll get this. But you, Nat. What about you?"

His eyes closed slowly and the brown gaze dropped to the ground, the lashes spangled with melting snow. "Give me time, Jake. If you can sort this, yeah. If not?" He shook his head. "I don't know what to tell you."

Chapter Eighteen

Abigail flexed her fingers as she pulled on her leather gloves. She gazed out at the swirling snowstorm with dismay, but she had to get her kit from Clancy's if she was to establish what had gone on in the living room of the private quarters.

The desk clerk arched his brows. "You aren't going out in that, are you?"

"I have to." Her dark eyes scanned the arctic wasteland with growing reluctance. "It can't really wait."

"If I was you I'd leave it," Sheriff Gibson said. "I ain't goin' out in it unless there's a murder."

"There *has* been a murder. A man was dumped in the church hall." She paused, peering out at the gathering tempest, and sighed. "I suppose I could speak to the staff. Is Eugene MacGilfoyle around?"

"He'll be in his workshop," the clerk answered. "He does a lot of woodwork in the winter. He's turning spindles to make chairs. Go through the kitchen and head left. Walk right to the end of the stables and there's a long shack painted dark green. That's his place. You'll see the smoke. He's got a potbellied stove in there to keep warm."

She left the warmth of the hotel and struggled through the snow, the chilled wind robbing her of her breath and beating her back with swarming flakes of ice which chipped into her flesh with biting cold. The storm had almost become a whiteout, but she could make out the edge of a building through the speckled tempest blurring her vision. Her right arm stretched out, feeling her way along the barn until she reached the end. She gasped at the frigid wall of cold air blasting around the corner, but fought on, her coat and skirts flapping angrily behind her.

Her hand fell onto a wall, the horizontal wooden slats feeling furrowed beneath her fingers. Abigail felt along, hand over hand, blinded by the driving wind and snow until she reached a door jamb. Her gloved hands groped the door for a handle, reaching a knob which she rattled and turned, bursting into the building without knocking. She gulped for air and shook off the confusion of the storm which swarmed around her until she leaned against the door and closed it behind her. When she pulled the snood from her head and looked around, all eyes were on the woman who had made such a dramatic entrance. A wiry man with sandy hair watched her with wry amusement. When he spoke it was in the sing-song brogue of the Irish.

"You're in the wrong place, missy. This is an outbuilding." He pointed. "The hotel is thataway. Maybe young Tom could help you over there?"

The boy stood, happy to oblige. She smiled, hoping he didn't recognize her from their conversation at the bank. "No, I'm looking for Eugene. Are you him?"

He frowned. "Yes, miss."

She turned to the burly, balding man in the corner. "Would you be Otto Schuster?"

The man stood, eyebrows like steel wire meshing together in curiosity. "How'd you know?"

"Jethro Walters told me you three handymen hung around together."

"Jethro?" MacGilfoyle's brow creased in surprise. "Walters has been holding out on us. Where would he get to speak to a lovely young woman like you?"

"My name is Abigail MacKay and I'm a Pinkerton Agent, Mr. MacGilfoyle. In fairness to him I had adopted a role, and he didn't know who he was talking to." She suddenly detected a new chill in the air which had nothing to do with the weather. "I'm looking into a murder. A Mr. Lymen Cussen, who was dumped in the church hall."

"What has this to do with any of us?" demanded Shuster.

Abigail scanned the men in the room. "Och, now, don't let's waste time playing coy. Jethro will have told you he had to change his beloved fur-trimmed coat because we recognized it. He led us to the bonfire where you drink and talk. Would I be correct in thinking your meeting around the fire is really a séibín, Mr. MacGilfoyle?"

"You speak Irish?" MacGilfoyle demanded.

"What's a *séibín*?" asked Schuster.

"I'm Scottish and a Gael if it answers your question, Mr. MacGilfoyle. The languages are related, so I think we understand one another. And a *séibín* is a drinking den, Mr. Schuster. People build their own still and sell alcohol informally." She walked in and sat on a barrel warming her hands on the stove. "I'm not interested in any way in your social arrangements, I assure you. It's no concern of mine if you brew your own moonshine. I'm here because a man was killed and his clothes were found on your bonfire."

"Well, that could've been anyone," MacGilfoyle said. "It's a public place."

"Technically, it's not. It actually belongs to the hotel, and you are rather particular about who trespasses here. They have to pay for the drink you make, don't they? We brought these stills from the Old Country where we avoided the tax."

MacGilfoyle scowled. "How did you know about that?"

"I didn't. I guessed from long experience." She tilted her head. "But you just confirmed it."

"It doesn't matter. Anyone could've dumped them clothes on the fire before I saw. It doesn't mean a thing."

Abigail nodded. "Indeed. I actually wondered if you'd seen anyone, but you jumped straight into being defensive."

MacGilfoyle placed his hands on his hips. "I've got a long legacy of dealing with the Brits and their laws."

"I'm sure, Mr. MacGilfoyle. However, we are all Americans here now, regardless of our accents. I'm not after you. I'm simply trying to answer the questions the man's family will ask. I agree. Anyone could have dumped those clothes there. Can I take it from your answers you didn't see anyone?"

"No, ma'am. We didn't." Schuster said. "We really didn't. I'll swear on a stack of Bibles, ma'am."

"Thank you. That's really what I came here to find out."

"That's it?"

"Yes, Mr. MacGilfoyle." She fixed him with curious eyes. "What else would I be here to find out?"

"I dunno. How am I supposed to know?"

She stood and walked over to the ornate wood in the lathe. "Beautiful workmanship, Mr. MacGilfoyle. You are skilled. My father used to work wood for fun, but it was nothing like this."

"Thank you. What does your father do?"

A smile played around her lips. "He was a distiller. Maybe I could give you a few tips for that still of yours?"

"Was?" MacGilfoyle tilted his head sympathetically. "I expect that's why you have to work? My sympathies."

"Sort of," she answered. "He was murdered, and the authorities weren't working hard enough on his case. Alan Pinkerton found my meddling in the investigation easier to control when he employed me. I now try to bring the comfort of resolution other bereaved families." She fixed MacGilfoyle with an intense stare. "It's not so unfeminine to want to bring comfort, you know."

MacGilfoyle's rugged features softened. "I'm sorry for your troubles, Miss McKay."

"And for yours, Mr. MacGilfoyle."

His brows rose. "Mine?"

"Your mistress has died, hasn't she? I understand you and she got on well. It must be a sad time for you?"

"It's a sad time for the whole hotel. She was a good woman, and well thought of by everyone. She gave everything she could to help others. There aren't many left like her."

"So I understand. Her daughter is distraught. It's a terrible business."

"It is, indeed." MacGilfoyle nodded. "A terrible accident. Her husband blames himself for leaving it there."

"Yes, it's terribly sad." Abigail examined the Irishman. "How tall are you, Mr. MacGilfoyle? Five-foot-eight?"

"Five-seven-and-a-half. What does that have to do with anything?"

"And you, Mr. Schuster? What height are you."

"I'm five-six? Why?"

"Nothing for you to worry about," Abigail answered. "I'm eliminating some things from the enquiry. Tommy? How tall are you?"

The boy frowned. "I ain't reached my full height yet, but I'm five-six. I reckon I'll be at least as tall as my pa when I finish growin'."

She ran a long finger across the grooves and gouges of the spindle. "How well did you know her? How long have you been in Pettigo?" She looked at both men in turn, making it clear she wanted to both to reply.

"Me?" Schuster shrugged. "I've been here fifteen years now. I only knew Mrs. Williams to tip my hat to. She looked like a nice enough lady, but she didn't mix with the likes of me."

"Were you born in the United States, Mr. Schuster?"

"Bavaria," he answered. "My folks came when I was little."

"Through which port?"

"Baltimore."

"And you, Tommy?" She turned to the boy. "Where did you come from?"

"New York. We came from Tipperary when I was two. I don't remember it."

"Why're you askin' him?" MacGilfoyle demanded.

"I'm trying to include everyone," Abigail said. "What brought you to Pettigo?"

"I worked on an estate back on the old country. I'm a trained gardener. I served my time there and specialized in roses. Mrs. Williams advertised for a proper gardener, and I was what she wanted. I've been here ever since. It's got to be, oh, ten or more years now. What do you say, Tommy?"

"About ten-and-a-half, I reckon. I was nearly seven, pa."

"What newspaper did she advertise in?"

"I can't remember. It was in San Francisco. I was working there for about two years before I came here, for a company who maintained the private squares. I left with great references. Ponderdine and Sons. You can check. There were more chances for an Irishman out West, so I headed there almost straight off."

"Did you know Lymen Cussen? He came from San Francisco?"

"Me?" snorted MacGilfoyle. "The whole hotel is talkin' about him, but that's all I know of him. How would an Irish gardener know a protestant banker? I didn't even go to the same church. I'm Catholic. No, Miss MacKay. I don't know him and never did. I'll swear it on a stack of Bibles if it makes you happy." He placed his hand over his heart. "Bring a priest. I swear I never met the man the whole time he walked on God's good earth, ma'am. May the Good Lord strike me dead on the spot if I say a word of a lie."

"I see." she paused. "Can you tell me where you were on the night of the eighteenth of December and the day of the nineteenth?"

MacGilfoyle snorted. "Here. What exactly I was doing I can't say as one day runs into another, but I was here or hereabouts on hotel business. I'm only ever here. So's Tommy."

"And you, Mr. Schuster?"

Schuster played pensively with his handlebar moustache. "I honestly don't know. I'll work as night porter here at the beginning of the week. You know the type of thing: watch the desk in case anything happens. On top of that, I work at the saloon three nights a week. What day was it?"

"The eighteenth was a Saturday. The nineteenth was a Sunday," she answered.

"Saturday I work until about two in the mornin' in the bar," Schuster replied. "On Sunday, I don't do nuthin'. I maybe have dinner out if'n I fancy it. I can't remember."

Abigail chewed her lip as she processed the information. "Thank you, gentlemen. You've been helpful."

"We have?" MacGilfoyle grinned. "I didn't think we'd told you anything."

A smile tugged at her mouth, not reaching into her eyes. "All the little details build to the truth. One more thing, Mr. MacGilfoyle. Are you familiar with *sloinneadh*?"

He frowned. "Of course I am. What does it have to do with anything?"

"What?" Schuster asked.

"It's the Gaelic way of identifying your lineage from father to son. For instance, you may have several John MacDonalds as it's a common name, Mr. Schuster, but they will all have different *sloinneadh*; a different father, a different grandfather, great-grandfather, and so on. It's your unique identity. It's who you are connected to, and who is connected to you. As the names are translated from the Gaelic, they can also be spelled differently in English. Our people can tell exactly who you are, and your lineage, right back to medieval times or before."

"So?"

"MacGilfoyle. There are a few English versions of that name aren't there? Mac Gilla Phoil? Sons of the followers of Saint Paul. There are many spellings and versions. Why did you choose yours?"

"Choose it? We have English names and our Gaelic names. You know that. I spell it the way I was taught. Why do you spell yours the way you do?"

"It's the accepted way for us to spell it in English in my family. We all spell ours the same." She persisted. "Do any of your family spell your name differently, Mr. MacGilfoyle?"

He frowned. "Tommy spells it the way I do. He's all I've got but for a few distant relatives back home."

"It's originally Welsh, isn't it?"

"Some say it was, way back about the eleventh century." MacGilfoyle raised one brow. "I'm an Irishman in blood and bone, miss. I'll never be anything else." He grinned. "I couldn't. I can't do any other accent."

"I'm sure you are, sir." She nodded and pulled her snood back over her head and walked to the door. "Thank you, gentlemen. I'll leave you to your work. I'm sorry to take up your time."

◆◊◆

Jake's foot rattled back and forth in impatience. He'd been waiting all day for Abigail to get back from wherever she had gone for hours. The need to talk to her burned a hole in his heart. The house was silent. Mrs. France had been escorted home because of the storm, Clancy was on his rounds, and the top of Nat's head was obstinately on show as he played wordless solitaire at the table. The flick of the cards crowded the thick silence with an irritating thrum, broken only by the crackling fire and the clock marking off the sluggish passing of time. Jake stood and walked over to the window.

The snow was getting heavier and the wind whipped it into a blinding dance of dazzling white. A dark figure struggled against the wind, leaning forward, and encrusted in ice. The man was mottled in snow as the gale whipped at his scarf and slammed the gate against the picket fence. The path was treacherous and he slithered over the steps until out of sight and a key was heard rattling in the lock.

"Hello!" Clancy banged the snow from his boots and shook off his coat. "I'm back. Who's here?"

"Good, I was worried about you." Jake wandered out into the hall. "I escorted Mrs. France home. This weather was getting so bad I was worried about her getting stuck here. She left us a pie and full instruction on how to cook everythin'. Real full instructions. She seems to think we're idiots."

"That's how men in the kitchen seem to her." Clancy grinned. "Thanks for that. She'd find it hard to walk at all now. What about Nat and Abi?"

"Nat's here. I've no idea where Abi is."

Clancy frowned and blew in his hands, heading for the fire. "Hmm. I hope she's okay. Don't you know where she went?"

Nat didn't even look up from his game. "She was heading to the hotel this morning. I haven't seen her since."

"Didn't you want to go with her?" asked Clancy.

"I sure did, but she was most particular about doing this on her own." Nat gathered his cards back into a pack and shuffled them. He frowned at Jake and looked back at the cards. "Most particular."

"She's still upset?" Steam drifted from the seat of Clancy's pants as he dried out by the fire. "I thought you were going to speak to her, Jake."

Nat banged his cards on the table and glared at his uncle. "You told him?"

"Yeah, he guessed. He deserved an explanation. This is his house."

Nat gaped in disbelief. "Everything? You told him everything?"

"No. Not everything," Jake snapped. "He's got a way of drawin' a man out."

Clancy glanced from one to the other in confusion. "What didn't you tell me?"

Nat glowered at Jake, challenging him to disclose exactly what had gone on. "Yeah, what?"

Jake dropped his head. "I called Abi a whore."

Clancy's brows arched. "You did? Hmmm... That's harsh. You called her that for laughing?"

"They were havin' a snowball fight," Jake said, as though it explained everything. "I know how bad it is, you don't need to tell me. I've been waiting to apologize all day."

"Good luck with that," growled Nat. "She's not talking to either of us." He stood. "I'll get you some coffee, Doc. You must be freezing."

"Thanks, I am. Mrs. Hamilton's baby came at last. I can't tell you how relieved I am I can relax and not worry about getting out to her place for a delivery in this."

A loud thumping at the door cut off their conversation. Nat

turned to answer it, the blizzard following Sheriff Gibson in with an angry flurry until the door was slammed shut. "Phew! It's fierce out there."

"Coffee?" Nat walked over to the kitchen door. "I'm getting some for Clancy."

"I ain't stayin'. I'm on my way home." Ben flapped his hat to remove the melting ice which had begun guttering down his neck. "I came to tell you Miss MacKay's at the hotel. She's gonna stay there and sleep on the floor. I offered to help her back here, but she said she still had too much to do and it'll save her fightin' her way back in the mornin'."

"She ain't comin' back?"

Gibson smiled at Jake's concern. "She's fine. She's bein' well-looked after. You don't have to worry about her."

"Yeah, I do. One of their guests was murdered."

"Oh, you heard about that? It looks like he was done in right in the Williamses' livin' room. She wants me to bring her bag of kit first thing in the mornin'. There's blood between the floorboards and on the carpet. Someone hid it by turnin' it so it was under the sofa."

"Blood?" Jake's jaw dropped open. "No. I didn't know that. Forget the kit, Ben. I'll take it to her now. I'm goin'."

Clancy watched him pull on his boots. "You can't go out in this."

"Why not? You just did."

"It was life or death."

Jake turned simmering eyes on the doctor. "So is this. There's a murderer on the loose, and she's diggin' him out."

"I wouldn't have left her if I thought it was dangerous," Gibson said. "She's fine."

Jake thrust his arm into his coat. "I know you wouldn't, but that woman has a way of findin' trouble wherever she goes. She could find a shark in a bathtub."

He wound a scarf around his neck and mouth, closing his sheepskin coat up to the neck and opened the door. "Don't wait up, Doc. I have no idea when I'll be back."

♦◊♦

The clerk hung a sign on the handles of the lounge door bearing the legend 'private' in gold lettering. "Here you go, Miss MacKay. The guests will have to use the dining room to socialize. This will be reserved especially for you. It's no hardship. They've used it all day and most are turning in themselves, now."

She looked around the lounge, and more particularly at one of the sofas already made with blankets and pillows for her. "Thank you. It looks cozy."

"I've sent for hot chocolate for you too." The clerk smiled. "Now, about nightclothes—"

"Oh, there's no need Mr. Nash. I won't be wearing any." He flushed bright red as she hurriedly continued. "*I mean* I won't be undressing at all. This is like camping, or a nap in the middle of the day."

He shrugged. "If you say so. I don't mind trying to borrow something from one of the maids for you."

"There's really no need to make a fuss, Mr. Nash. I'm quite used to roughing it. This is positively luxurious compared to what I'm used to."

"There's no need to be so formal. We're all working here after all. Everyone calls me Dick."

She arched one brow. "They do? That's mean of them."

"No, my name is Richard. It's Dick for short."

"Oh, I see." Abigail walked over to the fire to hide her smile. "Thank you, Dick. You have been helpful."

A knock at the door brought a maid with the promised hot chocolate. The clerk took it and placed it on the side table next to the sofa. "There you go. May I presume to call you Abigail?"

"If you like. If it helps you to tell me everything you know about Lymen Cussen."

"Me? All I did was check him in and out like any other guest. I don't remember anything about him. If he left on a Sunday I wouldn't have seen him at all. Mr. Williams does Sundays."

Abigail lifted her chocolate as he sidled onto the sofa beside her. "You work right in front of the private quarters. Don't you remember any fuss or disagreements?"

"I can't say I do."

She sipped at the delicious concoction. "Do many guests at the hotel visit the owners in their rooms?"

"Not many." Abigail's eyes slid sideways to watch him stretch out an arm and drape it along the back of the sofa behind her. "It's mostly local people who come to see them."

"And Lymen Cussen wasn't one of them?"

"Not that I remember. I can't even remember him leaving, but he must have."

"Do you work on Saturdays?" she asked.

"Eight until eight. Monday to Saturday." He leaned in. "Do you ever get lonely doing this work?"

"Chance would be a fine thing." She stood, warming herself in front of the fire. "So you didn't see Mr. Cussen go back there at all,

Nash stood. "You know I didn't. I'd have told you."

Abigail's brow creased. "I know nothing of the sort, Mr. Nash. Our acquaintance is short."

"You could get to know me better. And I told you to call me Dick."

"Mr. Nash, you are in great danger of being called any number of things. Can we keep this relationship on a purely professional standing, please? Mr. Williams deals with guests?"

"Yes. Every Sunday. Not that it's busy on a Sunday. There's only one train in and out. It's dead."

"What about evenings. Who covers nights?"

"That'd be either Tommy MacGilfoyle or Otto Schuster. They have a camp bed behind the desk. They share it. There isn't much to do at night other than give a few people their keys or messages."

Abigail paced. "Thank you, Mr. Nash. You've been helpful."

"Don't you want me to stay and keep you company?"

She turned to the rotund little man with a thick dark brows

meeting in the middle. "No, thank you, Mr. Nash. You have been most kind, but I must insist you leave now. I really must get some rest."

The desk clerk's face fell. "If you insist."

"I do." She crossed over and opened the door. "I insist most strongly. Good evening, and thanks for the bedding and chocolate. That was thoughtful of you."

He nodded silently and stalked from the room. "Just let me know if you need anything."

"You'll be in bed. It's after your finishing time. You told me you finish at eight. I wouldn't dream of bothering you. Sleep well, Mr. Nash."

His brows peered in through the gap in the door as she pushed it closed. Her fingers felt around the handle and she grimaced at the discovery there was no lock. She turned back to the fire and what was left of her chocolate, rubbing her temples. She was tired. She hadn't slept well after Jake's comments yesterday. She was ready for a deep sleep and was extremely grateful for the hiatus away from Clancy's house. The storm had been perfectly timed. If she could just find some of that calm everyone said came after it, she might get some sleep.

♦◊♦

Jake practically fell through the door to the hotel. His body was encrusted with ice and snow from head to foot. The walk from the doctor's house generally took about twenty minutes, but it had taken over an hour, and Jake was a fit, muscular man. It would have been dangerous for anyone less prepared to be out in that blizzard. Jake shook the pile of snow from his hat and stripped off his coat and scarf, scattering frozen chunks over the large, woven rope mat which served to take the worst of the debris from the public as they entered the building.

The blue eyes scanned the dimly lit reception area. The desk was empty and there was nobody to be seen, so he strode over to the desk and whacked the button on top of the butler bell enough times to vent a little of his excess adrenaline and sprinkle glistening spots of melting snow on the counter. The boy he'd seen talking to Abigail in the bank wandered out from the kitchen. "Can I help you, mister? We ain't got no rooms, but I can let you wait out the storm in reception. We wouldn't send a dog out in this weather."

"Tommy? You're the handyman's son?"

"Yeah, I'm Tommy MacGilfoyle. Pa's a gardener. How'd you know my name?"

Jake smiled and showed his badge. "I saw you at the bank a couple of days ago. I'm lookin' for the Pinkerton lady. I've got the bag she wanted."

"I don't know nuthin' about no bag, but she's sleepin' in the lounge, mister."

He followed the boy's pointing finger over to the closed double doors. A sign hung on the handle declaring it private.

"She's in there."

"She is?" Jake bent and picked up the bag at his feet. "Great."

Tommy scampered out from behind the desk and blocked his path. "You can't go in, mister. I've got orders."

Jake inclined his head to stare at the lad obstructing his way and grinned. "And do you really think you're gonna stop me?"

The boy gazed at the wall of muscle before him, tempered only by the twinkle of humor in the eyes.

"Well, I've gotta be able to say I tried."

"Great work. You tried. I'll shout it from the rooftops for you." Jake indicated back toward the kitchen with his head. "Go back to your supper."

Tommy shrugged the shrug of the pragmatist. "Just don't disturb any of the guests, huh? We've got all the women and children here. When one baby starts hollerin' they set the rest off. Then they starts poopin'. It's a nightmare. I can't wait till we get back to drunks and gamblers. They only cry when they lose."

"We'll be as quiet as mice," said Jake, moving the lad aside before adding under his breath. "Although, knowin' Abi, it'll probably be more like the kinda noise a granny makes when she steps on one in the dark."

He tapped gently on the door with his knuckles. There was a pause before a female voice called out. "Who is it?"

There would never be a good time to face her, so he braced himself and called out. "Make yourself decent, Abi. I've got your bag, and I'm comin' in."

The firelight illuminated the room, showing her pushing herself to a sitting position on a sofa, covered in a patchwork quilt.

"Good, you're dressed." He sighed in relief. He glanced around the room, instinctively checking for danger. "Here's your bag."

She silently glared at him as he placed it on the floor beside her.

His moue of discomfort which ghosted across his face was both long and excruciating as he fought to find the right words. "Abi, I'm sorry. Sorrier than I can ever say. I had no right to call you that. I was about as wrong as a man can be. Can you forgive me?"

Her dark eyes narrowed. "Fine, you're forgiven. Now go away."

He hooked his thumbs in his belt, his eyes downcast. "It ain't that simple. There's the mother of all storms out there. It took me over an hour to get here. I can't get back. I'm stayin'."

She blinked as she considered the options. "This is a big place. Find somewhere else to wait it out. I don't want you around."

"So you haven't forgiven me? Look, I spent the day Mrs. Williams killed herself walking about, seeing pictures in my head, mixing up that woman's brains spilling out with my sister's. I was in distress, angry, and all kinds of wrong." He paused. "I invited Nat to punch me in the mouth. You can do the same, if it helps."

Outrage flashed over her face. "I don't go around hurting people to make myself feel better. I believe that's your prerogative. What do you think I am?"

"Since you ask, a real fine person. Brave, honest, and honorable. You're also irregular, free-spirited, and the most singular woman I met since my ma. You told me you were still gettin' used to us bein' out of the ordinary. The same goes for me. You need to give me time to find the words for a woman like you. And for the record, I think you could hurt a man real bad if you put your mind to it. In fact, you're doin' it right now."

"I'm not doing anything."

His brow creased. "You know you are. You're closed down and cold. That ain't you, Abi."

"Of course I'm cold." Her voice was crisp and sharp. "I came here with some fantasy of an impossible life. I already know what people think of respectable women who take up with criminals, but in a wildly inconceivable brainstorm I believed we could carve out a world where none of it mattered. Then you showed me it did. It always will."

He dropped his head. "Please, Abi. If I could go back in time and change it I would, but all I can do is put it right."

"You can't unring a bell. I'm leaving as soon as I can. I advise you to do the same."

He walked further into the room and sat, although unbidden. His earnest eyes glittered in the firelight. "You can't."

Her hostile glare pinned him to the spot. "What do you mean, I can't?"

"You're one of us." His eyes burned intently across the half-light. "Like it or not, fate made you from the same stuff as us. You're the light, we're the dark, but you'll always be drawn to what's in your soul. It's why you're here. My grandpa told me the Irish used to believe souls were created in circles. That's your clan. When you meet a stranger and you feel connected, it's because they belong to the same soul circle. Circles never end. You're a Gael. You know this stuff."

"Very colorful, Mr. Conroy, but I am a modern woman and I have free will."

"Sure you do. So does Nat, and he doesn't give up on things easy. Why are you calling me *mister*? Call me Jake."

"Our relationship is no longer informal."

"Abi, I was a horse's ass yet again. That ain't a change, it's more of the same, and you showed me I've got to do somethin' about it. I think you could change everythin' for Nat. You'd be good for him." He paused. "He could be good for you, too. Look how happy you've been."

"Or, he could ruin my life. This has focused me on how dangerously close I came to being sucked in."

He leaned forward, resting his forearms on his knees. "Fine. What if I disappear and leave you and Nat to it? *I'm* the problem, not him."

Her forehead creased. "You'd do that?"

"If it meant you and Nat could be happy, I'd do whatever it took. I brought him up since he was four. I kept us together and got him the best education I could, but he still never had a chance. I kept bad company. I was a bad influence." His eyes burned into her. "I love him like my own son, but I'll walk away and leave you two in peace if that's what you need."

An array of emotions fluttered across her face before she spoke again. "Nat would never do that."

Jake snorted. "He's already told me he's goin' away from me the minute this place thaws. The way I figure, he might as well take you with him and be happy."

"He said that?"

"And more. Most of it not fit to share with a lady. Sleep on it. Think it over."

She played idly with the quilt, her fingers working at the fabric at the center of a colorful swirl before she nodded curtly. "Goodnight, Mr. Conroy."

He took off his jacket and settled back on the sofa. "I'm goin' nowhere, Abi. Not only is it cold enough to freeze off a man's whiffles, you're diggin' out a murderer. I ain't leavin you in an unlocked room in the place the killer is likely to live." He punched a cushion into shape. "Besides. There's a fire in here.

I'm only dumb, not a complete dunderpate."

He draped his jacket over him and lay back. "If I could get you to understand how seein' the body affected me. Sometimes, I wonder when the forgettin' will ever begin. When you've seen a loved one smashed up, it haunts a person, but I guess I'm just weak."

The silence lay heavy with unspoken thoughts as the fire crackled in the hearth, throwing a cavalcade of flickering shadows dancing around the room. He sat to pull off his wet boots, placing them on the hearth to dry out, and glanced over at the silent woman, who had turned her back on him and pulled the covers over herself. "Goodnight, Abi. I hope this isn't another regret to add to a lifetime of mistakes. I'm a damned fool, but don't let Nat pay the price for it."

He removed his gun belt and dangled it over the arm of the sofa so it would be close, then lay back on the opposite sofa and closed his eyes. Their conversation played over and over in his head, irritating him as he found countless ways to have posed a better argument. The glowing fire was comforting, and he soon succumbed to the soporific effect. His breathing slowed to a deeper, calmer rhythm until he sank into a drowsy, torpid state. Something softly touched him and his eyes darted open. The colorful quilt had been delicately spread over him. A smile tugged at his lips as he discreetly watched her climb back under her remaining blanket and turn on her back to him. Abigail had clearly waited until she thought he was asleep to share her bedding, but share it, she did. Maybe this visit hadn't been a complete disaster, after all.

Chapter Nineteen

Almost every man in town was engaged in digging out the roads the next morning. At least three feet of snow had fallen overnight and the wind had carried it in shifting drifts which scaled walls and over roofs like sifted flour. The loose snow caught the wind in glittering shards which danced over the surface in tiny, shimmering whirlwinds, underscoring the biting wind chilling bones and burning sinuses water wherever it hit.

But Nat wasn't cold. Sheer hard work was his furnace and, for a man who had dedicated his life to finding ways to collect money which were light on the back, he was certainly throwing himself into hard labor. He had stripped off his coat, and was battering through the banks of snow like one of those clockwork automatons he'd seen in books. It was cleansing; living in the moment instead of dwelling on his emotional problems. They didn't disappear, but his mind focused on the repetitive work and gave relief from the pressure. Work as a way ahead was new to him, and the thought made his lips twitch into an involuntary smile. He'd always heard hard work was its own reward, but didn't think it was worth the risk to find out.

He paused to wipe sweat from his brow, screwing his eyes against the blinding sun glinting off the hoary whiteness of the banked-up snow, and rested for a moment on his shovel. Abigail wouldn't listen to reason, but she'd have to listen to him if he solved this damn thing. There was a huge piece of evidence sitting in a bag in the doctor's consulting rooms. Pettigo had a tailor; a good one, who made bespoke clothing.

Surely, he could tell him a little more about the suit moldering away in the packing box? The corpse had been dressed in it before being dumped. That meant it belonged to someone local. All they'd really done was look at the debris it had collected. Maybe it was time to look at the garment itself.

♦◊♦

The bell above the door tinkled and bounced around on the brass spring to announce the arrival of another customer to the emporium, causing a ferret-faced youth to emerge from the back of the shop. Nat hesitated, unsure what to even ask. He showed his badge.

"I wonder if anyone can help me? I need an expert to tell me as much as he can about a suit of clothes. They belong to a murder victim, and it might help us know more about him."

The boy's eyes widened and he darted back to the door, bellowing into the shadows beyond. "Pa. Ma! There's a lawman here. He's got questions about a murder." He turned back to Nat, his chest rising and falling in anxiety. "Why'd you think we're involved?"

Nat smiled to lighten the spiraling panic of the gathering knot of people. "I don't. I thought a tailor could tell me how old the suit was, maybe where it was made, or even about the type of person who got suits like this made for them. Anything at all, really. There's nothing to worry about. You know clothes, I don't. I want to pick your brains."

"Oh!" The tall man said as he followed a tiny, sandy-haired, beige-faced woman into the main shop. "That's a relief. Taylor Nessmith, this is my shop. This is my wife, Elly. How can we help?"

"Taylor? Really? You're called Taylor and you're a tailor?" Nat placed the box on the counter, his most charming persona in play.

"Yup. My pa was a tailor, too. He never had much in the way of imagination. Ma was always surprised he had the gumption to leave England at all."

"Is this a bad time? I don't want to impact on your business."

"It's slow as hell since we've been snowed in. The apprentices are working on ready-made for the summer, but we need the folks through here to be busy. The tourists comin' to the hot springs and the gambling tournaments are a big part of our business. Wealthy folks like to go back with a fine new suit of clothes, especially when they win big. Whatya got? I got time."

Nat lifted off the lid and removed the jacket, placing it on the counter. "What can you tell me about this?" He pointed out the dark spots. "Not the stains, more how it was made and what it tells you about who would have had this made."

The couple pored over the fabric, moving it around and fingering it. "This was expensive back in the day." Mr. Nessmith declared as his wife nodded in agreement.

"Yes, Harris Tweed. Imported fabric," she answered. "This belonged to someone wealthy."

"The cut is old-fashioned. The legs are wide, like in the fifties. They got much narrower in the sixties. The watch pocket is hand-stitched. A button fly, not a fall front, so keeping up-to-date mattered to the owner. Both types were made in the fifties, but the modern man went for the button fly."

The tailor's practiced eyes narrowed as he peered at the stitching. "Some of this is sewn by machine and the rest hand-finished. That was fairly normal for tailors in the fifties. Machines were startin' to come in, but they still did darts and tricky bits by hand." He raised his head and grinned. "Look at this, Elly. Look at the finish of this knot."

The woman peered at the tiny stitches. "It's a bullion knot." She smiled at her husband. "Just like your pa used to do. You don't think he did this do you?"

"It is, ain't it? A bullion knot." The tailor looked Nat full in the face. "My pa always ended visible hand stitching with an ornamental knot. A tiny little thing, something nobody but a tailor would notice, but he insisted it all added to the quality of the finish. This looks like his work. I can't say for certain, but not all tailors do this. It's not common. It looks like his work."

"Your pa made this? How much of a coincidence is this?"

"Well, not too coincidental. You are in the same town as his shop. It's not too much of a stretch to think a lot of the best suits locally come from the only local tailor."

"I guess." Nat scratched his head. "Is your pa around?"

"Yeah, he's in the graveyard on the outskirts of town." Nessmith chuckled. "The ground's a bit hard right now, so you might have trouble raisin' him before spring."

"Oh, hush, Taylor." Elly admonished him with a wave of her hand. "Stop being disrespectful."

Nat sighed. "Darn. I don't suppose he'd have remembered who he made it for anyway."

"Nope, but we keep all our records." Elly arched both brows. "You're welcome to look at those."

"Records? What records do you keep?"

"A tailor has a manual for all his bespoke customers. A good fit doesn't just rely on the basic measurements. It takes a trained eye to spot all the little nuances in posture, all the little imperfections a shoulder higher than the other, a slight hunch, or a bit of a belly. Excellent tailoring can disguise all that, and we take detailed notes to ensure a man looks the best he can. If we keep them the first time we don't have to do it again." Nessmith eyed Nat's broad shoulders. "I could make you the most wonderful suit of clothes you ever wore. With a physique like yours, I could make you look like a Greek god."

"Yeah, but I think it'd be more than I earn as a deputy in a year." Nat's cheeks dimpled. "And it's too cold for a toga."

Nessmith chuckled. "You'll be earnin' every penny of it if you go through our records back to 1850. That's a lot of readin'. Pa kept a manual, but I find a card system easier. Every customer has his own card and the measurements are amended with little changes on every visit so it's all up to date. The older records are much harder to read because they're by date, not name."

"I guess I'll have to go through them." Nat fixed on the man's laughing eyes. "You're enjoying this, aren't you? I bet you get a lot of fun out of people's imperfections behind the scenes."

"Nooo." Nessmith laughed. "If I wanted to profit from other people's misery I'd have become a florist."

Nat's dimples deepened as he warmed to the man's dry humor. "So, if I go through the records to identify this suit, what am I looking for?"

"Well, I'll give you all the measurements. The fabric's called Harris Tweed and it's hartwist plain herringbone in barleycorn." He led Nat through a room full of young men laboring away over pieces of fabrics to an office. "We keep all the manuals in here."

The dimples fell from Nat's dismayed face at the stacks of huge leather-bound books crowning the shelves. "These?" he asked. "All of these?"

"Oh, no." Nesmith pulled a bolt of material away and unveiled a tea crate. "There's all these, too." He folded his arms and arched his brows. "Are you sure you want to do this? There has to be an easier way of identifyin' this man. We've dressed thousands of people over the years."

Nat dragged out a chair. "Oh, we've identified the man but someone had dressed him in an old suit to make him look like a saddle tramp. If I can find out whose suit it was, I might stand a chance of finding out who did it."

"Good luck with it. Will coffee help? I'll measure it for you and Elly will fix the coffee."

He pulled out the first ledger and flicked it open. "Yes please. A large vat of the stuff."

♦◊♦

Jake started awake at the sound of the door closing. The blanket was neatly folded on the opposite sofa and the pillow placed squarely on top. He pushed himself to a sitting position in the empty room and frowned aimlessly into the gray ashes of the dead fire in the hearth. The lack of resolution sat in his gullet like a ball of lead. She had thawed only slightly, but today would be pivotal. Had she warmed enough to stop the only family he had from walking out of his life forever? He cursed under his breath and stood, bolstering himself to face possibility of the rest of his life alone. Seeing your own children a couple of times a year and hearing them call you *uncle* was just an extra spike in the heart. It'd be just him and the specters of the lost.

The reception area was quiet with Dick Nash ensconced behind his desk. The dark brows gathered into a tight line of disapproval at the sight of a male deputy emerging from the room he'd reserved for the female Pinkerton.

Jake scowled. "Let's get somethin' straight. She's as respectable as your own mother. I came here through the storm to make sure she was safe. There's a killer on the loose. I wasn't leavin' her alone to face him. She's been hurt doin' that before. Understood?"

The steely determination in the blue eyes was enough to make the desk clerk flutter nervously and fumble with the ledger. "I never said a word, sir."

"You didn't need to. I saw the way you looked at me. Where'd she go?"

"The private quarters. She wanted to get to work right away. I'm sending in breakfast for her while she works." Nash's moustache twitched in agitation. "Shall I get them to add to the order?"

The gunman nodded and headed straight for the private quarters. He thrust the door open and strode in to the sight of Abigail lighting an oil lamp.

His greeting was terse but he attempted to sound conciliatory. "Mornin', Abi."

Her dark eyes slid sideways, her hands still on the crown of the lamp. "You're up. I left you sleeping."

"I ain't been sleepin' too well the last few nights, Abi. I'm grateful." He frowned. "A lamp? It's broad daylight."

"I need a flame to purify instruments." She replaced the

shade. "I'm testing for bloodstains. The Williamses have been staying with the Morgans, and need to get back in their home. I have to finish today."

He paused. "Can I help?"

She still didn't look him in the eye. "The women have been itching to clean so it looks decent for them. I need to get on quickly."

"So? Let me help."

She turned her back on him and bent over her bag. "There's no need. I can manage. You don't know how to do this."

Jake huffed in irritation. "Abi, enough. I was a horse's butt, but we need to put catching this man first."

She turned to look at him at last, her dark eyes reflecting more than they revealed. "We don't know it's a man. Why do men always assume it's a man?"

"Probably because it usually is. We get angry and do dumb things."

"So do women." She strode across the room and pushed at the heavy sofa. "Anger is a human emotion. It's not male or female. Hasn't occurred to you that women feel every emotion that men experience? We do dumb things, too."

"Yeah, like not lettin' go of stuff." Jake seized her arm as she strode by. "People do dumb things when they're angry. Ain't you ever been stupid?"

She stood staring his grasping hand with an eerie calm. "Many times. Recently, I've been more stupid than ever." She shook him off. "But you're right. I forgive you. I really do. Now, can we get on? If you want to help, push the furniture back so I can assess the layout of the room when it the carpet was stained from the indentations left by the furniture."

His face split into a smile. "Thank you, Abi. I promise nothin' like that will ever happen again."

She glowered at him. "If it does, I might just shoot you in the foot."

"It won't." He slapped his forehead in frustration. "I need to do somethin' about my damned problem. Someone must know how to cure irritable heart. Soldiers get it all the time. Some doctor must have studied it."

"I found it helps to talk." Abigail lifted the side table away.

"Folks don't want to hear about things like that, besides you ain't related to the folks you saw dead. You don't understand."

She continued to work, her face stony and resolute. "I found my father, Jake. He was shot through the head by his killer. I *do* know." She paused before sighing. "Of course, you were a child trying to protect another child, and life was uncertain for you. That's way worse. It's also acceptable for women to show emotions." She heaved at the Chesterfield sofa. "Get the end of that, will you?" She grunted with exertion as she hauled at the furniture. "Find someone to talk to. Instead of freezing people out when you get overwhelmed, go with it instead of shutting it down. Experience the feelings and work through them, even if you have to pay a prostitute to listen to you, or smash something to get rid of your aggression. Work through *them* instead of letting them work through *you*."

Jake dragged the settee to the side. "Is that what you did?"

She glinted at him beguilingly. "I didn't hire a prostitute, if that's what you mean. I spoke to my older sister. I also used my father's squash racket." She paused, her eyes drifting off to the left, unfocused on everything but her memories. "And I walked. A lot. It used the energy. I think if you added up all the miles, I could've walked all the way back to Scotland. In the end, I decided to bring his killers in, and Alan Pinkerton hired me so he could at least control me a little. I was clodhopping all over his investigation, but it helped me."

"I can't talk to Nat. It's his family, too."

"You decided that, did you?" She watched him nod. "Ask him. He's a grown man now, and he has no memory of it. He might be able to help you get it off your chest. Maybe you need to do a little looking after yourself now? It'll make you a better uncle to him if you stop these angry outbursts. "

Jake paused, staring at her intently. "When'd you get so smart, Abi?"

"Smart?" Her laugh was mirthless. "I fight my own demons. I understand what you're saying, but all I know is, you can't take them out on others." Her eyes darkened. "I learned the hard way, too. We all live with the storms of our past. Why do you think I'm out here on my own? We can sit alone in a shelter or we can ride it out to get to the other side. That's all I know. I haven't beaten my demons, but they don't control me. Not anymore." Her sigh was heavy, laden with disquietude. "Not always, anyway. Look, can we leave this here? I need to get on."

His brows met, his mind running like quicksilver behind the bright blue eyes, but he merely allowed a smile to ghost across his features. "Sure. What's first?"

She stepped back, hands on hips to read the dents on the carpet before dropping to her knees. Her head tipped sideways at floor level. "So, the sofa has six dumpy feet. Two at either end and a pair in the middle. The existing dents means it was along the wall on the left, with the back toward Constance's bedroom. The two chairs were on the opposite side of the room, with their back toward the parents' room."

She stood again, her lips pursing as she perused the scene, and flipped back the rug to observe the underside. She strode over to her bag and took out purple chalk. "So, if I mark on the top of the rug to correspond with the stains underneath—"

She drew on the top of the carpet, marking out where blood had seeped in, but had been either cleaned or lost in the pattern.

"Why purple?" asked Jake.

"It's all that was left in the box."

"There's a dent." Jake pointed. "A long one. It matches the foot on the table."

She nodded and drew the table over to fit into the groove. It matched exactly.

"So there was a table at the end of the sofa near where the bloodstains are? Here at the same end of the room as the door." Her eyes lit with a memory. "The shepherdess. The staff told me about an ornament which went missing around the week before Christmas, or so. Mrs. Williams eventually admitted it was broken after pretending not to know anything about it. If the stabbed man knocked over the table and then bled into the carpet, it could fit with her lying about it. I must ask what table it usually sat on."

She took a magnifying glass and examined the area, seeking out tweezers to probe at a tiny piece of white matter. She delicately pulled it out and held it aloft, turning the shard behind the lens. "Porcelain. One side glazed with pink and gold. It does look like something was broken in this area."

She stood and dropped it into an envelope, labeling it with a pencil and logging it on a rough diagram of the room.

"Now, the carpet." She flipped the edge of the carpet over and moistened it with a bottle marked 'Distilled Water' and placed a piece of blotting paper on top. She dropped more on top until the paper was soaked. She then dropped the hydrogen peroxide oxide on the dark stain. It fizzed into a foam almost instantly. "Hmm, now the guaiac." She raised a dropper over the foam and carefully dripped it on the froth. It gradually turned blue. Her dark eyes turned to Jake. "It's blood."

"Yeah. I thought it might be."

"Looking at the stain, it seems more like it seeped it rather than dripped. There are no tails or splatters on the pattern I can see." She turned, still on her knees, and glanced at the floor boards. "Now, where else did it drip?"

There was a knock at the door and Nash strode in, bearing a tray. His heavy brows arched and his back stiffened at the sight of the carpet pulled up and the furniture in disarray. He put the tray on the table and scowled. "The accident was in the bedroom, not here. What are you doing?" His gaze landed on the carpet. "Is that a purple mark? It'd better come off."

"It's chalk. It'll come off." Abigail climbed to her knees. "We're tracing all the blood in the room."

"Why?"

Jake folded his arms and glared at the clerk. "Do we tell you how to do your job?"

"Everybody tells me how to do my job," said Nash. "That's

working with the public for ya. Just don't be too long. The women'll be here at noon to clean."

He turned and stalked from the room with his nose in the air, closing the door behind him with a loud clatter.

"So? What now?" Jake asked reaching for the toast.

"We carry on." Abigail poured them both a coffee. "Can you eat over on the other side of the room? The hydrogen peroxide works on proteins, and crumbs might interfere with this."

"Shooor—" Jake mumbled through a mouthful of toast. He lifted the tray and headed for the window seat. "I'll take it over here. Want one?"

♦◊♦

Nat had limited himself to local addresses in his search, figuring if the suit had remained in town since the early fifties, the owner probably had, too. Given most of the trade came from tourists, his search was a lot quicker than he'd anticipated since he ignored non-locals. It had been a mere two-and-a-half hours of soul-sucking, banal ennui which flew by like the visions of a drowning man going under for the third time; but it had been worth it. He eventually found an order for a suit made from hartwist plain herringbone Harris Tweed in barleycorn with all the right measurements. The suit was in the box under his arm, and he was headed to see the man who'd ordered it.

And that was why he was here; at the Jagged Tick Palace, the most popular drinking establishment in town. It was less cultured than the Regal Hotel, but it was a huge draw for the less wealthy and less sophisticated end of the market. And as most people in this town were uncultured and poor, business was booming. Nat reckoned that included him and Jake since they'd passed more than a few hours in there themselves.

He clunked over the steps to the wooden sidewalk, which was gritted with ashes as the dank, frozen wood could be treacherous in this weather. He pushed open the door, instantly noting how uninviting a bar was in the cold morning light. The usually ubiquitous jangling music, a constant cacophony in the background, was gone. The large room was silent but for the slopping of a mop against a galvanized bucket and the distant tinkle of bottles somewhere in the distance. The stale stench of old beer and foul tobacco mingled with washing soda into a sickly miasma.

The mop sloshed over his boots before the hunched drudge of a washerwoman wordlessly pushed him aside to catch the spot where he had been standing.

"We ain't open yet."

Nat turned, trying not to stare at the woman before him, as unreal in the harsh light of day as plaster of Paris figurine left out in the rain. He'd seen her before and the paint and powder was colorful enough by oil light, but in daylight, she had a cosmetic fortitude rarely seen outside circus folks. He pasted on a smile to mask his reaction. "Good morning, ma'am. Is there a man called Noah Washburn around?"

"I told you. We ain't open."

"I'm not here as a customer. I'm here to see the owner."

She propped both hands on her hips and raised her chin. "He don't see travelers until it's gone noon."

"Travelers?"

She frowned, causing Nat to wonder if any of her face would flake off. "Yeah, travellin' salesmen. Come back after twelve."

He pulled back his coat, displaying the star on his jacket. "I'm not selling anything. I'd like to have a word with him if he's available, please."

The penciled in brow arched toward a mop of bright red curls which sat slightly askew atop her painted head. "The law? Why ain't I seen you before? I know them all in this town."

"I have drunk here, and it's a great place. Maybe you didn't notice me? I'm helping out Ben Gibson. Mr. Washburn? Is he in?"

"Honey. When I don't notice a man like you, it's time for me to get some of them there spectacles." She paused, drinking in the chiseled cheekbones, the chocolate eyes, and the square shoulders. "Yeah, he's in, but this had better be important, callin' at this ungodly hour."

"Ungodly?" Nat grinned. "It's past eleven."

She gestured with her head for Nat to follow him, and he watched to see if the wig would turn at the same time as she did. The wobble gave it a life of its own.

"Yeah. We don't get to bed till after three. Eleven's as good as a sparrow's fart to us."

She opened the door to reveal a bald man in an extravagant purple dressing gown topped off with a satin paisley cravat.

"Noah, we got a lawman here to see you."

His fork hovered inches from his open mouth as his lips dropped open at the sight of an unfamiliar face. "You're not Ben. Who are you?"

"I'm Nat. Ben recruited me and a friend to help him with the body dumped in the church hall because we've been involved with the law before," he answered with suitable economy for the truth. "We've identified the man, but he was redressed in a suit which wasn't his. I tracked the original owner, and you had it made at Nessmith's in fifty-one." He tapped the box under his arm. "This is it."

Washburn dropped his fork. "My suit? From seventeen years ago? You're sure?"

Nat nodded and placed the box on the table. "Pretty sure. It fits all the measurements, and has funny stitching the tailor, Taylor, recognized as his pa's work. It was made here, and is the only one in their records made to these dimensions and in this fabric."

"They have records?"

Nat rolled his eyes. "Thousands of them, and I went through them all." He opened the box. "Anyway, you're not a suspect. We know it's been passed on and used as work clothes, but I wondered if you could tell me who you gave it to?"

"Oh, look, Noah." The woman gasped, poking him with a lacquered nail. "I remember you in that. You were somethin' back then."

Washburn scowled. "I'm somethin' now, Dolly."

Dolly's throaty laugh was both contagious and slightly-sullied. "Sure, ya are; but back then, your *somethin'* weren't hidden by your belly."

"Do you remember the suit, sir?"

Washburn nodded. "Sure, I do. The first suit I ever got made. I loved it back in the day. Then it got outta date." He patted his expansive gut with a smirk. "And too small. It didn't fit." He turned back to the woman. "Who'd I give it to, Dolly?"

"One of the staff, weren't it? The barman. Weren't it Bart?"

Noah nodded. "Yeah. I gave it to my head barman, Bart Dunkly. When did I give it to him, Dolly?"

"It was about the time we built up the place and had the stage put in, weren't it? Maybe sometime in fifty-seven?"

Washburn masticated on his eggs while musing. "Yeah. The hotel was openin' under new management and bringin' in a better class of visitor. We wanted the staff to look smarter. Bart had to have worn the suit for another five years or more. Then he got another one. That dark brown one he still wears. I dunno what he did with it after that. I never gave it another thought."

"Is Bart around?" asked Nat.

"He starts at four, but if you want to speak to him urgent he lives over in Clark Street. Little red house with a bent chimney. You can't miss it."

"Thanks. You've been real helpful." Nat tipped his hat and turned. He strolled back out to the bar where a bent hairpin of a charwoman dragged out a sack of fresh sawdust and began scattering it liberally on the floor to soak up the spills and spittle in the day ahead. He stopped to watch for a few seconds while buttoning his coat and heading back out into the caustic winter sunshine. Sawdust. There was sawdust on the suit, wasn't there?

♦◊♦

Ben Gibson stared at the wet gobs on the floor circled with purple chalk and squinted a questioning look at Jake and Abigail.

"Purple?"

"It was the only color left in the box," said Jake. "I asked that, too."

"But why the circles?"

"These are all the areas the hydrogen peroxide bubbled between the floorboards." Abigail climbed to her feet and dusted off her knees. "I found a shard of broken porcelain too. The maid told me it went missing about a week or so before Christmas, and Mrs. Williams only admitted it broke when Constance kicked up a fuss and accused the staff of stealing it. She had bought it as a present for her mother."

"So it sounds like Constance can't be the one Mrs. Williams is coverin' for," said the sheriff. "Constance drew attention to it when she didn't have to."

"Double bluff?" Abigail shook her head. "It could be a diversion and the fuss was to cover for her. It could still be her."

"There doesn't seem to be much blood." Gibson stared at the floor. "If a man was stabbed in the heart I'd expect him to be covered in the stuff."

"Dr. Fox confirmed most of the bleeding was internal," said Abigail. "These are spots, probably where the weapon was pulled out. It starts here, beside the coat rack." She followed the trail across the room. "He staggered a few steps, dripping as he went, and then seems to have fallen face-down on the rug and bled there until he was moved. There's not too much blood on the rug, so I think the body was moved fairly quickly." She laid a hand on the small table. "The rug shows this table was beside the chair. It's also where the bit of porcelain was found between the floorboards. It looks like he tipped over the table as he fell. I checked with the staff, and the broken shepherdess was in a pink dress. The piece I found has pink glaze on one side."

Gibson frowned, placing his hands on his hips. "I've gotta say, it all fits. Any sign of a weapon?"

"Nothing so far." She walked over to the desk and collected the brass letter opener shaped like a dagger. "I'm going to take this to test, but I'm fairly certain it's too wide. I'm going to take the rug and everything on the rack to examine more closely for blood splatter. The scene looks like it started beside the hat rack, he staggered a few steps then fell, taking the table down with him. He probably laid face-down for a very short time, and was then flipped on his back so the bleeding continued inside the thoracic cavity. I can do the coats while the women clean, as long as I note where they were on the rack. I'll take those, too, to see if there was any splatter."

"It's weeks since Cussen was killed. Those coats ain't gonna be in the same place as they were when he was killed," said Jake.

"I have to check." Abigail shrugged. "I can't take anything for granted."

"It's gotta be Percy Williams," said Gibson. "Kathleen would cover for him and it fits with Constance gettin' annoyed at the ornament goin' missin' And not knowin' her pa was involved."

"But what's the motive? And how could Williams or anyone else get Cussen's body out of here without being seen? It took two to bring the body into the church. Someone else is involved. They have to be."

"Maybe Williams and his wife in disguise? Could've dropped the body out of the window, I guess." Jake flicked the latch and slid open the sash window. The warmth leeched from the room almost instantly, dissipating into the freezing void outside. He peered out at the snow covered bushes forming arctic mounds below. He reached out and dusted off the ice. "It don't look like anythin' heavy landed on these, though. They ain't squashed, and nuthin' regrows in December."

"So they must have taken him out via the door, which is right behind the front desk. The night porter has a camp bed off to the side, so either Dick Nash, Otto Schuster, Williams, or Tommy MacGilfoyle must have been around when the body was taken out. The night cover may have been asleep though, so they have an excuse." Abigail sighed. "And we have no motive. None."

"What if the Williamses hid the body in their room until Constance and the night porter were sleepin'?" asked Gibson.

"They could've snuck the body out through the kitchens. The door is only a few yards away."

"It's possible." Abigail paced. "I can't test for blood in the bedroom, though. There's too much of it there already, and I have no way to say whether any of the blood is from Cussen or Mrs. Williams."

"So I guess we go and find out what the Williams family did on the night of the eighteenth of December." Jake slid the window closed. "Constance mentioned Cussen talking about riots in the church."

Abigail's brows rose. "There were riots in Pettigo?"

"Nah." Jake shook his head. "Massachusetts, years ago. Constance heard Cussen talking about Catholics riotin' and her mother told her off for listenin' to unladylike things. Maybe we can ask the preacher if he was at the church his last night here. He might know other people who had dealin's with him."

"Catholic riots?" Abigail frowned. "Cussen was talking about Catholic riots? Do you know what he said?"

"No idea." Jake thought back. "Somethin' to do with us being drunken louts and animals. The usual rubbish about Irish folks. I ignored it."

"Are the Williamses Catholics?" asked Abigail.

"No, they go to the Methodist church. Pettigo has a Catholic priest who comes through here about once a month. They get to use the Jagged Tick Palace for services on a Sunday mornin'." Gibson fixed them both with disbelieving eyes in turn. "Kathleen Williams wouldn't be seen dead in there. She ain't never been anythin' but Methodist."

"So we can dismiss them disagreein' over insults to Catholics," said Jake. "Even if she heard it at all."

"I'm missing something." Abigail strode back and forth. "Something big."

Jake nodded. "Could Cussen have walked in on somethin'? Is there a chance any of the Williams could have had a lover or a secret? If he was religious, he might have been tryin' to put them on the straight and narrow and things got ugly?"

"The Williamses?" Gibson snorted with laughter. "Nah.

Percy is too interested in his family and business. He loved his wife like it hurt. Adored her. He didn't even use the brothel like everyone else. Neither of them would have had the time, anyway, since they worked together. Constance used to be a bit flighty, but she's pretty stuck on the doc."

"When I was disguised as a boy, the cook and a maid were discussing how close Mrs. Williams was to MacGilfoyle. Could there have been anything going on there?"

Gibson exploded with laughter. "MacGilfoyle and Kathleen? Are you kiddin'? How can I put this delicately? Mrs. Williams was a dry old stick. Real religious and pious. She was known for bein' picky and demandin' everythin' be real clean. The idea of her with a rough laborer with dirty fingernails is too wild to be true."

"Some of the most proper ladies have been known to fall for the more rough and ready man." Abigail avoided Jake's penetrating gaze. "You'd be surprised."

Gibson shook his head. "Ma'am, let me put it this way. I'd be surprised if Kathleen Williams saw that as more than a Christian wifely duty. MacGilfoyle grows good roses for displaying in the hotel and keeps the garden nice, is all. Carnal stuff with others don't matter as much to folks who really enjoy bein' with their spouse. They did more than love each other. They *liked*, too."

They turned at a tap at the door and Dick Nash thrust his head inside. "The women are here to clean. Can I let them in?"

"Sure. Let them in." Abigail said, gathering the coats from the stand. "We're finished here. Have you any boxes? We have to take a few things away."

◆◇◆

The chimney atop the red house was more than crooked, it was lurching perilously. Some new mortar showed a half-hearted attempt had been made to repair it, but it really needed knocking down and rebuilding. Nat tapped on the door and waited, his gaze constantly drifting over to the slanting stack while he listened to a muffled voice shouting about the imminent opening of the door and swearing at the clothing he was falling over on his way. A hirsute man appeared, his wide eyes blinking off sleep over a bird's nest of a beard.

"Bart Dunkley?"

"Who wants to know?"

Nat swept his coat aside, wishing he'd had the forethought to put the damned star on the outer garment in this weather. "I've spoken to your boss. Can I come in? This won't take long."

"What won't? I ain't done nuthin' wrong."

"Mr. Washburn gave you a suit around about fifty-seven. It's turned up in something we're looking into, and we wondered who you passed it on to."

"Suit?"

"Yeah, brown tweed. I've got it here if you want to see it."

"There's no need. I can tell you easy. I gave it to Otto Schuster. He works at the Palace three nights a week. It was pretty done in then, but he worked in it for at least five more years. I thought he still had it. He was usin' it for rough work after that; yard work and the like. I used to see him comin' back from the brick factory in it."

"Otto Schuster? He does yard work for the Morgans, too, doesn't he? He works at the brick factory, too?"

"That's the fella. He's all right ya know. If someone stole the suit he'll be pleased to get it back. Yeah. He's worked at the brick factory for years. Just seasonal, though."

"Thank you, Mr. Dunkley. You've been real helpful." Nat stepped back. "I'll let you get back to sleep."

"Nah, I'm up now. I might as well eat."

"Well, enjoy it." Nat frowned and stared at the wonky stack above them. "Doesn't the chimney worry you?"

"That thing? Nah. It's been catawampus since I moved here. It'll probably see me out."

Nat shrugged. "It will if it comes down. It'll bring half the roof with it, but it's your call, sir. Thanks for your help."

♦◊♦

Nat strode into the building, stopping in his tracks at the sight of Abigail through the doorway of the back office with Jake and Gibson. They were deep in discussion with the lawman, without a glimpse his way. His heart dropped like a stone. They had made good with one another, but she had clearly made no effort to seek him out at all.

He watched them chat, the muscle in his jaw flinching as his tension built into a burning anger. They were deep in conversation, poring over a box full of who-knew-what. Business as usual was the order of their day, while his world fell apart. Whatever was in that box was way more important than seeing him. Well, they could go to hell. After all, that's where they'd sent him without a thought about how he was doing.

He dumped the box on the deputy's desk and turned on his heel, slamming the door behind him.

Jake's head appeared around the door, frowning at the deputy whose bemused smile greeted the questioning blue eyes. "What was that?"

"Your partner. He musta been in a hurry. He dumped this box on my desk and darn near ran outta here."

"Nat?" Jake hurried over and thrust his head out the door. He looked both ways along the street but there was no sign of his nephew. He turned back to the deputy. "Did he say anything? Where he was going?"

"Not a word. He came in, stuck this on my desk and walked out."

Jake opened the box, fingering the suit pensively. "So what was he doin' with this?"

"Dunno," answered the deputy. "I didn't ask."

"Thanks." Jake scooped up the box and strolled back to the office. "Abi, Nat brought this back. What do you think he's been doin'?"

♦◊♦

Nat trudged up Climax Hill, the powdery snow almost coming to the top of his boots. He was too irate to care about the icy melt seeping into his flesh as he swept through the drifts. Abigail's face swam around and around in his mind, her eyes flashing as she declared she was done. Why was she concentrating on this damned case with Jake instead of him? It had been a kick in the guts for him to see them talking together in the office as though nothing had happened. Maybe Jake had been right and she was simply dallying with him; enjoying a fling. She had already said she was going back to work, so how were they meant to build a future together?

The realization that she was probably flirting with danger hardened in his heart. Of course he was just a diversion. She had always been going back to work, and had told him as much right from the start. His breath quickened, spiraling along with his mood. He was going to solve this damned case and prove she wasn't as clever as she thought she was. Once the case was out of the way, she'd have no excuse to push him aside. Was he just a bit of rough, an adventure? If she was going to walk out of his life forever she was going to have to explain why everything seemed more important than he was. Talking about love sure came easier to her than showing it.

♦◊♦

Clancy turned from his book. "Nat? No. I haven't seen him for ages. He was out early this morning shoveling snow, then he said he was going to look into something. He looked pretty pleased with himself so I thought you'd sorted everything out."

"Did he have the suit with him?" asked Abigail.

"The box? Yeah. He hasn't been back since this morning." His brows rose, examining them in turn. "Have you lost him?"

"Yeah, we got split up stayin' at the hotel and all."

"I'm sorry. I have no idea where he's gone. Have you tried the sheriff?"

Jake's downcast eyes betrayed his concern. "We just came from there."

The doctor placed his bookmark in place and closed the textbook. "I take it you two have sorted things out between yourselves?"

Abigail glared at Jake. "You told him?"

"He picked up on the atmosphere." The gunman cast an arm towards the doctor in protest. "This is his house, and he was entitled to an answer."

"Yes, I was." Clancy steepled his fingers and sat back. "So I also deserve an answer to this one. You two are fine?"

Abigail bridled at Jake. "How much did you tell him?"

"He told me he called you a whore," said Clancy. "He also told me about his sister and how badly it affected him. The death of my prospective mother-in-law caused old issues to come back to haunt him."

"Yes." Abigail pursed her lips and decided to tread carefully in this conversation. "That has come up before in another investigation. I understand it. We've decided to put it behind us. The doctors called it 'irritable heart'. We don't really know what to do to help."

Clancy nodded, his eyes narrowing. "I've heard of that. What treatment have you been given? Some people say it's to do with strapping on equipment which damages the nerves in soldiers, but others have observed symptoms in civilians. A man called Scheuchzer used to send them for mountain air and relaxation in Switzerland. Saltpetre in new wine helped, along with congenial company."

"It did?" Jake frowned. "Maybe I'll head off to the mountains for a bit when this is over."

"Good idea." The doctor paused. "Saltpetre is potassium nitrate. The salt we found on the body."

"So the powder could be something to do with irritable heart?" asked Abigail.

"I doubt it." Clancy mused. "It was more like he'd lain in a pile of it. You'd use no more than a few grains for medicinal purposes. It affects the nervous system, but it can be poisonous if you take too much. It's just a coincidence, I guess." He looked at both Jake and Abigail in turn. "So it was worthwhile you heading to the hotel after all?"

"About that." Abigail sidled over and sat opposite. "Clancy, I did a full scientific examination of the private quarters. There was old blood on the carpet, which had been turned to hide it under the sofa. There were also blood spots between the floorboards from the front door to where the stain would have been before the carpet was moved. It's a complete trail. It looks like the Williams place could have been the scene of the murder. I'm so sorry."

The doctor's eyes widened as he processed this information. "Could the blood have been tracked through from the suicide? Could it be a false trail?"

Abigail shook her head. "We know it wasn't blood from Mrs. Williams as the boards were clean. It was the spaces between the planks which reacted to the chemicals, and they weren't where people went in and out the door. They were drops left over after a cleaning, and we could still see Mr. Williams's footsteps on the floor. The carpet had been deliberately turned to hide it and was well away from anywhere people could have stepped. It was hidden under the sofa. The tracked spots look like a murder scene behind the door when everything was put back in the original position."

"The dents in the carpet where the legs had been was a clue to the carpet bein' moved," said Jake. "It wasn't from Mr. Williams. It was the other side of the doorway; near the hat rack."

"I have a diagram of the stains if you want to see it. I can talk you through the scene." Abigail examined him intently, judging his reaction. "I took the rug. It's at the sheriff's office."

Clancy remained mute, staring straight ahead, shaking his head, but they were unable to read if it was denial or refusal.

She stood, biting her lip at his reaction. "Does that mean you want us to leave? We understand if it's the case. You've been more than kind."

Clancy blinked away the thoughts crowding for his attention

and melted into a watery smile. "No, of course not. You must stay. It means I don't want to see it. I don't want to compromise you. Do your job. I know these people are decent. Any truth will speak to that."

"That's real good of you, Doc."

"Nope, it's the right thing to do."

Abigail arched her brows. "Are you sure?"

"Positive. I know my fiancée and she couldn't hurt a fly. Nor could her father. I don't know what happened there, and I'm not going to interfere. I'm sure you'll get to the truth and it'll vindicate them."

"Let us know if you change your mind," said Jake.

Abigail pressed on. "I need to ask you something else. What were you doing on the night of the eighteenth of December?"

"Me?" He rose and walked over to the desk and began flipping over pages of a diary. His fingers traced the paper as he read. "I saw my last patient at five, so I would have written it up, and then had dinner." He paused, a smile of relief washing the tension from his features. "It was the night of the Christmas ball. I remember it. Constance and her mother were helping at the church where there had been a party for the local orphans. I collected them from there about seven and walked them to the hotel. I had a drink with Percy Williams in the bar while the ladies got changed." His smile widened. "Constance was stunning that night. She was in emerald green and was the most beautiful woman in town. I never left her side all evening. We danced till we dropped. There'll be dozens of witnesses. Everyone who was anyone in town was there. It went on until about midnight."

"Did the women meet you together, or did one take longer to get ready than the other?"

"Almost together. Constance was first, and her mother arrived soon afterward."

"How quickly?" asked Abigail.

"Fifteen minutes? Maybe twenty. Nothing significant. Certainly not enough to kill a man, dispose of his body, and clean the room."

"And a man like Cussen would have been tucked up in his room by midnight." Abigail stretched out a hand. "I'm so pleased for you. I'm glad I asked now."

"So am I. That's a weight off, I can tell you."

"What about Mr. and Mrs. Williams?" asked Jake. "Did they leave before the end?"

"Oh, they were there the whole time, too. They were at the head table. I honestly don't think they left, although I was dancing and enjoying myself. They were the host and hostess. People would have noticed if they disappeared."

"Was Cussen at the church when you collected the ladies, Clancy?" Abigail asked. "I know his face wasn't looking its best by the time we saw it, so you might not have recognized him."

"There were all kinds of folks there." Clancy closed his diary and held it out. "I honestly didn't pay any attention. Do you want to check my diary for yourself? It's important to me that you can see I'm telling the truth, and you believe me."

"No, thanks. I believe you." Abigail walked over to get her coat. "We'd better get over to the church, and then the hotel. I don't know when we'll be back."

"No rush, I'll be here. Do you want me to speak to Nat about this if I see him first?"

She pulled on her gloves. "Oh, yes. Could you? You can tell him where we are in case he wants to join us, too."

"Yeah, I think we're getting close to sortin' everythin' out." Jake buttoned his coat and put on his hat as he headed for the door. "I'm glad your loved ones are in the clear, Doc."

♦◊♦

Nat's mood was ever fouler by the time he reached the Jagged Tick Palace. The arduous struggle up the steep hill to the hotel in polar conditions had been a failure. Schuster wasn't there. As this was Thursday, he was working in the bar. He had cursed under his breath when he'd reached the top only to find he had to slither all the way back again. His fall had been the final straw. The melting was now seeping into his flesh and the dank long johns sticking to his butt did nothing to improve his disposition as he battered aside the door and entered the tavern.

The scene could not be more different to the empty, soulless place he had walked into that morning. The golden glow of oil lamps were muted by a fog of tobacco smoke, a huge fire burned in the grate providing the comforting aroma of pine resin, and the hum of patrons melded with the tinny piano jangling cheerfully away in the corner. A joyless dimple pitted his cheek as he scanned the room and picked out the bald man pouring beer behind the bar alongside the man he knew as Bart. That had to be Otto Schuster. At last.

"You're back, honey?"

He turned to see Dolly grinning at him with rouged lips.

"Yeah. I wondered if I could speak to Otto Schuster? Bart told me the suit was passed on to him."

"You're still chasin' the owner of that tatty old rag? Ain't the law got nothin' better to do?"

"Yeah, but I've got a point to prove. Any chance of a quiet word with him?"

"Sure, honey. Go take the table by the fire and I'll send him over. We always cooperate with the law. How about a drink?"

"Oh, Dolly. That's music to my ears. Bourbon?"

He reached into his pocket but was stopped by the hostess. "Put it away. This one's on the house. Go get a seat. You look freezin'."

Schuster arrived at the table with the promised drink, his bottom half swathed in a snowy apron and the top in an extravagant, but stained, waistcoat. Only the grubby fingernails betrayed the other side of his employment. He sat, the chair scraping across the wooden floorboards as he leaned in to present Nat with the most impressive set of hairy brows he'd ever seen.

"Otto Schuster? My name's Nat. Bart Dunkley said he gave you a suit years ago, a brown tweed one?"

The brows meshed together. "That old thing? So what?"

"It was found on the body of a dead man. I wanted to know how your suit ended up on a murder victim."

"Mine? No. There must be some mistake. My suit's still hanging in Morgan's hut. I leave it there because it's my old rough workin' clothes. I usually change out of them into my bar clothes 'cause I got all them jobs in the same day." The barman nodded over toward Dolly. "She's real strict about us lookin' smart. Anyhow, those rough jobs are seasonal and I ain't worn it for months."

"So you work at the brick works, then the Morgans', and then here?" asked Nat. "How many hours a day is that?"

"We start at eight at the brick works and I finish around two in the afternoon. It's only a few days a week and casual work. I don't work there all the time, only when they're busy. There ain't much buildin' work in the winter, so it's spring and summer only. The yard work tails off in the winter, too. At this time of year, all I really got is the bar work three nights a week and the night porter the other three more. I take Sundays off."

"So you work all day and all night in the summer?"

"A man's gotta take the work while it's there. Besides, there's nothin' to being night porter. Just hand out a few keys until about ten and sleep in the cubby hole around the corner. It's less work than my wife was, God rest her soul. It's company for me."

"So when did you last wear the suit?"

"October, I reckon. That's when the yard work dries up for the winter and the brick works slow. Until spring it's the bar and night porter, and I wear this for night porter, too. I ain't even checked on that suit for months. I reckoned it was too ratty to steal." Schuster's moustache bristled. "So it got stole? I've got to find me another set of clothes for dirty work now?"

"Maybe." Nat sipped his bourbon. "What were you doing on the eighteenth and nineteenth of December?"

"That lady Pinkerton already asked me. Don't you talk to one another? I was working here till about two in the morning. Then I had a day off."

"And people can testify to that?"

"I ain't had a day off work since I broke my ankle back in sixty-three, and even then I still did the night porter work. I was here. I'm always where I'm supposed to be. Ask Dolly."

Nat sat back, defeated and out of questions. "I guess that's it. I'm sorry to bother you, Mr. Schuster." He threw back the drink and clattered the empty glass on the table. "You've been really helpful."

"Thanks. You want another?"

Nat peered ruefully at the empty shot glass. "Why not? I'm done for the day and I've got nowhere else to be."

Chapter Twenty

"Oh, good. You must be the Mr. Cranshaw and Miss Reger I've been expecting. Congratulations on your engagement. You make a lovely couple."

The spindly preacher looked at Jake and Abigail in turn. "No time to lose, come this way. Do you have witnesses? You can't get married without witnesses."

"Reverend Gilmour?" Abigail caught the arm of the man ready to bustle them away. "We're not those people. I'm Abigail MacKay, and I'm a Pinkerton. This is my identification. Jake, show him your badge."

Jake dragged off his hat in respect of being in a church, his tousled hair flattened into a peculiar circle by the brim. "We want to ask you a few questions about a man who was killed and dumped in the church hall."

"A woman?" The minister peered over his beak-like nose at Abigail. "In the law?"

She squared her shoulders in an assertive posture not matched by her words. "I'm afraid so. Is that a problem?"

"But why?"

"Why what?" Jake demanded.

"Why have a woman in the law?"

"I've gotta say I asked the same question when I met her, Reverend." Jake scratched his head, rumpling the matted dirty-blond hair. "She's good at surprisin' people."

The slim brows arched in question. "What? Like jumping out at them?"

"No. More like overhearin' stuff. The things folks won't say when a lawman is around."

"I don't say anything I mind a lawman hearing. Why have you brought a woman?"

"I didn't," answered Jake. "She brought me. Does it matter?"

Gilmour pursed his thin lips over his considerable overbite. "Well, it isn't appropriate, is it? Doesn't Timothy say, 'Do not permit a woman to teach or to exercise authority over a man; rather, she is to remain quiet.'"

"I guess Timothy slept in the barn with the cows a lot, huh?" Jake grinned. "You don't like women. I get it. I've run into men like that before. You think what you need to—but she's here, and it's official."

The preacher's lips gathered in a tight line. "I simply think a woman's place is in the kitchen."

Jake folded his arms, staring at the pinch-faced man with amusement. "You want to put them where the knives are when you speak to them like that? You're a braver man than me." Jake shook his head. "I don't really care what you think of her. I didn't come here to ask you about that. Tell me what you know about a man called Lymen Cussen. His body was dumped in the church hall, stabbed through the heart. We were told he came here each time he was in town. He was a bank auditor. Do you know him?"

"Mr. Cussen?" The pastor's mouth dropped open in dismay. "That devout model of piety and devotion is gone to meet our Lord? Whoever could do such a thing?"

"That's what we're trying to find out, Reverend Gilmour," said Abigail.

"And they send a woman? *A woman*! That man saved more souls from eternal damnation than anyone I know. He deserves the attentions of Alan Pinkerton himself."

"I'll be sure to mention it to him when I next see him." Abigail's tense face betrayed her growing irritation. "Can we focus, please? Did he have anyone he saw regularly in town? Who did he know? What motive could anyone have for killing him?"

"No, he lived quietly. He either attended to his work, read the Bible in his room, or he attended services in Methodist churches wherever he found himself. He preached here twice. He was quite a magnificent orator, and his knowledge of the Bible was simply staggering. There was none of this namby-pamby preaching you get from modern preachers. His heart was full of fire and righteous anger. He could set a room alight with just a few sentences. It was amazing. He was so quiet as the mere man, but as an instrument of God, he was magnetic."

"When did he last come here?"

Gilmour's eyes slid upward as he searched his memory. "About a week before Christmas. It was the orphans' Christmas party. They had been worthily endowed by the town, and I agreed it was right that Mr. Cussen remind them to be grateful for the charitable bounty bestowed upon them."

Jake turned his head to roll his eyes as Abigail continued. "Was anyone upset with him? Anyone at all?"

The preacher's brow wrinkled. "Why would anyone be upset? We could all learn to find more humility."

"Indeed." Abigail nodded in agreement. "Quite apart from his preaching, did he ever discuss anything else? Anything from his past?"

"No." The minister shook his head but paused, staring off to the side. "He did talk about where he found the Lord and where he started preaching, but other than that, no."

"When did it happen?" asked Jake.

"The last time he was here. He talked about studying under Chivington Miller himself. That's where he learned his firebrand ways. He told us how necessary it was because the creeping rise of Catholicism in the country. As a young man, he spoke at a meeting which resulted in a gang of drunken Irishmen going on the rampage in protest. Mr. Cussen and his friends were trying to force the release of young women being kept against their will in a Catholic establishment when a mob set upon them."

Abigail glanced cautiously at Jake before turning back to the preacher. "Where was this?"

"Massachusetts…uh… I think he mentioned the Endellions? They sounded like a strange sect. Anyway, they were totally out of control. It was obviously a shocking time for him. He was injured and left the group. That's when he came out West. It changed him."

Her brow creased. "Who heard him saying that? Who was within earshot?"

"Just me. Oh, and Kathleen Williams was pouring his drink when he said it. She might have heard, but I doubt she'd have understood. Her daughter's such a lovely girl. Engaged to the doctor. Have you never considered marriage, Miss MacKay?"

It was Abigail's turn to look at Jake and silently roll her eyes. He stepped into the void. "What about her mother?"

"The dear departed Mrs. Williams. Oh, no. She was on teas."

"And people serving tea can't hear?" asked Jake.

"Well, pouring tea takes concentration. Cake means just handing out plates. There's always more conversation from those handing out cake. It takes less focus. Wouldn't you say, Miss MacKay?"

"I really couldn't say, Mr. Gilmour. I don't serve much cake in my profession. One more question. Do you have any other denominations in your church?"

"We may have a few who were Lutherans or Baptists when they came out West. They took advantage of the first established Protestant church, and we welcome them."

She nodded. "What about Catholics? You do have Catholics? I haven't been able to find a Catholic church in Pettigo."

"Are you Catholic, Miss MacKay? Father Peters visits once a month. He shares a number of parishes as a peripatetic priest. In fact, the Williamses are such Christian folks they allow him to stay at the Regent free of charge. He couldn't afford accommodation like that otherwise. They are special people."

Jake's eyes flashed with interest. "Was Father Peters here at the same time as the orphans' party?"

"Oh, no. He always comes at the beginning of the month but he missed January due to a funeral. He would never come to this church anyway."

Jake nodded sagely. "Anythin' else you want to ask, Abi?"

Her eyes glistened with intensity. "What time did Mr. Cussen leave?"

The spindle-shanked, sharp-elbowed man tugged at his jacket, as black as a raven's wing. "Oh, about ten or fifteen minutes to eight, or thereabouts. He was among the last to leave, and I always dine at eight."

"And what did you do after the orphans and everyone left?"

His long finger tapped at his temple in a steeple of thought. "Well, I cleared up with my helpers. Then I retired to my rooms to dine and read the Bible. What else would I do?"

"Thank you, Reverend Gilmour. You've been helpful. We'll try not to bother you again."

Jake walked ahead of her, pushing open the door to a world suddenly bursting with light and life after the subdued twilight of the church. "Well ain't he a bucket of chuckles? I bet he sent those children back to the orphanage feelin' like they were made of worms because a few folks showed them a little human kindness. Men like him are the reason Nat and me are criminals. We had to do more than *survive*. We had to *live*."

Abigail sighed. "Your criminal activities go way beyond living, Jake. You could have dropped out of gangs in your early twenties and lived honestly. You didn't. I'm not having a go at you. It's the truth. Don't try to sugar-coat it for me. It won't work."

"Sugar-coat it?" Jake slammed the door behind them with a snort of disdain. "Let me know when you're prepared to put your kids' lives in the hands of men like that. They bully them, then they sell them as housemaids and farm boys—and that's if they're lucky. Nat was real smart., almost a genius. He deserved better. It ain't his fault I was a bad example." He crunched though the snow, his hooded lids on his bright blue eyes showing how much the encounter had enervated him. "So, anyhow. Where are we headed?"

"I don't know about you, but I'm headed to the telegraph

office. I want the office to tell me what happened at the Endellion riots in Massachusetts. You told me Mrs. Williams told off her daughter about listening to such things, but what if it was to mask her reaction to the subject matter?"

"Why would she? She's not Catholic."

"She was Christian, though." She turned to look at Jake's profile, her brows gathering in thought. "Very much so, and it makes you impervious to the divide and conquer techniques of partisan politics. She welcomed the priest, she employs Catholics, and she worked hard at charity work. I want an impartial version of what happened there. I also want to know if she, or anyone she knew, was involved in it."

♦◊♦

The night had closed in hours ago, and all Abigail could see was a bubble of golden light punched into the frigid darkness by the oil lamp on the sill, her ghostly reflection inches from her nose. The lamp made a shadow mirror of the window, and projected the room into her field of vision. Abigail couldn't really see a thing.

There was no fresh snow tonight, just the descent of a freezing fog which hung in the air, a debilitating glacial miasma which caught in the chest and masked the world from view.

"No sign?" asked Jake.

Abigail turned with a concerned smile. "I'm worried about him. Where do you think he is?"

"Well, maybe he's avoidin' both of us. He was real angry, and we haven't managed to talk him round yet."

"Could be, but where would he go? The town is full since the avalanche cut off the railroad. Surely he wouldn't go back to sleeping in the church hall just to spite us?"

"He can be real ornery, Abi. Stubborn as a mule. You want I should go and look for him?"

Her gaze drifted back to the window. "It's horrible out there. I can't ask you to do that."

"You didn't. I offered, and I reckon I should 'cause I'm to

blame for all this." He lifted his coat from the hook and slid in an arm. "I won't be long. There ain't many places he could be."

♦◊♦

The firelight flickered over Nat's face, deepening the dimples and flooding into the lines, shadowing his profile into a silhouette. The wrinkles around the eyes had been etched by laughter, but today they were only remnants of better times. The brows gathered over dark eyes swirling with injured pride; a dose of wrathful fury filtered through the morose lens of bourbon until his perspective was well and truly out of kilter. He wasn't used to losing, and he most certainly wasn't used to women walking out on him. He was starting to find out how much it cut to the quick.

Dealing with this case was more important than him. Sorting out her problems with Jake was more important than him. From where he was sitting, it looked like damn near everything was more important than him. The bottom had fallen out of his world, and she had simply walked away without looking back.

She had come to him so full of hope and life, but all she really wanted to do was to take from him like a succubus. Abigail wanted to throw herself at life and feel alive, and she fed off his energies and loyalties until it hurt. Once she had boosted her own pride in winning him over she moved on to her work, just seeking sensation where he'd dreamed of a future. It burned in a way nothing had ever had before. He'd considered giving up everything for her, even his family, yet she couldn't take ten minutes to tell him she'd come to terms with Jake's outburst. They'd been in town. Why not find him instead of the sheriff?

A female voice shook him from his phantasm. "Need anythin' else, honey?"

He turned to face a smiling Dolly, the light from the fire brightening the auburn tints in his brown hair. "I guess I should really think about getting back. I can't say I look forward to going back out there in the cold. It's fine and toasty here, and there's nothing but coldness where I'm going."

A penciled-in brow arched. "We got rooms, but they come with company."

His eyes narrowed. "Company?"

"Yeah, twenty dollars for the room, breakfast, and services. Ya got a hankerin' for a woman? We don't employ trash here. Only the best, and nobody'll roll you for your cash. We got a new girl in a few weeks ago. Italian, dark hair, and eyes like a baby deer."

"No dark ones." He spat more vehemently than he intended. "You got any blondes?"

"Sure we have. Let me go fetch Lizzie. She's as pretty as they come, and almost a virgin. You want more drink, too?"

He paused. The idea of indulging in sensual pleasures was becoming increasingly tempting when compared to the frigid welcome he expected. He needed a distraction from that hellion, and the light from the burning bridges might as well light his way. "Sure. If all I gotta do is get upstairs, I guess I can manage another."

A pudding-faced girl with brittle peroxide hair appeared, her eyes disappearing beneath a mass of paint. The tattered feathers in her hair quivered when she moved. "Hi, I'm Lizzie. I hear you want company."

He stared at her, his eyes glittering with intensity as he noted her torn stocking and bruised knees, wondering what had caused them before realizing he didn't really care. She couldn't be more different to the prim and proper virago who had played with his feelings so lightly. Why the hell not? He stood and tossed back his drink, towering over her by at least a head. He grasped her hand and pulled her to the staircase. "Come on. Show me this room of yours."

♦◊♦

Jake pulled off his hat at the entrance to the saloon, closing the door behind him. His bright blue eyes narrowed in on his nephew's back as he disappeared up the staircase with a working girl.

"Can I help you?" A middle-aged painted woman appeared at his shoulder. "A drink? Food? Maybe some company?"

His head titled back at the sight of Nat striding along the open landing and following the girl into a room. "Yeah. I'll have a beer. I need time to get my story straight."

♦◊♦

Nat's hands lingered on her thin shoulders, pushing at the cheap frills to expose her pale skin. Her small breasts crested from her bodice, pale, milky, and enticing. Nat's fingers tightened into the flesh as his breath rasped in her ear. "Take it off."

"The dress? Sure, honey."

"Yeah, but I was talking about the muck on your face. It's horrible, and makes you look like a clown. Take it off."

She pouted. "Dolly said the men like it."

He scrutinized her, his intense dark eyes glittering with hunger. "Dolly's wrong. Take it off."

She sniffed prettily and walked over to the washstand, pouring out water into the bowl. He watched as she scrubbed at the paint, the mess splotching the washcloth. She wrung it out and tipped the water away, repeating the process with clean water until her face was fresh and pink. She turned and smiled at him but his brow creased with alarm. "How old are you?"

"Nineteen."

"Don't lie. You're nowhere near that. What are you? Fourteen, fifteen?"

"I'm nineteen—"

He stood, the feral side coming to the fore in a snarl. "I told you not to lie."

She stepped back as he advanced on her, cowering with a cry of fear at the sudden change. "I'm sixteen."

He grabbed her shoulders, shaking her. "The truth!"

She dropped her head, her body folding into submissive acceptance. "I'm fourteen—"

"You're a child." He stood back, his jaw set in anger. "And

that's why she told you to put all the paint on your face."

"I'm old enough to get married. Why're you here if you don't like me?"

"How'd you end up here?"

"Pa got me the job." Her face was alight with tears. "Enid already runs home and tends the little 'uns. They don't need another girl. They need money."

Anger made his accent slip. "Doin' this? What kind of father is he?"

"What else can girls do? It brings in ten times what I could make cleanin'."

His fists clenched in anger and he swung around. He strode back to the bed. He sat there his chest rising and falling as his breath quickened. "He sold you to be a whore? At fourteen?"

She didn't cry prettily. Her eyes were red and her nose ran with snot. "I make good money. Leave me alone."

"I've got news for you, Lizzie. Whores have a short life. Usually brutal and often used every which way. What're you gonna do twenty years from now when they've turned you into a drug addict to make you easier to control and nobody wants you anymore? Your family will reject you because you're soiled goods." The dark eyes burned into her. "I've seen it time and time again. A few years of good money, then a long, slow death in the gutter."

"What are you? Some kinda preacher?"

"Me? I'd burst into flames if I went near a church. I know how young 'uns get used. I was orphaned."

She propped a hand on her skinny hip. "So what do you want, mister? I ain't got all night."

"Yes, you have, Lizzie. I paid for this room and I paid for you." He nodded toward her cut knees. "How'd you get those?"

"A farmer. He wanted me on my knees." Tears streamed down her face. "He wanted things he didn't pay for, and when I wouldn't, he forced me. Dolly threw him out." She fixed him with eyes full of pain. "What d'ya want, mister? I ain't never met anyone like you."

He ran his long fingers through is brown hair in frustration. "I don't want a thing from you, Lizzie. You're too young. I want a place to sleep."

"Ain't I good enough? You ain't bein' fair. They'll throw me out."

Nat shook his head. "Lizzie, you're *too* good. You're too young, and they're using you. Once you're all used up, they'll throw you away and find another. I'm not gonna complain, but you're too young for me, so I'm not…not interested in you that way. I've got scruples about using people."

"You're a fiddle-headed loony, mister."

"Yeah, sure I am. When was the last time you got an undisturbed sleep, Lizzie?"

She paused. "We don't keep regular hours here."

"So a long time? Lizzie, I'm tired and I'm heart-sick. A woman's giving me a hard time. I ain't gonna bother you. When I see Dolly, I'll tell her you're the best and all you have to do is sleep for the same money. How does that sound?"

"Strange—"

He rubbed his face. "I'm tired, Lizzie. I'm going to sleep. You can either do the same and get the longest sleep you've had in months, or you can go screeching to Dolly and get another John who'll keep you up all night. Your choice."

She approached cautiously. "Just sleep?"

"Yeah, sleep. You can sit over there by the wash stand or you can try to get eight hours full sleep. Your call."

"You promise?"

"I promise." Nat kicked off his boots and slid out of his pants and hung his gun belt on the bedstead. "You're too young. I'm sleeping. You do whatever you want." He rolled on his side. "G'night, Lizzie."

She paused, unused to this reaction from a man. Eventually, there was a swish of her disrobing and she joined him in bed, stiff as an ice sculpture.

He lay on his side, facing the wall. "Goodnight, Lizzie."

"Goodnight, John, or whatever they call you."

♦◊♦

The tinkering of the lock alerted Abigail to Jake's return. She turned to him expectantly, her eyes widening at the sight of him entering alone.

"You couldn't find him?"

"He's got a room. I didn't get the chance to speak to him, but he's safe. He's gone to bed. I guess he's still real angry and didn't want to come back here."

"Where is he?"

Jake hung his hat on top of jacket. "He found a place doing rooms by the night. He's fine. We can talk to him tomorrow."

She stood, closing the book and placing it on the side table. Her glittering eyes betrayed the calmness in her voice. "I'll ask again. Where is he?"

"He found a place that does rooms."

"In Pettigo?" She frowned. "The place is full because of the avalanche. There are no rooms."

He shrugged. "What can I tell you? He's Nat. He's resourceful. He found somewhere, but it ain't permanent. He'll be back tomorrow and we can straighten out this whole thing then. Go to bed. I'm gonna get my head down. I'll see you in the mornin'."

He disappeared off into the kitchen as Abigail watched him intently. She walked over to his jacket and raised it to her nose, sniffing it.

The aroma of tobacco, stale beer, and wood smoke still clung to the sheepskin, and she instantly knew where Jake had been. By association, she could guess where Nat was and what he was probably doing. There was only one way a man could spend the night in the town bars.

She closed her eyes and gulped back a knot of pain as she dropped the sleeve. Distress whirled in her chest until her the caustic tears burned at the back of her throat. She steeled herself to stay in control, bracing her shoulders and raising her chin with a defiance she didn't really feel as she walked over to the bedroom and quietly closed the door behind her.

Jake stood at the kitchen door, concealed in the darkness as he observed the whole scene unfold. He cursed under his breath at the knowledge he'd set of this whole chain of events in motion. She knew. How could he put this right?

Chapter Twenty One

"Bacon, eggs and lots of coffee." The plate clattered with a sonorous clang on the table in front of Nat, causing him to drop his head into his hands.

"Headache?" the cook chuckled over a well-upholstered bosom. "We see a lot of them. You want some willow bark tea? We put fever few in it, too. That'll fix you right up." A stubby finger pointed to the breakfast. "That, and food to soak it all up."

Nat rubbed his weary face and fixed the cook with bloodshot eyes. "Yeah. That'd be good, thanks. Oh, and maybe ice? An ice pack on the temples might help."

"Ice." The cook sniggered. "Yeah, how many tons d'you want?"

"About four I reckon." Nat played idly with his eggs. "Does that tea really help?"

"It sure does. That's why I brew one every mornin'. I'll go get it."

Nat sat back, nursing his head and shoveling in food to help soak up the booze. Somehow the saltiness of the bacon and the blandness of the eggs cut through the alcohol, and dampened the worst of the stale bourbon repeating on him. Fresh baked bread also served to soak up the remains of last night's excesses. An hour later, he was sitting with an icepack on his forehead, a packed belly, and starting to feel considerably better.

His mind wandered to yesterday's turn of events as he turned them over in his head. It looked like Schuster couldn't be guilty unless Cussen was killed on Sunday morning, but if he was killed then, almost anyone could have done it.

He carefully sorted through the substances found on the suit; brick dust, sawdust, and potassium nitrate. The fertilizer he'd taken from the Morgan place didn't fit the bill. The pharmacist had told him it was bone meal. MacGilfoyle used a compost pile where he rotted down horse manure and vegetable peel. Where did the grains come from? Maybe that was the link?

"You look more human." The cook removed his dirty plate. "That tea did the trick, huh?"

"Sure did. What was in it again?"

"Willow bark and fever few. The pharmacist here makes it." She grinned, her plump cheeks forming into joyous balls. "If you make a habit of this you might want to buy a packet."

"I might do that. It sure evens out the aches without addling the mind."

"The ice helps, too," she said. "We're lucky here. The hotel makes it in the summer and sells it to us. It gets real warm here in the summer months and it's real welcome, I can tell you."

"So how do you make ice?"

"Dunno. I wish I knew how to make it. It'd save this place a fortune in the summer. MacGilfoyle keeps that secret real close. It's the one thing only he can do. As long as he can make ice, we all need him."

Nat stroked his chin. "Yeah, well, I'm gonna get myself along to the pharmacist to get some of the tea. Thanks for the tip. I've got a feeling it'll make a big difference."

◆◇◆

"Are you all right, Abi?"

Her smile was bright, a little too bright for it to be credible. "Of course. Why wouldn't I be?"

His breath hung in the cold air as he spoke. "Because you sniffed my jacket last night and knew I was in a bar."

"You're entitled to go for a drink, Jake. I have no call on you, and you've been working hard on this case."

He narrowed his eyes. "You know, Abi. Drop the act."

"Know? Know what?"

"Where Nat went last night."

She stared straight ahead as they trudged across the frozen earth, avoiding his eyes. "I have no call on him, either. He can do as he pleases. In fact, I'm pretty sure that's *exactly* what he has been doing."

His mouth firmed into a line, unsure what else to say without making things worse. The air was filled by the crunch of their feet through the harsh frost laid down in last night's freezing fog which formed a shell over the soft snow underneath.

Abigail tilted her head back to look at the vast sky, bright and azure since the wind had blown away the mist and clouds. The light diffused and glinted off the snow, making icicles gleam and frost glisten. It all looked new and enticing after such a long period of low heavy clouds. It was a brand new day and a brand new start, darkened only by the heaviness of a grave error of judgment deep inside her heart.

Jake stepped forward and held the door open to the telegraph office in a show of chivalry, smiling at the clerk behind the desk as he followed Abigail to the desk.

"Good morning. Have you a reply for me from Chicago? The name's Abigail MacKay."

The clerk nodded. "Do I ever! I ain't never had a longer one." He rifled through a drawer handed over the missive he picked out. He picked up a book and entered the reference number. "Sign here, please."

She dipped the nib in the ink and scrawled a signature with a scratchy nib and took the proffered document. Her head inclined as she tore open the envelope to read the contents.

Jake peered at the lashes forming crescents against her skin, waiting for her to share the contents, his impatience growing as the seconds felt like minutes.

"What? What do they say?"

Her eyes darted to him. "The Endellion riots took place near Boston in 1843. Cussen's mentor, Chivington Miller, was active in the Native American movement and used his pulpit for political ends."

"Native Americans? You mean, like Cherokee and Sioux?"

"I mean Protestants like the Know Nothings. I mean politics and religion, mixing into a toxic blend to stir up hatred and violence. Miller is known as 'The Chiv' in criminal circles due to his ready use of a knife to help settle scores. He also runs a gang who extorts money from businesses."

Jake stared at her in silence as she continued.

"Lymen Cussen preached at one of the meetings which inflamed the mob. He repeated allegations of young women being forced into Catholicism in order to receive aid. That was a lie used to provoke hate. It was a boarding school and they were already Catholics."

"So? What happened then?"

"There was a riot and the building set on fire. Teachers and pupils fleeing the building were pelted with bricks until a mob of Irishmen arrived to see them off. Nobody was killed, but one young woman was left with brain damage and died three years later after being terribly injured. It couldn't be considered as murder legally as she'd have to have died within a year and a day of the actual injury taking place."

The blue eyes burned into hers. "Does it give you her name?"

"Margaret Mary Foyle."

Jake's brow creased. "You mean—" He paused, shaking his head in confusion as he pronounced the name carefully, "is that like MacGilfoyle?"

She nodded. "Yes. The names have the same root. *Sloinneadh*. Us Gaels have names in Gaelic. When we translate our names, there can be many versions and spellings. We understand that better than the English, because we know the translations. Son of Guilfoyle is Mac Giolla Phóil. It means son of a follower of Paul. Foyle is another version. I suspect MacGilfoyle was related to the poor woman."

Jake gestured with his head toward the door. "Aw, jees. Do we need to get the sheriff to bring him in? Any man'd want to kill for that."

"Not everyone would actually follow through on those feelings. We can't have people taking the law into their own hands. Look at McCully. We need to speak to him, Jake. You go and get the sheriff and bring him in. I need to get my bag from Clancy's. Don't forget to bring in the boy, too. Two people carried the body in and one was much smaller than the other."

"Nobody could blame them," Jake answered.

"Indeed." She paused. "But it's not over yet. If they say what I think they're going to say, it may change everything. Especially when we can get the real killer identified."

♦◊♦

Nat strode to the edge of the hotel grounds where two structures had been cut into the steep hillside. One was the root cellar for the hotel, the other was the ice house. He scanned the snow near both doors. One was well trodden-down, the other deep and soft. It was fairly obvious which was which. The root cellar was more in demand for stock than the ice house because the cold stuff was readily available all over the damned place, so he strode over to the least-used door confident he'd accurately picked the correct door. Cussen had been dead for weeks, frozen solid, yet not as much as a mouse had nibbled on him. Where better to stick a body than somewhere it would be preserved and private? Nobody needed to go into the ice house until at least spring.

He tugged at the padlock securing the hasp. It was locked, but it was no problem to a man of his talents. He pulled out the lock pick and flicked it open in seconds. Satisfied brown eyes slid from side to side, checking for witnesses. The hasp creaked back and Nat dragged the door open against the gathering snow piling at the bottom. It was time to examine the hotel's outbuildings.

♦◊♦

MacGilfoyle's blue eyes fixed on Jake, narrowing as his gaze drifted to the star on his chest. The gunman's brows arched in mute challenge, holding the stare until the Irishman looked out the window.

Sheriff Gibson strode in with Tommy MacGilfoyle. His father turned, burning with indignation. "What's he doing here? He's just a boy."

"He's sixteen," answered Ben, casting out a hand to the empty chair beside his father. "Sit down, Tommy. There's stuff we need to clear up."

"He has nothing to do with it."

Jake's eyes flashed. "To do with what?"

"Anything. He's a good honest boy."

"I'm counting on that," said Abigail walking in carrying a box which she placed on the floor. "It's best for you both to be honest. I know you are honest too, Mr. MacGilfoyle, even when you are trying to mislead. I noticed it when you and I spoke. You talk all around the truth trying to hide it." She examined the boy who fidgeted next to his father. "Hello, Tommy. I take it you remember me?"

"Yes, miss."

"Good. We are going to ask you a few questions about a man who died. I want you to tell the truth."

The boy shook his head in denial. "I don't know nothin' about anythin' the law might be interested in."

"We'll be the judge of that." Sheriff Gibson eyes glistened with cautionary lights. He looked over at Jake. "Do you want to start the questioning? You brought him in."

"Sure." Doubt glimmered over Jake's face. "Tell us about the night of the eighteenth of December. It was a Saturday, and they held the Christmas Ball."

MacGilfoyle snorted. "Tell you what? I don't go to balls. Neither does Tommy."

The boy glanced at his father and bit into his lip. "If it was a Saturday, I'd have been covering for night porter."

Abigail cut in. "From eight. We know."

"Yeah, until eight the next mornin'."

"Were you at the desk when Constance and her mother came out of the private quarters to join Dr. Fox and Mr. Williams in the bar?" she asked.

Tommy's mouth clamped shut.

MacGilfoyle's shoulders squared in aggression. "He doesn't remember."

"Let him speak for himself," Jake barked.

The Irishman ignored him. "Tell them you can't remember, Tommy."

"Think hard, Tommy." Abigail leaned in with both hands on the desk. "This wasn't any Saturday night on the desk. It was the Christmas ball. People were arriving in carriages and the ladies were wearing beautiful gowns. Constance was wearing emerald green and looked absolutely stunning, didn't she? She walked from the church with Doctor Fox and her mother about seven, so they must have gotten here about half-past. That was before you started on the desk." She stared intently at the lad. "Now if you didn't see them, it either means Dr. Fox is lying for no good reason or they got ready for one of the biggest social occasions of the year in less than thirty minutes and went to the ball before eight. I refuse to accept that ladies would dress for a huge occasion so quickly. Think harder, Tommy. You did see them. You even spoke to them, didn't you?"

The lad gulped hard, caught out by her determined certainty. "I—yeah. I guess I did."

"Who was first?" Her eyes glinted. "Before you answer, I want you consider the fact we already know."

Tommy's cheeks colored with little spots of pink. "Miss Constance. She was first. She was lovely. Mrs. Williams was second, because she'd been helpin' Miss Constance get dressed, and then did her own hair."

"And what happened then?"

"Nuthin'."

Abigail pushed herself back from the table and stood upright. "What do you mean 'nothing'? There was a ball going on. A lot happened."

Jake cut in. "Mr. Cussen was also at the church and left after the ladies did. You must have fetched his key from the board for him. He couldn't have got there before you started."

"I don't remember," the boy answered. His eyes glittered with tears which he blinked back.

MacGilfoyle frowned. "He doesn't remember, and you've got nothing to link us to this."

"Not so fast." Nat's dark velvet baritone drifted from the doorway, causing every head to turn. He strolled in with the confidence of a lion and dropped a half-full hessian sack on the desk.

He turned to stare at MacGilfoyle. "Saltpetre. I've had it tested by the pharmacist, and there's no doubt." He turned to Abigail with a satisfied smirk. "It's potassium nitrate and it's been used to make ice for hundreds of years. I checked. Mr. Rumbelow, the pharmacist, is real helpful and he knows how to make ice, too. He knows all sorts. All you've got to do is walk into the pharmacy and ask." Nat turned to the sheriff. "Not only that but I went into the icehouse and it looks like someone knocked over a bag of the stuff so it's all over the floor. If a body was dragged out of there it might have picked up a lot of it in the fabric. You might find it's a damned good place to hide a body for weeks without anything having a chew at it. It was frozen solid, wasn't it? Like it's been in an ice house, maybe? I bet we'll find traces of brick dust, hair, or even blood if we go through it with a magnifying glass. Won't we, MacGilfoyle? It'll have come off the suit."

The Irishman's Adam's apple bobbed as he gulped. "I don't know. I haven't been in there for ages."

"No?" Nat's eyes narrowed. "Why do you keep it locked?"

MacGilfoyle folded his arms in indignation. "You can't search without a warrant. You just messed up."

"Warrant?" Nat's cheeks dimpled. "The padlock fell to pieces in my hands. The cold must've gotten into the works. In any case, the icehouse belongs to the hotel, not you, and they're cooperating with us. We don't need a warrant."

The gardener's face fell as he slumped back in the chair and stared obstinately ahead. "Whatever happened in there, you can't pin it on me. I haven't been in there for months. There is no need to go in there with all the snow."

Nat's eyes glinted in feral determination. "Fine. Let me draw you the line connecting you to the body in the ice house. He was stripped of his own clothes and they were found burning where you and your friends have your bonfires and drink hooch. It was burning at a time of year nobody is doing any yard work, so there's nothing to burn. Everything's stopped growing. He was dressed in a tattered suit kept in a nearby hut, used by Otto Schuster for all his dirty work. He changed out of it for his less dirty jobs." Nat paced. "Only you, your son, Schuster, and Jethro Walters knew the suit was there. Jethro drew attention to himself by wearing the coat, and the scorching says he definitely rescued it from the fire. If it was him, he'd have kept it without damaging it. If Schuster did it, he wouldn't have dressed the body in clothes which could be linked back to him, and I tracked them right from the tailor who made them, right through every man who ever owned the damned thing."

"You did?" Abigail's surprise appeared to have made her forget to blink.

He glanced at her dismissively. "Yeah, I did. In any case, the body was left in the ice house you guard so jealously and carried into the church hall by a man and a smaller figure." He stopped, his eyes glittering with intensity. "That's you and your son. It couldn't be anyone else. In this whole town."

MacGilfoyle's lips curled. "It's not proof. It doesn't link me or my boy."

"No? I think it sounds pretty conclusive, but maybe I can push it further." Abigail walked over to the box she'd brought in and deposited it on the desk. She picked out the black straw hat and held it out. "Black straw. It's hard to see stains on this. Hard, but not impossible."

"Stains?" asked MacGilfoyle. "I don't know what you

mean."

"Blood stains. Practically imperceptible against the black straw, but if you look really close with a magnifying glass, you can see it. There isn't much, but Dr. Fox has confirmed most of the bleeding would have been internal."

She pulled out the pin; long and thin, and tested the point against her finger. "Ten inches long, and certainly could puncture the heart with a lucky strike." She stared at both MacGilfoyles in turn. "It was thrust back into the hat which smeared the hat where it was stuck back into it. I asked the doctor and he confirmed it could have been the murder weapon. I'm about to test it for blood. Here, right in front of you."

MacGilfoyle snorted. "So? You think I wear that?"

"No. I think Mr. Cussen came into the private quarters, and it was hanging on the hat rack by the door. It's possible he saw someone was upset with him and wanted to talk to them. He came in and an argument ensued and the hatpin was used in a fit of anger." She stared hard at Tommy. "Isn't that right? You saw Cussen go in. You heard shouting through the door. She called you to get your father didn't she? Talk to me, Tommy. Helping is not the same as killing. She's dead, but she left a note. I didn't give it to the family, but she admitted it."

"A note?" The boy sniffed and backhanded away the tears. "She admitted it? Yeah. She came out to go to the ball and Cussen was there gettin' his key. He said somethin' about Sodom and Gomorrah and how drinkin' and women dancin' wasn't the Christian way. Mrs. Williams asked to have a word with him. She weren't happy at all. He went in and the door closed." Tommy's cheeks were alight with the tears streaming down his face. "There was shouting. I couldn't hear the words, just the noise." He paused, looking at his father before continuing. "It all stopped real sudden, and then she came out. She were cryin' and she asked me go get my pa. The man was lyin' on the floor. I flipped him over, but he was a goner. It was an accident, mostly. Nobody meant for anyone to get hurt, let alone killed."

The boy dissolved into a moist ball of distress, his hunched shoulders heaving as he buried his head in his hands.

Abigail sighed and shook her head. "She admitted it to us in her note. But you covered the whole thing up, didn't you, Mr. MacGilfoyle? And you know I know why. When I asked you about *Sloinneadh* you said the only family you had here was Tommy, and that was true…right after Mrs. Williams died. She was related to you. The rumors of her being besotted with you circulating through the staff were true, but it wasn't romantic love, it was familial. I found her maiden name in a Bible, and it was Powell. That is also one of the translations of Mac Giolla Phóil. It's fairly common for Irish people to try to pass as Protestant to escape the prejudice and make better lives. I've come across it many times, and it's why I asked you if any other members of your family used different translations. Your answer was so precise and guarded about your son being your only living kin. She was what? A sister, cousin?"

MacGilfoyle's clenched jaw spoke of his refusal to assist. Abigail continued. "Her name translates to the same as yours in Gaelic. So does the name of the poor young woman who was killed in the riots Cussen helped provoke. You can claim that's all a coincidence, but it's not that common a name. You are all connected, and we can telegraph the authorities in Boston and Ireland to check if you force us to. We'll find out the names of your sisters through church records. Mrs. Williams spoke of a dead sister, and I think she was Margaret Mary Foyle as Kathleen Williams came from the same area. When Cussen's sanctimony put a damper on Mrs. Williams's Christmas ball she'd had enough. She confronted the man responsible for whipping up the mob and lashed out when he was uncaring and pious. I'm sure it wasn't intended to kill him, but the pin ended his life in one ill-considered blow. She was a gentle person who found it impossible to live with. The priest hasn't even been through here to give her absolution. She turned to her brother for help. You are older and still have your accent. She had no accent, and could pass as an American Protestant as she was younger when she came here. She could get a better job, meet different men, marry better. Basically, she took the easy way. Most people would. I don't blame her one bit. She thought about protecting others right up to the end, didn't she? That's why she left the note. She didn't want anyone else to be accused."

She stared at the reticent man and his wretched son. "I'm so sorry for you all. You lost your sister to a mob, and justice deserted you. I think she only wanted Cussen to understand the pain the family went through, but he cared more about the next world than this one. What did you do? Whip the body out through the kitchen? With Mister—" she glanced over at Nat and thought the better of using a surname, "my *colleague's* findings, it couldn't have been anyone else. We can check the ice house minutely. I'm sure we will find evidence Cussen was stored there."

"Laundry basket." MacGilfoyle spoke at last. "Kathleen was in bits but I sat her down and gave her a firm talking to. She had to go out there and put on an act to give her an alibi. She was my only living relative in this country apart from young Tommy, so I had to protect her. I told her we'd clean the mess. I pulled out the hatpin and stuck it back in the hat after a quick wipe. He went in the basket and I burned his clothes to stop him from being identified. I took him to the ice house later and then didn't know what to do with him. The ground was frozen too hard to bury him. I took a train to Lattimer the next morning to send a telegram, after checking Cussen's room to see where he was headed next, and left his luggage there. Tommy only did what I told him. It's not his fault."

Nat frowned. "And you took Schuster's suit?"

"Yeah. I had to get rid of the body and I couldn't bury him until spring. Out of desperation, I dumped him in the church hall dressed like a tramp. I thought he looked fresh enough to fool them into thinking it was somebody else and that he just got killed." He glowered at Nat and Jake. "I didn't count on you lot."

Ben Gibson paced. "So Kathleen Williams really did do it? She was protecting a secret brother." He rubbed his face. "Does the evidence prove she did it?"

"A hatpin isn't generally a male weapon," answered Abigail, lifting the bottle of hydrogen peroxide. She dripped it over the glass beads and it fizzed into a foam around the ornate setting of the glass beads. She then applied the fizz to paper already prepared with guaic and watched it darken to blue. "See? There is blood on there, deep in the burrs and prongs. We can see it using the magnifying glass, too. There's no reason to believe a gardener would be in the private quarters while ladies got ready for the Christmas Ball. The height and trajectory shows a shorter person than Mr. MacGilfoyle did it, but someone around the height of Mrs. Williams." She glanced at Tommy before looking over at his father. "We can only follow the evidence."

"I need to speak to the mayor." Ben Gibson shook his head. "This is a small town and MacGilfoyle and the Williamses are well thought of. If she lashed out, nobody in the West would blame a brother for protectin' her. Not after a family member died because of Cussen."

MacGilfoyle's keen eyes fixed on the sheriff. "Are you sayin' there'll be no charges?"

"I'm sayin' I can't see the point in any. It'll destroy the Williamses if they find out it wasn't an accident. You didn't kill anyone, and you ain't a danger to public safety. We found the killer and she killed herself. That's really all there is to it. We can tell Cussen's family who and why. I can't see the point of no trial for hidin' a body. It'd ruin the boy's life and ruin the Williamses' reputation."

"I gotta say I agree with you," Jake said. "I feel for you, MacGilfoyle. Cussen's past came back to haunt him, and his killer's dead."

"The past's got a way of doin' that. It can change your whole future." Nat's wry smile was dry and joyless. "Well, I came here to deliver my findings and I've done it. If anyone wants me I'll be in the Jagged Tick Saloon." He turned on his heel and strode out of the room without a backward glance. "But I can't see why anyone would."

Abigail and Jake shared a look of concern. Jake shrugged. "I'll talk to him."

Chapter Twenty Two

The mayor swung back on Sheriff Gibson's chair, his grim face cheerless and pensive. "So who knows all this?"

"Just my team, the sheriff, Dr. Fox, and the MacGilfoyles. Nobody else," answered Abigail.

He nodded. "I've spent a lot of time with the Williams family. It doesn't seem right to rip up Kathleen's memory based on a moment of madness. How sure are you she really was the killer?"

"She was the right height. She had the motive, the opportunity, and the means. It was her hatpin," said Abigail.

"So she was Irish, huh?" The mayor arched a thick brow. "My wife is Irish, but if that happened to her folks as a young 'un I can see why she'd hide it. What would we gain by prosecuting the MacGilfoyles? Are they criminal? Dishonest?"

Ben Gibson shook his head. "Nope. They're hard workin' and no trouble at all. The young 'un can be a bit of a scrapper, gettin' into fights and stuff, but I ain't had to shout at him for at least a year now."

"Yeah, well. You had to kick my Hiram's butt a few times. That's boys for you. It doesn't mean a thing. Them hidin' the body is a protective family reaction, it ain't like they do it for everyone. I think a jury out here would feel sorry for them; a secret family looking after a sister who lashed out through grief? I say we tell Percy Williams the truth and let everyone else forget about it."

"Except for Cussen's family." Abigail cut in. "They need to know who killed him, and why."

"Sure. I ain't got a problem with that." The mayor stood and buttoned his coat. "Send the body back and tell them the killer committed suicide and why. They don't need to know anyone hid the body. Let them think it wasn't found in the snow. I doubt they'll want to make a fuss when they hear he incited riots and got a girl killed. I'll go talk to Percy Williams so he knows the gardener is family. The rest of us need to shut our mouths about this for the Williamses' sake. They're good folks, and this'll destroy their reputation." He strode over to the door, the Astrakhan collar on his coat snug around his thick neck. "You let the MacGilfoyles go with a warnin'. It should keep them quiet."

His hand landed on the round brass knob, staring at Abigail as he leaned against the jamb. "We don't get many like you in town. I didn't know what to expect when the doc told me about a female Pinkerton. You ain't the rough piece I expected. You're almost decent enough to be invited to meet the wife."

"Almost?" Her brows rose along with her hackles. "I'd be delighted. You'd be surprised how many politicians' wives I speak to, Mr. Barfelt. They take up quite a considerable part of my time, professionally speaking."

The mayor's brow furrowed. "Hmmm. Well, you explain our decision to them MacGilfoyles And I'll take care of telling Percy Williams."

The door closed behind him and the sheriff turned to her, a mischievous grin playing across his face. "Politicians' wives take up your time, huh? Best keep away from his, she never uses one word when twenty'll do. You'll never have time for anything else."

"When people assume I'm a whore because I work, they deserve what they get." She shrugged. "I'm appointed, not elected, so I don't have to court popular causes or toady to politicians." She walked over and dragged open the office door. "Come on. Let's get the MacGilfoyles warned so I can get this case behind me." A dark foreboding fell across her spirit at the memory of Nat striding from the room without a second glance. "This isn't why I came here."

"Yeah." Ben turned back to her as he headed for the cells. "Why *did* you come here? You never did say."

"Unfinished business. That's all I'm prepared to say."

They clattered along the corridor toward the cells where the older man rose to meet them with an air of expectancy, tempered by desperation. "Well? What did he say?"

Ben rattled the ring of jangling keys in the lock and gestured towards the street with his head. "You can go, as long as you keep your mouth shut about this, or everyone'll want the mayor to do them a deal."

"Really?" The gardener turned excitedly back to his son. "We're free to go with no charges?"

"No charges, as long as you both keep your noses clean." The sheriff pulled the door open and stepped back to let them leave. "And the mayor is gonna tell Percy Williams you were kin to Kathleen, so don't be surprised if he speaks to you in private."

"He is?" MacGilfoyle's mouth dropped open. "That's not a good thing. We'll get sacked."

"That's the least of your problems." Abigail cut in. She stepped forward, staring at the two males loitering in the cell corridors. "Tommy MacGilfoyle, I know."

"What? What do you know?" MacGilfoyle demanded.

Her eyes glittered through the half-light of the corridor. "Tommy stabbed Cussen. He was the right height, and he was the one with a history of anger and impulse control. I was warned about hanging about with him while dressed as a boy due to his propensity for fighting, not to mention all the other reports floating around town. I know it was you, Tommy."

The sheriff's mouth dropped open while the boy gasped and ducked behind his father with eyes like a hunted rabbit.

"Don't let them hang me, Pa! Please don't let them take me away."

MacGilfoyle thrust out his chest aggressively. "I thought you said Kathleen did it."

"Nope." She shook her head. "I was most careful to avoid that. I described how Cussen died and said she'd admitted to it. I didn't say it was actually her who struck the blow."

Beads of sweat spangled MacGilfoyle's upper lip. "You said we were free to go."

Abigail inclined her head. "And you are. I just want you to know I'm aware of what really happened here. I can't prove it, but I know it. I also want Sheriff Gibson to be aware too, in case there are any more 'accidents' around Tommy. He needs to get a hold on that temper of his, and fast."

The sheriff finally found his voice. "What's goin' on? Tommy? Kathleen admitted it."

"And everyone said she couldn't possibly have done it. She was covering for someone. They were right. She was covering for her nephew. He was the person of the right height who also had the means, motive, and opportunity. He is also the only one with a record of being short tempered and ready to lash out. He was also right outside the door and would have heard any argument between his aunt and Cussen. For the record, I want you to know I cannot prove who struck the fatal blow, but you confirmed it by your reaction."

"We need to tell the mayor." Ben ran his hands through his hair in dismay. "This changes everything."

Abigail shook her head. "No, it doesn't. I cannot prove it beyond all reasonable doubt, and I have no wish to see a sixteen-year-old hang. This would never stand up in court. I want him to be aware we're watching him, though. I will place your name in the Pinkerton intelligence files, Tommy, so don't think for a moment you can leave town and behave as you want. This is a chance for you to start again. Take it, and watch that temper of yours. You will never get another chance."

The lad peeked out from behind his father. "I will, missus. I will. I'll be good."

MacGilfoyle's brows gathered. "You can't prove it?"

"Nope." Abigail held his gaze, registering the attempt to stare her down. "And I have no intention of delivering a poor investigation. I only act on what I can prove in a court of law. Don't make me regret it."

Confusion reigned in the Irishman's eyes under gathered brows. His breath quickened and his lips curled into a cold smile. "I don't rightly know why you did this."

"I did it because I'm honest. I can't prove it. Now, go."

The MacGilfoyles didn't need to be told twice. They scattered toward the door like ball bearings on a steep hill. The slam of the door was still ringing behind them when the sheriff turned on her, his eyes bulging in disbelief. "We should've charged him. We could've broken him into confessin'."

She shrugged. "It'd still fall at trial. A good lawyer could ride a coach and horses through that confession, and you know it."

"They hid a body. We'd have got them on that."

She folded her arms, her frown underscoring the determination flaring in her breast. "And what would it achieve? In my experience, prison only teaches young men to become better criminals. He has a much better chance of living a decent life with a warning and a father ready to teach him how to earn an honest living. We both know how juries work, especially out here. They're loathe to convict children or women for capital offenses at the best of times. If you throw in an admission from an aunt ready to protect her nephew, along with him being the noble protector, and we're right back where we were. Not to mention the Williamses' name is no longer protected from the scandal."

Ben threw up his hands. "Why didn't you speak up and tell the mayor?"

"Because it'll never stand up in a fair court, let alone a provincial one." Her eyes widened. "There's a problem with the court system when there's a noose at the end of it. We all know that. I could name dozens of cases where they obviously did it, but the courts felt sorry for them or were swayed by a sob story. There's Madeleine Smith, Constance Kent, Mrs. Howard acquitted for killing her husband's mistress, and that's just off the top of my head. There's a strict moral code, and if you appear to work within it, and belong to the established community, you can get away with almost anything. It's not how it should work, but it is what happens. We can get further with a warning and being known to the authorities than we can with him strutting around proclaiming his damned innocence to the world. That's what he'll do if he's acquitted."

The sheriff's mouth hardened into a line. "Yeah, you're right. They'll see him as the boy who protected his aunt. They'll never convict him. Not in Pettigo."

"Not here, and not in most of the world." Abigail shrugged. "It's reality. I have no way of proving who struck the fatal blow, and his aunt admitted to it. A lawyer would destroy the case in an instant. Besides, Kathleen Williams was willing to protect him, too, and not one of you had a problem with that."

"Do you think he's a killer?" asked the sheriff. "A cold-bloodied one?"

She shook her head. "No. He's a hot-bloodied ruffian. Maybe his father will be more aware and keep him in check. Even if he did stab Cussen, he was defending his aunt from a bully. He had a better defense than Cussen did, and he was allowed to get on with his life after causing that girl's death."

"Nobody deserves to die for bein' a bully."

Fire flared deep in her eyes. "And nobody deserves to die for being a Catholic. It was a hatpin, not a cutlass. A sixteen-year-old boy wielding it to protect his aunt was less likely to see the consequences of his actions than a grown man inciting a hateful riot based on lies. The mayor didn't want the Williamses' good name dragged through the mud because of this, either. Nothing's changed, except that I voiced my suspicions."

The lawman paused, running out of steam. "He admitted it."

"And his lawyer would say we scared it out of him." Her face softened. "It'll never stick, and everything else remains exactly the same. Aren't we better to try and reason with him rather than release another hardened criminal on the world? There's no jury in the country who would hang a boy for this. Even if we got him to jail, he'd come out of prison as criminal as the worst of them. It's a university of crime."

Ben Gibson's heavy sigh signaled the end of the debate. "What's the point? You're right. We'd never find a jury to convict him. Hell, most of the jurymen would want to shoot Cussen in broad daylight when they heard the full story."

Abigail strolled and lifted her coat from the hook. "Don't get me wrong. I hate to see a killer walk free, too, but what else can we do? Life isn't black and white, it's shades of gray. If I really thought he was a danger, I'd have told the mayor." She pulled on her gloves, wriggling her fingers into the sheaths of leather. "Besides, I suspect they'll disappear soon. The road to the north is now open again and the railway won't be far behind. They'll be long gone, and so will the name MacGilfoyle. That's a family with a whole lot of aliases. They'll soon find an alter ego."

She thrust out a hand, proffering a handshake. "It's been a pleasure doing business with you, Ben."

He took it, his strong fingers closing around hers. "You too, Abi. Would you and your friends like to join me for dinner tonight? Celebrate the end of the case, maybe?"

She delivered a crisp, professional smile. She needed to think, not talk, and Nat was a powerful presence brooding behind every word and action. She needed to process this mess now that she had the freedom to concentrate on one thing at a time. "That's so kind of you, but I must decline. I have other business. The men are in the saloon, and I'm sure you'd enjoy a drink with them better, anyway. Have a great evening and thank you for all your help once more. I'm glad we have gotten to the bottom of this."

♦◊♦

She walked out into the street, snuggling into the collar turned against the biting freeze settling in as darkness fell. The clear skies had brought much-needed sunshine, but the temperature dropped like a stone as soon as the sun set. So now what? She had come here to speak to Nat and to dig deep into the tangled Gordian knot of feelings buried somewhere in the fathomless gulf between them. Some green shoots had begun to grow, only to be trampled underfoot by Jake's emotional outburst.

She loitered on the wooden sidewalk, looking aimlessly one way, then the other. There was still life in the frigid town; stiff people bundled against the cold were scurrying home after a day's work; mercantiles and businesses were concluding deals. Then there was her. Abigail MacKay was all alone with nowhere to go. No, it was worse than that; she was lonely again. Alone was nowhere near the same as lonely. Lonely was the screaming void of emptiness she'd inhabited until that man trespassed into her heart.

A trapezoid of golden light fell over the wooden sidewalk opposite, gleaming through the gathering night. The restaurant looked warm and inviting against the backdrop of monochromatic shades of gray and ice. She wasn't hungry, but it was something to do and somewhere to go. She looked both ways in preparation to cross over. She always said hell would freeze over before she tried to tempt a man out of a bar, or anywhere else, to spend time with her. Her dark eyes caught the frozen drifts and icy ruts as the chilling irony hit her.

It already had.

◆◊◆

The high ceiling was painted dark brown, mostly because the choking tobacco smog was turning it a tarry ochre, anyway. The jangling piano was a quarter-tone out of tune, but the singer pitched at least an octave out, so it was the least of the problems. She was loud; not good, just loud. She battered out 'The Royal Wild Beasts' with an impressive array of suggestive winks, nudges, and unwholesome finger wagging through a veil of smoke and a buzz of gabbing patrons. A group of men gathered near the stage, displaying either an impressive auditory fortitude, or it could be more simple: the ability to shut out the cacophony to concentrate on the chanteuse's enormous breasts and long legs beneath a shockingly short peplum attached to her pinched-in bodice. One leg was white and the other black to carry through the Pierrot theme of her scanty costume, but it merely served to make one thigh look fatter than the other. Jake scanned the bar, where an array of men leaned, slumped, and listed, depending upon how long they'd been consuming the wares on offer in the Jagged Tick Saloon.

His bright blue eyes fell on the familiar long-legged man in the black hat at the end of the bar, his taut shoulders turned toward the door. He strode over and tapped his nephew on the shoulder. "Buy you a drink?"

The head turned, the brown eyes dripping disdain. "Go to hell."

"Done. Care to join me?" Jake ignored the dismissal and bellied up to the bar beside him. "I've been tryin' to talk to you for days now, but you disappeared."

"I was working. I wanted this damn thing solved so we can all get on with our lives."

Jake raised two fingers to signal to the barman how many drinks he wanted. "Yeah. You really tracked who made the suit and all the folks it was handed down to? Impressive."

"Well, now we know who did it, we can put this nightmare behind us?"

"Nat, I spoke to Abi, and she accepted my apology. She wants to speak to you, but you never hung around long enough for us to tell you. It wasn't easy, but I eventually got through to her. She understands."

"Lucky you, but actions speak louder than words. Everything and everybody in this town mattered more than me. It wouldn't have taken long to have a talk. It wasn't going to make Cussen any more dead if she took an hour for me." Nat stared at his shot glass as though it would leech the bitterness out of him. "This is the first time I cared about a woman more than she cared about me. It's the shittiest feeling I ever had. I now think back on women like Allie and Florrie and feel real bad about the way I walked out on them."

"Florrie? She was loco. She was gonna shoot you if you

didn't marry her." Jake sipped his drink and stared straight at the huge picture of a nude above the bar. "She wasn't even pregnant. Allie, yeah. That was sad."

Nat sighed. "It was for the best. I couldn't settle down and be the man she wanted."

Jake turned. "You couldn't settle down and be the man *I* wanted, either. I wanted you to get a proper job and be respectable."

"I tried. I apprenticed with a locksmith, didn't I? It wasn't for me."

The fair eyebrows arched. "You learned all there was to know in about a year. You were a genius at it."

"Yeah, but the hours didn't suit. I can't live a regular life. I'm not cut out for it."

Jake scowled. "I was a bad example. I got caught up in a life of crime. I blame myself."

"I blame you, too."

Jake's grip tightened on his glass. "Huh?"

"Every time you came back from a job you were excited and bursting with energy. Compared to twelve-hour days sitting in a shop, it was my idea of heaven. You weren't a bad example, you were a great one."

Jake shrugged. "I did it to pay for your education. You did real well. You could have been anything. Listen to the way you talk. You can keep up with the best folks."

The dark eyes glittered with doubt. "Yeah? Then why're you still doing it? Are you saving to get me a doctorate in locksmithing from Harvard?"

Jake rolled his eyes. "Nat, Abi got snowed in at the hotel. It's the only way I got to keep her there long enough to get through to her. She would've been there to talk to you the next night, but you stayed here." He paused, eyeing the young girl in the feathers and snagged stockings approaching with her hands on her swaying hips.

Nat nodded a smile of recognition to the girl and returned to his drink. "So? She told me to go. I did."

"You need anyone for tonight?" Lizzie wiggled her pelvis and eyed Nat. "I ain't wearin' the paint, the way you like me."

Jake's jaw dropped open. "Nat, you didn't. She's a child."

"I'm fourteen," she protested.

"You're a child. What the hell, Nat? You didn't, did you? Fourteen?"

Nat's brows met in consternation as his temper took the polish off his accent. "What do you take me for? I slept. I ain't into children."

"I'm old enough to get married," said Lizzie.

Nat glared at her. "You keep saying that, but it doesn't make it any better. It's 1869 in Pettigo, not 1809 on the frontier with no law. You can't get married without the consent of your pa, and if he gave it, I'd punch his teeth out. Where's he live? I've a good mind to go and have a good long talk with that low-life right now. I'm just in the mood for him."

"Well, the joke's on you. He ain't got no teeth." She sniffed in annoyance and sashayed off, leaving behind the sickly scent of cheap perfume unsuccessfully attempting to cover stale sweat and old sex.

"I can find him if I put my mind to it," Nat snarled. "I ain't got anythin' else to do."

Jake watched the younger man glower at her back as she flirted and toyed with patrons as she worked her way around the saloon. "Calm down. You can't save the whole world, Nat. If you want to worry about women, I'd suggest turnin' your mind back to Abi. Back off from that girl's pa."

"Abi's done. So am I."

Jake's brow furrowed. "She reacted to me bein' a butthole. Who wouldn't? She took a big risk comin' here, and I rubbed her nose in the dirt. It's my problem, and I need to get help. It's just plain selfish to keep lashin' out at people. I gotta deal with this. I can't keep makin' it everyone else's problem, especially when it's tearin' apart the lives of everyone who matters. Give her a chance."

"It sounded pretty final, Jake."

"For cryin' out loud, speak to the woman, will ya?" Jake clattered his shot glass on the bar in exasperation. "Why do you have to look behind every word and action like a damned old biddy?"

"I can't help it if I'm a thinker."

A muscle in the older man's jaw flickered as it clenched. "If you want to analyze anythin', do somethin' useful and explain that picture."

Nat glanced at the painting over the bar. It was an unclad Rubenesque blonde covered in fruit in a sad replica of a sylvan nude buried beneath a disgorging cornucopia. "What's to explain? They're trying to make her look classy like the pictures in the museums and grand houses. They failed."

"What's classy about bein' covered in fruit? It don't even look good on a hat." He arched a brow and nodded toward an area under scrutiny. "Let alone on that bit. I ain't sure those grapes will be wholesome enough even for the goat to eat." A wicked smile simmered. "I ain't complainin', though."

Nat's cheek dimpled in spite of himself, recognizing his uncle's old tactic of distraction. "I dunno. I suppose it's a tasteful way of hiding the worst bits, and it titivates."

"Titty what?" Jake's eyes glinted. "And there are worst bits? That's news to me. I like them all."

The brown eyes warmed and properly engaged with his uncle's at last. "It means to make her look better."

"She'd look better without them damned grapes gettin' in the way." His eyes gleamed with hunger. "Do you think she was painted from a model? Who got to polish the apples?"

"Maybe that's the type of work I need?" Nat mused over the lip of his glass. "Except I can't draw more'n a stick man."

"Why's there a goat there?"

"I dunno." Nat shrugged. "Maybe it was hungry, and the fruit attracted it."

"You leave all your food outside and it's gonna attract livestock. Why's it lookin' straight at me? It's real distractin'. You take a beautiful woman, cover her in fruit, and stick a damned goat in there with its eyes followin' you around the room. If you ask me, the man who painted it didn't know what to do with her once he got her clothes off."

"At least he got them off."

Jake ignored the bitter reply. "Maybe that stupid goat got in the way. It'd be real dumb to give up on a beautiful woman because of a dumb goat."

Nat sighed and rolled his eyes as Jake continued. "Look at it, starin' out at us as like it's king of the world because it found a pile of fruit when the real treasure is underneath." Jake tossed back the remains of his drink. "And that artist wants us to see he's real clever with all them shiny apples and that thing there with the pointy leaves." His eyes scrunched as he peered at the huge picture. "I don't even rightly know what that thing is. My point is, he's concentrated on the wrong stuff. Look at all the time he spent on fruit and goats when the whole point is the woman. That's a man who took his eye off the prize, that's for sure. Ya gotta be real dumb to concentrate on the goat more than the girl."

"You're about a subtle as a brick to the side of the head, Jake."

"Good. That saves me diggin' through the snow to find one."

The brown eyes slid sideways. "You've made your point. Let's go back to Clancy's, Jake."

The older man smiled and slapped Nat on the back. "It's about time. Come on. Finish your drink and we'll go."

"Sure, and on the way, I'm going to remind you who was the goat in the analogy."

♦◊♦

Clancy ushered them in, closing the door to crush the sucking cold slithering in behind them. "The sheriff told me who did it. Shocking, huh? That boy. Who'd have thought it? Ben Gibson must've missed you or he went to the wrong bar. He wanted to celebrate."

Nat's brow creased. "Boy?"

"MacGilfoyle. Tommy MacGilfoyle. It was him who really stabbed Cussen, and that's who Kathleen was really covering for. MacGilfoyle was really her brother, and she changed her name to pass as Protestant. Cussen was shouting at Tommy's aunt and he lashed out. MacGilfoyle covered for them both."

"That wasn't what was being said when I left," said Nat, his brow creasing. "I thought his pa did it."

"Abi surprised Tommy and he admitted it." Clancy ushered them toward the kitchen. "He was protecting the woman nobody knew was his aunt. We told the mayor, and he's keeping it quiet because they can't make it stick. They get to head off and have a second chance at life. Cussen preached a hate sermon and provoked the riot which killed the sister. Tommy stepped in when Cussen got angry at being confronted, but he didn't kill intentionally. It's all a bit of a mess."

Nat and Jake exchanged a conversation in a glance.

"So, no charges are being brought?" asked Nat.

"What's the point? Kathleen admitted it and she's dead. The case is closed, and pushing it further will probably ruin the Williamses' good name. They've been punished enough. It's how things are done in this part of the world. This isn't New York. Everyone called for jury duty will know Tommy. They're also likely to be very sympathetic to him. "

"I guess." Jake nodded. "If the mayor's decided that's it. Have you seen Abi?"

Clancy shook his head, frowning. "She didn't tell you? She's gone. A couple of men came and collected her chest. All I've got is a note thanking me for her room and the help."

Nat's eyes widened. "Gone? Gone where? The town's shut off."

Clancy shrugged. "I've no idea. The road's passable with care to the north now, and they've been working on the avalanche for over a week. The railway should be open soon. Maybe the agency arranged something for her? She did say she had another matter to deal with."

The young doctor turned back to the sideboard where a few bottles and decanters glittered in the lamplight, failing to notice the consternation on the faces of his remaining guests.

"On the bright side, it means one of you has a bed. Who's for a brandy? We've got the end of this to celebrate, and I'd like to drink to Kathleen's memory. Who knew she was carrying so many secrets and lies? You really can't judge a book by a quiet little cover." The amber liquid gurgled into one glass before he turned. "Gentlemen?"

"Sure." Jake nodded. "That'd be great. Nat? You might as well. She won't get far at this time of night. We'll find out tomorrow."

The dark eyes dimmed with resignation before he pulled himself together. Nat's cheeks dimpled and he smiled at his host. "You must have a lot of mixed feelings. Your mother-in-law died, but she was protecting the boy who was protecting her. She was angry at injustice. She looked after her family. On top of all that, she gave you a fine woman to marry. It'd be my honor to raise a glass to her memory."

Clancy's eyes misted over before he cleared the caustic lump from his throat. "Thank you." He handed the glasses out to his guests. "That means a lot."

Jake raised his drink for the glasses to chink against as they gathered in front of the roaring fire. "To Kathleen."

Clancy nodded. "To Kathleen, and also to her poor sister, Margaret Mary."

Jake silently swallowed, his Adam's apple sliding behind his collar. "To all the dead sisters. May they rest in peace, and may they allow us to have peace, too."

Chapter Twenty Three

She gathered her tatty skirts and climbed the few steps into the railway carriage, smiling at the guard welcoming her aboard. Her red wig suited her skin tone and lifted the drabness of the homespun dress, which looked even dowdier when topped by a shabby gray coat. The glass in her spectacles was plain, and designed to distract from her features, as was the deep brim of her frayed bonnet. She settled into a seat and her stomach lurched as she glanced out of the window. That man in the long coat had a familiar gait, both strong and graceful, but was it him? He turned and she released a sigh of relief at the portly figure with a moustache peeking over the turned up collar. It wasn't Nat. He was at least twice his weight.

It had been the longest week of her life, loitering among the single women being put up at the schoolhouse. Chattering aimlessly was not one of her strengths. She hated it, but she maintained the pretense of an abused wife hiding from her husband to ensure nobody gave her away.

Her cover had allowed her to work through the emotions she had bottled up; to be withdrawn, anxious, or even tearful. And she had been all these things in the last few days as loneliness engulfed her. Nothing sucked the life from a soul more than hungering for someone who didn't need them.

She had travelled across the country to see a criminal; a man who forced people to hand over their money at the point of a gun. Men like them had murdered her father.

Except they weren't like those men. It was more convoluted,

and *way* more complicated.

Yes, they could be dominating and demanding, but then they were kind, generous, and perplexingly contradictory. They were dishonest, but they were brutally honest about it. They cared about people, but Jake, in particular, cared so much it broke him.

From the moment she'd bumped into that infuriating man, Nat had found a way of worming right into her heart as though made for it. He had invaded her world and made himself a permanent fixture in her heart almost immediately. Part of her resented Nat's constancy in a world where her husband's short life had only been temporary. Nat's ability to permeate her thoughts grew to the point of obsession. Her husband had been a choice, where the magnetic pull of kindred spirits was not.

She had to walk away from this folly before it destroyed her life. There were only two places he could have found a bed in the packed-out snowed-in town; back at the church hall or in the bed of another woman; probably one he paid for. He hadn't stayed at the church, but he had stayed at the Jagged Tick. She'd checked. The barman had even pointed out the provocative child he'd purchased for the night, and it had hit her like a kick to her stomach.

The train juddered to a start and her eyes darted around the carriage which contained just her and four men rows away, preparing to start a card game on the flat side of a suitcase they used as a makeshift table across their knees. She watched the countryside flash by as the train gathered speed, leaving Pettigo and its misadventures behind.

With any luck, Quinn and Conroy would have gone in the opposite direction so they could all put this embarrassing misjudgment behind them. She would head back to New York and go back to work. There was no doubt in her mind she would be requesting to work as far away from The Innocents' territory as possible.

♦◊♦

They'd been travelling for hours and the afternoon had faded into a blue-gray twilight with ripples of silvering clouds crowding the low sky. The journey had been punctuated by only a few comfort stops at various icy stations with primitive facilities and even more primitive staff in the hill settlements between the largest towns. They were cursory habitations with basic latrines and poor food. In such places, it was a common ploy to take payment upfront and fail to deliver the food before the train departed. She was too experienced to fall for that, and had left with enough supplies to last her at least a day until she reached the hotel at Silverville.

She glanced at her pocket watch. Nearly three hours before they reached the last stage of today's journey and she could sleep in a real bed again. All those disturbed nights on a cold draughty floor with nothing to do but overthink had drained her energy. The gentle to and fro of the train was comforting and subtly rocked her until her breathing slowed and her eyelids drooped. Her head dropped onto her chest before she abruptly snorted in a most unrefined manner and jolted upright. She blinked her bleary eyes and glanced around the carriage. Only two men remained. One of them, a mustached bear, snuggled into his great coat with his hat pulled over his eyes. The other was slumped across the aisle where she could only see the top of his gray head over the back of the seat. He was wedged into a corner trying to grab a little much-needed sleep himself. She sighed and leaned against the wall, gradually allowing herself to drift off. She didn't feel the book drop from her hand and she certainly didn't notice the gloved hand which caught it before it hit the floor. Most of all, she didn't notice the dark eyes which smiled at her before he turned and walked away.

♦◊♦

The shrill blast of the whistle shocked Abigail back to life. She blinked and shook herself awake, then took stock of the carriage once more. The burly man was still in the corner, snuggling under his hat. The door behind her rattled open and a smiling conductor strode though the car. "Just takin' on more water, folks. Nuthin' to worry about. We'll be on our way shortly. Next stop after that'll be Silverville." He paused and looked at the set of seats opposite the mustachioed man and arched a brow. He chuckled under his breath at the sprawled figure and continued on his duties, departing through the clattering door at the other end of the carriage. A gray head bobbed up from the seats and the stout man wedged on a hat and stood. He spoke quietly to the burly passenger and headed out of the door the conductor had used toward the viewing platform.

She glanced at the book beside her and a frown flickered over her brow. She hadn't put it there. Or had she? She was so tired she couldn't be sure. She bent and rummaged in her bag, pulling out a little package wrapped in waxed gingham and stared at the bread and cheese. Nope, she didn't fancy cheese and couldn't stomach all that heavy brown bread, so she picked out the boiled egg.

She carefully peeled the shell into a handkerchief and ran her fingers over the smooth silky orb, feeling for grains of shell left behind. The rubbery albumen gave slightly under her touch. She worked at it until she was satisfied it was clean. It gave way at her bite, the neutral white soon melding with the slightly salty, sulphuric savoriness of the yolk as she chewed. Her stomach growled in anticipation like a grumpy beast prodded from a deep slumber. It had been a long time since she had eaten.

The train lurched and the whistle sounded once more, and they were soon on their way again. It was now dark, and the oil lights in the carriage made it difficult to see anything outside, so she picked up her book once more and flicked through to find her place, wondering why she hadn't marked it before putting it aside. She must have been more tired than she realized.

She caught movement out of her peripheral vision as the burly man removed his hat and dropped into the seat opposite. He pulled off his moustache and wig, and leaned forward, his dark eyes glittering with devilment as her mouth dropped open in surprise.

"You didn't think I was going to let you sneak off like that, did you, Abi?" Nat reached over and placed a long finger under her chin and pushed her gaping mouth closed. "Egg, huh? How sophisticated."

She gulped down her mouthful. "What are you doing here?"

"The same as you. You're not the only one who can use disguises."

She tensed. "I'm going home. You can go to hell."

"Been there." His grin became brighter. "They threw me out for bad behavior." He stood and unbuttoned his coat, removing the huge padded under-jacket which had provided his bulk, and tossed it aside. "Phew! You wouldn't think you could be too hot in this weather. I could sell these if they weren't so ugly."

She looked at the rough stitching, binding old clothes together with rudimentary stuffing. "You made that yourself?"

"Yeah. I can't see it catching on, though. It makes you look fat."

She scowled at the hairpiece. "Where did you get that? And the moustache?"

"I thought you might recognize them. They're from your chest. The one you hid at the railway station. We needed good disguises and you've got them all." He frowned. "Did you think I wouldn't find it? Really? Don't underestimate me. It's an insult to my intelligence."

"You didn't seem interested in bothering with me." Her brows met in indignation. "Where's Jake?"

"He was here. We were playing cards with two other men, but they got off. He's in the next car, now. He thought we needed to talk. Oh, and he has some of your stuff, too." His face fell into a mask of faux innocence. "A gray wig and a beard. I wouldn't want you to accuse us of stealing from you. We only borrowed them. You can have them back, but I was surprised to find out how many male disguises you have."

Her fists tightened, her breath shortening with irritation.

"What do you want?"

His fixed her with a hard stare. "What do I ever want?"

"You're wasting your time. I'm leaving. I know you took me at my word when I told you to leave me alone after Jake's outburst. That's fair enough." She paused and bit into her lip. "It's what you did afterwards which confirmed you weren't good enough for me."

He frowned. "After that? I tracked every owner the jacket ever had. I found out where the saltpetre came from. I proved MacGilfoyle was linked to the killing."

Her eyes narrowed. "You stayed at the Jagged Tick."

"So? You stayed at the hotel."

"With your uncle! You absolutely know I did nothing to be ashamed of."

"Hey, he fought his way there through a blizzard to apologize to you. Once you accepted it, you didn't give cuss about talking about putting things right. You ignored me."

"No, I didn't. I waited at Clancy's for you to come back so I could speak to you, but where did you go?" She sat back and folded her arms, leveling elbows at him like gun barrels. "And before you answer, I already know. I made it my business to find out."

"So?" He shrugged. "I got a bed at the saloon."

"I saw her." Her jaw firmed defiantly. "You disgust me."

"Who did you see? Lizzie? Good. I hope you spoke to her, too."

Her eyes flashed with anger. "A child! She's what? Thirteen? I could lay you out right here, right now. Get out of my sight."

"Lay me out?" His smile broadened. "Any time you want to try. I'm getting mixed messages, here. Did you speak to her or not?"

"Of course I didn't. What am I going to ask her? Your predilections? Your best moves? *Sean-dhruisire!*" She observed his arched brows and explained, 'It means dirty old man. Get out of my sight."

He leaned forward and fixed her with determined brown

eyes. "Abi, I didn't sleep with her. I wanted a room, and it was the only way to get one. I don't get involved with kids. What do you take me for?"

"A low-down, double-dealing, bottom-feeding, perverted, *bod ceann*—dickhea—"

"Fine." He cut her off with a raised hand. "So you've had time to mull it over. Abi, the town was booked out, and paying for the whole night gave her time off and me a bed. I never touched her."

"You expect me to believe that?"

"Yes, because it's the truth."

"You wouldn't know the truth if it bit you in the butt."

"Unless it was grown up, I wouldn't let it." Nat rested his forearms on his thighs, suddenly serious. "Abi, it felt like everything in the world was more important than me, and you'd already told me to go. You didn't want to see me or hear me. I had to find somewhere else to stay."

"You could've gone back to the church hall. Either that, or I could've gone to sleep with the women at the schoolhouse."

"And then I look like a heel for sending you to sleep on the floor? Or I get the floor in a draughty hall where a corpse didn't even thaw out? Yeah, that's a great idea." He shook his head. "No, I had to find somewhere. I'd taken refuge at the saloon and I could get a bed. It was freezing outside, and I didn't want to leave. I admit it was tempting to get a woman, but it wasn't a woman who turned up. It was a little girl." He tilted his head underscoring his words with an arched brow. "I've done all manner of wrong in my life, but that ain't one of them. Ask Jake. He talked me down from going after the father who sold her into the life."

Her face simmered with suspicion. "He did?"

"Yeah. He did. In any case, he persuaded me you were finally open to talking again." His eyes narrowed. "But then you up and disappear on me. You weren't hard to find, Abi. There weren't a whole lotta places you could be. If I wasn't already so angry at you for putting me last I'd be furious at you for that."

Her almond eyes widened. "You're angry at *me*? *You* bought a prostitute."

"I bought a *room*, but so what if I did look for a woman? The one I thought I had told me to leave her life forever. If you think that means I'll walk away and be celibate for the rest of my life, you can think again."

She leaned forward to face him nose-to-nose. "Feel free to go off and buy as many women as you want. Bear in mind, they are generally free if you're a halfway-decent human being."

She felt the warm puff of his snort of exasperation. "For cryin' out loud, woman. You came across the country to see me. We were doin' great until Jake blew his stack. So, we went off to lick our wounds, but neither of us actually did anythin' wrong. Now, we can walk away, or we can act like reasonable people and take up where we left off."

His accent strengthened, a sign of stress she now recognized. This clearly mattered to him. She stared into the chocolate eyes, dancing with devilment and temptation, and felt her resolution waver. Once more she had no control over the warmth growing deep in her center. It blossomed, as though truth was the seed, and he was the sun. Her resolve weakened.

When she spoke, it was with less coldness. Emotion crept in, causing her voice to waver. "Reasonable? You're a thief and a liar who walked off to spend a night with a prostitute. You could call this lots of things but reasonable isn't one of them."

Shades of venal hunger gleamed in dark eyes over a smile so innocent it hurt. He reached out and took her hand. The rush of his magnetism hit her, making her heart beat faster and melting her resistance like waves washing away sand. His honeyed tones drifted through her consciousness. "Yeah, but you make me want to tell better lies. I want to lie about stuff like givin' the children too much candy." He dropped his auburn head, the long dark lashes masking the roguishness in his eyes before he turned back to smile gently at her. "Almost every man in the place was married. They all lied about what they did, and do it regularly. I didn't, and I won't. I admit I was tempted, but I never went near her or any other woman. She was a child. If she hadn't been?" He shrugged. "Well, who knows? We weren't a couple, and I'm allowed to look at other women, especially when the one I wanted rejected me." He stared deeply into her soul. "I was hurting. Why did everything matter more than me, Abi? None of it would have happened if we'd sorted things out. We'd have been together. Give me one good reason why we can't talk about it now?"

Her breath quickened. "She was a child—"

"Do I need to get Jake in here to convince you? Better still, let's go back to Pettigo and you can ask her yourself?" His brows met in a scowl. "Abi, you studied me. Was there ever anything in my notes that said I used people? Or I liked my girls young? For God's sake, I'm drawn to you like cash in a safe. I hate to break it to you, but you're not young, compliant, or even easy to be around, and it looks like you're my type. Do you think she'd cut it? If you really think I did that I'll take you there, face down over a horse if I have to, so you can ask her yourself."

She paused, staring at him; reading him. He was a good liar. Could she trust him? It wasn't that he lacked morals, it was more a case of him having a code all of his own, but she had to concede he was principled when it came to women.

"Will you look me in the eye and swear you didn't go near her?"

He scowled. "Isn't that precisely what I've been doing? Are you going to talk to me? Are we both going to spend the rest of our lives wondering what might have happened if we'd just talked? Even if this doesn't work out, at least we'll know we tried." His face softened along with his voice as his fingers tightened around hers, his eyes flashing with determination. "Abi, if you think I can't be trusted with a fourteen-year-old girl then speak now and I'll walk out of your life for good. I know you can't trust me with money, but you *can* trust me with people."

She blinked pensive eyes which suddenly looked as black as

jet in the lamplight of the carriage. "No, you wouldn't. I trust you."

His lips spread into a wide smile, pitting his cheeks with dimples. He released her hand and moved over to sit beside her on the bench. "Thank you. That means a lot."

"I reacted when I saw her." She shook her head and sighed. "I was angry."

"Yeah, I can understand that. I was angry about you putting everything before me. I wanted to do something to spite you, but I couldn't go through with it." He reached out and stroked her cheek. "Let's take time in Silverville. Time to just be normal."

Incredulity crowded her face. "Normal? Us?"

"Yeah, normal. Somewhere we can be a man and a woman. We can get to know each other instead of the random corpse someone dumps beside us."

She nodded. "That would be rather pleasant. Test the waters somewhere quiet and peaceful. But we can't."

"Jake can go and play cards and relax. He spoke to Clancy and he's going to try the saltpetre and wine cure for his irritable heart problem. A Swiss doctor had some success with it, so it's worth a try. I think he quite likes the drink."

"He's found a treatment? That's wonderful. I hope it works."

Nat nodded. "Me, too, but I didn't come here to talk about Jake." He leaned in taking her face in both hands, dropping butterfly kisses around her lips. She felt his hands drop to her shoulders and stroke her as his tongue slipped between her moist lips and danced with hers. Her hands rose along with her desire, running down his back and slipping through his thick hair. He pulled back, taking her face in both hands once more and a wicked smile licked across his face. His chocolate eyes glittered with devilment. "No, Abi. Don't close your eyes. Look at me. I want to fill as many of your senses as possible."

She pushed him back into his seat with a groan of reluctance. "No. I need to get back. I've run out of time. We need to go our separate ways."

"That's why we can't waste time."

"Or why waste this reconciliation? Let's part as friends. Fate doesn't seem to want us to get together."

He pursed his lips pensively. "I don't believe in fate."

"Me, neither. But I don't believe in falling into bed with men, either." She settled back with a sigh. "There's no point in making enemies by creating another bitter parting, leaving us wondering what we're missing or if we've been used. It's for the best. It's also a lot better than we had about an hour ago. We both know you're not going to give up crime. That's what it'll take for me to give up the law."

"Abi—"

"No, Mr. Quinn. It's madness. Don't blame Jake. I'd have come to my senses eventually. It's just not going to work. He touched a nerve because he shone a light on the truth, but I would have gotten there on my own. My life is hard enough. I can't take up with a criminal."

He frowned. "We'll find a way."

"I *have* found a way. We accept reality and move on with fond memories. That's all there can be. I'm pleased you came to see me, but we leave it here." She reached out and grasped his hand. "It's for the best. It'll only bring misery to both of us. Being friends is better than we had. You were right to seek me out. At least we now know it's best to walk away. We're not adversaries. Mutual respect is our future. That's how we leave this as equals."

Nat's face dimpled in amusement. "Equals? You're a tiny woman. I could lift you with one hand."

"So? Is that supposed to impress me? There are plenty of men you could best physically. You still treat them as your equal."

"Do I?" Nat chuckled. "I guess I see them as more likely to be worth robbing. If you want me to treat you like a man you're out of luck. You're way better than almost any man I ever met, Abi." He shrugged, devilment still playing in his dancing eyes,

"I move in very dodgy circles so that's not setting the bar very high. You're stopping in Silverville?"

"Yes. But not for long."

"Good, we can have dinner and take more time to discuss this."

♦◊♦

Jake stood in the hotel dressed in his suit watching Abigail descend the stairs in a cobalt evening gown. He let out a low whistle as she arrived in the lobby, her décolletage enhanced with an ornate sapphire pendant.

She smiled. "It's lovely to dress up and just be a woman again."

"Sure is." Jake nodded, evading Abigail's admonishing glance.

"Shall we go in? Where's Mr. Quinn?"

He walked across the lobby toward her, his glittering gaze wandering over her hourglass figure.

"Abi, you clean up real nice. You look smart enough to be called Abigail."

"How about *Miss MacKay* if I look that good?"

He grinned and slipped an arm through hers. "I'm just relieved you decided not to go with a moustache."

They were seated at the table as the waiter handed out a wine list and took their drink orders. He was a sprightly, well-groomed man with effete manners who had swished his way around on the balls of his feet. He beamed at the little company, especially when Abigail conversed with him in French, and engaged with the chef who came out of the kitchen to join in an animated discussion full of gesticulations and animated expressions.

Nothing was too much trouble and everything was perfect. They relaxed into a convivial evening of conversation and sociable banter, unhindered by their polar positions in the world of crime.

"Just how many languages do you speak, Abi?" asked Nat.

Her eyes twinkled mischievously. "How many do you speak, Mr. Quinn?"

"You're hearing it. Now answer me? How many?"

"Why?"

"It could be a clue to your next persona. We know you speak French and Scottish. Anything else?"

"Actually, I *am* Scottish, so technically I speak my own language along with English and French. I didn't learn English until I was about eight. I learned French from the age of four, years before I learned English."

"Really?" Jake's incredulous frown met between his brows. "You speak English real well. Better'n most folks who speak nuthin' else."

"Thank you, Jake. It was almost all Gaelic on the island. My teacher was a clever and educated man who had taught in France. We moved to Glasgow when I was twelve and I had no choice but to make English my main language. We came to the States when I was sixteen."

"You kept your accent," Nat said.

"It's a hard accent to lose, even when you try really hard—and I worked incredibly hard at it."

"So? What else do you speak?"

A smile played around her lips. She was not about to tell him French was commonly spoken amongst well-educated Scots and she had no other linguistic tricks to fall back on other than the smattering of Latin and ancient Greek which came with a classical education. "I've always found it better to keep you guessing. What do *you* think?"

"I think there's a still lot to find out about you." Nat sat back, his eyes burning across the table.

"A woman should have a little mystery, surely?"

"There's mystery and then there's just plain annoyin'."

Shock widened her eyes. "Jake? Do I annoy you?"

"Abi, do you know how worried we were when you were shot and we had no way of knowin' if you were alive or dead? We didn't even have anyone to ask. That ain't fair, and you've done nothin' about it. We split up tomorrow, and we still don't know how to find out if you're alive or dead."

She dropped her gaze. "I'm sorry. I'll sort something before I go." She looked Jake straight in the eye. "Does that help?"

"Not really. You're goin' back to work. I wish you were goin' home."

She stretched out a hand and grasped his fingers. "I won't go after you now, anyway. Mr. Pinkerton wouldn't send me because you know me too well. I plan to stay out East, so it's unlikely we'll meet again."

"Don't go back, Abi," said Nat

She looked at both men in turn. "Why don't you give up? Go straight?"

Nat tilted his head at her. "Abi, I can't tell you how much we'd like to roll back the clock, but it's not as simple as that. We'll still be wanted. Wyoming has no statute of limitations. We'll be wanted 'til our dying day. We can be extradited from almost anywhere we settle."

"So, live quietly and make it hard for them to find you." She shrugged at their impassive stares, and grimaced. "You can't help some people."

"So—" Nat was not about to pass on her earlier comment. "You aren't going to come after us anymore?"

She sighed. "I certainly wouldn't if you gave up crime. But I can't promise not to be on the opposite side."

"You won't come after us. That's what you said." Nat grinned. "We're safe from your investigations? I guess that's better than admitting you couldn't manage to bring us in."

"Don't push me." She was beginning to regret her rash words. It had been made in a rare, unguarded moment, and they had leapt on it like children on fresh-baked cookies.

"I don't think you would." Nat laughed, sitting back. "You've changed. Things have changed. We'll walk out of here tomorrow without a worry and that's a good thing, Abi. It means we've moved on to another level."

Her dark eyes fixed on him, laughter floating around in their inky depths at his challenge. "Why? Just what am I going to be handcuffed to this time?"

"You shouldn't ask men those sorts of questions while you look as good as that." Nat dimpled into a meaningful grin.

She threw him a censorious look as she flicked up an eyebrow. "You're too good for the lives you lead, but you still choose to lead them. Let's enjoy the moment and stop this."

"So?" Nat eyes glinted with feral lights once more. "What do you think I'd do to you if you crossed me? Do you think I'd do nothing?"

"Do you think *I* wouldn't?" She demanded. "You're pushing me tonight. Why? You know this is over. Are you trying to prove I'm useless? Impotent?"

"What is there to gain by locking us up?" asked Nat. "You'd never get to convert us."

"I think the question is what the banks and railroads wouldn't lose."

Nat shrugged. "What's the point, tonight of all nights? I hope you never lose your edge, darlin'. It's what makes you special. We'll walk away tomorrow. I promise you we'll do nothing to you. I know you can't do anythin' to us. We're stronger, and you certainly can't outdraw us. The law'll never believe we're Quinn and Conroy. Not when you've dined with us."

She bridled at them, Nat's insouciance getting under her skin. "Don't patronize me. Will you two never learn? Pride comes before a fall, you know."

Nat raised his chin in challenge. "Let's not ruin the evenin' with idle threats, darlin'. You got no back up here and you can't overpower us, so you ain't got a hope. It's best to part as we mean to go on. A woman is no match for two men. That's why it's good we all part as friends."

She frowned before she raised her glass and threw them a broad smile. "You know, I couldn't agree more. It's no match at all."

♦◊♦

Quinn and Conroy walked out of the restaurant after breakfast, into the caustic winter sunshine glinting off the snow on Silverville. Nat pulled on his gloves. "It's a shame she never showed. It would have been nice to say goodbye. I guess she was worried what would happen after the way I left her in Bannen."

"Yeah." Jake nodded. "To say goodbye, real civilized-like, would've been nice. Just for once."

"Yup, Jake. I guess she couldn't face us. The ladies are weaker than we are, and she couldn't bear another indignity."

"She's had a hard time lately. First she got shot, and then you solved the link with the clothes and the saltpetre. Maybe we were too hard on her last night? What did you have planned this time, Nat?"

"Just my charm." His smile crept up at one side. "And maybe a little extra, if it was needed. I had the feeling she had somethin' planned, but I guess I was wrong."

He stopped short as the sound of clicking metal told them the guns pressed against their heads were cocked and ready to fire. Their hearts dropped like lead as a sharp chill cut through them. The sheriff stepped out in front of them, his pistol drawn as he fixed them with a determined glare.

"Hands where I can see them, boys. Lemual! Take them guns."

Jake Conroy's blood boiled as he felt a hand remove this weapon from his holster and Nat began a major charm offensive. His most glittering smile spread over his face as he hooked the sheriff with his most manipulative sparkle. "There's been a mistake."

"No mistake. We know exactly who you are. There's a warrant out for you, and you're comin' in."

Their shoulders slumped at the determination in his voice while the sound of rattling metal signaled handcuffs. Their arms were swiftly pulled behind them and their hands were tightly fastened behind their backs with bitingly cold steel.

"Move, and remember there are guns aimed right at your heads. One wrong move, and you're dead. We don't hold with your type in Silverville."

"Sir, there's been a terrible mistake."

"Nope. You're William Pettigrew and he's James Miller. You smashed the bar in Montgomery and caused nearly a thousand dollars worth of damage. The descriptions are very detailed and accurate, not to mention we got information you were in town. There ain't no doubt. You were identified by an eyewitness."

The two outlaws darted a look of relief at one another. It *was* a mistake, but they were far from being out of the woods yet if they were taken to the wrong jail. They might be recognized for who they really were.

"Pettigrew and Miller?" Jake shook his head in confusion. "You're wrong. That ain't us."

"Was this eye witness a woman, by any chance?" asked Nat. "There's a female who might want to settle a few scores with me by sending me to jail. I'm not Pettigrew."

The sheriff grabbed the top of his arm and led him across the road to the jailhouse. "Nope. It were a man. A Frenchman. The waiter who served you last night. He knew you right off. He worked at the restaurant next door to the bar when it was trashed."

"He's wrong, sheriff. It's mistaken identity." Nat shouted. "We've been stuck in Pettigo. Both the sheriff and the doctor can back that up. We did some work for them."

"Yeah, well. I got the owner comin' in, and if we're wrong, you'll be free as a bird in a day or so. Come on. Over to jail, and behave yourselves. We'll treat you as well as you behave."

Nat turned and smiled at the sheriff. "As soon as he gets here you'll know you got the wrong men, Sheriff. How long's he gonna be?"

"Town's twenty miles away," he answered with a shrug. "I'm waitin' for him to reply to my telegram."

"So not long, then?"

"Depends. Ain't a train till tomorrow."

"We didn't do a thing," said Jake.

"Got any identification boys?"

They shook their heads dumbly as the sheriff smiled at them. "I guess we'll have to wait until the bar owner gets here."

Nat's smile dropped from his eyes. "That's a long wait for innocent men, but I guess if that's what it takes to persuade you. We won't give you any trouble, Sheriff. We're honest men. All I can say is, contact Dr. Fox and Sheriff Gibson. We just got stuck in Pettigo and worked there. They can confirm it."

"If'n the owner can't get here, I'll do just that. Thanks, boys. Just relax. If you're as innocent as you say, you've got nothin' to worry about."

♦◊♦

Nat lay back on the hard, lumpy mattresses in their shared cell as Jake paced about like a caged lion.

"Will you sit down, Jake? There ain't nothin' we can do about this, but as soon as the manager gets here, they'll know they got the wrong men and let us go."

"I hate places like this!"

Nat placed his hat over his face. "You think I like it? There's nothing we can do but wait."

"You can pick the lock."

"We're law abiding men, remember? They don't pick locks. We have a different identity when we're relaxing, and we don't need them looking at what type of men *could* pick the lock and send a posse after us. It's snowy outside. A one-eyed toddler could track us through that. We'd do best to spend a night in jail and then head off with an apology when the manager gets here."

"And what if they don't let us go?" growled Jake.

"They will."

"You don't know that."

Nat huffed under his hat. "Nope, but it's a waste of energy to worry too much about what we can't change. Let's see what we're dealing with before we start planning an escape. I've got a lock pick in my boot. We'll get out when we have to."

"We shouldn't be in here at all."

"Lot of folks would disagree, but we're warm, fed, and saving money. All we've gotta do is wait until someone who was sober comes along to say we ain't Pettigrew and Miller."

A voice rang around the cell corridor. "Visitor for you."

They leaped to their feet and gathered at the door. "The bar owner here early?" Nat asked.

"Nope. A lady. A real attractive lady. I don't know what she sees in you two."

He stepped back and Abigail walked into the cellblock dressed in a dark red suit, nipped in at the waist, with flashes of white lace trims at the neck and the cuffs.

"I can't let you in with them, ma'am. It's against the rules. You speak to them from outside the bars."

She nodded in acquiescence. "Of course." The deputy hung around in the corridor as an impatient Abigail hooked him with an intimidating glare. "I wish some privacy."

"I gotta stay. It's the rules."

She arched a brow. "I would suggest you go and fetch your rule book and show me the piece of legislation that says a perfectly innocent woman cannot have an unsupervised conversation. I have committed no offense. I'm not even accused of one."

"But, ma'am—"

"No 'buts'. Go and fetch it. Show me in writing, then I will allow you to stay."

The deputy shuffled and looked at the ground before he spoke again. He was used to women who were in awe of his badge, but an imperious Abigail was an unknown quantity to him. He was as intimidated by her self-confidence as he was by her allure.

"Do I have to make a complaint?" She raised a challenging eyebrow.

"No, ma'am. I'll go get it."

He turned and walked back to the main office to rifle through the books and documents to search for the legislation as so commandingly demanded by the scary harridan in the cell block.

"Get us out of here." Nat pushed his face between the bars. "We thought you'd left town."

She smiled. "I'm sure you did. I was avoiding you."

Jake grabbed a bar. "Tell them we didn't smash that bar. Tell them who you are and get us out of here."

Her eyes glittered with amusement. "Now, why would I do that? I put you in here."

"What?" Jake's mouth dropped open.

"Jake. Keep your voice down. He'll come back in and he won't be so easy to get rid of this time."

"What the hell are you playin' at, Abi," Jake hissed through clenched teeth.

"It was the waiter." Nat's frown visibly transformed into a gasp of realization. "The sheriff told us it was the waiter."

She smiled with irritating faux sweetness. "Yes, at least he *thought* it was. When they go back to the hotel he'll realize the man he spoke to was considerably shorter than the actual waiter. He'll also realize slightly effete men are not the type of men he pays a lot of attention to until now. As soon as he sees the real thing he'll know it wasn't him. He's four inches taller than me and has blue eyes, for a start. The waiter and the chef told me all about the bar being smashed up. It was the most exciting thing they'd seen in years. It was easy for me to slip a fake warrant with your descriptions in amongst his papers under the guise of trying to help the sheriff find it."

He sucked in a breath. "You? Why would you do this to us?"

"Why? Because you spent all last night crowing about how clever you were and how I couldn't compete. Not only that, but you told me you were ready to use a prostitute if a grown woman had been available to you. What do you think any woman would do when she hears that?"

Jake's jaw dropped open and gawped at his nephew. "You

told her that? How dumb are you? I raised you better'n to tell a woman you wanted a prostitute."

"I was trying to be straight with her."

"Straight to jail, you saphead."

Abigail cut in. "Gentlemen, you'll have plenty of time to argue when I'm gone. You taught him not to *tell?*" She glared at Jake. "How about not using them in the first place? Women may not hit as hard, but we hit lower, and you needed a gentle reminder not to take me for granted. This is it."

Jake's hands closed around the bars. "As soon as I get outta here, Abi, I'm gonna teach you a lesson. Nuthin' like we had before; I'll treat you decent, but somethin' where you eat some crow. I'm caught in the middle of you two and your dimwittery. This ain't right. You need to sort this out."

She smiled and stroked his hand before pulling back quickly as he clutched out at her. "This is no worse than anything I've been through at your hands, and you *did* contribute to this."

Jake folded his arms. "And what if we're recognized? We could do twenty years."

"Relax. I'll stick around until I know you're released, and I'll step in and identify you as innocent parties if it goes wrong."

"And if you can't?"

"That's not going to happen. Trust me. Those men have already been arrested. The waiter told me that, too. As soon as the bar owner responds to the telegram, you'll be released." She held out a green book. "I brought you a book so you don't get bored." She reached out and slipped it onto the bunk before scuttling back out of arm's reach.

Nat examined the cover. "The Count of Monte Cristo?"

"Yes, it's about a man unjustly imprisoned." She chuckled. "I thought it was apt."

"I've read it." Nat's dark eyes burned through the bars. "It's mostly about his revenge. Even more apt."

She shrugged. "I needed to teach you a lesson. You'll be fine."

"Fine?" Jake kicked the cell door. "How many times have I

heard that from Nat? I don't need it from you, too."

"Look, you've lost respect for me and made it clear you think I'm either unwilling or incapable of locking you up. Did you really think I'd let you get away with that? I'm going back to work, and you need to take me seriously. A few hours in jail should focus your minds nicely on what I could be capable of. I'll make sure it's no more than that."

Nat shook his dark head and glowered at her. "I thought we'd reached an understanding."

She grinned at him. "We have now. I'm perfectly able to deal with you two. I think I've proved my point as neatly as you did when you handcuffed me to the door. We can fence, but we both have power."

Nat huffed with irritation. "Abi, is this all about you tryin' to prove you're equal to us?"

Her eyes widened in outrage. "Equal? I would never want to be equal to you. It's far too much of a drop."

Jake dropped onto the cot in resignation. "Very funny."

"You've got your strength, cleverness, and your ability with guns." She flicked a look at them both in turn. "I've got different talents, just as viable as yours, and I won't be patronized. Take me seriously."

"Abi, get us out of here now, or I won't be responsible for my actions." Nat's lips drew into a snarl.

She narrowed her eyes. "You should have thought of that last night. 'We'll walk out of here tomorrow without a worry. You're weaker than us, Abi—you're not going to come after us anymore.' What did you think I'd do? I won't let you or anyone else walk all over me, and you'd better realize that before I go back."

Jake turned and slumped on his bunk. "Nat, you're supposed to be the brains of the outfit. Where'd you get off makin' her so angry?"

Abigail's eyes twinkled fondly at him. "You're better than the brains. You're the heart."

"Yeah, right." He dropped his head into his hands. "What

was it you said about being patronized?"

She stepped forward with an envelope. "As promised. An address. It's a friend. If anything like that ever happens again, get a friend to contact that lady. She's a lady surgeon who used to train female Pinkertons, but she's retired now other than a few choice patients. I hope you never need it. She'll be sympathetic, but well able to deal with any of your tricks. She's impartial and you can trust her. I do. There's also money for a train ticket each to get out of here."

The deputy came clattering back into the cell block bearing a book as Nat snatched the letter and hid it under the lumpy mattress. "I found it." He thrust the book in front of her and pointed to a section with his cracked, grubby finger nail. "See. Females are to be attended at all time with male prisoners to prevent impro—impr—improperty."

"Impropriety. Do you know what that means?"

He fixed her with a vacant, open-mouthed gape as uneven, discolored teeth oozed methane like a malodorous, broken piano. "No, ma'am. Is it givin' them stuff?"

"In a way, yes. How would you know if we did it if you don't understand the word? And that's a book of guidelines for you. Since when was it legislation? That's not the law. It's only a book."

Confusion swirled in his eyes as he stabbed at the words with a dirty fingernail. "But that's what it says."

"Don't beat yourself up about it, pal. She's always like this. She's a nightmare." Nat glowered at her.

She patted the deputy's arm. "Well, you don't have to worry about it. I'm leaving. I got tired waiting for you to come back."

"You sure, ma'am? I'll see you out."

"Abi."

She turned as Nat called out after her with a menacing smile. "This ain't over."

"Threats? We have a saying in Scotland. The cock crows but the hen produces."

Nat's eyes flashed. "What did you just call me?"

She tinkled with soft laughter. "What did you say as you left me in Bannen? Until next time?"

"Will you two leave it out?" Jake said. "Otherwise, I'll lock you both in a room and not let you out until you sort this once and for all!"

Nat and Abigail turned to him, surprised at the vehemence in the blue eyes which burned into them, in turn. "You think I don't mean it? Try me. I'm fed up with the pair of you. Ain't neither one of you gonna hurt the other, so face it and treat each other with some decency. Now, I'm gonna have a sleep until dinner and when we get outta here, we're even." He threw himself back on the bunk and stared hard at Abi. "It's a clean slate Abi, one for us, and one for you. I hope you got that. Let's keep it that way."

"Got it. Goodbye, Jake." She nodded and smiled at Nat before she slipped away along the corridor.

"Sheesh." The deputy stared after her. "She's a looker, but I ain't sure she's worth the bother. Find an easier one." Their jailer turned on his heel and strode back to the office. "That'd be almost anyone."

An almost imperceptible tinkle of metal made both men glance at the floor. Nat's brows met as he leaned over and picked up the thin metal tool. His cheeks dimpled as he turned to his uncle, grinning with delight. "It's a lock pick. It was in the spine of the book. She passed us a lock pick."

"So? You've already got one."

"She doesn't know that, Jake. She's making sure we're okay. She's gonna make sure we get out of here in good shape." Nat's face dimpled with delight. "Oh, she's in for it when I catch her. She'll pay for this."

Jake turned on his side, wrapping his pillow around his head. "Dear Lord. Will it never end? Keep me out of it, Nat. That's all I ask. Now, shut the hell up so I can get some sleep."

About The Author

Chris Asbrey has lived and worked all over the world in the Police Service, Civil Service, and private industry, working for the safety, legal rights, and security of the public. A life-changing injury meant a change of course into contract law and consumer protection for a department attached to the Home Office.

In that role, she produced magazine and newspaper articles based on consumer law and wrote guides for the Consumer Direct Website. She was Media Trained, by The Rank Organization, and acted as a consultant to the BBC's One Show and Watchdog. She has also been interviewed on BBC radio answering questions on consumer law to the public.

She lives with her husband and two daft cats in Northamptonshire, England—for now. She's moving to the beautiful medieval city of York.

Blog - The Enigmatologist - all things obscure and strange in the Victorian period https://enigmatoligist.blogspot.co.uk/

Facebook - https://www.facebook.com/mysteryscrivener/

Twitter - https://twitter.com/CAASBREY

Printed in Great Britain
by Amazon